Swan

I was home within an hour of landing at JFK, whisked through immigration and into a waiting limo. After the frenzy of Paris, the serenity of my apartment seemed like a safe and welcoming haven to which I had finally managed to escape.

Until I went into my bedroom.

The red light on my answering machine was blinking in the darkness, signalling to me that he was back, there was no escape and, unless I took decisive action, there never would be.

I sat down on my bed, mesmerised by the flashing light. When the phone rang I jumped. Could it be him? No, of course not. He never rang when I was actually there. Somehow he always knew when I was going to be out or away.

I called him the Messenger.

Naomi Campbell, born in 1970, is one of the world's most successful supermodels. She was working for *Elle* at fifteen and in a matter of three years she was the first black model to appear on the front covers of both French and British *Vogue*.

Naomi was born in Streatham and educated at the Barbara Speake and Italia Conti stage schools in London. Talent-spotted while shopping in Covent Garden, she has experienced a truly extraordinary rise to fame.

She has starred in pop videos with chart-topping musicians such as Boy George, Bob Marley, Aretha Franklin and George Michael, and also appeared in Madonna's internationally bestselling book *Sex*. Her first album, *Baby Woman*, was recently released by Sony.

Swan

NAOMI CAMPBELL

Mandarin

A Mandarin Paperback

SWAN

First published in Great Britain 1994
by William Heinemann Ltd
This edition published 1995
by Mandarin Paperbacks
an imprint of Reed Consumer Books Ltd
Michelin House, 81 Fulham Road, London SW3 6RB
and Auckland, Melbourne, Singapore and Toronto

Reprinted 1995

Copyright © Naomi Campbell and Caroline Upcher 1994
The Author and the Writer have asserted their moral rights

A CIP catalogue record for this title
is available from the British Library
ISBN 0 7493 1830 9

Printed and bound in Great Britain
by BPC Paperbacks Ltd
A member of The British Printing Company Ltd

My very special thanks to:

Caroline Upcher

and to Geoff Mulligan and Chris Owen.

Also to Carole White and Sophie Wood at
Elite Premier Model Agency, London.

The help of the following is gratefully acknowledged:

Annie Veltri at Elite Model Management, New York.

Eileen and Jerry Ford and Joseph Hunter at Ford Models,
New York.

Eric at Ford Models, Paris.

Bethann Hardison and Christine at Bethann Management,
New York.

Alexandra Shulman, Carlton, Tom Weldon, John Potter,
Richard Grable, Sally Brampton, Rupert Everett,
Vivienne Westwood, Peter Howarth, Mak, Polly Mellen,
Jenny Asiama, Jenny Nichols, Tish Clyde, Beth Humphries,
Kari Allen, Roger Eaton, Robert Holmes, Ashley,
Christie Denham and Christopher, Claire Ferris, Lisa Snowden,
Lois Samuels, Helen Millet, Sarah Birch, Stephanie Pierre,
Sandra Sperka, Julie Graff, Tracey Gascoyne, Valerie Ambrosio,
Lisa Smith, Gavin Boardman, Cheryl Gordon, Paula Whiteman,
Niki Carter.

Contents

Contents

Part 1

Swan 1994

Part 1

Swann 1904

October 1994

I shall begin my story – or my nightmare, as I think of it –
at the Paris ready-to-wear collections last year. It all started
way before then but things came to a head in Paris.

I arrived for work at the last show on a rainy October
morning. They'd sent a chauffeur-driven Mercedes to collect
me and I scampered through the rain wearing nothing underneath my raincoat but a towelling robe over my bare skin. I
decided years ago that it was crazy to get dressed since the
whole day is spent running from one designer's show to
another, being whisked in and out of clothes by the dressers.
'I might just as well arrive naked,' I explained to the press
when I did it for the first time, giving them yet another
opportunity to print a story about how outrageous I am. That's
just fine by me. The further away from the real me their
stories are, the more I like it.

As I hovered backstage waiting for the show to begin I
could hear the good-natured slow handclap and the intermit-
tent wolf whistles from the impatient audience. There were
probably 2,500 people out there: at least 500 buyers, say 1,500
journalists and at least 300 photographers all crammed into a
hot tent for forty minutes' worth of theatre which would set
the designer back a quarter of a million bucks. I glanced at
him. He didn't seem too unhappy. After all, he'd got me.
They'd come to see his clothes but they'd also come to see

3

me. I was the one who had to make it all happen. Once upon a time the clothes were shown by anonymous house models, well-bred society girls trained only to walk gracefully along the catwalk, look elegant, turn at the right places, and paid a mere pittance for their trouble. Now, we don't just show the clothes – we sell them. The fashion industry, like any other, has become so competitive that the designers can no longer get the attention they've been used to by themselves. Now they have to use models as a draw for their clothes. Elegant catwalk mannequins have been replaced by lissom, streetsmart runway girls with accessible looks all conveying the same message: 'I look sexy in these clothes, buy them, and you will too.' Sexy has become the new marketing buzz word. I may be a well-bred English girl but I'm also a supermodel. A supermodel can make anything look sexy, and they say I'm the sexiest of them all.

The lights dimmed and through a crack I watched as the vast cellophane cover was removed from the runway and bundled clumsily backstage enabling the photographers to thrust their cameras on to the edge of the stage. The slow handclapping increased.

'Send out someone,' yelled a wag.

'Anyone,' yelled another.

The music swelled, the red curtains parted and I felt the designer give me a little push in the small of my back.

'Get ready to glide, Swan,' he whispered and I was off, climbing the steps to the runway, moving out into the spotlight with what the press have dubbed my 'Swan's glide'. I hooked my thumbs into the pockets of my tight silk pants and began to saunter down the runway, one foot dead in front of the other, hips wiggling subtly, right to the end, pause, turn to the right, turn to the left and return. I remembered to pause briefly in front of Anna Wintour, editor of American

Vogue, sitting there in the front row in her habitual dark glasses, and other key members of the audience I recognised, and I know I played instinctively to all the important photographers. It's always been a mystery to me why anyone wants to sit in the front row. Surely they can't see anything with all the photographers clicking away in front of them.

Over half an hour later I was almost through, coming up the steps for the last time to show the penultimate dress. Then the show would be closed in the traditional way with a bridal gown.

Patsy was coming down the runway towards me and it was Patsy who would be the bride. While I made my final run Patsy would be backstage, frantically changing into the wedding dress to be ready to go back out for the finale as I made my exit. In a few seconds Patsy and I would pass each other. Poor Patsy! I had been worrying about her for some time. She was relatively inexperienced and very young – only sixteen – and yet her agency had pushed her into doing collections. It was easy to see why. Patsy's waif-like looks epitomised the current fashionable look. She was Kate Moss gamine and Claudia Schiffer flirt all rolled into one, and as she came towards me, tottering imperceptibly on her seven-inch platforms, Patsy was irresistible. But inside her perfect body she was a flake. Nervous, excitable, she was a chain-smoker whose stomach was constantly upset. Only minutes before the show I had found her throwing up. Poor Patsy! A year ago she had been a green little teenager from a hick town in Oklahoma and about as streetsmart as an ear of corn. Now she was at the mercy of urban barracudas, and not only those in the fashion industry. I had witnessed Patsy's never-ending stream of shady-looking dates and I knew that this sweet undisciplined country girl, so far away from her mamma's protection, was on a one-way trip to disaster.

5

We were about to pass on the runway like we'd done so many times before, our long arms swinging loosely, our long hair rising and falling behind us, our long legs striding in tandem and then . . .

CRACK!

A shot? Patsy crumpled, almost in slow motion, and collapsed. I heard the crowd gasp, but nobody moved. I glanced quickly around me. What was going on? Hadn't anybody heard the shot? Didn't they realise what had happened? I could hear people coming down the runway behind me. I continued to the end, made my turn, saw that they had whisked Patsy away and began to walk back as if nothing had happened.

Patsy would not be able to show the wedding dress. There was only one thing to do. Patsy and I were the same size. As I arrived backstage I was already half out of my last garment ready to slip into the bridal gown and take Patsy's place for the finale.

An assassin at the Paris Collections might be a first but I knew the show must go on.

My name is Swan and I'm a supermodel.

It sounds simple but it isn't, not at all. Apart from my looks and my income, I'm quite sure I couldn't be less like the public's idea of a supermodel. They only see what's on the outside, my professional image. If only they knew what I'm like inside.

They never will. I am an intensely private person. I know that's what all celebrities say these days but in my case it's true. My mother's words – or were they Nanny's? – still resound in my ears as if they're coming out of my Walkman: 'Discretion is the better part of valour.' Exhibitionism was the cardinal sin, and my grandmother firmly believed that one should only ever be in the newspapers twice in one's life: to announce one's birth and one's death. Well, I've blown that one sky high, but I've noticed that it's dear old Granny who keeps the biggest scrapbook of my tearsheets and proudly displays them to anyone who goes to see her.

Swan is not my real name, of course. I was christened Lavinia Charlotte Christopher Frederick Crichton-Lake. There may appear to be something rather odd about the choice of these names for a baby daughter but it's easily explained. My father wanted me to be called Lavinia after his mother. My mother favoured Charlotte because it was her mother's name. In the end they gave me both names and added those of my two grandfathers to ensure fair play. Throughout my childhood my father always called me Lavinia and my mother called me Charlotte. My older sister Venetia (my parents' first child, named for their idyllic honeymoon in Venice – 'Thank God they didn't go to Positano,' remarked Granny), and my brother Harry called me Skinny-Lavinny. It is the understatement of the year to say that as the youngest, no one in my family took me very seriously but I think I knew even then that one day I would grow up to be somebody, one day I would show them! And I really was skinny! Nobody could understand where I'd come from. My father was fair-haired, my mother liked to describe herself as Titian, Venetia was ash-blonde and Harry's hair was a kind of butterscotch colour. Mine was black. Think ink, jet, coal, raven and take it from there. Then there was my skin. Dead white. Not creamy-milky but alabaster-ivory saved by twin bright red blobs on my cheeks. My hair was always cut in a fringe – bangs, as my American Granny Charlotte called them – and for the first seven years of my life I had two long black pigtails. Then my mother took me to Vidal Sassoon and I emerged with a very short, perfectly geometric bob. Everyone said I looked like a little Japanese doll. I've often wondered whether it is this particular aspect of my appearance that prompted a powerful Japanese conglomerate to offer me a multimillion-dollar five-year contract to endorse a new range of products they proposed to launch when they took over an American beauty empire. I accepted the offer (although naturally I reserved the right to bow out after three years if I so chose) and they paid me the ultimate compliment by naming the products SWAN.

So if my real name is Lavinia Crichton-Lake, how did I come to be called Swan? It was after I'd had that Vidal Sassoon bob. Somehow it did something to expose my neck in a way

8

it hadn't been exposed before. I went into school and I was walking down the corridor when one of the teachers grabbed another teacher's arm and pointed at me.

'Look at Lavinia Lake. I've never seen such a long neck!'

The other teacher taught English and went in for a lot of over-the-top flowery language which I suppose she thought was poetic. 'Such grace!' she agreed, 'such elegance. She'll never go through the ugly duckling stage. With that neck she's already a swan.'

Well, of course, my classmates couldn't resist it.

'Swan Lake,' they greeted me every morning, 'here she comes. Swan Lake, will you look at that neck. Swan Lake. Swan Lake.'

And Swan I stayed. Now that I'm a household name I read about my former classmates clambering over each other to tell the press: 'I gave her her name. It was me. It was my idea.' I don't mind. At least it stopped Venetia and Harry calling me Skinny-Lavinny although my parents still persist with Lavinia and Charlotte.

I was born on 6 June 1968 in Queen Charlotte's (Mummy loved that!) and I weighed 7lb. 4oz. My father just said 'D-Day' rather typically but my mother was always struck by the fact that she gave birth to her youngest child on the same day that Robert Kennedy, way over on the other side of the world, was gunned down in the Hotel Ambassador in Los Angeles. Mummy mentioned it so many times during my childhood that I imagined 'Bobby' Kennedy must be a family friend and took to referring to him as 'Uncle Bobby', as in 'I was born the day poor Uncle Bobby was killed in California.' When people started dropping casual enquiries into the conversation about an 'Uncle Jack', I rose heroically to the occasion and produced all kinds of fabrications about Uncle Jack coming to spend Christmas with us and what Uncle Jack

9

had promised me for my birthday until somebody took me aside and pointed out that 'Uncle Jack' was dead and had in fact died several years before 'Uncle Bobby', that is, before I was born.

Years later when I was working in New York, my cousin Felicity, who was at Brown with John Kennedy Junior, brought him to meet me and, to my intense embarrassment, told him the whole story. He thought it was a huge joke and to this day still calls out, 'Hi, Cousin Swan, how are you?' whenever we run into each other. Yet for whatever reason I do feel I have some sort of kindred spirit with the Kennedys and it's probably why I choose to live in an apartment at the top of the Carlyle in New York, knowing that that was where they once based their headquarters. I know it's probably funkier to live downtown but I'm just not a downtown girl. I grew up in a five-storey town house in the Boltons, which is probably one of London's most exclusive residential areas. To reach the front door you had to climb twenty-five steps guarded by four giant stone lions. It used to take Nanny half an hour to get me inside the house for tea on returning from my afternoon walk as I methodically climbed each step and stopped to pat the lions and feed them the bread I'd refused to throw to the ducks in Hyde Park. They were very literary lions, having been given names by my (real) Uncle Walter who was a terrible poet who had somehow landed the job of literary editor for a Sunday newspaper. He dubbed them Conrad, Swift, Proust and Amis. Amis sat at the top of the stairs on the right and had lost a chip off the end of his nose. Poor Nanny! Just when she thought she'd almost got me inside, I always had to go and kiss Amis's nose better.

We also had a weekend place in the country. My parents talked about going to 'the cottage'. *The Oxford English Dictionary* defines the word cottage as 'Labourer's or villager's small dwelling; small country residence'. Our house in Wiltshire had seven bedrooms yet it was always called the cottage. It was pretty shambolic and that was what we children loved about it. We could run wild down there, whereas in London Nanny made sure we were always properly turned out and on our best behaviour. The cottage was always full of animals. As well as dogs and cats, lambs strayed into the kitchen and cows ambled up to the ground-floor windows at the back of the house. When the Kennedyesque tragedies began to strike our family, my parents began to spend more and more time down at the cottage and once I left home they moved down there altogether. When they finally sold the Boltons and moved the furniture from that house to Wiltshire, I begged them to hang on to the furniture in the cottage until I found my own home. I have it with me now in my apartment at the Carlyle: the chintz sofas and armchairs, the Sheraton tables and chest of drawers, the button-backed velvet chairs, the oval mahogany dining table and chairs, my parents' old four-poster bed. Some of my friends in New York don't quite get it. I know they think it all looks a tad shabby and they're wondering why I don't get a designer in to make it all look a bit more Ralph Lauren. But I don't care. I need the comfort of my roots around me. I love New York but I am still English and it is possible to have a little bit of England high above Madison Avenue at 76th Street. And I believe that however successful a model becomes, she should try to stay in close contact with her family. If only I could practise what I preach! I love my parents very dearly but since the scandal my family has fallen apart and until everything is resolved, I must content myself with old and treasured family belongings as a poor substitute for the love and warmth of my mother and father.

Of course, I do have someone to console me. It is a source

of constant delight to me that I have been able to keep from the press the fact that I have been married now for six months.

If only that were my only secret.

I flew back to New York on Concorde.

I remember the first time I travelled on Concorde. I was totally in awe of the number of internationally famous faces on board and it was some time before I noticed that the other passengers were in fact casting surreptitious glances at me. It was then that it dawned on me that of course mine was the most famous face of all, because whilst everyone else was known for what they did rather than how they looked when they did it, I was a celebrity for my looks alone. Nothing else. Just my face and my body and the extraordinary way they photograph.

I was home within an hour of landing at JFK, whisked through immigration and into a waiting limo. After the frenzy of Paris, the serenity of my apartment seemed like a safe and welcoming haven to which I had finally managed to escape.

Until I went into my bedroom.

The red light on my answering machine was blinking in the darkness, signalling to me that he was back, there was no escape and, unless I took decisive action, there never would be.

I sat down on my bed, mesmerised by the flashing light. When the phone rang I jumped. Could it be him? No, of course not. He never rang when I was actually there. Somehow he always knew when I was going to be out or away.

I called him the Messenger.

13

It had started six months ago. I had come home from a job in the Caribbean to find the first message waiting for me. It came out of the blue, speaking to me from across the room as I unpacked my bags and wandered in and out of my walk-in closet, putting away my clothes. I was just about to sling my bags into the upper closet when the low seductive voice of a man began to talk to me.

'Swan? You there? Did you have a good trip? I sure hope so because what I have to tell you may upset you just a little. It's too bad *New York Magazine* did that pictorial profile on you recently. You know why? There was this picture of you when you were much younger, about seventeen, eighteen, not long after you got started, I guess. Anyway, if I hadn't seen that picture I wouldn't be calling you today. Now you have to do something for me. Switch off the answering machine and look through your mail till you find a blue airmail envelope with the postmark London Heathrow airport. Open it then listen to your messages again. I'll be waiting for you.'

The strange thing was I obeyed his instructions mindlessly. He had a beautiful voice, soft, melodious, hard to place – not English, not American, something in between, unidentifiable mid-Atlantic. I found the envelope immediately with my name and address typed on it and the Heathrow postmark. An airport meant he was just passing through from one destination to another, giving no clue as to where he actually lived.

Inside the envelope was a photograph and when I saw what it was of I began to shake. I rushed back into the bedroom and switched the machine back on. Then I pressed the fast-forward button until I found his first message coming to an end. I listened to the click and the whirr and then his second message began.

'Found it, did you? Pretty little thing, weren't you? Still are, of course. I was the one who took that photo in the envelope. I've kept it ever since. The image has stayed with me. I couldn't get it out of my mind. I've often wondered who the girl in the picture was – she seemed so familiar somehow, and I only needed to see that picture of you in that magazine profile and I knew. I recognised you straight away. The same young girl in that photo I snapped all those years ago. But what were you doing, Swan? Who's that guy in the picture with you? He's older than you and why is he handing you that huge bankroll? What did a pretty little girl like you have to do for him to earn that? It looks bad, Swan. It's no use asking for the negative, by the way. You can take a print from a print and I've got plenty. And when you place it beside the picture of you in New York, it's easy to see it's the same girl. You. No, I haven't sent it to a newspaper. I haven't told anyone. I think I'll just wait and see what I want from you first. You'll be hearing from me. 'Bye now.'

His messages have become pretty regular ever since, never threatening anything specific, but gradually growing more and more menacing and always ending with the same warning.

'If you don't tell anyone about these messages, Swan, I won't either and I won't do anything with the photo, but if you so much as think about calling the police or asking anyone for help, there's one thing you ought to know: before I hurt you I'll go for your mother, your family. Oh yes, I will! Think about it. If that picture ever reaches the press, your current reputation will be ruined, let alone anything you might have planned for the future, but how would you feel if your mother were to suddenly have a nasty fall down a flight of steps? And you so far away in New York. I'm not asking you for money,

Swan, that would be extortion, but sooner or later I'm going to ask you for one big favour and you'd better come through quickly for me or else. Now, push the erase button. No playing this back to anyone. . . .'

He took risks leaving messages for me. Anyone could be standing in the room with me when I played them back. I wondered if he knew about my husband. I had kept on my apartment at the Carlyle because eventually, when our marriage was out in the open, we would live there together, but for the time being he stayed in his own apartment at the Gainsborough on Central Park South. Then I began to notice that the messages were only left for me if I returned home alone, never if someone was with me. Did he live in my building? Did he keep a close watch on me? Who was he? Was he moving closer? I felt like Whitney Houston in *The Bodyguard*. Did I need a bodyguard? Maybe I should give Kevin Costner a call. . . .

The first tragedy occurred on Venetia's eighteenth birthday.

As a child I was deeply anti-social. From the minute I learned to read I always had my nose stuck in a book and the only thing that would get me downstairs and out of the nursery was any kind of dressing up. Being allowed to delve into the dressing-up box and transform myself into anything from a fairy princess to Charlie Chaplin was my idea of heaven. Even when I was very young, I was shrewd enough to know this was the only way I was ever going to get any attention.

The reason everyone ignored me was that Venetia was a ravishing beauty. She had eyes the colour of lapis lazuli, a fine straight nose and a wide mouth, but her crowning glory, quite literally, was her ash-blonde hair which hung to her shoulders in a sleek page boy. She was terribly classy, even I could see it, and she was always Princess Grace in the dressing-up competitions which meant she always won, because I suppose that's what she was in real life.

For her eighteenth birthday my parents gave her a midsummer ball. A marquee was erected in the garden at the Boltons and the guest list numbered over 400 people. I was only eight but the thought of dressing up for the ball had made me beg to be allowed to stay up for the beginning. Nanny and I had been working on my costume – I was going as a swan – for weeks and I was determined to make an entrance.

Venetia had been incredibly soppy all summer. Mummy explained to me that this was because she was in love with Oliver Fairfax, and when you fell in love it sometimes made you soppy. On her birthday, after she'd been served a champagne breakfast in bed and opened all her presents, Oliver arrived to take her out to lunch at the Waterside Inn. He had a BMW convertible and they drove off with the hood down and Bryan Ferry's 'Let's Stick Together' blasting out on the car radio.

By six o'clock they hadn't returned and my parents were hysterical. It was so inconsiderate of Oliver – they never blamed Venetia for anything – he knew there was to be a dinner party before the ball and the guests had been asked at eight for 8.30. If Venetia wasn't back soon she wouldn't have time to bath and change in time to greet her guests. By 7.30, we were all sitting in a row in the hall, biting our nails with worry.

I shall never forget the policeman who came to tell us. They shouldn't have sent someone so young. It wasn't fair. He would have stammered whatever he had to say to us. His face was scarlet with distress. I opened the door to him, jumping up and down in my swan's outfit, thinking it must

17

be Venetia. He must have thought he'd come to a house full of nutters.

'They didn't have a chance. Car going at ninety. Motorway. Removal van coming the other way. Family moving to London from . . .' He realised we didn't give a damn about some family moving house but he didn't know how to get out of it. 'Your son pulled out to overtake the car in front of him. Another car pulled out to overtake the removal van. They collided. Not a chance,' he finished lamely.

Everyone looked at Harry standing there very much alive.

My mother moved forward. 'Constable, this is our only son.'

The policeman went puce and consulted his notes.

'A Mister Oliver Fairfax?'

Everyone shook their heads in horror.

'A Miss Venetia Crichton-Lake?'

We stood there, staring at him, the awful question mark hanging in the air below the chandelier. He nodded miserably and then the doorbell went again and the first guests arrived for dinner.

I don't know what we would have done if it hadn't been for Harry. As I watched him telephone as many of the 400 guests as he could reach by ten o'clock, and then stand at the top of the steps between Amis and Proust and gently head the others off at the pass, I began what would become a lifelong devotion to my older brother. He was only sixteen yet he took the burden of grief off my parents' shoulders that night, as he did the following day when the press arrived on our doorstep.

We were never quite the same as a family after Venetia's death. My parents retreated to the country as often as they could in order to avoid the well-meant expressions of pity on their friends' faces. The only good thing to come out of it was that Harry and I became very close. He still called me Skinny-Lavinny and Titch and other nicknames I found offensive, but

18

I sensed in him a genuine ally in my struggle with approaching adolescence. Because it was a struggle. I was gawky and moody and I was obsessed with the thought that I was a hopeless substitute for Venetia in my parents' eyes. If it hadn't beeen for the fact that Harry made it clear he thought I was 'a good kid', I don't know what I would have done.

And then Nanny retired. She was seventy-four, after all – she'd been my father's nanny – and in a way she had become a kind of family retainer and now it was time for her to go. I was secretly quite excited by the thought of her going. I imagined I would be able to run riot without her supervision, but I was wrong. My parents decided that since they were away so often and we had no live-in servants, I couldn't be left in Harry's sole care so they hired a new nanny. It was a pretty ridiculous thing to do but I suppose a twelve-year-old girl couldn't be left to look after herself.

Molly Bainbridge was from Liverpool. She was twenty years old and she was not, she told me five minutes after she'd arrived, a nanny. She was a model. Nannying was something she did to get a roof over her head. I suppose I must have said something like 'Fine by me'. All I can remember is that I was too busy gawking at her to really take in what she said. I'd never seen anything like her. She was incredibly tall with very long legs in tight black leggings, and huge tits. I could see her nipples through her T-shirt. Looking back on it I realise she must have been incredibly vulgar. She always wore far too much make-up and kept going on about how she had to be prepared in case her agency called up and sent her on a casting. They never did, and in any case if they had she shouldn't have worn so much make-up because the client always wants to see what sort of shape your skin is in.

I probably would have settled down quite happily with Molly Bainbridge if it hadn't been for the devastating effect she had on Harry. On her first night my parents, who were in town for the night, invited her to dine with them in the dining room and insisted that Harry join us. I know I shouldn't notice such things, but she didn't know which fork to pick up or which wine glass to use. She was completely at sea and I felt really sorry for her.

But not for long. Harry, I noticed, had gone very quiet. He was, quite simply, drooling. He gazed adoringly at her all through dinner and when we had coffee (Horlicks for me) in the drawing room, he sat on the sofa beside her and asked her seven times if she'd like another cup.

She was no fool. She led him on. She left her bedroom door open so he would often catch a glimpse of her in a state of undress. Then she left the bathroom door open when she knew he was coming up to the nursery floor to see me and he saw her lying in the tub.

Now, even though I was twelve years old, nobody had ever really had *that* conversation with me about sex. What I knew I'd picked up from the TV and from all those books I'd read. All I understood was that Harry, who up to then had been my friend, had suddenly become strangely distant. It wasn't as though he didn't come to see me. As soon as he came home from work – he was now working for a commercials production company – he would race up to the top floor, but once he got there he didn't seem to pay me much attention any more. We had a little self-contained apartment up there, Molly and I, left over from the days when Nanny ruled the nursery floor. The nursery kitchen and bathroom had been her domain and woe betide anyone who went up there without a prior appointment. My bedroom had in fact been moved to the floor below since Nanny's retirement but I had my meals and shared a bathroom with Molly upstairs. I caught snatches of conversation between Harry and Molly in her kitchen or on the landing: 'Just come out with me one night. I want to take you out for a meal.' 'How can I come out when I'm supposed to be a bloody babysitter?' 'Well, I'll get a video and we can eat in, watch it together up here. . . .'

I suppose it was inevitable that I had to wake up one night with a desperate need to go to the lavatory, and I suppose it was equally inevitable that Molly had yet again left her bedroom door open. I hadn't seen Harry naked for a number of years, not since we were young kids larking about. As I came up the stairs I heard this peculiar noise he was making. It sounded as if he was in pain and that was what made me rush to see what was wrong.

They weren't in her bed. They were on the floor with their legs half under the bed. Neither of them had any clothes on and she was lying on top of him, biting him. I thought she was trying to hurt him and I rushed over and kicked her.

'Get off!' I screamed, 'get off him. Leave Harry alone, you're hurting him.'

'Oh, you stupid little kid.' She rolled off him and got to her feet. 'Go on, get out of here. Beat it.' She gave me a shove and I stumbled towards the door. I turned, waiting for Harry to leap up and thank me for saving him but all he did was laugh and say 'Go to bed, Titch.'

I know I shouldn't have told Mummy when she called but I was so hurt by Harry's behaviour, I wanted to get my own back on him. The next thing I knew I had been whisked down to Wiltshire and Molly Bainbridge had been given the weekend to pack her bags and move on.

Except she didn't move on. She couldn't. When my parents brought me back to London on Sunday night, we found her lying stark naked on the landing with the pillow that had been used to smother her to death still covering her face.

And there was no sign of Harry.

My father did his best to keep it quiet but the press were back on our doorstep and this time there was no Harry to deal with them. Mercifully, they never got hold of that aspect of the story. Molly was dead so she couldn't tell them she'd been carrying on with the son of the house, and as for Harry, well, he'd disappeared.

The family was portrayed in the tabloid press as being tragedy prone, what with Venetia's death and my nanny's murder. They hinted at dark events in the future, speculated as to who would be the next victim. My mother thought she had succeeded in keeping the papers away from me but I went and fished them out of the dustbin and it was the sight of those lurid stories that made me swear never to make myself vulnerable to the press if I could help it.

Molly's murder was never solved but, worse, Harry never reappeared. My father refused to go to the police for fear that they would link Harry's disappearance to the murder, but of course they knew he lived with us and they expected to question him. It was ghastly because as time went by we began to wonder if Harry was still alive. The police mounted a discreet manhunt for a missing person rather than for a murderer. It wasn't quite like Lord Lucan where there was someone left behind claiming he had tried to murder them and got the nanny instead.

I was so totally distraught at having lost Harry – I missed him so dreadfully – that at first I didn't care if he had murdered Molly providing the police found him. Then I came to my senses and was appalled at how disloyal I'd been. Of course Harry wasn't a murderer.

But where was he?

After seven years you can be declared legally dead if you haven't turned up. I was nineteen years old but I still looked about fifteen. I was beginning to wonder if I was now an only child. My parents had discovered that Harry had removed the first part of his trust fund from the bank. Being a boy, his was more than mine and Venetia's (the age of feminism had done nothing for trust funds). We received ours when we were eighteen but Harry had only received a small portion of his on his eighteenth birthday and he wasn't due to come into the balance until he was thirty. Those were the regulations laid down by our grandfather and there wasn't a great deal we could do about it. Poor Venetia hadn't had a chance to enjoy any of hers. I wondered what my parents were planning to do with it.

So on my eighteenth birthday I was, as they say, comfortable, having come into £150,000. I had left school with a burning desire to work with books and absolutely no clue how to go about it other than to offer my services to the little bookshop in Chelsea where we had an account. To my amazement they took me on as a sales assistant and I thought I'd died and gone to heaven. From 9.30 to 5.30 every day I was surrounded by books, all I talked about was books and then I went home and fell into bed with a pile of books. I had decided that in order to be a good sales assistant I should be in a position to personally recommend books to the customers. So that meant I had to read my way through the stock as it came in.

One day I was up a ladder, stocking the top shelves with Penguin Modern Classics, when I suddenly lost my balance and fell, landing heavily on my right ankle. The next thing I knew I was being hoisted up by a broad, hairy arm.

'I'm truly sorry, gel. It was my flash. I saw you through the window from the street, at least first I saw your legs and then

I saw the rest of you. I couldn't resist it. I had to come in and get a picture. I'd no idea I was going to surprise you like that. All right now?'

I was all right but I was also pretty angry.

'Who gave you permission to take a picture of me? What's it for? Some kind of publicity for the shop? I don't know anything about it.'

'Listen, I didn't know anything about it myself until just now. Thing is, you're beautiful. You must know that. I wanted to see what you'd be like on film. My guess is you'd be sensational. Nobody ever told you you ought to be a model?'

I winced at the word. It reminded me instantly of Molly Bainbridge. Of course, by now I knew there were plenty of models who looked nothing like her, several of my friends, for instance, and they were all rather well paid. But my life was in books.

'Do you have a card or something?' I was aware that I sounded terribly snooty and grand but I just wanted to get rid of him. He fished in his camera bag and handed me something. I looked at his name.

'Willy O'Brien.'

'Right. I've got my own studio. Give me a call.'

'Sure thing,' I said and gave him my best smile, moving him closer and closer to the door as I did so.

'Seriously. I mean it. You've really got what it takes. When will you call? Tomorrow? I'm at the studio all day.'

'OK. Fine. I'll call tomorrow.' Anything to get him out the door. Then as soon as he'd gone I tossed his card in the bin and picked up three copies of *Catcher in the Rye*.

I fell off the ladder again two months later when a voice behind me said, 'Would you by any chance have a copy of *Skinny-Lavinny Grows Up*?'

24

He caught me as I fell and the first thing I noticed was that his butterscotch hair had grown long over his collar and it was filthy.

'Who's it by?' I asked as he put me down. 'I have a feeling she grew up and went out of print when you left her.' And then I fell into his arms and burst into tears. We were alone in the shop but I suppose he'd waited for that.

'Oh, Titch, don't. I know, I know.' He patted me on the back as if I were a baby he was trying to wind.

'Sorry,' I snuffled, 'but you must admit, Harry, it's a bit of a shock. Who else have you seen?'

'No one. I've only been in London an hour and a half. I've come straight from the airport and I'm going into hiding as soon as I leave you.'

'Where've you been?'

'Can't tell you that, Titch.'

'Oh, stop bloody calling me Titch.'

'Lavinia?'

'Swan.'

'OK, Swan. Now listen, I want you to meet me at a hotel in north London. I'm going to stay there until I can get myself sorted out.'

'Why north London? Do you know someone at the hotel?'

'I know absolutely no one, you idiot. That's the whole point. I don't want anyone to know I've come back. You're the only person I can trust and I'm not even going to tell you where I've been.'

'You mean I can't say anything to the parents?'

'Particularly not them.'

'Harry, have you any idea what they've been through? That girl was found dead in their house. You disappeared. They're beginning to think you might be dead . . .'

'Best that they do. Now, I'll give you a choice, Swan. You

25

can come and see me at this hotel – ask for Mr Charles Gordon, by the way, I'll be registered under that name – but I won't tell you anything. In fact, I am going to ask you for a massive favour. Or you can get on your high horse and say you have to tell my mother and father and everyone about me and you'll find I'm not at that hotel and you probably won't ever see me again. It's up to you. . . .'

Of course, I went to see him but when he told me what he wanted from me I almost wished I hadn't. He wanted me to give him my trust fund. He needed money to make a fresh start. He admitted he'd been abroad for the last seven years – somehow I suspected Australia – but he'd run through the small amount he'd had of his own money and he couldn't think of any other way of getting his hands on a sizeable amount of cash without being found out. He was going to make a fresh start and clear his name, he had plans and no, of course he wasn't going to tell me what they were.

I couldn't start making inroads into my trust fund without my parents' knowing and they'd want to know what I was spending it on. I decided the simplest thing was to tell them I wanted to move out of the Boltons and buy a place of my own. My mother insisted on traipsing round with the estate agent and wittering on for hours about everything we looked at. It must have seemed rather strange to her that I appeared so unenthusiastic about finding this apartment I had set my heart on having. Finally I settled on a little flat at the back of a mansion block in the Old Brompton Road just around the corner from my parents. The original fourteen-foot-high ceilings were still in place and there was an unusual gallery sleeping area which appealed to me.

The next stage was really tricky. Over the next few weeks while I waited to exchange and complete I systematically removed huge sums of cash from my account and passed them to Harry. That was the irony of the Messenger's threat. He had it all wrong and he didn't know it. He had not taken a photograph of a man giving me money. I was handing money to the man, and that man was my own brother. Yet here I am still protecting Harry. I have to. Of course he told me long ago what happened that weekend when Molly Bainbridge died but he still hasn't been able to prove his innocence. So he has to go on lying low. He wasn't able to surface when he turned thirty and claim the balance of his trust fund so he still hasn't been able to pay me back. But that's not important. Together we are still working to get to the bottom of the mystery of who killed Molly Bainbridge and until we do I will support him. But I cannot let that picture taken of us together seven years after his disappearance be shown to anyone. That is why I have to take the Messenger seriously.

So there I was, my cash handed over to Harry and the down payment on a new apartment looming. I went to see the bank and I must say Mr Harris was extremely nice about it all, not that I told him anything near the truth. I spun him a ridiculous yarn about having lent a lot of money to a man I was hopelessly in love with and would he please not tell my father and could I have a loan until I could get it back. Mr Harris knew my father and his father before him. He knew my family had banked there for years. He knew what my father was worth. He turned the proverbial blind eye and probably would have patted me on the head had I not been at least four inches taller than he was.

For the first time in my life I had to earn money. Real money. I'd thrown the card away but it was an easy name to remember. I found Willy O'Brien's number in the phone book and the rest, as they say, is history.

The phone was still ringing. Any moment now the answering machine would cut in. I snatched the receiver from its hook.

'Hello?' It was barely more than a whisper.

'Swan? Is that you? What's the matter? I can barely hear you. It's Patsy.'

'Oh, Patsy . . .' my relief was overwhelming. 'Where are you?'

'London. I would have called earlier but I didn't think you'd be back till now. Wasn't all that stuff in Paris wild?'

'Patsy, are you insane? I didn't think it was wild at all. I thought we were being shot at. I thought you had been killed!'

'Oh, Swan, you always fuss so about me. I just fainted. I mean, sure, I heard a crack and I thought for one tiny second that maybe something was going down but the reason I fainted was because I felt bad. I always get nervous before a show and I was so frightened about being the bride and all. I just knew I was going to throw up all over that pretty wedding dress. Anyway, I just wanted to thank you for being the bride in my place. I know you must have looked so pretty. I wanted to see you but they made me go straight home to rest. My agency is not real pleased with me right now, as you can imagine. Here in London they're keeping a real strict eye on me. They got me staying at the head booker's home, won't let me go to a hotel.'

I couldn't help smiling. Poor Patsy. It sounded like she was being taken in hand at last: no men, no late nights. It would be a terrible shock to Patsy's system but it could only work out best for her in the end.

'Thank you for calling, Patsy. You'll try to take care of yourself, won't you?'

'Swan, that is one thing I do not have to do. I've got nannies all around me. We're working together next month in Rome. I'll see you then, 'kay? Bye-bye.'

I hung up and without thinking pressed the playback button on the answering machine.

It was almost as if he had been listening in on my conversation with Patsy.

'That really fooled you, didn't it? I really enjoyed the look on your face. Even though you kept on walking you still looked terrified.' The Messenger's voice resounded in the room as if I had lifted the lid of a box and let it out. 'You thought someone was trying to shoot you. Well, it could happen. See how easy it is. Think about it, Swan, when you next go down the runway with all those cameras pointing straight at you: one of them could be a gun. I was there in Paris. I was at the show right up there in the front row! I was close enough to you so that you heard the shot being fired. And it was a shot being fired – except there was no gun. It was a tape recording. I had a little recorder on the stage in front of me between the photographers and I leaned forward and pressed PLAY just as you were going by. The clicking of all those shutters disguised the sound to everyone except you and Patsy. See, I know her name too. She probably doesn't even realise what happened. She fainted instead of you. So you're tougher than I thought. But next time – if there is a next time – it won't be a recording, it'll be the real thing.'

29

By this time I was crouched down on the floor beside my bed in fear, listening with my eyes closed, unable to move.

'Now it's nostalgia time,' the voice continued. 'Remember the first time I ever called? Remember what I asked you to do? Well, I'm going to ask you again to go and look through your mail till you find another blue airmail envelope postmarked London Heathrow. I mailed it to you before I – and you – left for Paris. It should be there by now. Inside you'll find a photograph, just like before. Don't worry, it's not of you this time. In my next message I'll tell you why I'm sending it to you. Switch off now and go and look.'

I found the envelope easily but the photograph inside was a mystery to me. I knew who it was, of course. The face smiling up at me was almost as well-known as my own, a beautiful girl who had recently rocketed to near-supermodel fame. But what did she have to do with the Messenger?

A week later I found out.

'A beauty, isn't she? Swan, you're going to have to forgive me if I say she's even more gorgeous than you are but then, you see, I'm biased. I'm in love with her. The truth is you're looking at my fiancée. We'll be married in a couple of months. I've asked her to keep it secret for the time being. I hope you're happy for me, Swan, happy for us, but that's not the reason I'm calling. I've finally decided what you can do for me to stop me sending that picture of you and that man to the press. You see, me and my fiancée, we have a prenuptial agreement. Her money will be my money and she's going to be making a ton of money, starting with the SWAN contract. That's it, Swan, that's what you have to do. I know you're stepping down as the SWAN girl. I know they have a shortlist for your replacement. My fiancée's on it and you just have to see that she gets it. Simple. I'll be calling you again soon. And one more thing: no calling her and asking about me, who I am, stuff like that. You do that and that photo of you and the man will appear on the front page of the *New York Post* and the *Sun* before you can count to five.'

Now I knew I was dealing with a deranged human being and – more dangerous – an ignorant one. He was right. I did want to give up being the SWAN girl and I had already told the Japanese. My husband and I had talked about having a baby and I wanted to try something new professionally. My love of books was as strong as ever and maybe there was still a way I could enter into the literary world. My three years were almost up, I had an out in my contract and they'd been scouting around for a new girl. In fact there'd been a shortlist for quite some time. I ran through it in my head: Tess Tucker, Cassie Dylan, Celestia Fairfax, Gigi Garcia and Amy La Mar. All fabulous girls in their own highly individual way. But his assumption that I could have any sway over the choice made by the Japanese for the girl to replace me had shown me that the Messenger was not someone who was really in the know. While the Japanese board might extend to me the courtesy of asking who I thought would be best, that was all it was: a courtesy. I had no real say in the matter.

So who was the Messenger?

He was in London in 1987 when he had taken my photo with Harry.

He could get a front row seat at the Paris Collections so did he work in the industry? Was he a fashion journalist? A buyer? A photographer? Maybe even a celebrity himself?

Yet even though he claimed to be the fiancé of an up-and-coming supermodel, he didn't know enough to realise that what he was asking me to do was impossible.

Four months from now, at the beginning of 1995, I would no longer be the SWAN girl. The board had in fact made up their mind about who was to replace me. Ironically they had chosen the girl I had recommended. There was one small problem: it was not the Messenger's fiancée.

Part 2

The Shortlist 1992–1994

London, 1992

'Telephone,' called someone up the stairs. 'Angie, it's for you.'

'Probably *Vogue* wanting to know if you'll do their next cover,' came the sarcastic voice of Angie's brother Patrick from his room.

'Cut it out,' yelled Angie as she ran down the stairs to the only telephone in the Doyle household, which took pride of place on the hall table. The only trouble was everyone in the house could hear what you were saying. Before Angie had even said 'Hello', a quick glance told her that all her brothers and sisters had moved to the top of the stairs to listen in.

'Hello,' she said hesitantly. She'd written to all the top London model agencies. Maybe this was one of them calling now to invite her in for an audition or something.

'Hi, Angie, it's Kevin. I was wondering if you would come with us to see Chris Isaak at the Hammersmith Apollo tomorrow night? They say he's really grand.'

The disappointment hit Angie hard, causing her to catch her breath. Kevin O'Connor. A nice enough boy. Liverpool Irish. An electrician's apprentice who hadn't been able to find work in the North so he'd come down to London. He had singled her out in the pub two weeks ago when she'd been having a night out with her girlfriends and she'd been aware they'd all been quite impressed.

But Chris Isaak! Too pleased with himself by far and not

35

her kind of music. Besides, Kevin was getting too pushy. She had other things on her mind.

'Sorry, Kev. He does nothing for me. He's too schmaltzy. Ask someone else.'

'Schmaltzy? What does that mean?'

'You see, we just don't speak the same language.'

Poor Kevin. She always confused him but what else could she do?

'Not *Vogue* then?' sneered Patrick.

'Or *Cosmo*?' Eleven-year-old Kathleen was lying on her stomach looking down at Angie through the banisters.

'Who's Cosmo?' asked Michael, seven.

'You wouldn't understand if we told you,' Jeannie told him. At nine she was vastly superior to poor Michael.

'Why don't you get yourself an agent?' Patrick was leaning against the door of his room trying to look cooler than cool. At nearly sixteen he thought he was the bee's knees and crossed her at every opportunity, but Angie knew that at the root of it all was the fact that he resented being younger than she was. He should be the one taking care of the family, not Angie. He was a man, wasn't he? Well, almost. When their mother had walked out four years ago Angie had stepped automatically into her shoes and taken it upon herself to look after her brothers and sisters. Their father, Joseph Doyle, had aged ten years overnight.

'What's an agent?' Michael kicked his football down the stairs and clapped his hands when it crashed into a picture of the Virgin Mary on the way and dislodged it from the wall.

'Michael!' everyone protested wearily in unison. Michael caused havoc day in, day out. Angie understood why. He was a very physical little boy and it was a terrible restraint for him living in the cramped little two-up, two-down with the girls all sleeping in one bedroom, the boys in the other, with their

36

father grabbing what sleep he could between his shift work on the settee in the living room. There were moments when Angie could see why her mother had upped and left. She herself hated having to share a room with Kathleen and Jeannie, hated, on the rare occasion when she had a date, having to get ready with the two of them watching her every move and keeping up a running commentary:

'You're never going to wear that. You've had it a million years. He must have seen it before. He won't want to marry you if he sees you in that.' They were already trying to marry her off.

'He'll think you don't have anything else to wear.' She didn't.

'Mum's not going to let you go out looking like that. You'll catch it. You'll see!' And then the inevitable realisation that Mum wasn't there any more, followed as always by the tears which Angie then had to mop up. Small wonder she was always left with barely half a minute to do her make-up.

'What's an agent?' Michael asked again, 'and why don't you get one, Angie?' Michael liked to echo his big brother at every opportunity.

Patrick had a point, thought Angie as she went into the kitchen to begin making the tea. They ate at 6.30 sharp and with luck their dad would be home in time to eat with them. Angie knew the children were happier if he was there, though they tried not to show it.

It had been two months since she'd posted the letters to the agencies enclosing two snapshots of herself, one a head shot and the other full length, and still she'd had no reply. It had been those snapshots that had started it all. Her father had taken them at the beginning of the summer when the whole family had gone to the seaside for the day. Maybe it was a trick of the light, maybe she really was better looking than she'd ever imagined, but when she picked up the developed prints she could hardly believe the girl in the photos was really her. Nor could her brothers and sisters, who teased her unmercifully – 'Suppose you think you can be a model or something now' – until she began to sneak looks at the pictures and started to wonder. . . . They didn't know, of course, that it had been her dream, her secret ambition, to become a model and she had read somewhere that what you looked like in the flesh didn't matter. It was how you photographed that counted. But it was the bit of information her father told her in a quiet, resigned voice one evening after she'd finally managed to get the rest of the children to bed.

'Your ma was going to be a model years ago. She'd just been accepted by one of them agencies when we met.'

'Dad, you're kidding! I know she was beautiful but what happened?'

'She married me.'

'Well, that shouldn't have stopped her.'

'She got pregnant.'

Suddenly Angie realised what he was saying. 'With me?'

'And then with Patrick. She lost her figure after that. She never got it back. But those photos, Angie girl, you're really good looking in them. There's so much money to be made and there's so many of you children. D'you see what I'm trying to say?'

After that Angie was determined. So what if the agencies didn't write back to her? She'd go and see them in the flesh. Once they'd seen her, well, that would be it.

She'd heard of an agency in Covent Garden called Etoile that had what they called an open casting. Anyone could go in between ten and twelve in the morning and if they liked the look of you they gave you a photographic test and if that worked out OK they took you on.

Jeannie and Kathleen became suspicious as soon as Angie didn't jump out of bed when the alarm went off. She wanted them out of the room so she could decide what to wear in peace, but they weren't buying it.

'Why aren't you downstairs getting our breakfast? You'll be late for school.'

Finally she had to tell them where she was going just to get rid of them.

'Our Angie's going to be a model today,' she heard Jeannie tell the neighbours as Patrick led them off to school.

'Patrick, do me a favour. Tell them at school that I've got the flu. Summer flu. Very nasty,' Angie called down to the street.

'Well, don't go giving it to Kate Moss if you're working with her today,' he called back.

'I'm not,' she said truthfully.

Everyone was talking about the Grunge look and Angie had been practising putting her own outfit together whenever she could get a moment's privacy in the bathroom. It consisted of a long navy and white floral print cotton dress, a pair of baseball boots, a back to front baseball cap and little round metal-framed granny shades with blue lenses. Finally she hung a big silver crucifix that had belonged to her grandmother around her neck. She felt a tinge of guilt, knowing that this had nothing to do with her Catholic upbringing and everything to do with the fact that crucifixes were a fashion accessory. The boots were Patrick's but she'd be back long before he noticed. The floating floral dress had buttons up the front. In her nervous rush, Angie didn't notice that she'd done up the buttons all wrong so one side of the dress hung down below the other, leaving her left leg exposed. She wasn't a great one for looking at herself in the mirror. Normally she never had time. The dress was fashionably long but there was a reason for this. It had been her mother's and her mother had been a tall woman. Angie had inherited her father's looks – and his height. She was only 5 feet 2 inches. Her legs were so sturdy that Patrick had taken to calling her Thunder Thighs until their father had stopped him. (Needless to say Michael had picked up the refrain and often came home from school chanting 'Thunder thighs, thunder thighs, what's for tea?') She was almost completely flat chested and her saving grace was her sweet round face with its huge midnight blue eyes fringed by her father's long black lashes. The baseball cap crammed on top of her mop of ebony curls looked ridiculous, the boots were too big, the dress hung unevenly and the granny sunglasses hid her best feature.

This was the picture Angie presented to the Etoile Agency as she stepped through their doors to make her family's fortune.

No one looked up.

Angie saw a couple of girls standing in front of her, trying to look nonchalant.

'Are you here for the open casting?' she asked one of them.

'Yes.'

'What happens?'

'You report to the receptionist and then she shows you to that girl over there. She does the New Faces. We're all together. Three of us came up from Croydon.'

'Oh,' said Angie, 'I'm on my own. Guess I'll have to wait.'

She looked around her. At a big circular table several people were frantically answering the phones and scribbling on clipboards which they snatched from a revolving hanger. Angie looked closer and saw they were calendars with girls' names on them at the top. Suzy Q. Amanda. Meghan. Claudia Schiffer. *Claudia Schiffer*! Angie squealed and now several people did turn to look at her, but they soon looked away.

As she watched and listened, Angie worked out what was happening. The girls at the round table were some sort of appointment makers since their phone conversations often resulted in them pencilling in a date for a model – and a fee: £350 + 20 per cent, $750 + 20 per cent, £2,500 plus first-class transportation were some of the figures she heard.

Behind her was a blackboard headed CASTINGS. Angie read what was written below in amazement.

11 a.m.–12	*Woman's Journal.*
	Gary Marlowe's studio, King's Road 'Classical looks and can you ride a horse?'
3–4	Casting at the agency for travel brochure. 2-week shoot in Botswana. Girl who's good with animals – especially snakes and monkeys.
4–5	Vogue Promotions. Sophisticated and classy.

Then she just stood and drank in all the hullabaloo going on around her.

'Listen, darling it's going to improve your book no end just to go and see him. He might want to take some nice piccies of you, in fact I know he will, you're just his type. You need his work to make your book stronger. He did Tia Maria with Iman. He's on a par with Bailey.'

'They want her to go to Milan for five days' casting and I just know she won't do that.'

'It's one day, you fly first class, $15,000 and you show the clothes to Ivana Trump.'

'There's something perfect for you. If you run you can just make it. It's 11 to 12 and they want someone who can ride a horse. When do you ever do anything else, Amanda? Listen, I'll give you the address.'

Angie looked behind her. Amanda, whoever she was, was

41

being told to go on a casting. Now she understood it. They were the day's castings for jobs coming up. Could anyone go on them? Maybe she'd better wait until the agency took her on. Anyway, she couldn't ride a horse. Did all models have to be able to ride a horse?

The longer Angie waited the more fascinated she became. There was an incredible rush of energy about the place, not to mention the overall feeling of glamour. The whole of one wall was covered with plastic pockets containing the girls' showcards: endless black-and-white photographs or photocopies of beautiful girls. Everyone who walked into the place was either tall and leggy and looked like they'd stepped out of a magazine or they were beat-up cool-looking guys who Angie reckoned had to be photographers or male models. Even the bikers delivering parcels, striding in in their leathers, seemed to have the required in-look. If someone turned up the blasting music, someone else turned it down, if someone opened the windows, someone else closed them, if someone made a huge pot of tea it would be left sitting on a chair undrunk while people shouted messages at each other over the noise without ever checking if they had been heard. Without a doubt Angie knew she wanted to be a part of this crazy world.

The other girls who had come to the open casting were leaving, giggling and bumping into each other. Angie went up to the receptionist, asked to see the New Faces girl and was directed to Sarah. On closer inspection Sarah was not at all glamorous. Although she was sitting down, Angie could see she was short and rather plump. She looked up at Angie and smiled vaguely before returning to her calls. Angie saw that she had an open, kind face, not particularly pretty.

'Eh, excuse me,' said Angie, 'they said you dealt with New Faces.'

42

'Yes, I do,' said Sarah without looking up.

'Here are some pictures of me. I did send them to the agency a couple of months ago. Maybe . . .?'

Sarah looked up and stared hard at Angie for a few seconds. Then she sighed and handed her a sheet of paper. 'Here's a list of all the modelling agencies in London.'

'No, you don't understand,' persisted Angie, 'I've already written to them but I thought I'd come and see you in the flesh. Am I not right for you?'

'I don't think so,' said Sarah. 'You don't really have our look.'

'Oh, well, I'll try somewhere else,' said Angie cheerfully. 'Which one would you recommend for me?'

'You want the truth?' asked Sarah.

Angie nodded.

'None of them. I think it's best if I tell you straight out. There's no chance you'd ever be a model. You need to be at least 5 foot 8 for runway work. You're the wrong shape for print work, you're about two sizes too big and your legs look like they're too short and too large. These snapshots are really sweet but they don't say model. It's best you know that now rather than go on trying in vain. You have a very pretty face, of course you do, but it's just wrong for modelling, that's all.' Sarah was smiling kindly and speaking very gently. Angie felt the tears of disappointment starting to well up in her eyes. How could she have been so stupid?

She asked where the Ladies was so she could recover herself in private but when she saw herself in the mirror it only made it worse. There was her dress all hoisted up showing her short stubby legs, and her silly cap squashing down all her curls. What must they have thought of her? She squirmed when she realised how out of place she must have looked amongst all the glamorous people coming and going. Yet when she thought

43

about it, Sarah wasn't glamorous. She was ordinary and fairly pretty, in fact she was rather like Angie herself without the ridiculous get-up. You've made a fool of yourself, Angie Doyle, she thought, but you're not beaten yet.

She washed her face and returned to Sarah's side.

'OK, Sarah, so I'm not a model but I make a fabulous cup of tea. I can sweep the floor. I can answer the phones and take messages. I can go out and get your sandwiches. I can do anything you want. I may not be photographic but I'm bright and I'm willing. Please give me a job here.' Silently she added: I've got four sisters and brothers and I need to help my dad look after them. He's depending on me.

'How old are you, Angie?'

'Sixteen. Seventeen next month.'

'Well, come back when you've left school.'

Sarah hadn't bargained for the Doyle determination. Angie left school at the end of that term, just walked out without even getting her GCSEs. For the next three weeks she turned up at Etoile every day.

'I'm going to show you who I am and what I can do,' she told Sarah. 'I know there isn't a job but I've got my big fat non-model's foot in the door and I'm going to keep it there until there is. I'm going to work unpaid and I'm going to be here every morning whether you like it or not.'

Which is exactly what she did for five weeks, making endless cups of tea and coffee (and making sure people found time to drink them), forcing people to give her errands to run, dogging everybody's movements, watching and learning all the time.

It happened one lunchtime.

The place was deserted. It hardly ever was but half the booking table were on their lunch break and the other four had nipped out for some cigarettes, gone downstairs to make a cup of tea, gone to the loo, whatever. Angie was on her own when the phone rang.

It was one of London's top photographers going apeshit in his studio about Marianne. Marianne was one of the agency's biggest earners, an amazing six-foot girl with peroxide hair and ice blue eyes who was never out of work. She also had the emotional resilience of a nine-year-old. Her love life was a permanent mess and depending what had happened with Roger, Mark, Gavin, Simon or whoever the night before, she was either a dream to work with or a complete wreck. Apparently she'd spent the morning standing in front of the camera like a limp rag saying there was nothing she could do until Roger rang to tell her he still loved her.

'Darlin', you're gonna have to have a word with her,' the photographer told Angie, 'or I'm going to get on the phone and book another model. There was a girl at Tempest we nearly booked and if she's not working today, I'm going to get her over. I'm not putting up with Marianne any more.'

'Put her on,' said Angie, trying to stop her hands shaking in terror. Tempest was Etoile's biggest rival. Angie checked Marianne's chart and saw a grand going down the tube if she lost the job.

'Hi, Marianne, this is Angie, what's the problem?' Angie tried to make it sound as if she'd been working at Etoile for years.

'Roger hasn't rung. We were in this club at one in the morning and he's dancing with this girl and I'm like, what's he playing at? I mean I know there's nothing going on 'cause she's with her fella but when I ask him what's he doing dancing with this girl, he goes: We're not married, leave me alone, I can dance with who I want, and like, I run out 'cause I'm all upset and I haven't heard from him since.'

'Have you tried calling him?'

45

'Oh, I daren't.'

'Give me his number, Marianne. I'll call Roger. Pretend I'm trying to reach you. See what his reaction is. Then I'll call back and let you know.'

Roger was a bit sheepish. Angie had seen it happen so often in arguments between her brothers and sisters, between her own friends. It was all a bit of a misunderstanding that had got out of hand. Both sides wanted to kiss and make up but neither dared make the first move.

'If I find her, Roger, I'll get her to call you,' Angie told him then she rang Marianne back at the studio.

The pictures of Marianne in *Elle* were fantastic.

Next time he was talking to the booking table, the photographer told them, 'That new girl you got's really great. She worked wonders with Marianne. You'd better hang on to her.'

What new girl?

Angie came clean.

Which is how when Sarah left two months later to go and work at Tempest, everybody agreed that Angie would be the perfect person to take her place with the New Faces.

Angie had become a booker.

London, 1993

Tess Tucker was a redhead like her father. She had his green eyes too but neither of them had the flaming temper usually associated with redheads. Terry Tucker and his daughter were obliging, easygoing people who sometimes drove Tess's mother Annie mad because they did so much for other people and not enough for themselves.

Terry Tucker had a newspaper stand at the bottom of the Earls Court Road where it hit the Old Brompton Road. It was right across the street from where Princess Diana used to live before she married, and Terry had often sold her newspapers and magazines. He was very proud of his stand. It had cost about £7,000 and had been built for him by the *Herald Tribune* whose name was emblazoned across the top, giving them free advertising 365 days a year. It was only a year old but the site on which it stood had been in the family, so to speak, for nearly a hundred years with newspaper stalls handed down from father to son. Only Terry didn't have a son to hand it on to, he only had a daughter: Tess.

And he had problems. He owned his stand but he didn't own the site on which it stood. Nobody really knew who did. Behind the stand stood a pub and the pub had recently changed hands. The new brewers didn't want a newspaper stand on their doorstep but they didn't own the pavement any more than Terry did, and he reckoned that they had no right to try to move him on so until they actually got him to court and won a case, he wasn't about to budge.

Tess helped him out after school and at weekends. She loved the stand. They sold sweets now and loads of magazines. Her dad had his off-to-work regulars who stopped to buy their morning paper on the way to Earls Court tube station and he had his lunchtime and afternoon customers who came for their *Standard*. The one thing that made Annie furious was the way Terry trotted off on a delivery round every morning without being paid extra.

'It's not even as if they're old people you deliver to. They could get up easy and come and get them. It's not right, lazy young layabouts with their bleedin' *Independents* and *Guardians*. All the old people come out to get their *Sun* and their *Mirror*. . . .'

'Yes, but that's because they're lonely and they like a chat with Dad,' Tess pointed out. 'It's probably the highlight of their day, poor old dears.'

'And they like seeing you too.' Her father smiled. It never ceased to amaze him how lovely his daughter was. Thick red hair and the palest pure white skin he had ever seen. And those green cat's eyes were so piercing they almost shimmered at you. She looked tougher than she was, did Tess, he often thought. Terry knew she was shy and sensitive like he was. Oh, he liked to stand and joke and gossip with his regulars but it was a front he had forced himself to adopt for the sake of his work.

'You should be on the cover of those magazines,' people told Tess, pointing to Cindy Crawford on *American Vogue* and Claudia Schiffer on *Vanity Fair* behind her.

'That's what I keep telling her,' said her father, but he knew Tess was far too shy and quiet to go off and be a model. It might be one of her secret dreams but she would never actually do anything about it.

As it turned out he didn't know his daughter quite as well as he thought he did.

Tess's mother was in a wheelchair, had been as long as Tess could remember. When Tess was only four years old, Annie had had a stroke which had paralysed her from the waist down and as a result she had not been able to have any more children. Tess had grown up an only child and in the early days she had helped out a great deal in the home. Then, as soon as she was old enough, she had started helping out her father after school. She had few friends and Annie felt that those she did have took advantage of her. She was worried about her daughter, worried about her ability to stand up for herself in the world. She was insecure and vulnerable despite her breathtaking looks. It was, Annie thought, quite remarkable that Tess had no idea how beautiful she was.

But Annie was wrong. Tess had been looking at herself in the mirror a good deal recently. She had been studying her own face and those of the girls on the covers of magazines. The remarks of her father's regulars had not fallen on deaf ears. And she had seen an advertisement in *Smash Hits* for a competition called Girl of the Year. They wanted you to send in snapshots of yourself but she didn't have any. She noted the address of the agency sponsoring the show. She'd go there herself and see what happened. She knew that with modelling it was possible to make a lot of money very quickly. Tess didn't waste time when she was working on her father's stall. She studied the papers every morning during the school holidays when she was often there all day and she had read about a new motorised wheelchair that was on the market, a wheelchair that could completely revolutionise her mother's life. But there was no way her father could afford it.

What she never knew as she walked down the street to the agency on the first day of the summer holidays was that someone on the booking table, who happened to be looking out the window, saw her coming, broke off from her telephone call and shrieked, 'Angie, there's a six-footer coming down the street, a redhead, who is the best-looking girl I've seen in months. Go out and grab her before she gets away. If she doesn't photograph like a dream, I'll give this business up by lunchtime.'

So when Tess walked in and nervously apologised for not having any snapshots of herself she was somewhat gobsmacked to find her wrist grabbed by a pretty, overweight girl with a mass of black curls who held on to it while she dialled a number with her other hand and said, 'Harry? Can you do a photographic test on someone, like, immediately? Can I send her right over? You won't regret it. OK, fine. She'll be there in half an hour. Her name is – hold on, I have to find out what her name is – Harry, you still there? It's Tess. Tess Tucker.'

Miami, 1993

Gigi Garcia was born chewing gum. At least that's what her mother Elena reckoned, not that she'd been present at Gigi's birth. But what did Elena know? She was just a *vieja chocha*, a silly old lady who didn't speak any English. How Gigi longed to shout out loud and tell the world that Elena wasn't her real mother but every time she threatened to do so, Elena sucked in her shrivelled lips and warned, 'Go ahead. Do what you want. Spit on the person who gave you a home. You tell them the truth, Gigi, and they'll throw you out just like they did your mother.'

The trouble was, the bitch' was right. Gigi was an illegal immigrant in America. Her parents had been 'Marielitos', boat refugees arriving in Miami from the tiny port of Mariel in Cuba in 1980. These refugees were not middle-class Cubans like those who had fled Cuba decades earlier when Castro came to power and had since worked hard and established themselves as respectable citizens in the Little Havana area of Miami before moving on to surburban life. 'Marielitos' were Cuba's misfits, poor, uneducated and many of them, including Gigi's father, criminals fresh from jail.

Her father never made it to Miami, or rather, he never made it to dry land. In his excitement he fell overboard just before arriving and was promptly attacked by a Portuguese man-of-war. He was dragged under and since he couldn't swim he drowned.

'You trying to tell me my father died by being stung by a fucking jellyfish?' Gigi simply would not believe it when, in answer to her question, 'What really happened to my father?' Elena had explained the details for the first time. 'I figured he died with a bullet in his head, a knife in his back, something he could have been fucking proud of. Something I could have been proud of.' Elena winced. She could barely speak English but she could sniff blasphemy in the air in the middle of a tornado. Besides, she could never understand why Gigi was so dissatisfied with her father's ignominious death, why the girl pretended to her friends that he had been a hero. Nothing was going to bring him back.

'I dint tell you before because you too young. I tink, she prolly go crazy if I tell her dis,' explained Elena in the Hispanic accent Gigi hated so much.

'And my fucking mother abandoned me,' Gigi always went on to insist, however many times Elena pointed out to her that Gigi's mother had been deported but since the authorities had not known of the existence of her eleven-month-old daughter she had been determined that at least one member of the family should have a chance of living in America. She had handed her baby to Elena Garcia, the wife of another refugee, whose own baby had died at birth back in Havana.

Unlike the refugees of the 1950s who by now had their own businesses, the 'Marielitos' only made it as far as South Beach, where they setttled down to terrorise the local community. Ironically, Elena Garcia's husband was killed in just the kind of violent brawl that Gigi would have wanted her real father to die in. She was eleven at the time and from then on the widow Elena more or less gave up on her own life. As a result Gigi began to run wild.

Deep down she was proud of being Cuban, but by the time she was seven years old she was sick of Elena holding up Desi Arnaz and Gloria Estefan as national heroes, sick of only watching WLTV (the Spanish-language channel), and sick of hearing about the Bay of Pigs as if it were something that had happened yesterday instead of nearly twenty years before she was born. Yet in her own way Gigi's passions ran as high as those of her country's early independence fighters. She was a true Latin, ready to go into instant action, violent or otherwise, to defend her views rather than settle down to a rational discussion. Elena's resigned attitude to life was anathema to her. As she grew up it was impossible to restrain her. Her eternal question was always: 'How am I going to get away from here? What am I supposed to do all day? Hang around shaking the palm trees and waiting for $50 bills to fall into my lap? No way, José! I'm going to party!'

She was only six years old when Bruce Weber hit Miami to shoot nudes on the hotel roofs for the Calvin Klein Obsession campaign but she heard about it and filed it away in her child's mind for use in the future. From that day on she couldn't wait to walk the few blocks to Ocean Drive, away from the run-down poverty-stricken part of South Beach where she and Elena shared two rooms above a launderette in a tiny street off Collins, where the houses were all backed up one against the other and the only view from the window was of drug deals being transacted in the shadows below.

It always came down to money. Gigi just couldn't see how they were ever going to have enough to live a better life. Elena had a job as a maid at the Park Central hotel on Ocean Drive. Sometimes Gigi had to go and find her to deliver a message and inside the art deco palace it was like entering another world. She invariably found Elena cleaning one of the guest's rooms and Gigi would simply stand and stare at the simple, stylish décor, the low bed on the floor, the mosquito net hanging above it and above that the hypnotic rotation of the ceiling fan. She liked to open the closets when Elena wasn't looking and feast her eyes on the rows of the hotel guests' designer clothes. Occasionally, when Elena was called away, she would whip out a dress and try it on, parading up and down in front of the mirrors.

At twelve years old Gigi already had breasts, two firm melons which jutted out beneath her T-shirt. She had creamy Cuban skin, dark coffee in colour. Her hair was a close-cropped helmet of jet black poodle curls some of which she had semi-straightened to hang in tendrils down her face. Her normal facial expression was a sultry pout due to the sensual fullness of her lower lip but when she smiled her mouth was suddenly stretched into a glare of dazzling white teeth, giving her the look of a Latin Carly Simon.

By thirteen, Gigi was all woman and sensationally cur-vaceous. She had tits and a 20-inch waist, an ass that wiggled when she walked and long silky thighs, and every weekend at seven o'clock she went down to Ocean Drive between Fifth and 14th Streets to show off her wares. The place was always a riot, cruise city for the ravers with cars moving at a snail's pace going round and round, bumper to bumper, stereos blast-ing, horns honking and guys leaping out of one car and into another and back again. Gigi jostled with the crowd and tried to look cool hanging around in the News Café but somehow she couldn't quite compete with the hordes of models who appeared to have flown in from all over the world. The unspoken message of the jocks driving in their sports cars seemed to be 'Why would we want a regular little Cubana when we can have our pick of blondes from Scandinavia or New York?'

Ultimately she always found herself walking up the sandhill

to the beach and staring out to the horizon. Somewhere out there was Cuba, the land of her birth, and her real mother. She loved it when it rained and the skies were stormy and the waves rolled in off the Atlantic and crashed on to the sand. The raw tempestuous beauty of the beach at that time was more in keeping with her own fierce Latin unrest.

It was during one of these walks on the beach that she saw what she thought was an old beach bum stoop and pick up a $10 note someone had dropped in the sand. That could have been me, she thought, just my luck he saw it first. It didn't really dawn on her that she had been following him until she realised she had walked all the way down the beach. She was almost at the German-owned Century Hotel, about two miles from South Point. Postmodern and ultra-smart, the Century was the last word in designer chic. Surely the bum wasn't going in there?

He wasn't. Opposite the Century was a derelict old building on the beach that had obviously once been a hotel. Now it was empty with an eerie feel to it. Gigi had never forgotten the remark someone had once made that if they ever killed someone and wanted to dump the body, here was the place to do it. Had the bum wasted someone, brought them here to do some dope deal and then blown them away? Gigi waited for about fifteen minutes then her curiosity got the better of her and she ventured inside. She saw the bum immediately, slumped on the floor, fast asleep with an empty bottle beside him and the $10 bill still in his hand. Gigi crouched down beside him on her six-inch mules and slowly began to tease the bill out of his hand. His mouth was open and his breath smelled foul, coming at her in waves along with the stench of his grimy clothes. He was a Cubano, one of her own. She shuddered in revulsion. Fucking lazy bastards. It was always the women who had to work as far as she could see; the men in her neighbourhood never seemed to do anything. Her growing rage made her tear at the money in the bum's fist and he woke up with a start. Before she knew what was happening he had grabbed her by the crotch, tearing at the denim of her cutoffs.

'You wan' eet?' He held the money high above his head. 'Beetch!'

His grip was strong. If she moved away from him her jeans would be ripped at the crotch.

'You can have eet if you do something for me.'

'Gimme the money first.' Gigi's hustler's instinct had surfaced before she had even asked what he wanted her to do. His fist relaxed slightly and she whipped the money away but when she tried to make a run for it she felt her jeans begin to tear.

The bum was fumbling with his flies.

What she had to do was disgusting but it was also easy. He came instantly. For Gigi, the thrill of earning money for the first time in her life far outshone the degradation of what she had just done.

She didn't stop there. She watched from her window for likely clients and raced down to service them right there in the alley. She called her savings her Alley Cat stash and kept it in a box under her bed. After a month she upped her rates to fifteen bucks and a month after that she encountered her first taste of violence when a john whacked her across the head. She screamed so loud she alerted a cop, who came running to her aid.

'How old are you?' was his first question.

'Thirteen,' she said without thinking.

'I see you doing this again I'm taking you straight down to the Dade County Jail. Understand? Now get on home.'

It was 5.30 in the morning and suddenly Gigi was frightened

to go back to an empty home. Elena was on night shift. Without fully comprehending why, Gigi made her way to Ocean Drive.

Outside the Park Central stood a never-ending line of motor homes. Gigi glimpsed inside and to her amazement saw toilets, videos, sofa suites and sumptuous breakfasts being laid out. Inside the hotel, expecting to find the place fast asleep, she was confronted instead by a bustling hubbub of activity. Another mouth-watering breakfast buffet had been laid out up the stairs from the lobby by the bar, people were rushing about carrying camera equipment and armfuls of clothes but it was only when she went upstairs in search of her mother that Gigi came across the strangest sight of all. In the balcony above the lobby were fitting rooms with clothes rails and make-up rooms with mirrors. Semi-naked girls were running around, dashing in and out of the clothes rails. More models sat staring vacantly into the mirrors while they were made up and their hair was piled on top of their heads in curlers. Some were still puffy-eyed from sleep and the moans of agony all told the same story.

'I mean, I was in Warsaw till two. I think I'm going to curl up and die and call you from hell.'

'I thought the only straight night at Warsaw's was Saturdays?'

'So I was with Fred and Ginger and they got me in. Terrible music! Gilberto Gil or someone. Give me a break!'

'Give me a cup of coffee. Where's the shoot today? Someone said something about Key Biscayne. Hi, you little cutie? Who are you and what are you doing here?' One of the models caught sight of Gigi in the mirror.

'I'm looking for my mom.'

'Does she have a shoot this morning? Is she a model, make-up, seamstress or what?'

57

'She's a maid,' said Gigi, embarrassed.

'Well, she's probably cleaning out our rooms back there, isn't she?' The model had lost interest and returned to the girl next to her: ' . . . so I'm on this giant dance floor, right, and this really butch guy comes up and stares at me and he asks: who did your op? and I say: what? and then I get it, he thinks I'm a tranny!'

Gigi wandered away down one of the long corridors. She couldn't see Elena anywhere. The girls finally departed in a mass exodus down the stairs, through the lobby and into the motor homes. Suddenly the place was quiet, deserted. Housekeeper's wagons with clean sheets had been abandoned in the hotel corridors. Gigi slipped through an open door. Within seconds she was indulging in her favourite pastime: trying on the fancy clothes she found in the closets.

'Is this your room?'

Gigi had her back to the door. The voice was low and male and sexy. Maybe if she didn't turn around he'd go away.

'I said, is this your room? And by the way you have the most photographic backview I've seen in years. You ought to make a plaster cast of your ass and sell the mould to plastic surgeons as inspiration.'

Gigi turned around slowly. She was wearing a skin-tight thigh-length Lycra tube with a scoop neck and three-quarter-length sleeves. She struck a pose without even realising what she was doing: legs wide apart stretching the Lycra as far as it would go, hands on hips, head thrown back, staring down at him arrogantly.

Then she crumpled. She had no right to be there. Maybe it was his room and this was his wife's dress she had on. Maybe any minute now he was going to call the manager and Elena would be fired. The Dade County jail beckoned yet again.

She sank to her knees before him.

'I'll give you special rate. Ten dollars. Seven-fifty.'

He looked puzzled. Then he held out his hand and helped her to her feet.

'My name is Charley Lobianco. I'm really pleased to meet you.'

Holy shit! thought Gigi. The guy turns out to be the first gentleman I've ever met and I'm offering to suck his dick. He was old, no not old, mature. Thirty-five at least. He had sunstreaked brown hair to his collar and he was wearing a light suede jacket over a black shirt. Gigi had never been within sniffing distance of expensive aftershave but she knew she was smelling it now. He was holding her with both hands at arm's length, appraising her.

'You're very beaooooutiful.' He spun the word out for several seconds. He had a slight accent but it wasn't Spanish. 'Tell me your name.'

'Gigi.'

'Don't be frightened. I can help you. I run model agency in New York. You hear stories. You think you got to sleep with me before I make you a model. Is not true. This does not happen any more. Is all very eighties. Is not necessary. I am getting very successful. I have very big girls now. You come to New York, I make you big.'

'You from Miami?' Gigi eyed him suspiciously.

'I'm I*tal*ian.' The emphasis came down heavily on the *tal*. 'You know what I do? I start new model war with John Casablancas. He has his agency Elite. Mine is Etoile. French for star. I make you a star. Is OK by you?'

He was stroking her now, running his long fingers down her face, her neck, feeling the tops of her arms, pushing her slightly, making her turn round for him, walk up and down like a racehorse in a paddock. He fished in his pocket.

'Here you are. My card. Call me when you come to New York. Right now you too young but I tell you what you do. You enter competitions, Etoile competitions, you tell them Charley sent you and you will win. 'Bye *cara*, I have to go to the shoot.'

He was gone, slipping off down the long corridor in his bare feet and moccasins. At the end he stopped and turned to call back: 'Take off that dress and put it back before they catch you. One day you're going to be wearing beaooooutiful clothes all day long and making me lots of beaooooutiful money. I see you later.'

She combed the beach up and down Ocean Drive but she couldn't find him at any of the shoots. He must have gone to that shoot in Key Biscayne one of the girls had mentioned and she had no way of getting there.

Gigi had two ambitions in life and they were not entirely mutually exclusive. One was to become a model and the other was to find Charley Lobianco again and make him treat her like a woman and not like a little girl.

She entered the Etoile competition and she came second. The winner was a tall, sun-kissed blonde with blue eyes. The same thing happened six months later and Gigi developed a ferocious hatred for tall, all-American blondes with blue eyes. Was she always going to lose out to them? As a Hispanic was she always going to take second place? Was there no demand for her sultry Latin looks? Charley Lobianco had believed there would be and she clung to that.

One day she finally won. When they presented her with the bouquet and hung the sash across her body they found they had to send out for a bigger one that would cover her breasts.

The first prize for the contest was to be flown direct to New York and be taken on to Etoile's books. She would see Charley

60

again. She rushed back to the two rooms on Collins and in the space of a few minutes she threw away her Florida life and packed a bag for her new one. She might not have a passport or any real status or identity but she was on her way and she had no intention of ever coming back. She felt a twinge of guilt about not seeing Elena before she left, so she wrote her a note and left it on the kitchen table. She would call her from New York.

'She's not my real mother,' she told herself on the plane to New York, frantically chewing gum to steady her nerves. 'She's not my real mother. She doesn't mean anything to me.'

Still, when she arrived at JFK, Gigi called Elena right away. She was suddenly freaked by the enormity of what she had done. It was late at night and she had her Alley Cat stash and the address of Etoile in New York but beyond that she was on her own.

Elena's neighbour answered the phone. Where was Gigi? They had been searching South Beach for her. Why? Elena had collapsed. Her heart, a brain haemorrhage, who knew what had happened? She had been dead on arrival at the hospital.

And to her own amazement, Gigi found herself spending her first night in New York, the first night of her brand new life, sobbing her heart out for the woman she had always pretended meant nothing to her.

London, 1993

'My dear, it's too exciting. I thought the day would never come when she'd be old enough to carry on the family tradition. Of course, she hasn't got anything like the looks her grandmother and I were blessed with – takes after her father, poor girl – but I'm determined to do what I can . . .'

The Hon. Celestia Fairfax covered her ears with her hands as her mother prattled on to her sister 'Pwimwose' in their daily telephone call. The youngest child of Lord Fairfax, the distinguished historian, Celestia was sixteen and home for the summer holidays from St Mary's, Calne, the exclusive Wiltshire boarding-school, and if her mother had anything to do with it she wouldn't be going back in the autumn.

Lady Prudence Fairfax – or 'Pwudence' as she called herself, being unable to pronounce her 'r's – gave new meaning to the term upper-class twit.

'Pwimwose darling, I can still remember the first time Bailey photographed me. It was too fwilling. . . .'

The *only* time, hissed Celestia through clenched teeth. Lady Prudence claimed to have been a sixties model and to hear her go on, a stranger might be forgiven for thinking she had given Jean Shrimpton a bit of competition when in actual fact she had merely tripped along the catwalk as a débutante at the Berkeley Dress Show and had once managed to be one of twenty in a group photograph for a cosmetics ad taken by

62

David Bailey. As far as Celestia could make out, her mother had been nothing more than an upper-class dolly bird (more Eaton Square than King's Road) before snaring the most eligible bachelor around in the form of Celestia's father, Hugo Fairfax, a devastatingly good-looking Cambridge undergraduate and heir to Trevane, a romantically Gothic house on a sprawling estate covering a large amount of land in darkest Devon. Nobody had been able to understand how someone as brilliant as Hugo could marry anyone as dim and irritatingly frothy as Prudence Pickering although no one could deny that between them, Prudence and Primrose Pickering, the Heavenly Twins from Henley-on-Thames, had made quite an impact during their season. Some said it was an attraction of opposites and others, more cynically, assumed that Prudence was after a title.

For Celestia, growing up at Trevane was like living at Manderley crossed with Wuthering Heights. Her father spent most of his time locked away in the library and to Prudence's eternal despair he seemed perfectly happy for their wild and headstrong daughter to roam the grounds all day either on foot or riding bareback in as filthy a collection of moth-eaten garments as she could muster. Worse, as she approached adolescence, Celestia's face began to develop her father's strong handsome features rather than her mother's fragile bones. She grew tall and angular with jutting cheekbones, a long nose and an extraordinary wide, slightly lop-sided mouth. Her long brown hair hung down her back in a constantly matted state of tangles.

Once, when Prudence was in the middle of an afternoon's flower arranging in the Great Hall (and being photographed by *Tatler* in the process), Celestia had wandered in looking so dishevelled that for a second or two her own mother had failed to recognise her and had dropped a glass bowl in shock

63

at the sight of what she thought was an intruding tramp. Prudence had subsequently been rather miffed when *Tatler* never ran her pictures but she would have been apoplectic with rage had she known of the excitement back at the *Tatler* offices over the two frames in which Celestia had appeared. Discerning eyes saw beyond the unruly vagabond (already 5 feet 8 inches tall) to the wonderful haughty bone structure of the face the camera had captured. A note was made to keep an eye out for the Hon. Celestia in a few years' time.

But while Prudence might only have played at being a model, Celestia's grandmother had been the real thing. For the last twenty years of her life she lived in the folly at Trevane and Celestia frequently escaped the stifling atmosphere of her mother's presence to spend an afternoon with her grandmother going through her scrapbooks. Fiona, Lady Fairfax, Hugo's mother had been a house model for Dior at the time when he created his notorious New Look which rekindled hope and fire in the fashion world in the depressing post-war years of the late 1940s and '50s. Fiona had been a catwalk queen, a forerunner of the fabulous supermodels of the 1990s, and she had also graced the cover of *Vogue* on more than one occasion. Her impeccable breeding had resulted in exquisite bone structure both in her face and her body and she had exuded such class and style that as Celestia lost herself in page after page of stunning black-and-white photographs bearing invaluable signatures – Horst, Beaton, Avedon, Penn – she slowly began to realise that if it were remotely possible, this was what she too wanted to be. The old lady sensed this and, insisting it remain their secret, began to coach her gawky, angular granddaughter for the future.

Fiona Fairfax was over seventy but she was still 5 feet 9 inches and had the carriage of a Grenadier guardsman. When Prudence was out – she could not abide her daughter-in-law

– Fiona let Celestia escort her up the drive to Trevane and into the Great Hall. Here Fiona would instruct her grand-daughter how to walk using the forty-foot hall as a catwalk – how to pause, swivel on the spot, walk back and then exit, how to lead from the pelvis, with the torso tilted behind and chin up, place one foot directly in front of the other in short steps to make the hips sway, swing each arm in time with the opposite leg – and to her delight Celestia was a natural.

The night Fiona Fairfax died – in her four-poster bed in the folly – she was brought up to Trevane and laid out in her favourite Vionnet and sapphires on the mahogany dining-room table with four tall white candles placed strategically at each corner. In the middle of the night Celestia crept down-stairs, dressed immaculately in a 1947 Dior coat and skirt her grandmother had given her, and walked up and down the dining room, pausing, turning, removing the jacket, saying goodbye to the old lady in the way she would have wished before an audience of five generations of Fairfaxes looking down on her from their portraits on the walls. There was no whirring of cameras, no flashes, no loud music, no hyped-up audience – only silence and candlelight – but it was Celestia's first show and in years to come she would conjure it up each time she was about to go out along the runway, and use the extraordinary image to centre herself.

'Who's in charge here?' bellowed Prudence, striding into the agency while Celestia stood in the doorway, embarrassed. She had begged her mother to allow her to go on her own but Prudence wasn't going to miss out on her one chance to re-enter the fashion world. As an act of defiance, Celestia had gone out the day before and had her long hair chopped off in a close-cropped feathery urchin cut which really accentuated her striking facial bone structure.

'Well, who is in charge here?' repeated Prudence even louder when no one took any notice of her. Several pairs of eyes swivelled automatically towards the far end of the table where Grace Brown sat.

Grace Brown owned the agency but still elected to sit with her team of bookers at the booking table and work alongside them. She was the one island of calm amidst the mayhem, rarely raising her voice, speaking constantly into her phone negotiating mega figures in a husky whisper. Grace was cool. She handled the supermodels and her stable was the best in town. She gave the appearance of being so laid back and unobtrusive as to be almost invisible to the uninitiated amongst her frantic underlings, but from behind this front Grace observed everything that was happening. She never ever missed a trick – although she would have been more than happy to have missed Prudence, who was bearing down upon her.

'You're in charge, are you? What's your name?' demanded Prudence, impervious to the fact that Grace was talking on the phone.

'Grace Brown,' mouthed Grace, motioning to Prudence to go and sit on a sofa and wait.

'Jolly nice name, Grace,' commented Prudence in a rare moment of flattery, 'there was an editor at *Vogue* called Grace. Was that you?'

Celestia winced.

'No, that was Grace Jones,' said one of the bookers. Prudence failed to notice that the entire table was about to collapse in giggles.

'Oh, yes, of course. Such a dear woman. We thought about the name Grace for Celestia but one look at my daughter and you'll see just how inappropriate that would have been.'

But Grace Brown *had* taken one look at Celestia and it had

66

been enough to tell her that here was a girl who could soar into the stratosphere. Those bones! Those huge grey eyes. That perfect Celtic skin. Those dazzling even teeth. That long, strong aristocratic nose. Those perfect clothes-hanger shoulders. Those long arms and even longer legs. That angry stare and stance. She had caught Grace watching her and had struck a pose the like of which Grace had never seen. The girl had class and the confidence that went with it, but most of all she had attitude – bags and bags of sheer, irresistible attitude. Corinne Day would die for her.

Even Angie, who ordinarily would have leapt up to claim a New Face, had instinctively left this one to be claimed by Grace. Grace always gave Angie a little nod if anyone with remote potential came through the door, just as she shook her head imperceptibly if someone was clearly hopeless – which most of them were – although Angie's natural judgement was becoming much more accurate. Except for Tess Tucker. Grace had been about to give the thumbs down to Tess Tucker but Angie had moved so fast. Not because the girl wasn't beautiful. She was. But Grace's experienced eye had known immediately that Tess didn't have any attitude. There was a vulnerability about her that Grace saw instantly and Angie didn't. This girl's going to get hurt, thought Grace. She doesn't look tough enough to go the distance, I ought to step in and put a stop to it right now. But instead she had merely delivered a mild admonishment to Angie for letting a girl go off to a photographic test without first checking it was OK with her parents. And Tess Tucker's test shots had been a big success. But Grace still felt uneasy about her.

But the same could not be said of this girl standing before her now.

'Well, now, I'm Lady Fairfax. But of course you will have recognised me as Prudence Pickering. . . . The entire table

67

looked blankety-blank. Who was Prudence Pickering when she was at home?' . . . and this is my daughter, the Honourable Celestia Fairfax. She's a huge great hulk, I'm afraid, poor darling, but if there's anything you can do with her. . . .'

Grace held out her hand to Celestia, smiling. 'You wouldn't – by any remote chance – be any relation to Fiona Fairfax?'

And Celestia grinned and said, 'I'm her granddaughter.'

'Well then,' said Grace, 'I think we'd be proud to see what we can do with you.'

Los Angeles/New York, 1992/1993

Cassie Zimmerman met the man of her dreams when he was thrown at her feet by the California surf. She had been watching him for some time, wondering what such an unbelievable jerk thought he was doing trying to compete with the surfers at Alice's Beach. He'd clearly never surfed in his life before yet he'd chosen a particularly dangerous spot to start.

Cassie needed distraction. For the first sixteen years of her life nothing bad had ever happened to her. Now suddenly her whole life had fallen apart.

She was a California girl with almost white blonde hair, violet eyes and a cute little turned-up nose, a Nordic beauty courtesy of her mother's Scandinavian ancestors. She appeared to have none of the Jewish blood of her father, Al Zimmerman, an entertainment lawyer with a client list of serious Hollywood TV talent. She had been raised an only child in a Beverly Hills mansion almost at the top of Benedict Canyon with a Filipino maid to wait on her hand and foot. Her classmates at Beverly Hills High competed with each other for invitations to her home because not only did she have the biggest pool but she was also the only one to have her own private screening room at her disposal. Her life appeared to be perfect. And so it had been, except for one nasty blip.

It had happened a year ago. She had not yet turned sixteen.

The boy was English, spending the summer in Los Angeles with his parents who had rented the house next door to the Zimmermans. Cassie had dated many of the boys in her class at school. None of it had been serious but she was pretty and she was popular and she was one of the gang. She was also a romantic. She had always imagined that her future would hold nothing more than a husband and kids whose lives would revolve around going to the beach, going to the movies, going to school and hanging out by the pool, just as hers had done. She loved children and she was looking forward to being a mother one day.

She lost her virginity to the English boy. In her girlish romantic mind, the fact that he was English branded him as special, worthy of being her first lover. It did not, however, make him special enough in her parents' eyes to be the father of her first child. The abortion was relatively painless. Al and Kari smothered her with love and attention and never once made her feel that she was to blame. She was their darling. These things happen. Once. Never again. The English boy went home and what nobody knew was that Cassie cried every night for the baby she had lost.

On the surface her life seemed perfect once again.

Until four of Los Angeles' finest beat up a man called Rodney King, and a plumbing company manager called George Holliday caught it all on his Sony Handycam. When the cops were tried and acquitted the subsequent riots of protest at the verdict left dozens of people dead and the city of Los Angeles in a state of devastation. Cassie's father promptly went into a state of panic.

'Call U-Haul,' Al Zimmerman told his wife, Kari. 'Call the realtor. We're selling up and moving. This town isn't safe any more.' What he didn't say was that his law practice was going nowhere. He might have started out with some of the biggest names in the business as clients but as soon as they became successful they started to drift away, poached by sharp young lawyers who seemed to inhabit a different world to the one Al was used to. He was old at thirty-eight. He'd come out to California from New York to seek his fortune after graduating from law school and for a while it had looked as if his dream was going to come true, but now he knew his time was up. The Rodney King riots provided the perfect excuse for him to move back east, to New York, to his roots and, most important as it turned out, to his mother.

Cassie was horrified. As far as she was concerned, the thought of giving up her pampered California lifestyle would mean the end of the world to her. Luckily for her, her mother felt the same way and for a while Al was too weak to overcome their resistance. But his partner was poised to buy him out and now, a year later, Al had put his foot down. At the end of the summer in 1992 he was sending Cassie and Kari ahead to live with his mother in New York while he wrapped up his affairs and sold their property in California.

Cassie was desperately making the most of what might turn out to be her last summer at her parents' house in the exclusive Malibu beach colony just in case she never saw it again. Nothing had actually been decided about the Malibu house and it was just possible that Al would agree to keep it on as a holiday home. Day after day Cassie roamed the shoreline, venturing beyond the perimeter of the colony, past the sign telling the great unwashed to keep out and on to the public beach, past Alice's Restaurant and the pier. Sometimes she went to Venice to go rollerblading and she was well aware that she turned more heads than most people as she glided smoothly from side to side. Above her minuscule sawn-off denim shorts resting snugly on her hips, her belly-button nestled in a long expanse of tanned naked flesh beneath her tiny bikini top. Her legs measured 38 inches and they too were perfectly tanned. Sometimes she went the other way, up the Pacific Coast Highway to Zuma, her favourite beach, but come what may, every evening as the sun went down, she sat out on the deck with her long tanned legs stretched out in front of her and drank in the view of the Pacific Ocean reaching all the way to Catalina and beyond. Only three more weeks and she'd be staring at concrete urban chaos. If only some prince would come riding in on the crest of a wave and carry her away.

Who was the nerd who couldn't surf? It was pathetic! He couldn't even stand up on his board for two seconds. Cassie decided, since she had nothing better to do, it would be fun to go down and take a closer look and then, just when she reached the place where the sea ran into a little inlet and she had to wade across it to reach the public beach, the surfer lost his balance and was plunged into the high waves. Cassie watched with some apprehension. The currents were known to be very treacherous just there. The boy could easily be sucked under. She looked around for the lifeguard and saw he wasn't in his chair. She saw the boy's seemingly inert body being tossed towards the shore and then in a matter of seconds he was lying at her feet.

As she knelt down beside him, all thoughts of what a nerd he was were swept out to sea. He had the most romantic face she had ever seen. Drenched strands of black hair lay across his forehead. His eyes were closed and his eyelashes were so long they cast shadows over his high cheekbones. His nose was long and straight and there was a shadow of dark stubble above his full, sensuous mouth and around his chin. To top it all his body consisted of six feet of hard tanned flesh and firm muscle.

He opened his eyes and looked up at her and for the first

time Cassie knew the meaning of the ridiculous word swoon that she had come across in historical novels. She wanted to sweep him up in her arms like Deborah Kerr holding Burt Lancaster at the water's edge in *From Here to Eternity*. Instead she asked: 'Are you all right?'

To her surprise he held out his hand and when she took it he rose out of the water and jumped to his feet, shaking himself like a dog. He grinned at her and she had to look away to hide what she knew was a stupid adoring look in her eyes. He was sheer unbelievable heaven. And then he spoke:

'Thought I was in serious trouble there for a moment.'

Cassie started.

'You're English!'

'You're American. Are you a model?'

'Am I what?'

'A model. You know, do you stand in front of photographers while they take pictures of you?'

'No way. I'm still at school.'

'So are loads of models.'

'What is it with this model thing?' Cassie was getting nervous. Would he now ignore her because she wasn't a model?

'Don't be so defensive. You're incredibly good looking. You're tall. Your skin is brilliant, so are your teeth and your hair and your legs and your bones. In fact, you're totally wonderful. Why aren't you a model?'

'Well, I'm just not. That's all. It's weird, you asking me like that. I mean, it's like I don't ask are you a Grenadier guard or whatever they have in England.'

'We have models in England too, you know. Besides, maybe I am.'

'A Grenadier guard?'

'Or perhaps I work at Lloyd's in the City of London or

73

maybe I manage my vast country estate and do a lot of hunting, shooting and fishing.'

'Really?' Cassie was thrilled. 'Do you have a snooty English name like Lord Whittington-Douglas-Fairbanks or something?'

'Just call me Tommy Lawrence.'

'Oh, sure. I'm Cassie. Cassie Zimmerman. So what are you doing in California?'

'I'm with my parents. We're staying at the Beverly Wilshire.'

That was it. No further explanation as to why they were staying at the Beverly Wilshire or what his parents were doing in Los Angeles.

'Are you studying in England, I mean, are you . . .?'

'You mean am I still at school? No. How about you? If you're not a model are you going to college or whatever they call it here when you leave school?'

'I guess,' sighed Cassie, 'right now I don't really know. See, we're about to relocate to New York.'

'Lucky you!'

'I don't think so. Listen, eh, Tommy, I'm running Brad Pitt's latest movie at my house tonight. I mean, if you're not doing anything and you'd like to come along . . .?'

She had no plans for a screening that night but if he said he'd come she'd call her father and swear to behave like a perfect angel about moving to New York if he'd use his contacts to get a print sent over as soon as possible.

'If you want to call your folks at the hotel why don't you come straight up to the house. I mean our beach house, right here. My screening room's at our Beverly Hills house. I'm afraid we don't have a screening room at the beach.'

She saw she'd impressed him. He was looking positively stunned. Surely, from what he'd said, he lived in a big house back in England, some stately home or baby palace.

74

'A party? That'd be fantastic. Give me the address. I'll be there.'

She hadn't meant it to be a party. She'd meant it to be an intimate little screening for just the two of them, but never mind.

Her father was putty in her hands.

'Daddy, I just can't bear the thought that it might be the last screening I'll ever have, it just has to be a terrific movie. Please get me Brad Pitt. Please get anything but just get it to the house by seven. Please, Daddy, I promise I'll try to learn to love New York, please don't let me down.'

Al couldn't help musing over the fact that once upon a time he would probably have had the power to get her Brad Pitt in person.

She never heard Tommy arrive, even though she sat by the window listening for the sound of his car. What kind of car would he have? Then the maid was tapping on her door and telling her he was downstairs, that he'd arrived on foot. On foot? Nobody arrived on foot in Los Angeles. Were all Englishmen so eccentric? Well, maybe he'd come by cab from the hotel. That was it. But why had he walked up the drive?

Cassie thought she would never forget the moment the gang walked into the screening room and were introduced to Tommy. She could see they were knocked out by him – by his stunning looks and the fact that he was English. She watched him shaking hands with everyone. Shaking hands! It was out of this world. And instead of saying 'Hi, how are ya?' he said 'How do you do?' very politely. It was quaint. There was no other word for it. But she loved it.

By the end of the evening she loved him too.

Throughout the film he held her hand. He just reached for it during the opening credits and hung on to it. When the movie ended and the lights came up she heard herself say,

'Thanks for coming everyone. See you around. Angelina will see you guys out.'

No invitation to stay for drinks, a moonlight dip in the pool or call for take-out. She wanted them to leave and she let them know it.

She and Tommy sat up and talked till two in the morning. She had never opened up like this to anyone before. She found she could tell him things she hadn't even admitted to herself. The only thing she couldn't bring herself to mention was the other Englishman in her life. Tommy just sat there and listened, still holding her hand, and he seemed a million miles removed from the square-jawed, straw-haired California beach boys she'd grown up with. There was only one way to describe both Tommy's looks and his personality: sensitive. He might have the body of a beach boy but his face was that of a romantic gypsy. He had tied his long black hair back in a ponytail and now he had gold hoops in his ears.

'I don't know how I'm going to survive in New York,' she told him. 'I'm scared. I'm scared of so many things. I'm an outdoors girl. I'll go mad in some cramped apartment.'

'You'd love the English countryside. Do you ride?'

'Every chance I get. I keep my horse at some stables in Topanga Canyon and ride him down on the beach. That's another thing I'm going to have to kiss goodbye. Do you have a lot of land over in England?'

'Acres and acres. You'll see.'

You'll see. For months Cassie would carry those words in her head. To her it meant that one day he would show her his land. Did it also mean that one day he would make her his? As they talked into the night he described his faraway English lifestyle and by the time he left Cassie could see herself striding over hard frozen soil in mysterious objects he called 'wellies' and sitting on something called a shooting stick.

76

(And getting married and having the English baby that she had lost.) It was a far cry from Alice's Beach.

He kissed her before he finally left in a cab. Cassie had had plenty of boys put their tongue in her mouth before but this was different and she was amazed at how much she liked it. She was amazed at the way her own tongue sprang to life and her lips pulled at his and how not only did she feel a sudden need to press her whole body against his hard frame but she also wanted to wrap her long legs around his jeans. She was reaching for his belt buckle when the taxi driver honked his horn.

'You still leaving, buddy, or what?'

'I'm afraid I have to. Now listen, Cassie, I have to go to the desert with my parents but I'll call you when I get back.'

'But we're moving . . . we'll be in New York . . . you won't know where to reach me!' she shouted after him.

He wound down the window and leaned out of the cab.

'Don't worry, I'll find you. You'll see.'

That was all she had to go on – two little words: you'll see.

In the weeks before they moved she seemed to see him everywhere. On a visit to her aunt who lived in Sherman Oaks she was convinced she saw him wheeling a trolley down one of the aisles at Hughes Market. But what on earth would he be doing in Sherman Oaks? Then another time she was lying on a lounger by the pool at the house of one of her classmates when the girl suddenly leapt to her feet and shrieked:

'Cassie, quick, cover up your breasts. I forgot we had a new poolman coming on a different day,' and as she ran into the house Cassie could have sworn that the new 'poolman' she glimpsed out of the corner of her eye was Tommy.

It happened twice more. She thought she saw him – but

77

always in the most unlikely places. And finally, the day before they were moving to New York, she called the Beverly Wilshire in desperation.

'When are you expecting the Lawrence family back?' she asked the concierge.

'We have no guests of that name.'

'No, I know, but you did, recently, and you're expecting him back – with his parents.'

But the concierge was adamant.

'I'm sorry, Miss, we have not had anyone of that name staying at the hotel recently.'

Cassie had not encountered Grandma Zimmerman very often. She had a dim recollection of an elderly woman arriving to stay in California at odd moments during her childhood, someone who complained the entire time she was there – the sun was too hot, the air conditioning was too cold, there was no one on the streets, the smog was unbearable – but nothing prepared her for the full force of Doris Zimmerman on her home ground.

She lived on the Upper West Side of New York on West End Avenue at 97th Street and had done so for fifty years. Cassie's father had been born and raised in her apartment. He had always maintained that it was the view of the Hudson River that made him yearn to go and live by the ocean in California. One look told Cassie that you might possibly be able to see the Hudson from Doris Zimmerman's apartment but only if you leaned out the window so far that your brains would be splattered all over the street before you'd had a chance to savour the view.

Grandma clearly didn't care for Cassie's mother, and Cassie soon got the feeling that this dislike extended to her too.

'Such a *shiksa*,' she would mutter all the time, never making it entirely clear if she was referring to mother or daughter, 'shame you're not *zaftig*, you'll never get a husband'. This was presumably directed at Cassie, whose slender, non-voluptuous looks were clearly anathema to Doris. Doris peppered her sentences with Yiddish (of which Cassie understood not one word): 'He has the brains of a *shlemiel*; it's time you met the family, the *ganze meshpocheh* will be here for dinner tomorrow; tell your mother she's lucky to have me for a *shviger*.' And on top of everything she observed the *Shabbes* on Friday evening, insisting that Cassie and her mother join her in covering their heads with a kerchief, lighting candles, circling the candles three times and intoning the blessing. And the food she served! Gefilte fish, herring, *knishes* stuffed with cheese, chicken soup with matzo ball dumplings – not a leaf of radicchio or a sun-dried tomato in sight.

Kari Zimmerman had always needed to be liked and she looked upon this period with her mother-in-law (which she imagined would only last a short time) as an opportunity to win Doris over. With this in mind she went along with everything Doris wanted. Cassie, on the other hand, began to feel seriously claustrophobic. The only thing that kept her sane was the thought of seeing Tommy again one day. Every night she rang her father in California to ask if he had called, and every night Al explained patiently that if he did call, the first thing he, Al, would do would be to give him Cassie's number in New York.

'But what if he calls when you're out?'

'For Christ's sake, Cassie honey, we own an invention called an answering machine. Here's what it says: 'You have reached the Zimmerman residence. Kari and Cassie Zimmerman have moved to New York where you can reach them on area code 212 221 6453. If you would like to leave a message for Al Zimmerman please speak after the tone. Thank you.' I listen

79

to the goddamn message every day. Your guy hasn't called. And if you want my opinion he won't ever call. Forget him, Cassie. So tell me, Mom says she took you to Macy's. What did ya buy?'

Cassie wasn't going to listen. She stormed out of the apartment and down to Riverside Park. How she hated the miserable grey Hudson River. How she yearned for the Pacific. How she dreaded starting school in New York. How she hated living with Grandma Doris and all her *kvetching*. How she hated *everything*!

'Do that again,' said a voice to her left.

He was tall and athletic looking. It was hard to see his face because of the camera in front of it.

'Go on, do it again. Stamp your foot and then hold the pose. Look at me like you'd like to stamp on me.'

'I don't want to stamp on you. I'm just upset because. . . .' Imagination had never been part of Cassie's make-up.

'Oh, forget it. Just look at me.' He sighed and clicked and rewound and clicked again and moved about in front of her.

'Give me your address.'

Cassie looked shocked. 'I never give my address to strange men.'

'Of course you don't. I'm not a strange man. I'm a photographer and if your pictures are any good I'm going to send them to a modelling agency – here's their card, take it – and ask them to let me test-shoot you for real. Now for the last time, are you going to give me your address or do I have to follow you home? What's your name, by the way?'

'Cassie Zimmerman.'

'Zimmerman. Not a good name for a model. Any relation to Bob Dylan? His real name was Robert Zimmerman. Just kidding. Hey, why don't you call yourself Dylan? Good catchy name right up near the beginning of the alphabet when people are going through the agency book.'

Cassie tried to look at him as if he had crawled out from under some disgusting Manhattan stone but something about the things he said made her hesitate. He talked about her being a model. That was the first thing Tommy had said to her: 'Are you a model?' Maybe meeting this guy was meant to be. Maybe it was a sign that would somehow move her closer to Tommy. So instead of stalking off with her head in the air she gave the photographer her address. And her phone number.

Two weeks later she got a call.

'It's Paul. Paul van Ash. I took your pictures, remember? They were just fabulous. They want to see you at the agency, so go by there tomorrow. You've got the address. Do it!'

Cassie did – but only for something to do to get her out of the house and away from Doris's moaning. The only glimmer of light at the end of the tunnel was that her father seemed to be having a hard time wrapping up his business in LA and was even making noises about them going back for Christmas.

'I'm Cassie Zimm – I'm Cassie Dylan,' she told the receptionist at the agency the next day, 'you wanted to see me.'

'Can I have your book, please.'

Cassie looked extremely surprised and handed over the battered copy of *The Bridges of Madison County* she had been reading on the subway. Now it was the receptionist's turn to look surprised.

'What's this? I don't need this. I read it already. I want your book, your portfolio.'

'I don't have one.'

'Are you here to be a model or what?' asked the receptionist, trying to disguise her growing irritation and not succeeding very well.

81

'I don't know,' said Cassie. 'Am I?'

There was a coarse guffaw from the banquette at the end of the reception area. Cassie turned to see a wild-looking girl sprawled along the seat with one leg resting on the coffee table. She was smoking a cigarette and popping gum at the same time. Her face was astonishingly beautiful and her head was shaved almost bald. Cassie had the uncomfortable feeling that she had absolutely nothing on under the tight black leather waistcoat.

'Ya don't wanna be a model, why ya here?' asked the girl. Cassie thought she was the most vulgar-looking creature she had ever encountered but she had been raised to be polite so she smiled and said, 'A photographer sent me.'

'Paul van Ash.'

The astonished expression on Cassie's face gave her away.

'Oh, don't worry about Paul. He does it all the time and they like him. He's got good taste. Couple girls have got started thanks to him. Hey, wanna go shopping? Wanna check out the new Barneys uptown?'

'Who are you? I don't normally fraternise with complete strangers.'

'Oh, get out of here. Nobody talks like that. I mean, like, excuse me, *what* did you say? Fraternise? I asked you to go shopping, not fratting. How 'bout it, Miss Cassie something-Dylan? Paul told you to change your name, didn't he? Well, I'm Gigi. We're leaving now,' she informed the receptionist, 'we'll be back.'

'But Gigi, you have a casting here in twenty minutes,' whined the receptionist, 'Gigi – '

'So where are you from?' asked Gigi on the ride uptown.

'California.'

'Disneyland?'

'Beverly Hills.'

'Los Angeles. Aren't you just crazy about Cypress Hill?'

'I don't know that area.'

'It's a band, stupid. You never heard of Cypress Hill?'

Cassie shook her head. 'Where are you from?' she asked, to change the subject.

'Who knows?' Gigi was evasive.

'You must have grown up somewhere.'

'Guess I must have.'

Once they arrived at Barneys Gigi raced ahead and Cassie lost her in the throng of shoppers, but when she did finally locate her, she felt her heart begin to hammer in her chest. Gigi was calmly slipping jewellery into her giant model bag. She glanced around quickly every now and then and when she saw Cassie staring at her she grinned, inclining her head as if to say: 'Come on, what are you waiting for?'

But Cassie had turned and fled.

They called it Hollywood's own towering inferno, whipped to fury by the Santa Ana winds off the high desert. Barely six weeks before they were due to return to California for Christmas, Kari and Cassie were woken in the night by Al's frantic phone call. Their Malibu house was now a shell. He described how the police had discovered the charred bodies of a couple so badly burned they were unidentifiable but he believed them to be their recent neighbours on the beach. He related stories of other friends who had cowered in their swimming pools, waiting to be rescued by helicopter, as the flames leapt higher and higher all around them.

Then, when he had calmed down, he said there was no way he was going to stay in Los Angeles. He had had enough. He would buy them a luxurious penthouse apartment in Manhattan from the proceeds of the sale of the Beverly Hills house and the insurance on the Malibu house. He could not wait to come home, he told them and home to him, they realised, meant Doris Zimmerman's apartment.

The next morning Cassie bolted, literally, like a runaway colt, long legs hurtling her out of the building to the only escape route she had encountered in New York: the Etoile model agency. She paid $50 for Paul van Ash's test shots of her and talked Kari into letting her move out of the claustrophobic atmosphere of Doris Zimmerman's apartment and into one of the agency's model apartments downtown. She struck a deal with her mother, the first stab at negotiation to enter her mind: if she hadn't been booked for a modelling job by the time Al joined them in New York for Christmas, she'd move back in with Doris.

Cassie almost changed her mind when she met her roommate. Talk about out of the proverbial frying pan and into her very own inferno right here in Manhattan. Two narrow single beds, one for her and the other for the half-naked gum-chewing Gigi Garcia, who greeted her as she walked in.

'Hi, blondie, remember me?'

London, 1993

My name is Amy and I have dreams. I mean, I know we all do but mine come true. Not the beautiful dreams about being a princess and a movie star and all that little girl rubbish. Those are just daydreams (except for my latest fantasy about becoming a supermodel).

I'm talking about my nightmares and how they have this weird habit of coming true. My teacher told me there's a word for what I have. They're not dreams, they're called premonitions. She says I'm psychic.

Take last week. I had this dream and in it I was on a Number 23 bus coming back from window-shopping in Oxford Street to Notting Hill Gate, where I live. The conductor on the bus, he was laughing and joking, he had a smile for everyone until he came to me. Then his smile disappeared. He grabbed me by the arm and told me:

'Girl, you have to get off this bus.'

I looked out of the window. It was dark outside. Suddenly we weren't in London any more but right out in the middle of the countryside, miles from anywhere.

'No,' I cried, 'I don't want to get off here. I want to go to Notting Hill.'

'We're not going there any more,' he told me.

Everyone in the bus turned round and screamed at me: 'WE'RE NOT GOING THERE ANY MORE!'

The conductor took me to the open platform where passengers got on or off the bus. They still have them on the Number 23. We fought and struggled until finally I was able to push him off the bus and as I watched him falling, disappearing into a void, his eyes fixing on me in horror, I woke up and realised it had been another nightmare.

The next day it was on the news on TV. A woman had had an altercation with a bus conductor on the platform while the bus had been moving and the conductor had lost his footing and fallen. He was said to be in a critical condition.

They showed a picture of the woman responsible for his fall, a white person like the conductor in my dream. Then they showed the picture of the conductor who was lying in intensive care.

His skin was black. Like mine.

It makes me so mad when people ask me where I'm from just because I'm black. I'm English, just like everyone else. I was born here and I've lived here all my life. I talk like all my friends do. If you asked me: 'What do you want to do when you leave school?' I'm not going to say, 'I know dat money is not all dat matters but me want try fe de best, try fe de modelling.'

I'm going to say, 'I dunno, I guess I'll have a go at modelling, see if I can make a bit of money somehow.'

My mum's Jamaican. That's true enough. She was born in Kingston and her parents came over here when my grandad was recruited by London Transport in 1955. My mum was only four. My grandparents went back to Jamaica when my mum married my dad. They didn't like it here, didn't like the cold and the wet. Then my dad took off and left her with three kids to bring up on her own. My brother Leroy, me, and my little sister Tootie. She had no money and we were so poor when I was little. They were always cutting off the electricity because we hadn't paid the bill. I'd come home from school and there'd be like pitch black everywhere and I'd keep little Tootie from being scared by playing 'I Spy in the Dark' with her, and then Leroy would get home and we'd huddle together and sing songs to cheer ourselves up. Leroy's voice was incredible. My mum always wanted him to sing in the choir in church but like I always told her, there was more chance of the Devil himself turning up in church than getting Leroy there.

He was wild, my older brother, Leroy Winston La Mar, always getting into trouble, skiving off from school and that. It got so my mum couldn't handle him, and when he was about seven she sent him to Jamaica to live with our gran. I know my mum must have been sad to see him go. We only heard from him at Christmas when my gran made him write us a card. I will never forget the Christmases I had as a kid. Often we were too poor to afford presents so we gave each other something that didn't cost anything. I would draw pictures. I was good at drawing and one year I remember I painted a black Cinderella going to the ball for Tootie. In return Tootie climbed up on a chair and sang Michael Jackson's 'Billie Jean' for me. She was such a cheeky little performer, with her pigtails sticking out, wiggling away and doing his moonwalk until she fell off the chair. She was always crazy about Michael Jackson and though she hasn't said anything, I know she's confused about what's happened to him and all the stories about what he's supposed to have got up to with those little boys at Neverland. She doesn't know what to believe. When I did the Cinderella drawing for her, she pasted a picture of Michael Jackson on to it as Prince Charming. Now all of a sudden he doesn't seem to be Prince Charming any more, although Tootie won't hear a word said against him.

I have my very own Prince Charming. His name is Marcus and he is called after Marcus Garvey, a Jamaican and black leader in America who urged all blacks to consider Africa their real home. He died in 1940. My Marcus wears his hair in funky dreads but that doesn't make him a Rasta. His elder brother went to school with Jazzie B when they lived in North London and passed on a lot of stuff to Marcus. Marcus is pretty heavy on black dignity and black pride. He calls us Afro-Caribbeans. That's OK. I mean, I'm still English but I can live with being Afro-Caribbean as well, I suppose.

Marcus is the strong and silent type with a proud face that says black male beauty to me, bit like Viv Richards, the cricketer. I fell in love with Marcus when we were in the fifth form and now we're sort of unofficially engaged. He's a Scorpio, pretty secretive. My mum likes him, probably because he likes her cooking. He comes round for Sunday dinner and mum really goes to town, plantain, chicken and rice, stew peas with beef and kidney beans, soups with great chunks of potato and yam – you name it! One other thing, I'm sixteen and I'm a virgin. I'm going to stay that way till I'm married. Marcus and me, we've discussed it and he's fine about it. He understands. And I know it makes my mum happy. I don't think Tootie's going to have that attitude. She's such a flirty little thing even though she's not even fully grown. Standing there in church I get quite embarrassed by her sometimes, the way she rolls her eyes while she's singing, sticks out her bum and grins at everyone. I don't know what Reverend Westbrook must be thinking, but she's so cute, no one can bear to get cross with her.

Actually, I can't help thinking Tootie is more cut out to be a model than I am. She's more sort of showy and extrovert naturally but Mum reckons she'll be an actress or a singer or something. I don't understand these girls I know who don't get on with their mum. To me and Tootie, Mum is the best friend in the world. She's always there for us. No matter how little money there is, our clothes are always clean and there's something to eat even if it's only once a day. Mum's an Evangelist. She goes to the Pentecostal Church. She's never thrust religion on me. She says what works for her may not work for me, and she's right. I go now and then but I don't feel I have to go to church although I do find prayer really helps. But I believe God is always there for me and I don't have to go inside a building to find him. That's all it is, a building, and you'd probably find half the people don't believe anyway, they're just there for the singing or because they think they ought to be there. Yet when I'm alone and praying, all of a sudden I can be overwhelmed with this feeling that He's right there with me, listening to me, looking after me. I don't have to go to church.

But Mum does and she's really pleased they're rebuilding the old Peniel Chapel in Kensington Park Road. It's just around the corner from where we live. We live in a council flat on the Portobello Court Estate. It's become a very fashionable area, where we live, loads of what Mum calls 'them white middle-class liberals'. I don't think she really understands the phrase even, it's just something she's heard over the years, going way back to the Swinging Sixties, and it applies to the kind of people she's not really sure she trusts. The kind of white people who like black people just because they're black and cool and funky or whatever we're all supposed to be, and not because of who we are as individuals. But there's the Portobello Market for fruit and veg, and antiques on a Saturday and it attracts the tourists. Also it's the area where we have the carnival every August Bank Holiday and that's the only time of year I can get really excited about being Afro-Caribbean.

There's a fancy restaurant called 192 which is always full of what they call media types. Tootie walks along behind them and imitates them when they come out on the street after their lunches that go on for half the afternoon. But my favourite place is Rococo. It's a newsagent and there's magazines from all over the world. I go in there every day after school and I read *Vogue* and *Elle* and *Clothes Show*, all the fashion magazines, then I put them back on the shelf and buy *Mizz* and *Jackie* and *Shout* because they're all I can afford. Marcus reads an American magazine called *Vibe* which was founded by Quincy Jones. That's got good fashion too.

I saw the ad for the Girl of the Year competition in *Smash Hits*. It said to send in a couple of snapshots of yourself and you had to be at least 5 feet 8 inches. I'm 5 feet 10 so no problem there. I talked to Marcus about it. He's not the sort of guy who'll say 'Yeah, go on, why not? Be a laugh.' He takes things really seriously and that's why I love him. He really talked me through it.

'What is it you're really interested in?' he asked me.

'Well, you know, clothes and that.'

'You mean fashion?'

'Yeah.'

'You like to draw and you're good at it, right? So why not think about dress design? Your mum's taught you to sew. You're always picking up stuff down the market and ripping it apart and putting it together again to make your own look. Why not do it for real?'

'What's this got to do with the Girl of the Year competition? I don't get it.'

'I might be prejudiced but to me you're a fantastic-looking girl and you've got model written all over you. You might, it's not certain mind, but you just might be able to make a bit of money from modelling over the next couple of years, stash it away, go to college and then start your own design company without the struggle for finance in the beginning.'

It sounded all right to me. It was a good job I had Marcus. I hadn't really begun to think seriously about what I was going to do once I'd left school. Marcus took care of the snapshots. In the end they weren't anything like snapshots. Marcus got his friend Joe to take the pictures. Joe was going to be a photographer one day. He'd saved up for years and bought himself a camera and he wandered round London taking pictures of people, on the street, on bits of wasteland, in schools, wherever he found interesting faces. Sometimes he took Marcus with him and gave him a go. Marcus was OK at taking pictures but he didn't have Joe's talent.

I had to send my Girl of the Year pictures to a modelling agency called Etoile and when they contacted me and asked to see me I was more or less convinced it was because of Joe's pictures. I'm not a doe-eyed, mixed-race light-skinned pretty pretty girl. I have a really positive black face and my hair is very short. He'd shot me with a kind of halo of light behind me and I looked really striking. When they saw me in the flesh, they wouldn't want to know.

I was wrong.

It was such a friendly place. I met this girl called Angie who had a sweet face. She sat me down and gave it to me straight.

'I'm not going to mess about with you, Amy. There's not a lot of work for black girls but we think you should enter the competition. The truth is we need to have a black face in it. It's frightening how few black girls have applied.'

I didn't like what I was hearing. I hadn't applied because I was black. It might sound strange but I'd never really encountered racism. Mum had raised us to understand we were people first and our colour came way way behind. Still, I wasn't about to get into an argument with Angie. She was saying I could get into the competition and that was the reason I'd come to see her in the first place. She explained what I'd have to do, when to turn up for rehearsals, what was in store for me. Meanwhile she was happy to use Joe's pictures as my test shots for the time being. They were that good!

Mum was full of joy at my news and cooked a special supper.

She had some news of her own for us. We made Tootie sit on her hands and bite her lips, she was so fidgety. All she could think about was that she had been asked to go and sing karaoke at a church fair. All week she'd been standing in front of the mirror singing into a hairbush for a makeshift microphone, miming and emoting for all she was worth. But Mum wanted her undivided attention. Just for once Tootie had to sit still. Mum had something to tell us.

'Your brother Leroy's coming back from Jamaica. He's coming home to live with us.'

That night I went to sleep and dreamed not of being crowned with glory at the Girl of the Year competition, but that when we went to the airport to meet Leroy, the Devil got off the aeroplane.

London, 1993

I shall never forget the first time I saw Amy La Mar. It was at the Girl of the Year competition hosted by my agents, Etoile and they had asked me to be one of the judges. It was held in the ballroom at the Hilton Hotel in London overlooking Hyde Park. When I arrived the usual swarm of paparazzi surged forward and it took my minder about ten minutes to clear a path through to the hotel entrance where the television cameras were waiting.

'Hey Swan, how are you?' called out one reporter.

'Fine thanks, Joey, how's yourself?' I knew quite a few reporters by name and sometimes it was comforting to see familiar faces waiting for me.

'Good to have you back in England, Swan,' yelled another. 'Why don't you stay here?'

This was a bit of a loaded question for me. Everybody knew models made more money in America but I didn't want to sound disloyal to my country by pointing that out. 'One day, maybe,' I replied, trying not to sound too evasive.

'Going to pop in and see your mum and dad?'

This was another tricky question, although not half as tricky as they thought. If I said I had no time it meant I wasn't caring but I could hardly tell them the truth. Since Harry's reappearance I had found it increasingly difficult to spend time with my parents without giving anything away. They

94

still spent an inordinate amount of time dwelling on the past. They had never recovered from the tragedy of Venetia's death and recently they had begun to lose hope about Harry. Each time I saw them I longed to tell them Harry was alive, but I knew I could not. I had given Harry my word. He had been adamant that he wanted to wait until his name was cleared before being reunited with our parents. In any case I had no idea where he was. He had promised to contact me again after I had given him the money (and been photographed doing so by the Messenger) but that was so long ago now even I was beginning to have a few qualms. I had begun to dread seeing my parents. Not because I didn't want to see them but they thought I was all they had left and sometimes their desperation to have me close to them was suffocating. It was one of the reasons I had made my base in New York. It was healthier. But I hated lying to them; at first I'd hated being unable to tell them that Harry was alive, but now that I too experienced tiny painful darts of doubt about Harry's safety, it was unbearably depressing hearing them talk about him as if he were dead. It was a dilemma that nagged away at me each time I came to London and I found it heartbreaking, particularly when I had to smile for the press and look as if I was having a good time.

It was a bunfight in the ballroom when I entered. Etoile always used the event to invite their clients to a wonderful night out. Hair and make-up artists mingled with PR people, artists, photographers, fashion editors and buyers, not to mention a generous scattering of models on the agency's books. A giant catwalk jutted out into the ballroom and I could hear the thump thump thump of a disco beat undercutting the roar of the conversation. The show hadn't even begun but everyone had already begun to party.

A spotlight picked me out and followed my path to the

judges' table as the photographers surrounding the catwalk turned around and went wild. I blew them kisses and got out my little instamatic to take my own pictures of them, which always drove them crazy. I was the judge of honour with a seat in the very centre of the long table running down one side of the catwalk. To my left I had an internationally famous hairdresser with salons in London, Los Angeles and Sydney, and with whom I had worked many times. On my right side was Charley Lobianco, the president of Etoile.

I adored Charley. His infectious Italian charm was so engaging. It was his unashamed delight in women that I found so endearing. Among women he was like a small boy in a candy store. He moved from one to another, caressing, whispering, kissing, you could almost hear him purring. Yet he had none of that smarmy playboy phoniness. He genuinely loved being around women. The other thing I liked was that he was so far removed from the reserved English boys with whom I had grown up. Charley was an emotional creature. I had actually seen him cry on several occasions with no shame whatsoever and I admired him for it. It wasn't a matter of loss of self-control; he had been genuinely moved by something. I also found his background rather interesting. His mother came from an old Italian family with a beautiful villa on Lake Como and this accounted for his impeccable manners and good taste. His father, however, was a shady Italian-American thug from New Jersey about whom not very much was known apart from the fact that he had seduced Charley's mother over thirty years ago and persuaded her to elope with him. Since Charley managed to embellish the story each time he told it, no one was quite sure of the precise details, but it accounted for Charley's occasional raffishness, something which only made him all the more attractive. I had heard stories about Charley's dalliances with young models in his stable but I chose to ignore them.

This evening he was playing his little boy role.

'Swan, my angel, I canta kiss you because I have a cold. I long for my mamma. When I was a boy she would make a fantastic drink each time I had a cold.'

'Poor darling Charley, what was in the drink? Maybe the Hilton can make it up for you.'

'They did already,' said Charley, grinning and taking a swig of whisky. 'They just forgot the hot lemon and honey. Anyway, you know me, as soon as the girls come on I will feel better.'

I imagined the scene backstage: frantic last minute make-up being applied, hair being combed out of rollers, nervous pacing up and down. Poor little girls. The last few minutes before a show started were bad enough for seasoned models but these girls had never been on a catwalk before. Not for the first time I reflected how easy it had all been for me. I had never had to go through all this. Willy O'Brien had begun working with me straight away and taken me to Paris. Within four months I was on the cover of French *Vogue* and Charley Lobianco was preparing New York for my arrival. These young girls we were about to see had written in to Etoile in answer to a competition they had seen advertised in *Smash Hits* magazine: twelve girls shortlisted from hundreds. Girl of the Year was televised and covered by the national press so it was a big chance for them. The winner would go on to take part in the Girl of the Year finals in New York, but what would happen to all the others?

'We've got some great girls this year.' As if she had heard my unspoken question, Grace Brown, who ran the London office of Etoile came to lean over my shoulder. I loved Grace. She was so cool and unruffled all the time. Together she and Charley had masterminded the international careers of half the world's supermodels, including mine, yet she appeared to have no ego whatsoever despite the fact that as a former model she was still staggeringly pretty at forty-four. 'In fact, don't tell Charley yet but we've already told five of the girls we'll almost certainly take them on.'

The girls came tripping out on to the catwalk in pairs as Madonna's 'Cherish' blasted into the room. I love 'Cherish', it always gets me going, but I found the opening lyrics about being tired of broken hearts and losing at this game before you start rather ironic given that this was supposed to be the night when these girls' dreams came true. Still, it was an upbeat catchy melody and the girls had to walk fast and really move along the catwalk. The audience began swaying in time to the music and singing along. Everyone was having a good time. Charley put an affectionate arm around my shoulders and hugged me to him. I couldn't help laughing, he was in such heaven; there was no place he'd rather be than sitting watching long legs and supple bodies parading above him. We had the girls' photographs and details in front of us but I resisted looking at them. I wanted to see if I could recognise the girls Grace was excited about.

I think we all knew who would win the minute she stepped out on the catwalk, and I know we would have chosen her in spite of what happened next. I think she would have stood out even if she hadn't been the only black girl. She was the last girl to come out even though they were walking in pairs. It wasn't that she didn't have a partner: Amy La Mar just exploded on to the catwalk in such a way that the other girl was instantly catapulted into her shadow. I knew she had to win. But I think we also knew even then in that very first moment that it wasn't going to be easy for her. Her face was too strong a look to be immediately acceptable in the

98

conventional fashion world. Nor was her skin a pretty, light coffee colour but dark, seriously black.

She didn't sport a long silky hair extension. She had a crew cut, dyed white, but the perfect symmetry of the bone structure of her face was breathtaking. Huge wide-apart hazel eyes blazed at the judges and even white teeth flashed a warm smile. She was wearing a slinky black silk jersey tube. Skin tight, off the shoulder, long sleeved and ankle length, it covered most of her superfit body while managing at the same time to leave nothing to the imagination. Yet there was an innocence about this girl, a freshness that made her stand out from the rest. Instead of a turn at the end of the catwalk, she executed a few hip hop dance steps. This girl was having fun! The crowd loved her and each time she came out the wolf whistles doubled. She was a star.

It happened just as the girls had made their final run down the catwalk. The only thing left was the line-up on stage when the winner would be announced. Suddenly a small black woman ran out of the crowd and jumped on stage. She seized the microphone from the master of ceremonies and let us have it:

'I want a word with you!'

Heads turned in Charley Lobianco's direction but he waved his hand as if to say: Let her speak.

It was some speech, and as far removed from the superficial fashion world as it could possibly be.

'As you may have noticed, only one black girl has been shortlisted in this competition and I want to know why. Why is there always only one, if that? Why not several? Naomi Campbell was the first black model on the cover of *Time* and French *Vogue* and this is the 1990s. Veronica Webb is the first black model to endorse cosmetics for Revlon – but is she being paid the same money as white models? My guess is that nobody is pushing hard enough for the black model. There ought to be twice as many of them out there. The work's there. Why don't they give it to the black girl? Tell me that? We have a beautiful black girl here tonight but she's nothing like Iman. She's nothing like Naomi. She's nothing like Tyra Banks. They're beautiful but so is she in her own way. Look at her. . . .'

I could see poor Amy La Mar was pretty shaken by this sudden intrusion. She was trembling slightly, not quite sure whether to stay where she was or slip backstage. I wondered if she knew who the woman was. A journalist? A black activist? Whoever she was she was only speaking the truth, and I was pleased that Charley was allowing it to be heard.

'There are jobs waiting for this beautiful girl and for hundreds of other black girls and Asian girls. Don't forget the Asian girls. Where are the Asian supermodels? There's Yasmeen Ghauri but she's mixed race, her mother's Canadian. The more the world sees pure black and ethnic girls coming up, the less of an issue it will be. The colour outside is just a shell. Everybody's an individual, it's what's inside that really counts.'

And then she was gone as quickly as she had appeared.

There was a short, stunned silence before the whole room burst into uproar. Everyone stood up to applaud her. The wolf whistles were going through the roof. The other girls had come out on stage to see what all the fuss was about.

'Let's get straight up there and present Amy La Mar with the winner's bouquet so the press can make a good story out of it,' whispered Charley, and together we slipped away from the table. Charley tapped the microphone and held up his hand for quiet.

'As you can see, Ladies and Gentlemen, we have a winner and her name is Amy La Mar. We're also lucky enough to have with us here tonight Britain's biggest supermodel, or should I say the person who is currently Britain's – and indeed the world's – biggest supermodel: Swan. Swan, may I ask you to present Amy with these flowers.'

'Get my number from Grace and let me know how I can help you, Amy,' I whispered as I kissed her cheek and laid the bouquet in her arms. She smiled shyly at me and I saw how young and vulnerable she was. Please God let her toughen up fast, I thought. It's an uphill struggle for any young girl starting out on a modelling career but for a black kid like Amy I knew it was going to be twice as hard.

Wiltshire, 1993

I read the papers in the car going down to the country the next day. Amy's face was splashed all over the front pages. The headlines – along the lines of VOICE OF THE YEAR and AMY TRIUMPHS – were fairly predictable but she'd got good ink. I wondered what was happening back at the agency, whether people were lining up to book her.

I was in England for the Girl of the Year competition and to do a shoot for an American fashion story using famous paintings as themes for each picture. I had already done Gainsborough's 'Blue Boy', wearing a blue velvet evening suit. Christy Turlington had done Botticelli's 'Birth of Venus' as a swimwear story, Claudia Schiffer had done one of the Degas ballet pictures as lingerie, Naomi had done a couple of Gauguins in Mizrahi sarongs and Ozbek chiffon, poor Kate Moss was booked to do the 'Mona Lisa' but history had yet to relate what the clothes would be, and now here I was on my way to do Fragonard's 'The Swing' in a country garden somewhere wearing a frothy tulle shepherdess dress from Vivienne Westwood. Not exactly Louis XV in keeping with the period, but what did they care?

I had had my first good night's sleep in ages. I had looked in at the party at San Lorenzo after Girl of the Year, posed for more photographs with Amy and then slipped discreetly away around the corner to the Halkin. I poured a mixture of essential oils – rose absolute and geranium – into my bath and soaked away the stress of flying in from New York (even if it was on Concorde) and going straight to the Hilton. Then I tumbled into bed and fell into a deep deep sleep knowing that for once I wouldn't have to be up for a 5.30 shoot. Grace had really pampered me. All I had to do today was be driven to the country for some fittings and then have another early night. What bliss! Tomorrow was 'The Swing' shoot and then the day after I was to do something totally different. It was a story called Salisbury Plain, which would also be the location. It was in stark contrast to the rich extravaganza of the first shoot. The budget was minuscule and I had agreed to work for nothing to support two new young designers whose clothes I adored. They were into deconstruction with a capital D, back to basics, tailors' chalk marks, raw seams, as recycled as you could get. The kids had written to me in New York in desperation because the fashion editors were being huffy stuffy puffy and turning up their noses at the clothes. So now I was going to meet them at Stonehenge along with Willy O'Brien. Any make-up artist would give their eye teeth to work with me and Willy and we had asked a lovely girl called Amber to come down. Willy would shoot a few rolls of black-and-white of me in the raw Salisbury Plain clothes and then we'd see if the fashion editors could be made to see sense. I liked to use the power of my name to help out in this way occasionally, especially when the fashion industry looked like it was ignoring real talent.

Suddenly I had an idea. We weren't very far out of London and I dialled Etoile on the car phone.

'Grace?'

'Swan, thank you for last night. Sorry you didn't stay for the party but then you never were much of a party girl. What did you think of our new discovery?'

'Extraordinary! Did you know that woman would pull a stunt like that speech?'

'No idea whatsoever. But it was the best thing she could have done.'

'Phone's been ringing then, has it?'

'Off the bloody hook.'

'Grace, listen, I know it's a bit of a cheek to ask but would Amy do a story for free? Day after tomorrow? With me?'

'Well, if it's for free you'd better ask her yourself. Here, let me give you her number. She lives with her mother and her little sister in Notting Hill Gate somewhere. Good luck, and Swan, don't tie her up for too long. Charley's whisking her off to New York next week for the Girl of the Year finals – although I can already see he's worried about what they're going to make of her there, she's so different – but I wouldn't mind getting her to earn a crust or two here before she goes. Still, pictures with you, that'd do her image no harm.'

Swan called Amy.

'This is Tootie La Mar. We're not in at the moment but if you'd like to leave a message please . . .' said a little girl's voice.

'Tootie, put that down. Sorry, who is this?'

'Amy? This is Swan.'

'Oh, Hi. Sorry about that. My boyfriend's just bought me an answering machine and my little sister's practising what kind of message to leave.'

'I expect you have a hangover, Amy?'

'Oh, I don't drink. Will you say hello to Tootie for me otherwise she'll never go away.'

'Hi, Swan.' The squeaky little voice came back again.

'Hi, Tootie, are you a model too?'

'No, I'm a singer.'

'Really? Sing me a song.'

I had to hold the phone out the car window as Tootie began a raucous rendition of 'What's Love got to Do with It?' When Amy retrieved the phone I quickly outlined what I wanted.

'These kids are just getting started and I want to help them. I know you'd look sensational in the clothes. They have no money so you wouldn't get paid but you could use them for your book.' I went on to explain about Willy O'Brien and told Amy to contact him so he could bring her down.

'We've got a great girl called Amber coming to do the make-up but you might want to bring your own base. I've worked with black models in New York and they always have to do their own because the make-up artists haven't a clue, but Amber's pretty smart. She might well be tuned in but it's best to be on the safe side.'

I settled back in my seat to enjoy the ride to the country. We were all staying in a private house which was not far from Salisbury Plain so I could stay on there for the next day's shoot. Willy was going to drive down for the day. As the car turned off the motorway and I was driven along the winding country roads, I suddenly realised where I was. The ridge of rolling downland on the horizon was terribly familiar. We were approaching the village where my parents lived in the 'cottage' with seven bedrooms where I had spent the happiest days of my childhood.

When they told me we would be staying in a private house it never occurred to me that it would be with people I knew. As the car turned into the drive of Woodbridge Mill, my heart sank. The Frasers were among my parents' oldest friends, although as it turned out I needn't have worried.

'Lavinia, sweet thing, how wonderful to see you. I'm so glad you've dropped in. Do stay to dinner. It's not just that I'm thrilled to see you after such a long time but you see, these frightful American magazine people have descended on us. They heard about the mill and how beautiful it was and this very bossy woman rang up from New York and asked if they could come down and take some pictures, and of course I got in one of my fearful muddles and kept worrying about her phone bill which must have been gi-normous, we'd been talking such a long time and so I said Do! We'd love to have you, when in fact I meant the exact opposite and Geoffrey's furious and hasn't spoken to me for days but you'll be the perfect foil at dinner, you can . . .'

I might have known! Lucy Fraser hadn't the first clue that I'd become a world-famous supermodel. She was so out of it. I stopped her in mid-flow and shepherded her inside her own front door.

'Actually, Lucy dear, I'm one of them. They're going to take pictures of me . . . now that I think about it, we must be going to use the old swing in your orchard. Do you still have all those little stone cherubs at the end of the walled garden? I expect they'll want to get those in somehow.'

'Good gracious!' Lucy looked as if she might fly into a prize flap, so to take her mind off it I took the plunge and asked, 'How are Mummy and Daddy? Have you seen them lately?' I held my breath waiting for her answer.

'They're fine. What a shame you won't see them. They miss you so much now you live wherever it is you live. I had a postcard today.'

'A postcard?'

'They're in Scotland. Somewhere in the Borders. I can't remember why.'

I suppose I should have been relieved I was let off the hook, but I wasn't. I loved my parents and sooner or later I'd have to find a way of spending more time with them and coming to terms with them.

But then Mary-Ann de la Salle, the fashion editor from New York, came running into the hall to greet me in her OTT southern accent.

'Swan, sugar, this place is to die for . . .' and she whisked me away, leaving poor Lucy standing there.

'The Swing' shoot was exhausting. In the painting the woman's shoe has come off and is flying through the air as she swings and Mary-Ann insisted on reproducing this exactly. It took quite a few takes before I managed to kick off the shoe and the photographer (a tetchy old French queen with whom I hoped I'd never have to work again) managed to catch it on film all in the same shot. Of course once I'd kicked it off it always landed miles away in the thickest brambles and the skinny bare-legged fashion assistant who was sent to look for it always came back with her pale skin scratched and bleeding. Then Lucy decided to enter into the spirit of things. She had sat up after dinner looking at magazines and by now she was completely *au fait* with the world of the supermodel – or thought she was.

'I do think that Claudia Fisher's most awfully pretty, don't you, Lavinia? Do you know her?' she asked me while flitting about dusting her stone cherubs and wandering into shot, which drove the photographer to call her an 'espèce de salaude' at which point Lucy turned round and told him he was an 'absolute cretin' and I couldn't stop giggling. We finally finished at about 7.30 and as they drove away to London, I can't say I was sorry to see them go.

'Your parents will be so sorry to have missed you,' said Lucy, kissing me goodbye the next morning. 'Why ever didn't you tell them you were coming?'

I huddled in the back seat, staring out of the window, miserable with guilt as my driver drove me to Salisbury Plain.

Willy and Amy had already arrived and Amy was being made up.

'That gel, I swear, she's very tasty. I'm gonna marry 'er, Swan, I am.'

'Watch it, Willy, she's only sixteen, less than half your age,' I pointed out. At thirty-four, the son of a barrow boy with a startling resemblance to Terence Stamp in *Billy Budd*, Willy had already been married twice before, first to a local girl when he was seventeen and subsequently to a bit-part actress who had run off with a stunt man. I loved Willy. He was one of the few good photographers who wasn't a prima donna and he was never temperamental.

'I've always fancied 'avin' a bit a cocoa,' he said with a nod to Amy, 'nice and soothing, like.'

'Willy, for Christ's sake!'

But Amy just laughed. 'Don't worry about him. We had a nice chat on the way down, didn't we, Willy?'

'Definitely. You know, Swan, there just aren't enough black girls modelling these days. Someone oughta be doin' summink about it.'

'Who better than you, Willy? Start spreading the word, start asking to work with black models, start telling the clients. Don't tell us, we know.'

'Right. Yeah. Right,' said Willy several times. 'So what we goin' to do today then?'

From the minute we got started I knew the pictures were going to be amazing. Amber used some special kabuki make-up which accentuated my ultra-white skin and contrasted with Amy's blackness. What with my black hair and her white crewcut it was all very ebony and ivory in tone. Stonehenge loomed on the horizon and even the sky obliged by turning grey and the wind came up and moved the clouds along very fast above and behind us. It was only halfway through that it dawned on me that this was Amy's very first photographic shoot. Willy was talking her through it.

'That's it, darlin', t'riffic, hold it, don't smile, no smiling today, all serious, stare right through me, that's it, reach up, go on, up, UP! Grab those clouds before they get away. You too, Swan, don't look at me like I'm daft, your hands are touching the clouds, give a little jump, NOW! It'll look like you're being carried away by the clouds. All right, turn around, back to back, look at me, look back again, give me a nice bit a profile. . . .'

I wanted to offer Amy a lift back to London and get to know her better but there was something else I knew I had to do. I thanked her on behalf of the designers for her time and made her promise to get in touch when she came to New York for the Girl of the Year finals. Then I watched with amusement as Willy, who had been hovering behind me, seized his chance and whisked her away.

'Got anythink planned for tonight then?' I heard him ask casually as he helped her into his car.

'Nothing special. Just family dinner with my fiancé. You want to join us?'

I didn't hear Willy's reply.

I had to go back. I didn't tell the driver where we were going. I just asked him to drop me off by the road at the end of the drive and said I wanted to go for a walk. He didn't know I was going for a walk in the grounds of my parents' home.

It was September and the leaves had not yet fallen. I walked slowly up the drive, breaking into a run to gather up speed to leap across the cattle grids as I had done as a child. The house is seventeenth century, built of rose brick and timbered. You turn a bend in the drive and there it is, down in the valley with the river running by it. The drive peters out into a dirt road which leads to the stables and to reach the house itself you have to walk across the fields that lead right up to the front door. It was even more wild than I remembered.

I didn't go in. I didn't want to play the intruder and besides, I didn't need to go inside to recapture the atmosphere of the place. We had always played in the fields. I walked past the house and soon I was following the narrow path along the river. I knew where I was going and I knew how treacherous the route would be.

We had all played there as children. It was our secret place: a deserted lime kiln. It was almost impossible to reach unless you knew of its existence. You had to walk across the weir, something we were expressly forbidden to do, then along the riverbank until you came to some woods rising steeply up a hill. Built into the side of the hill, totally hidden from view unless you came across it by chance, was the kiln.

I saw the smoke rising before I saw the kiln itself and then I reached it and found that someone had put on a brand new wooden door that stood open. As I stood there I realised that all around me a clearing had been made. I knocked on the door. There was no answer. I stepped inside and saw immediately that someone was living there. The kiln was conical and its roof rose to a point in the middle. The round floor made an awkward shape in which to arrange furniture but somebody had tried. The oven of the kiln was clearly being used both as a fireplace and for cooking. A futon bed stuck out into the middle of the room. Books were piled up on the floor along with tapes and a giant ghettoblaster. I loved it. It was the perfect hiding place, just as we had always wanted it to be as kids.

Then I saw it, taped to the wall with a Band Aid: my first

Vogue cover. My own face stared at me in the midst of this strange little dwelling and I stared back, bewildered.

Suddenly I heard the voices coming up the hill behind me. I was trapped. I had no time to get out of the kiln before they reached me. I would have to stay and be caught trespassing.

His shadow against the September evening light filled the doorway.

'Well, you took your time, Swan,' my brother Harry told me. 'I thought you would have found me ages ago.' And then he stood aside and a young woman came into view. There was something terribly familiar about her.

Oh my God, I thought, it's Molly Bainbridge.

London, 1993

'Angie, here's one for you,' said Grace one morning: 'a commercial for a new hot dog chain. DAX. Short for dachshund. Get it? They're casting for kids. New faces. It'll be split screen, six different boys and girls walking along the street eating hot dogs. I told them they could have the casting here next Thursday after school. That way we can case the competition alongside our girls. Tell them to dress simply – white T-shirt, jeans, Keds, the natural look. No one over sixteen. Off you go now, get on that phone. Call your little girls.'

Angie smiled. She still couldn't quite believe that she had her own girls to look after. And did they need looking after! The models were supposed to call in to their bookers every day between five and six to find out what work was available and get details of castings, but Angie soon realised that her New Faces liked to call in for a chat anyway. Often they dropped by in person and just hung around talking to each other, making cups of tea, trying to be cool.

Angie had been plunged right in at the deep end from day one, taking calls from clients – fashion editors of teenage magazines, co-ordinators of fashion shows for high street stores, ad agencies, PR companies – searching for girls. She sent girls to castings and learned that if the client liked the girl, they would call and put an option on her, a pencil, a first refusal. Once they confirmed that they did indeed want her

they would then talk money. The agency got a commission –
20 per cent – from the client *and* the girl.

In her first week Angie confirmed a girl on the wrong day
and it was sheer chance that the girl rang up ten minutes
before the client was expecting her and asked, in all ignorance,
'Anything for me to do today?' But after a month or so she
settled into the job and began to build up a stable of New
Faces. She could see a girl in the open casting, chat with her,
ask her about school, how she was getting on, suss out
her personality and then, providing she was the right height
(5 feet 8 inches plus) with good features and reasonably photogenic in the snapshot she had brought with her, Angie would
send her on a test shoot. The girl would have to pay for it
herself – £50 – but Angie sent her girls to a former model
who had become a photographer who would do the test shots
in her flat and knew just how to make the young girls feel at
ease. If the test was OK, instead of printing them for £10 to
£15, the agency had the facility to laser them for £5 – and
of course Mum got one for the album. Then there were
photographer's assistants also trying to make their mark, who
were often happy to do a girl's test shoot for nothing just so
they could have pictures of a gorgeous girl, even though she
might be a very young one, to beef up their own books.

Then it was time to try to start making up the girl's book,
sending her off to get print work, editorial pictures in magazines so she could put the tearsheets in her portfolio. Angie
found that one of the biggest problems with girls in her age
group was weight. Often a girl who had tested really well
would go off on a casting and the word would come back that
she had really put on weight. The weight fluctuation was
invariably related to emotional disturbances, boyfriend
trouble, and Angie soon realised that her job spilled over into

113

the evening when the girls started calling her at home for comfort.

Tess Tucker was the most constant caller. Angie had been bewildered by the fact that Tess didn't get work immediately but when she called to find out why it was always the same story: 'The girl's a beauty. She's really fit! Personally I couldn't wait to photograph her,' said a photographer who had been present at a casting Tess had gone to for a Kookaï show, 'but she doesn't sell herself at all. She's so shy and hesitant. She's not a good walker, she doesn't walk tall, and she sort of clutched her book to her chest and they almost had to prise it away from her.'

'She looked terrified! I thought she was going to burst into tears any second. She was up for a tampon ad and you know what they're like – all hop, skip and a jump in the sunlight and isn't life wonderful! This girl looked like she had the worst cramps in the world. Her looks were stunning but she just had no confidence,' reported someone on a magazine.

'Angie, it was horrible. I had to strip down to my bra and panties and they kept looking at my thighs and talking about me as if I wasn't there.' Tess was almost hysterical down the phone the evening after her tampon casting. 'They hated me from the minute I walked in the door, I could tell.' It was like listening to Jeannie, her little sister, when she came home from school all upset because one of the older kids had teased her. Angie knew that she had to be very patient. She mustn't get ratty with Tess – or any of the girls, for that matter – she must work on her confidence, get Tess to trust her.

'Tess, that's going to happen over and over again but it's their problem, not yours. You're a beautiful girl and if they can't see it, they're mad. We'll find someone who will, you'll see. Now there's a casting tomorrow I'd like you to go to. You'd be perfect. It's lingerie again but your body's a dream and your skin tone's great. If you stand up straight and act really confident, you should have no problem at all. Now, take down the address. . . .'

When Tess arrived for the casting at the photographer's agent's office in a converted Victorian workhouse in a remote part of the City, she was dripping with sweat. The heat wave at the beginning of June 1993 had knocked London sideways. While New Yorkers were used to working in air-conditioned offices and going out at lunchtime to be blasted by 97-degree heat, Londoners were completely thrown when the temperature rose to what was for them a staggering 85 degrees. On top of everything the casting turned out to be for six to eight black-and-white pictures in the national press for – thermal underwear!

Tess was early. She was so obsessed with being on time for her appointments that she was always early. The office was deserted but she could hear voices upstairs. It was a narrow Dickensian building with one room on each floor. Tess made her way nervously up the spiral staircase to the next floor only to find that too was deserted. She saw a door marked Ladies and slipped inside to wash away the surface sweat. Somewhere up above her the old ceiling had cracked: she could now hear the voices quite clearly through a hole.

'So what we looking for then? Bras and knickers? Nice bit of skin tone? Really firm boobs?'

Tess realised it must be the photographer and the client waiting for the girls to arrive. She was just about to go out when she heard footsteps on the spiral staircase. Someone was there before her.

'Hello, come on up, that's right. Now, who are you? Have you got a card?' A new voice, a woman's: must be the client.

'Here you are,' said a bright, confident voice, 'I'm Zara. How are you all today?'

'We're fine, darling. Don't you look lovely. Done lingerie before, have you?'

'Oh, lingerie's my main thing. I do it all the time.'

'Well, aren't we lucky. Now, could you pop downstairs and change into this all-in-one bodystocking and come back up and show us, there's a love.'

Tess heard the girl coming down. She was about to go out when she heard them talking upstairs.

' "*Lingerie's my main thing. I do it all the time.*" She's got to be joking. She's got no tits to speak of. Oh, whoops, here's another. Morning, darling, got some cards for us? Thank you. Not shy doing lingerie, are you, what's your name, Maggie? OK, take this bodystocking, Maggie, and come back up when you've put it on. And you, sweetheart, oh, I've worked with you before, haven't I? Nice to see you again. . . . Oh you're back, are you? Fits you perfectly, doesn't it? Do you want to parade up and down for us like one does, bit of a strollette so we can see how you walk. Lovely. . . .'

Then Tess listened in horror to the comments when the client and the photographer were alone. No matter how warmly the girls were greeted, once they were on their way back down the spiral staircase it was non-stop put-down:

'Droopy tits. Ropey skin. Not a hope.'

'She just hasn't got enough up top and did you see that cellulite on her thighs?'

'Who did her tests? Made her look like an old hag, poor thing, not that she's much better in the flesh.'

'This card says she's 5 feet 8 inches and she's a bloody midget!'

'The top half's brilliant but when it comes to the legs, forget it. Thighs like pregnant whales. . . .'

116

Yet when Tess peeped out at the girls coming down the staircase they all looked perfectly beautiful to her.

I haven't got a prayer, she told herself and ran away without being seen.

What am I going to do with her? Angie asked herself fifty times a day, it's Catch 22 with Tess. She's perfect for Laura Ashley but her book just isn't strong enough and until it is they're just going to send her back every time. But how am I going to strengthen her book if she never gets any work? I've got to find someone to give her some confidence.

The last person she expected this to be was her brother Patrick. Angie had a constant battle with Patrick. The fact that he was still at school while she was now a wage earner was almost more than he could bear. Every night when she came home exhausted in time to cook the family's tea, Patrick sniped at her non-stop.

'So how's the queen of the fashion world? How's Miss Angie Doyle who thought she could be a model but they only made her a secretary?'

'I'm not a . . .' began Angie, furious, but then she stopped. She mustn't let him get to her. He wanted to be out there supporting the family. His frustration was mounting daily. She could feel his tension, coiled up and ready to be released in bitter attacks of resentment, most of them directed straight at her. But what could she do? He was still so young and he hadn't even got his GCSEs yet. She knew what the real problem was. Patrick had worshipped their mother and of all the children she had made no secret of the fact that he had been her special favourite. When she had left he had been utterly devastated despite the fact that he had been the only one to receive anything from her. She had left him a box of oddments, an old fountain pen, her father's watch, her first camera, a cigarette case, a pack of cards, a water pistol and a magician's wand. Crazy things, very personal to her and perfect for Patrick, who was a clown and an inveterate practical joker. Yet he had gone into total denial, refusing to believe that she would not come back for him. Every day he was the first to rush for the mail, never giving up hope that she would write to him. She never did.

So as Angie walked back from the underground to the Doyle household, she prepared herself for the usual Patrick onslaught the minute she let herself in the door.

'I'm home!' she called as she always did.

'What's for tea?' yelled back Jeannie, Kathleen and Michael before she could even get her coat off, but from Patrick there was silence. When she went into the kitchen she saw why. Tess was sitting at the table with a big pot of tea in front of her. Opposite her, staring at her in apparent adoration, was Patrick.

'Oh, Angie, please forgive me for coming to your home but I just had to talk to someone and I knew you'd have left the agency by now. You won't believe what happened today. It was so disgusting! I went for this casting, you know, the one for that magazine story about kissing in public, should you or shouldn't you? Would you or wouldn't you? Oh, Angie, they made me kiss the male model right there in front of everyone and do you know what he did? He sort of grabbed me while he was kissing me and I could feel him pressing against me really hard. . . .'

'Well, didn't you say anything?' asked Angie.

'Oh, I didn't dare. And he followed me out after the casting and said all sorts of filthy things to me.'

'What things?' asked Patrick eagerly.

'Shut up, Patrick. What was his name, the model?'

'Oh, I never asked. I just ran. I came straight here. I was

in such a state and Patrick has been so sweet and made me a cup of tea.'

'That's a first,' muttered Angie. 'Tess, next time anything like that happens you call me straight away from wherever you are and I'll talk to the client there and then. I'll find out that model's name first thing tomorrow. He's obviously a menace. So has Patrick been boring you to death?'

'Oh, *no*, nothing like. He's been telling me how much like your mother I am. I'd never have guessed your mother had red hair like mine, Angie.'

'Well, she did,' said Angie shortly. It had never occurred to her that Tess did indeed have a look of their mother about her.

'And Patrick's been telling me how it'll be no time at all before I'm working non-stop. He says it's always hard at first but one day someone will take a shine to me and appreciate my particular look and I should just be patient and try my hardest to present a confident open front when I go to castings and keep telling myself I'm wonderful until I believe it. He's been so supportive, I just can't wait to get back out there in spite of how awful it was today. . . .'

All the things I've been saying to her for weeks, thought Angie, and just because the words fall from Patrick's sweet lips she finally understands them. Angie turned away so they wouldn't see the look of amusement on her face. Patrick must have been listening to everything she said about Tess and repeated it as if it were his own advice. Well, what did it matter where it came from providing it worked?

She'd never seen her brother with a girl before. He was such an odd-looking bloke with his big nose and long, sad face. Not really ugly because his eyes were so beautiful, dark blue with long lashes. Angie knew her father worried about Patrick. His teachers at school had often called Joseph Doyle in to have a chat about his son. It had even been suggested that Patrick should get some professional help, that his mother's departure had left him more disturbed than his family might realise.

'My lad see a shrink? Get away!' Angie's father was outraged at the idea.

But Angie wasn't so sure. She sensed her brother was deeply unhappy, but because of his resentment of her she was the last one to whom he would turn for help.

When it was time for Tess to leave, Patrick was on his feet. 'Come on, Tess, I'd better walk you to the underground in case anyone leaps on you in the street.'

Angie was about to warn Tess that Patrick was only playing at being a gentleman, she shouldn't take him seriously, but Tess was already on her feet and smiling at him. 'I'll call you tomorrow, Angie,' she said as she walked out the door with him.

Well, well, well, thought Angie.

London, 1993

As a teenager Linda Johnson had always dreamed of being a model. Her bedroom wall in the surburban semi-detached in Ashton-under-Lyne outside Manchester was plastered with pages torn from fashion magazines depicting models both super and regular. When she was fourteen two things happened: her father, a newspaper man, got a job on a national tabloid and the family moved down south to London and simultaneously, although the two things could not possibly be related, Linda began to put on weight. She became fat, so fat that she took down all the pictures from her walls and put all thoughts of modelling out of her head. Her father got her a job in the newsroom of his paper and she began to channel her energy into another dream: to become a highly respected journalist.

The one constant thorn in her flesh was her older sister Alice. In a way Alice had succeeded in making a variation of both of Linda's dreams come true. She had grown up tall and slim with her own innate sense of style, she had gone to Durham University and then she had entered and won the *Vogue* talent contest. Now at the age of twenty-six, although everyone always said she could have been a model, Alice was fashion editor of *Carter's*, which in Linda's envious eyes was just a rip-off of the other big glossies but she could not deny that it had *Vogue* and *Harpers* on the run. So Alice was both a journalist of sorts and she was working in the midst of the fashion world, just where Linda wanted to be. Alice lived and breathed clothes twenty-four hours a day. She hung out every night with other fashion editors, photographers, models, designers. Her conversation revolved around the eternal question of how she was going to come up with a fresh look for a white shirt story, a denim story, a really good black polo neck story or a new corduroy story, or whether one of her arch-rivals on a magazine would pinch one of her ideas for a story and run it before Alice's own copy date.

In a pathetic attempt to keep up, Linda changed her name to the more stylish Lindy and added her middle name to make it Lindy-Jane Johnson. Her new aim in life was to become an investigative reporter and expose celebrities. Using her father's contacts she managed to get a job on a sleazy Sunday paper that paid pretty well but just as she was about to dangle her impressive rates in front of Alice, whom she knew was paid very little by *Carter's* despite the importance of her job, Alice announced that she had landed a lucrative bit of moonlighting as stylist on a well-known designer's ad campaign.

Lindy-Jane longed to stumble on the Prince of Wales in a gay bar, to uncover evidence that Hillary Clinton had been born a man, to learn that the wholesome, toothy boy who had grown up next door to her in the other half of the Ashton-under-Lyne semi-detached had grown up to be a bigger serial killer than Dennis Nilsen and had thoughtfully obliterated half of Kentucky as well so she could sell the story in New York and be invited to be a contributing editor on *Vanity Fair*. Then gradually, as she watched with seething, silent envy as her sister began to make a spectacular success of her career, a germ of an idea began to formulate itself in Lindy-Jane's manipulative little mind. The more she listened to Alice wittering on about her own ethereal world, the more Lindy-Jane began to realise that Alice's wretched stories depended more and more on the model or, if she could get her, the supermodel. Throughout the 1980s the photographers had been the people who gave the magazines their own image – the Steven Meisels, the Bruce Webers, the Patrick Demarcheliers – they made the pages look the way they did and the fashion editors had depended on them. Now, it seemed to Lindy-Jane, in the 1990s the supermodels were taking over. They had the power – just a small cluster of them, but who knew how fast they would rise? Or fall. Lindy-Jane had found her new goal: she would bring down a supermodel.

The only trouble was she knew absolutely nothing about models, so there was only one thing to do: swallow all her vitriol and jealousy and sibling rivalry and invite her darling sister to lunch.

'My bitch of an editor's on my back,' growled Alice when Lindy-Jane walked into her office at 12.45. 'Some poxy French designer who shall remain nameless is going to withdraw £250,000 of advertising if I don't use some of his disgusting clothes in a story. So where are we going for lunch? I rather fancy Lebanese.'

Lindy-Jane's stomach heaved. That was another thing about Alice. She always wanted to eat exotic food. Plain Cal-Ital or French was much too boring. Still, if she wanted Alice to give her the dope on supermodels she'd have to go along with her, so she trudged dutifully after her sister through Mayfair to Shepherd's Market. Alice was on one of her 'I haven't got time to go to the gym so I'm going to walk' kicks.

'What are you getting Mum for Christmas?' Lindy-Jane resented the way Alice always plundered the boxes of freebies sent into the fashion department.

'No idea. I've done Daddy – he's getting that box of Givenchy Gentleman eau de toilette that's been sitting in the fashion cupboard for the last six months – but God knows what I'll give Mummy. What about you?'

Lindy-Jane winced at the Mummy and Daddy. Pre-university, Alice had never called their parents anything but Mum and Dad.

'Oh, a book, I expect.' They were passing Heywood Hill in Curzon Street.

'For a woman who will only read a magazine if it teaches her to knit her own royal family?' Alice raised her eyebrows and stopped to look at the books on display in Heywood Hill's window. 'My God, that's it! Look!'

'What?' Lindy-Jane could only see a window of books.

'*Mrs de Winter*.'

'Who?'

'It's a book, stupid. There, right in front of you. Top of the bestseller list. Sequel to *Rebecca*.'

'What about it?'

'That's my story. Hats and veils. It opens with a funeral. Beatrice's funeral. She was Maxim de Winter's sister and they have to come back for the funeral.'

'What happens?'

'Oh, darling, for heaven's sake. I don't read books, just the reviews. We gave it rather a good one. I'll have to dig it out for reference. Come on, about turn, back to the office. We'll do lunch next week. It'll be a hats and veils story, very moody and sexy round the grave, Maxim de Winter and that little mouse he married after Rebecca. We'll put her in some dark suit or coat by the wretched French designer and focus on the hats. Call Philip Treacy.'

Alice had whipped out her mobile and was shouting into it as she charged back up Curzon Street and into Berkeley Square.

'It's going to be back to black, hats and veils and long black gloves and great big silver crucifixes and a ton of white lilies, it's going to be black and white moody retro and the photographer will be Peter Lindbergh if we can get him. No, darling, it certainly won't be studio, it'll be Manderley or as close as we can get. Check out English Heritage. See what they've got. Tell Geraldine to look up my notes from the collections and go off to that unspeakable French designer's showroom and pick me out a few of his dreary charcoal suits and tell that little work experience creature – what's her name? She can't be Geraldine too – well, tell her to go through the piles in the fashion room and find me some dramatic hats. And have someone start thinking of some good ideas about which house we can use – find one that's got a good chapel and a good graveyard. I'll be there in five.'

She turned to Lindy-Jane.

'Did you see those pictures based on famous paintings in American *Carter's*? No, of course, you didn't, you're worse than Mummy when it comes to magazines. Well, there was this place where Swan was photographed in Vivienne Westwood in a take-off of Fragonard's "The Swing". Now that house was divine, I wonder if it has a chapel. . . .'

'Where was it?' Lindy-Jane feigned interest. It never ceased to amaze her how Alice managed to take all the credit while getting all her fashion assistants to do all the work. It seemed the lower down the pecking order you were, the more you had to do.

'Wiltshire somewhere. Lucy Fraser's place. Friends of Swan's parents, apparently.'

Lindy-Jane's ears pricked up like a Jack Russell's. Swan was the one supermodel who was a closed book. No one knew anything about her other than the fact that she was obviously top drawer. Lindy-Jane realised she didn't even know her real name.

Back at the office, Alice sat down to tackle the most important question: the model. Who would they get to wear the
clothes?

'It's a real bitch. She's got to be mousy and timid with no
attitude whatsoever but at the same time she's got to take our
breath away. Any ideas anyone, before we call the agencies?'

The work experience girl came forward. Alice looked at
her very suspiciously. She didn't take these people on to speak.
'Yes?'

'I was having lunch with a friend on *Just Seventeen* yesterday
and . . .' Alice looked as if she was going to be sick. ' . . . and
they were having this casting for a "Would you kiss your
boyfriend in public?" story. There was this girl there who
would be just perfect. She was terrified, she cowered in fright
and jumped when she was kissed, she was just like a mouse
but she was the most beautiful mouse I've ever seen. The
thing is, well, I stole a Polaroid and – '

Alice snatched it out of her hand.

'Geraldine, darling,' she said after a minute or two, 'why
don't you call your little friend on *Just Seventeen* and find out
who this girl's booker is. Oh, thank you. . . .' Someone had
just handed her the issue of American *Carter's* with Lucy
Fraser's house in it. She flipped through her Rolodex for
Lucy Fraser's number. 'Lucy, how are you? Tell me, do you
have a chapel? No, darling, a chapel. No, I'm not getting
married, it's for . . . you don't. No, well, never mind. 'Bye
Lucy.'

Standing behind her, Lindy-Jane copied Lucy Fraser's
number.

That evening she called her. '. . . .writing a book on Fragonard. I understand your house was even used in a fashion shoot
based on "The Swing." Why was that? Do you happen to own
a Fragonard? Oh, you own a swing, oh I see, how silly of me.

Did the shoot go well? Really? Lavinia? Lavinia who? Lavinia Crichton-Lake? Lavinia Crichton-Lake is Swan? Oh, of course she is. Any relation to the Crichton-Lakes whose nanny was found murdered – yes, wasn't it dreadful? – their daughter? Thank you, Mrs Fraser, you've been most helpful.'

Well, well, thought Lindy-Jane as she put the phone down, Swan was none other than the sister of Harry Crichton-Lake, who had disappeared so mysteriously right after the murder. Well, well!

'Look sweetheart,' yelled the photographer, 'I'm here to do a job. You're here to do a job. You're probably being paid quite a lot of money. I know I certainly am. I don't care about your emotional life. Now let's get on with it.'

Tess stood shivering in the middle of a rain-sodden grave-yard, her shoulders hunched over as she hugged herself to keep warm.

'For Christ's sake, stand up straight. I can't even see the bloody clothes. Oh, no, not again . . . !'

Tess had dissolved into tears for the fourth time that morn-ing. This was her one big chance and it was all going horribly wrong.

Amber, who was doing the make-up, rushed over to Tess.

'Now, now, take it easy. We don't want tears all over that pretty face. You'll be OK. He's a bastard. Just don't let him get to you. Just keep remembering how pretty you are. He needs you just as much as you need him.'

Tess flashed her a faint smile of gratitude.

'Why don't you say something?' Lindy-Jane asked her sister. 'You're in charge, aren't you?'

'Not on the shoot. It's the photographer's territory.' This wasn't strictly true on every shoot but it was typical of Alice to pass the buck. What Lindy-Jane didn't know was that a really professional fashion editor would have sorted it out herself. But Alice was Alice. 'I knew he was a right pig but I didn't think he'd be this bad. We should have got Peter.'

'Peter?' said Lindy-Jane.

'Peter Lindbergh. We're not going to get any pictures at this rate, not that she's exactly helping matters.'

'She's so thin, Alice. I saw her when she was getting changed at the hotel. She's all skin and bone and ribs sticking out all over the place, it's pitiful.'

'Who cares? She'll photograph like a dream. What's your story on anyway? Anorexic models?'

Lindy-Jane had spun Alice a yarn about actually having been commissioned to write a story about models otherwise she knew her sister wouldn't have let her tag along to watch. Now that she thought about it, a story about the scandal of anorexia among young models wasn't a bad place to kick off.

'Look at her, Alice. Her teeth are chattering. If somebody doesn't do something soon that girl's going to faint.'

Somebody did.

Bobby Fox ran up to Tess with a giant umbrella. He put his arm round her shoulders and led her away to the shelter of a mausoleum with a stone bench. He was the photographer's assistant and it had been his job to give Tess a wake-up call at the hotel at 5.30 that morning, half an hour before everybody else so that her eyes would have time to get rid of their sleepy puffiness. She had not responded to the call and he had had to go up to her room. The sight of her creamy white back, spattered with tiny freckles, and her long red hair spread out over the pillow had stopped him in his tracks and it was a moment before he could summon up the courage to gently tap her on the shoulder to wake her. She had woken with a start, sitting bolt upright, and he saw she had been in one of those deep sleeps where it takes a minute or two to realise where you are when you come to. She had grabbed the sheet to cover herself but not before he had seen her tiny pointed nipples on an almost flat chest. He had been stunned by how much he had been aroused by the sight of them. It wasn't as if he never saw naked breasts but this girl's flesh was a dream.

'What's the matter, love?' he asked as she stood and shook with cold. 'Had a row with the boyfriend?'

'I haven't got a boyfriend.'

'What is it then?'

'This place. . . .'

'Yeah, bit spooky innit? Still, it's only the location. All the bodies are safely buried six feet under. No one's going to rise up and get you. Besides, I'm here to look after you.'

'I only became a model to help raise the money to buy my mum a new wheelchair – she's crippled, you see, paralysed from the waist down, and look at the mess I'm making of it all. I haven't earned a penny, I'm about to blow this job, I owe the agency for my test shots. . . .'

'I would have done those for you for free. Now listen, love, you've got to get a grip. This photographer's a real hothead and any minute now he's going to blow his stack and walk off the shoot. It's all up to you. Come on, let's get back there and show 'em what you can do. OK? Look at me, give us a little smile. OK?'

Tess gave him a shaky smile. He was gorgeous looking with long fine silky hair, and his face was pretty, almost like a girl's. He bent forward and kissed her softly on the neck.

'I think you're the most beautiful person I've ever seen,' he whispered.

Those were the words that got Tess through the shoot. 'You're the most beautiful person I've ever seen.' She kept repeating them to herself over and over like a mantra while

Bobby moved about, reloading cameras, winking at her every now and then and holding up his thumb in encouragement.

Somehow, with Bobby's help, she got through the day. At the end the male model hired to 'play' Maxim de Winter standing behind her at the grave jokingly made as if to push her into it and she screamed. Amber came to her rescue once again and escorted her back to the hotel to change. Tess was so rattled that she asked Amber to wait for her in her room while she went to take a quick bath down the hall. It was one of those old-fashioned English hotels with no bathrooms *en suite*.

'I think I'm going mad,' she told Bobby who joined them later when he had finished packing up all the camera equipment. 'I could swear I heard the whirr of a camera as I was getting changed in the bathroom. I'm seriously paranoid.'

'You sure are,' said Bobby, 'and I'm going to do something about it.'

Instead of dropping her home, he took her back to his place and cooked her a large bowl of spaghetti carbonara.

'I can't eat this.' Tess looked horrified. 'If I put on weight I'll never get another job.'

'I could give you four bowls of this and you'd still be totally photogenic. Now eat, that's an order, and take your medicine.' He handed her a bottle of Corvo. 'It'll thicken your blood.'

'Where do you get your confidence? If you could cook me a bowl of that I'd eat you out of house and home.'

'It comes from knowing what you want to do and getting on with it. I always knew I wanted to be a photographer. I did an HND – a Higher National Diploma – for two years; you arrive and they point you at a studio, and now I'm an assistant, working with a load of big names, learning as much as I can on the job. As soon as I can get a good enough book together – maybe in a year or so – I'll go on my own. That's what your problem is with modelling. I don't get the impression you really really *really* want to do it. You have to want to succeed for yourself, you have to believe in yourself. You took the first step by going to the agency so what's stopping you now? You could be huge. That photographer today gave you a really hard time but he does that to all the girls. I heard him talking about you. He thinks the pictures are going to be amazing.'

He went on and on, coaxing her, building up her ego, refusing to listen when she tried to voice her insecurities. Finally he took her to bed but it was another two hours before he took her virginity. He placed tall lighted candles around the bed and gave her an aromatherapy massage, gently rubbing the oil over her creamy skin until she was totally relaxed, then slipping a hand between her legs and stroking her fine red-haired mound until she was wet.

Just before dawn he entered her and just as he had talked her through her crisis of confidence, now he talked her through sex, pausing between sentences to lick the tiny nipples on either side of her flat chest until they rose up in stiff little points.

It was inevitable that she should fall in love with him. It was a given that she would become totally dependent on him. She continued to be shaky at her go-sees and in the end Angie just gave up and let her only go for castings where they thought there was a chance Bobby would be working on the shoot. If they knew who the photographer was going to be, and it was someone who regularly used Bobby as an assistant, they were ahead of the game. Just knowing that she might be working with him seemed to give her the necessary confidence to get herself the job.

Yet despite Angie's reassurances that Tess was finally sorting

131

herself out, her mother, Annie Tucker, was worried about her daughter. Then something happened to confirm her worst fears.

On the news-stand one morning Annie could not understand why all her husband's regulars were giving her odd looks. Suddenly no one seemed to be able to look her in the eye. Finally one of them patted her arm and said:

'Don't you worry, love, she's only young. She'll come through it.'

'Who will? Come through what?' asked Annie, bewildered when the customer handed her a copy of the *Mirror* and walked away.

The headline in the centre pages was giant: WOULD YOU LET YOUR DAUGHTER TURN OUT LIKE THIS? And underneath: 'The sad story of a young model's battle with anorexia. In her constant battle to keep her weight down for the cameras, teenager Tess Tucker has become a pitiful anorexic. . . .' But it was the grainy photograph of Tess in the nude, her ribs and vertebrae caught sticking out in skeletal fashion, that caused Annie Tucker to close up the news-stand for the day and make someone take her to Etoile.

It wasn't true, of course. Tess was no more anorexic than Mr Blobby, and Annie knew it. The byline to the muckraking story was that of Lindy-Jane Johnson. There was no photographer's credit but Bobby had a pretty good idea when the pictures were taken: Lindy-Jane must have called someone down from London and had them hide and take pictures of Tess in the bathroom when she was getting changed. This would set Tess's confidence back months, not to mention her career, and he was about to go off to Milan for three weeks' work. She would have to face it on her own.

Grace Brown had other ideas.

'Take her with you, Bobby. Do us all a favour. Best thing

in the world if she's out of the country now, and it could be they'll love her in Milan. They love Titian hair and pale skin. It's what Italian men are crying out for. They rarely get it in their own women. Besides, the one place a girl can beef up her book is Milan. There are so many magazines and they all come out so fast, if she gets a few jobs she'll come home with loads of tearsheets. Take her with you, Bobby.'

'OK,' said Bobby and secretly began to wonder just exactly what he'd taken on in Tess Tucker.

' . . . so we're sending her to Milan with Bobby Fox. Let's hope the Italians love her and she gets loads of work,' Angie told the family that night as she prepared the evening meal. To Kathleen, Michael and Jeannie, hearing about the ups and downs in the life of Angie's discovery, Tess Tucker, was like watching a soap opera, the latest instalment of which they demanded every evening. But Angie was not prepared for Patrick's outburst.

'She's bloody left me! First my mother and now Tess. How could she go off like that without telling me, and who's this Bobby Fox character?'

'Patrick, for God's sake, that's over-reacting a bit. Bobby Fox is her boyfriend. She barely knows you. She only met you that one time – '

'Oh no she hasn't!' chorused the other three.

'What do you mean?'

'He's been seeing quite a bit of her, haven't you, Patrick? They have coffee together in espresso bars in Soho or Covent Garden. Coffee! Wild, isn't it?' Jeannie was laughing and Angie was astonished when Patrick slammed his fist down on the table and left the room.

'Patrick's in lo-ove. Patrick's in lo-ove,' sang his little sisters until Angie shut them up.

Her father called her the next day.

'Whatever did you say to Patrick last night? He's gone and left home. Walked out. Says he's gone to find his mother. You're going to have to give up that model agency job of yours, Angie, and come home and help with the little ones. They're in shock. You're going to have to be here. No more work; your place is with them.'

New York/ Miami, 1993/1994

Stacey Stein, working on the booking table at Etoile New York, was in despair about her two newest girls. They were the only ones without a mother or an older brother in tow to keep an eye out for them, but that was not the real problem.

Cassie Dylan ought not to have been a problem at all. She was the perfect New Face. At her Orientation, where the new girls in town were told how to get around New York, never to give out their home address or telephone number, never sign a release, always refer it to the agency, how to behave and what to wear at test shoots and go-sees, how to stay in shape and be well groomed, how to avoid tanning and tan marks and where to go for other general advice, she had listened intently. She was never late with her rent at the model apartment. At her go-sees she was always on time. No one had a bad word to say about her, she was pretty, she smiled, she was polite – but after a month and a half nobody had even put an option on her, let alone booked her for an actual job.

At last Stacey had to face the truth: the girl was boring. Gradually she was getting some comeback from fashion editors and photographers that gave her clues. Dylan was a pretty girl, her hair, skin and teeth were in good condition, she was the right height, her figure was fine, her legs were great. So what was wrong? She was too apple-pie, too all-American, her look just wasn't exciting. *She* wasn't exciting. The most interesting thing about her was the fact that she rollerbladed to her castings, charging in and out of the traffic up and down the avenues, but of course no one ever saw that once she was inside the building with her long hair neatly combed and Paul van Ash's test pictures ready to show in her book on her lap.

Finally Stacey decided what the problem was: the long hair had to go. With a short sharp bob, Dylan would be a new person. Shock tactics were called for. But the girl was resisting. She dug her heels in and showed a stubborn side of her nature that gave Stacey hope that it might be converted into the kind of determination a girl needed to get her to the top. Stacey could go on till she was blue in the face about the way Linda Evangelista's short hair had been so successful but Dylan just wouldn't listen. Her excuse was always something about her boyfriend liking her with long hair. Well, said Stacey, they could get the boyfriend in and have a chat with him. No, they couldn't apparently because he lived in England. It was all a bit weird but there was nothing Stacey could do to make Dylan change her mind. It was a waste of time sending her to *Vogue* or *Harpers* or *Elle*, so Stacey just kept on sending her to *Mademoiselle* and *Just Seventeen* and even to *McCall's* and *Ladies' Home Journal* and all the apple-pie catalogues she could think of.

Gigi Garcia was a different story altogether. She was in mega serious trouble and sinking deeper every day. It wasn't that nobody wanted to use her. She was being booked every other day but within a month she had earned herself a sensationally bad rep. She had been perfect fodder for the gossip-mongers the second she stepped off the plane from Miami. The story going round Manhattan had it that she had been on the same flight as Marlon Warner. Marlon Warner was a photographer whose style, while totally individual, fell somewhere between that of Bruce Weber and Robert Mapplethorpe. In the late eighties he had emerged as a serious contender in the area of the sensual advertising image, with a particular emphasis on male fashion. The thing about Marlon was that female models were crazy to work with him because if he could make men look that good, think what he could do for them.

The story went that Marlon had discovered Gigi in a phone booth at the airport, tears streaming down her face, and started shooting film on her there and then. He had delivered her to Etoile four days later and what had happened between them in the intervening period was anybody's guess. Speculation was rife. The only positive proof of their association emerged in a steamy GQ men's swimwear story Marlon had shot during those four days at Atlantic City. When the pictures were delivered to Condé Nast, all anybody wanted to know was who was the sultry, pouting Latin chick in the background whose semi-naked body was covered in sand.

When her book started going the rounds, these pictures, plus a few selected solo shots clearly part of a private shoot at Marlon's studio, made Gigi the most wanted New Face in town. Yet every day Stacey was subjected to the same incessant flak:

'Stacey, it's 10.30 already. Gigi Garcia didn't show. She was booked for eight.'

'Stacey, your girl finally shows up four hours late and we're all set and I tell her, Gigi, lose the gum. You know what she does? She goes next door and I think she's throwing it down the toilet and the next thing we know she's gone, out the window, down the fire escape . . . can you send me someone else?'

'Stacey, we have this wig for her and we've just got it fixed and then, you'll never believe this, she doesn't like it so she takes the fire bucket, fills it with water and before we can stop her she's bent over with her arse in the air and she's ducking the wig in the water. It's ruined, of course. . . .'

On top of everything Gigi couldn't be bothered with the subway and took cabs everywhere. She hadn't paid more than a week's rent since she'd been in Manhattan. She was running up a gigantic bill with the agency and the word was spreading about her unreliability. Yet people kept booking her. She was everything Cassie Dylan was not: she had triple-A edge.

As for the House Rules pinned up in the hall in the model apartment, Gigi broke them as steadfastly as Cassie kept them.

YOU ARE NOT ALLOWED TO INVITE MALE FRIENDS TO THE APARTMENT. NO SMOKING OR ALCOHOL ALLOWED AT ANY TIME.

Gigi chain-smoked and drank Jack Daniels and lemonade and the only friends she invited to the apartment were men.

RESPECT YOUR ROOMMATES! KEEP THE APARTMENT CLEAN AT ALL TIMES. DO NOT LIVE OUT OF YOUR SUITCASE.

Gigi didn't live out of her suitcase because she didn't own one. She lived out of the five or six carrier bags in which she had brought her stuff from Miami, and left them littered around the room she shared with Cassie.

PLEASE DO NOT EAT OTHERS' FOOD. YOU WOULD NOT LIKE IT TO HAPPEN TO YOU.

Cassie took to eating food within an hour of buying it. If she left it in the fridge, Gigi helped herself.

IF YOU WOULD LIKE THE MAID TO DO YOUR LAUNDRY PLEASE PUT IT IN THE LAUNDRY BASKET PROVIDED.

Gigi dumped hers on Cassie's bed.

Cassie realised she had never actually hated anyone before she met Gigi. She had never met anyone who put her down quite so much as Gigi seemed to enjoy doing and the fact that Gigi was booked several times a week and Cassie had yet to land a job made it even worse. Cassie couldn't help noticing that Gigi was being sent to Condé Nast for castings on a regular basis whereas Stacey had only sent her there once at the very beginning. Still, she knew Stacey was there for her. Cassie called her dutifully at the agency every day on the dot of four o'clock as she had been told to at Orientation, and Stacey was always encouraging, always told her something was about to happen for her, to hang in there, never lose hope.

'Going to see Mom and Pop again, are we?' sneered Gigi each time she saw Cassie getting ready to go out in the evening. 'Make sure you're home early, bed by 9.30, got to get that sleep to be fresh for all the work that's coming your way.' Gigi of course was generally at an after-hours club till four each morning She couldn't hide her delight that at last the tables were turned, at last she, a Hispanic from nowhere, was in demand when a blue-eyed all-American blonde was not. Then there was the other way in which she scored: 'Heard from the boyfriend recently?'

Cassie's passion for a seemingly mythical English guy from whom she never heard was a source of constant amusement to Gigi. Where the other girls had pin-ups of Hugh Grant, Keanu Reeves and Pearl Jam by their beds, Cassie's wall was covered with pictures of English stately homes, the English countryside, Buckingham Palace, the Princess of Wales, Kate Moss, Seal, Emma Thompson, anything so long as it was English.

Apart from Stacey's faith in her, the other thing that kept Cassie going was her dream of seeing Tommy Lawrence again. She had made up her mind: as soon as she had made enough money she was going to go to England to look for him.

Except she wasn't making any money at all and in the meantime she had to contend with Gigi. The day she finally lost it was when she came home and found that Gigi had eaten all the precious English food – Marmite, Jaffa Cakes, even the Cooper's Oxford marmalade that she had bought at the store on Hudson as part of her research for her future life in England.

'I feel sorry for you, Gigi,' she screamed. 'You know why? Because you don't have a dream like I do. You don't have anyone special to dream about.'

But she was wrong. Gigi lived for the day when she would run into Charley Lobianco again. She never ever called in to Stacey like she was supposed to. She just dropped by the agency now and then and it was on one of these visits that she glimpsed Charley at the end of a corridor. Of course, he had an office there. Why hadn't she thought of that? She started dropping by more regularly but then discovered he had gone away on one of his frequent trips abroad. Tentatively she asked if he would ever handle her direct.

'In your dreams, sweetheart,' Stacey told her. 'OK, so people are interested in you, but that's because Marlon took those pictures of you. You've still got a lot to learn, you're still a New Face, you've only been working for six weeks. Charley only looks after supermodels.'

'Well, that's what I'm going to be,' declared Gigi.

'No, you're not, dear,' sighed Stacey; 'not at the rate you're going. People are beginning to get sick of always seeing those pictures of Marlon's in your book. It's looking suspicious that you have so few new tearsheets. I don't tell them it's because you always fuck up the shoot and they have to call for someone else to finish the job, but the word's getting around all on its own. Watch it, Gigi. Time's running out.'

For a couple of days Gigi was mildly worried. One of the things that had always concerned her was the dusky colour of her skin. Maybe there was a sub-text to what Stacey was saying. Maybe people weren't booking her because of her dark Cuban colour.

She called Marlon to ask if he would take some new pictures

of her, get her booked for a shoot he was working on, told him she'd make it worth his while, but even Marlon was wary of her reputation by now. His wife had heard the stories and seen the Atlantic City pictures and had begun asking awkward questions. What Gigi didn't know was that he had actually requested that she not be booked for any shoots with him.

Then Gigi got the call she had been waiting for.

'Gigi, can you come by the agency tomorrow around five?' asked Stacey. 'Charley wants to see you.'

It wasn't what she expected. For a start Stacey came in with her to see him. He wasn't in his office when they arrived and Gigi wandered around taking a good snoop at everything despite Stacey's pleas for her to sit down. Predictably the walls were covered with photographs of Charley with all the big supermodels, whether he represented them or not, but stashed in a corner Gigi was surprised to see a pile of sports gear: tennis and squash racquets, fishing tackle, weights. She picked up a framed photograph on his desk of a beautiful older woman, her hair tied back in an elegant French pleat, a pair of giant sunglasses pushed back on to the top of her head, her hand holding a branch of bougainvillaea away from her face. In the background there was a sun-drenched Mediterranean villa. The wife, thought Gigi. I suppose there has to be one.

'Who's this?' she asked Stacey casually.

'His mother. His upscale all-Italian mamma. Put it down, Gigi. He goes ballistic if anyone touches his things.'

Then Charley came in suddenly and Gigi skipped away from his desk and quickly sat down beside Stacey. Her heart was going thump thump thump and she found to her amazement that she was staring down at her lap, she couldn't bring herself to hold her head up and look him in the eye. For the first time in her life Gigi was actually shy.

'Charley, this is Gigi Garcia and here's her book,' said Stacey. 'I spoke to you about her.'

Why's she doing this? wondered Gigi. He knows all about me, surely. She looked up at him, waiting for him to tell Stacey that he knew all about Gigi, that he'd personally hand-picked her down in Miami, he'd be taking over her book from now on.

'Thanks Stacey. I remember. OK, I'll take it from here.'

Stacey left the room. Now we're talking, thought Gigi. He wants me but he's smart. He doesn't want Stacey to know he thinks I'm special. He is so dreamy. He is so cute.

And deep down in her subconscious a voice she didn't hear added: he's the daddy I never had, he'll take care of me.

She waited for him to come around the desk and embrace her. Instead she got a nasty shock.

'Now listen, young lady, we had an agency meeting about you yesterday and you're in pretty serious trouble. Stacey only refers her girls to me when she feels it's absolutely necessary, and in your case it clearly is. You're going to have to listen to me and you're going to have to listen good if you want to stay on our books. You're outta line. I'm looking at your account sheet here. I see charges here for tests from Marlon Warner – oh, you look surprised, you thought Marlon wasn't going to charge for those pictures? Get real, honey. Then we've had to bill you for taxis, Fedex, your Z card, Xeroxes, laser copies, faxes, Polaroids, postage for mailing, telephone calls and last but by no means least, you don't appear to have paid any rent since you've been here. You owe us over $11,000 and as far as I can make out from Stacey you're blowing out virtually every single job you get and we're getting you plenty. But not for much longer. We're working really hard on your behalf but your reputation in this town is zero. So what do you have to say for yourself?'

She had barely heard what he said. None of it made any sense anyway. She had been mesmerised by his voice. His words had been harsh but nothing could mask his silky slight Italian accent. She could still hear him telling her: 'You're very beaoooooutiful. Tell me your name.' She stared at him, willing the tears not to roll from her eyes as she slowly faced up to reality.

He didn't remember her.

'Hey kid, you listening to me? I don't hear you coming up with any answers. Look at it this way. You think I'd be wasting my time talking to you if I didn't think you were worth it? These pictures Marlon took of you are sensational. You're sensational. You've got a future, no question. And I understand, you're what? Fifteen? Sixteen? You've never been away from your parents before and here you are in New York. Where are you from?'

That did it. The fact that he had to ask confirmed he didn't remember Miami.

He was around his desk and kneeling beside her proffering a large white handkerchief.

'*Cara*, please don't. We are here to look after you but you gotta help us. We gotta find a way for you to pay us back our money and we gotta find a way for you to make much much more, you understand?'

Gigi nodded and resisted the urge to fling herself into his arms when he patted her head.

'We gotta get you out of this town. I tell you what we gonna do. We gonna send you to Italy, to my home country. We gonna send you to Milan. You work hard in Milano, lots of magazines there, you bring home lots of tearsheets, you make lots of money and you make your book superstrong and we start again in New York. OK?'

She said yes, of course, she had no option but what she

was really thinking was: if I go away and be what you want me to be in Milan, when I come back you will love me, won't you, Daddy?

There was one small problem about sending her to Milan: she didn't have a passport. The agency had been asking her for it ever since she arrived. Now she had to come clean and tell them she didn't have one, assuming they'd sort it out for her. To do that, they said, they needed her birth certificate.

Here there was an even bigger problem. If they saw her birth certificate they'd know she'd lied about her age, just as her Z card didn't give her correct height. When the attention of the booker who had measured her on arrival at Etoile had been distracted for a second, Gigi had leaned over and altered her height to 5 feet 9 inches from 5 feet 7 inches and had made sure she wore heels to castings ever since.

There was only one thing to do: she'd have to find a way to go back to Miami and look for her birth certificate amongst Elena's things.

To Stacey's eternal amazement Gigi appeared to turn over a new leaf overnight. She promised to sort out her passport herself and she rang in every day to ask about castings, but it was too late. No one would book her. Then Gigi slipped in a seemingly innocent question: 'What about Miami? Any work down there?'

'After Christmas, January, February it never stops. Want to play the homecoming queen?' laughed Stacey.

'Something like that,' said Gigi.

It was only two weeks to Christmas and Cassie was almost hysterical. Her mother kept reminding her of her promise to come back and live at Grandma Doris's if she didn't have a job.

She washed her hair, did her nails, rubbed in moisturising

cream to give her face a glow, swallowed her vitamins and as usual left for her go-see with an hour to spare. She mustn't be late. She must not be late whatever happened. It was an exclusive. They had seen her book and they liked her but with her luck once they saw her in the flesh, they wouldn't like her any more. Stacey had been vague about the details. It was catalogue work, it would pay $1,200 for the day and it didn't really matter what she wore to the casting providing she looked healthy and glowing.

She was never ill. She was one of those lucky people who would still be up and about when everyone else was down with the flu yet as she walked along Madison Avenue looking for the address, Cassie felt a strange churning sensation in her stomach. By the time she had reached her destination and announced herself at Reception, she knew she couldn't hold out much longer.

It had to be that filthy Cuban food Gigi had forced on her last night. For some strange reason Gigi had become overpoweringly friendly. Suddenly it was Gigi who was buying all the food and doing all the cooking – only Gigi couldn't cook and Cassie was terribly afraid that the meat she bought was not always fresh. Cassie didn't eat red meat in any case but she hadn't wanted to offend Gigi. Now it seemed she had food poisoning as a result.

She got as far as handing her book to the woman before she bolted out of the room and down the hall to the bathroom. She threw up over and over, cursing Gigi in a most un-Cassie-like way. She hadn't a prayer of getting this job now and it was all Gigi's fault. Yet when she returned, ashen-faced but smiling bravely, all the woman said to her was, 'All right now, dear? I hope you're not trying to take this job too seriously.'

She couldn't believe it when Stacey called and told her:

145

'You've got it, Cassie. You're on your way. Tomorrow at 7.30 a.m. at the Sunshine studios at Broadway and Prince.'

'What about a fitting?'

'Well, this is one job where you won't need one of those. Gotta go, bye-bye,' Stacey laughed and hung up.

Cassie was mystified; it sounded shady but then Stacey would never let her do anything like that.

That night she couldn't help casually letting slip to Gigi that she was working tomorrow. She tried to make out it was a big job but the minute she mentioned the word catalogue Gigi lost interest.

'Bread-and-butter work, pays OK but it doesn't have the prestige of editorial.'

But no amount of put-downs from Gigi could dampen Cassie's feeling of pure joy as she walked into the huge daylight studio the next day. The winter sunshine was flooding in through the giant windows. She sat happily while the make-up girl worked on her, a little disappointed that she was made to look rather wholesome and countrified and not glamorous and sophisticated as she had imagined. Then they showed her to a rail on which were hanging several dresses. Cassie picked one out. It was several sizes too big. They must have given her the wrong rail, one for an outsize shoot.

'Excuse me,' she said nervously, 'where are the clothes?'

'Right here,' said the stylist. 'Now let's get you ready.'

And so for her very first job in the glamorous world of New York modelling, Cassie Dylan spent a day with a pillow tied round her stomach while she did sixteen changes for twenty-four pages of a maternity catalogue, smiling bravely at the camera while the tears for her unborn baby shimmered in the corners of her eyes.

Barely a month later Gigi was standing in the middle of the

146

stone quarries outside Miami doing, of all things in sun-soaked Miami, a ski clothes story. She was dressed in a parka and ski pants and giant sunglasses and the stylist was about to pour a bag of fake snow all over her while the wind machine blew it at her from behind.

It was hard to keep her mind on the job. She kept on thinking over what she had seen – or rather heard – the night before.

She had gone over to Etoile late in the afternoon and hung around till everyone had gone home in the hope of catching Charley Lobianco on his own so that she could tell him about her Miami job, about how she was really going to turn over the proverbial new leaf once she got to Milan, how she was going to make him proud of her.

She could see the light was still on in his office and she edged nervously down the corridor towards it but as she was about to knock on the door, she stopped.

Charley was not alone. She could hear a woman's voice and the reason that she could hear it was because it was raised in anger.

'Mr Lobianco, there are two things you should know. First, my husband's brother is Arthur Kraft. The girl you have made pregnant is Mr Kraft's niece. If he should get to hear of this I have no doubt that he would instruct the staff on the various magazines in his publishing empire never to use your clients again. Second, my daughter is only fourteen years old. She is under age.'

'I swear to you, Mrs Parrish, I have never met your daughter.'

'Well, of course you would say that, given what I have just told you. Look, here's her photograph.'

'Mrs Parrish, I meet hundreds and hundreds of girls, literally,

147

it's my job. Your daughter is very pretty but I do not recall ever having met her in person.'

'And you imagine I'm going to leave it at that?'

'Well, what do you want me to do?' Gigi heard Charley ask. 'Get down on my knees and propose to her?'

'I'd advise you not to be so flippant. The situation is deplorable enough as it is. For the time being I am not going to press charges, you will no doubt be relieved to hear, but only because the family name cannot be linked to scandal of this kind. You will be hearing from my lawyers. In the event that Victoria is required to give birth to the child I shall hold you financially responsible for its welfare. In any case we shall have to come to some arrangement to prevent the matter reaching the ears of my brother-in-law. . . .'

Mrs Parrish left soon after and Charley saw her out. Gigi emerged from the shadows. It seemed she wasn't the only girl Charley had forgotten, but then he hadn't tried anything on with her. Maybe he was telling the truth to Mrs Park-Avenue-sounding-Parrish. Out of curiosity she slipped into Charley's office and picked up the photograph of Victoria Parrish.

She looked at it for a second – it was taken on a beach, a very familiar beach with an equally familiar art deco building in the background – before stuffing it inside her bra as she ran out of the office.

At the end of the day's shooting, Spike, the driver of the motor-home hired from the production agent Randee Phillips, took her back to the hotel. Spike was a Colombian with a 30-inch neck and gold teeth who dressed in commando gear and was particularly popular with incoming film crews.

'Where you from?' he asked Gigi. 'You don't look like no fancy New York chick.'

148

'Gee, thanks a lot.' Gigi smiled. 'I'm from around here as it happens.'

It had been weird coming back to South Beach with an official role to play in all the hullabaloo. Her first night she'd had dinner at the new in restaurant, Pacific Time because she wanted to say hello to the owner (and chef) Jonathan Eismann who used to be at the China Grill in New York. And then, of course, he modelled on the side. But it didn't feel right. Suddenly she was little Gigi Garcia all over again, illegal Cuban immigrant forever looking over her shoulder in case the authorities came after her. She didn't have Elena looking out for her any more. This was brought home to her when she went back to the disgusting little apartment on Collins. The new tenant, a dirty old man in shorts, opened the door and suddenly Gigi was reminded all too vividly of the bum on the beach who had enabled her to begin her Alley Cat stash. She fled. It had been too much to hope that the place would still be empty.

She went next door to a neighbour and asked what had happened to Elena's belongings. The woman screamed at her for a few minutes about how she hadn't even bothered to stick around for her own mother's funeral and Gigi had to force herself not to scream back that the silly old woman hadn't been her mother in the first place. Finally the woman handed over a pathetically small bundle, including a cardboard shoebox containing a few papers In it Gigi found what she was looking for and discovered that she had in fact been born Gina Garcia on 9 November 1978 to Maria and Ernesto Garcia in Havana. Was everyone in Cuba called Garcia? It had been her foster mother, Elena's name. The only Cuban movie star anybody had ever heard of was called Andy Garcia. Yet as she stared at her birth certificate, Gigi began to experience a sense of identity about herself.

She took the box back with her to the hotel and sat up in bed with it. At the bottom she found a bundle of formal-looking papers and an envelope with her name on it. The letter inside could not have been written by Elena herself, since Elena had never learned to write properly. She must have dictated it to someone who couldn't speak English; the letter was written in spidery block capitals in Spanish.

Dear Gina,

Your mother wanted me to call you by this name. I don't know how we call you Gigi. This box for you when I die. It will tell you who is your real mother and father but also you will see I was your mother too. You need these papers for when you get married or get in trouble with police.

I hope you get married and have babies. I hope you are happy now.

I love you, Gina.

Your mamma Elena

The papers were adoption papers. Elena had formally adopted her so she would have official status in America. As Gigi lay on her futon under her mosquito net in her room at the Park Central, she dissolved into soundless, heaving weeping as she realised what Elena had done for her and how selfishly she had repaid the tired little woman's kindness with rudeness and contempt. Elena had loved her, not with the kind of love Gigi wanted but, she thought wryly, it was the only kind of love it looked like she was ever going to get.

In the morning the maid came in with her breakfast and found her in a heap on the floor, the contents of the box spread out all around her. The sight of the maid dressed in the same uniform as Elena used to wear and looking so like her only sent Gigi into another paroxysm of sobbing.

'Dios mío! Qué pasa? Mal?' The maid dumped the breakfast tray by the bed and rushed to put her arms around Gigi.

'Soy OK,' Gigi tried to assure her and then burst into tears again. Finally she gave up and told the maid the whole story. After all, she was never likely to see her again and the woman was probably one of the few people in the world who would understand. She was, she told Gigi, an immigrant just like her. It was good that Gigi had got away, it was good that she was making her mark in New York, she must be proud of herself, she must remember that she was doing it for all the poor Cubanas who had had to stay behind. She would become their idol. Elena was dead but maybe one day her real mother, Maria, would open a magazine in Cuba and see her face.

'But she won't know who I am,' protested Gigi.

'So one day you become so famous you tell your story to the newspapers and then she know who you are.'

'You watch too much TV,' grumbled Gigi as she began to clear up her papers. The maid helped her, reaching under the low wooden base of the futon for a stray item. It was a photograph.

'You know this girl? She a friend of yours?'

'No way. Why, do you know her?'

'Sure. She stay here two, three months ago with her uncle. Very nice man. Very very nice man. Very handsome. Leave big tip. He come here often. Same work as you. Mr Lobianco. Very nice man.'

'Is that so?' Gigi leaned over and gently removed the photograph of Victoria Parrish from the maid's nicotine-stained fingers.

London, 1994

The fashion cupboard at *Carter's* was a very hallowed place and only Alice Johnson as fashion editor and Geraldine, her assistant, were supposed to have keys. However, any time anybody laddered their tights a number of people were suddenly and mysteriously able to produce keys, the door would be opened and mounds of tights by Charnos and Elbeo and Marks and Spencer and Lord knows who else, supplied by eager-beaver PR ladies, would cascade on to the floor, offering instant replacement legwear for the staff in the fashion room.

Which is how when Geraldine went to the fashion cupboard for inspiration when she was captioning a story, she found it to be tightless.

'Black net fifties skirt from Cornucopia, 12 Upper Tachbrook Street, London SW1; rubber T-shirt from Joseph, 77 Fulham Road, London SW3; shoes by. . . .' Geraldine paused and sucked the end of her Pilot Fineliner. There were no shoes in the picture as the photograph had been cropped at the knee but Alice had been adamant that Marky Shoes be given a credit in return for their very lucrative advertising in the last issue. 'Shoes by Marky,' wrote Geraldine dutifully and added, 'Fragrance by Amber.' It amounted to the same thing. Amber was a new perfume that had been advertised and you couldn't see that either. 'Earrings from Van Peterson, Walton Street, London SW3, diamanté ankle chain from Kensington

152

Market, 49–53 Kensington High Street, London W8; tights by. . . .' She paused again, nothing in the fashion cupboard – she usually credited the first pair to fall on the floor – so to which PR did they owe a favour? She selected someone, recalled which tights they looked after and wrote down the name. Now what about the make-up? Did they owe Clarins a favour or did they owe Chanel a favour? 'Oh, God,' said Geraldine and wrote, 'Make-up by Boots No 7.' Now she was finished. No she wasn't. The wretched girl was wearing a load of bangles up her left arm. 'Oh, fuck it,' muttered Geraldine and wrote, 'Bangles: model's own.'

Geraldine was pretty hopeless at merchandising, as crediting was called in the magazine business. Alice could never make her understand that anything mentioned in the credits had to be available throughout the country. Geraldine never remembered that the stockists had to be finalised after the buyers came back from the collections. She was always gaily writing things like, 'Suit by Romeo Gigli from Browns, South Molton Street,' without checking whether the buyers at Browns had actually bought the suit. Alice was always having to cross things out and put, 'Jacket made to order' or something equally vague.

So Alice was keeping half an eye on Geraldine as she credited while at the same time she worked her way through a pile of model books she had called in for an undies story – for what she had in mind, she couldn't really call it a lingerie story. She had arrived at the office that morning in a state of high excitement.

'Gerry, angel, I had this brilliant idea in the bath this morning. We'll call it My Beautiful Laundrette. We'll have this drop-dead classy-looking girl in a grungy, backstreet launderette doing her washing only it'll be with a difference. In the background the door will be open and you'll be able to see that she's just ridden up on her Harley or whatever. . . .'

'Motorbike by Harley Davidson.' Geraldine made a mental note for the future.

' . . . and has come running in to do her washing. She's in the process of actually stripping down to her T-shirt and undies – different in each picture, they're the clothes in the story – and throwing them into the machine as she stands almost naked, maybe even completely naked in the last picture.'

'It sounds vaguely familiar,' said Geraldine.

'Oh, Gerry, you say that about all my ideas,' moaned Alice. Now she held up a picture for Geraldine to see.

'I must say this girl has the most spectacular body, what do you think, Gerry?'

'Divine, definitely. Who is it?'

'Girl called Celestia. From Etoile. Give them a ring, there's a love, better get her in if only to check it is her. I remember years ago when I was on *Woman's Journal* and we did this lingerie story and an agency sent this girl's book in while she was out of the country and we thought she had a fabulous body and booked her sight unseen – silly thing to do, I know. We nearly had a fit when she turned up on the shoot. Turned out she had a sister who was also a model who looked very like her but the sister had the great body. What this girl had done, don't ask me how, was to get someone to doctor some pictures of her sister so that her own head was on top of her sister's body. She had literally stolen her sister's torso.'

Grace Brown punched the air in jubilation and shouted a silent 'Yes!' as she listened to Alice Johnson's plummy voice telling her that she wanted to see Celestia for a shoot she had in mind where she needed someone with a sensational body.

'She's a star, Alice, let me send her round right away and then . . .'

She stopped in mid-sentence as she remembered that the Hon. Celestia had celebrated being signed on by Etoile by rushing out and diving straight into an orgy of body piercing, starting with her nose, moving on to her navel and finally, as she had announced to all and sundry on the booking table, she had gone and had her pussy pierced and it hadn't hurt a bit.

'Alice, I think there's something I ought to tell you. She's had her body pierced, her navel, you know, that sort of thing. . . .'

'What sort of thing?' Grace was sure she could hear Alice's breathing growing heavier.

'Well, there's another part of her anatomy, you know, lower down. . . .'

'In that case we'll definitely do some nude shots. This girl, Celestia, will she do nude?'

Suddenly the voice of Prudence Fairfax whining at her every day on the phone flashed into Grace Brown's head: 'When is my daughter going to be in *Vogue*? When is my daughter going to be on the cover of *Carter's*? When is my daughter going to Paris? When is my daughter going to . . .?' She pictured Prudence's face when she saw a fashion spread featuring the Hon. Celestia and her pierced labia, and told Alice Johnson with a certain amount of relish:

'She'll do nude. I shall personally guarantee it.'

In the weeks prior to her departure for Milan, Tess continued to slog round London on exhausting rounds of castings.

Sitting in a corner of the agency, trying to chill out while she waited to hear if any of the people she'd seen the day before had put an option on her, Tess watched the mounting excitement on the booking table as the word spread about Celestia's first major booking.

'I know exactly what you're thinking,' whispered Angie, coming over and crouching down beside her: ' "The Hon. Celestia Fairfax, who does she think she is? All lah-di-dah from a posh background, walking in here and getting six pages in *Carter's* without even trying. All right for some." '

Tess blushed, her fair skin going scarlet. That was exactly what she had been thinking.

'How does she do it, Angie? I mean you're not looking after her. She's gone straight to Grace. It's not. . . .'

'It's not fair? Is that what you were going to say? Tess, this is one of the most unfair businesses you could ever be in. To many people it might not seem fair that some girls can make loads of money because they're prettier than others. And then you ask yourself is it fair that the camera loves some girls and not others who seem just as pretty? Take a good look at Celestia next time she comes in and listen to her too, talk to her, get to know her a bit. She's a nice girl, Tess. OK, so she comes from a classy background but she hasn't got any airs and graces and in your own way you're just as classy as she is. If she does have an advantage over you as far as modelling goes, it's that her background has given her a kind of built-in confidence about herself. Be positive, Tess. Don't envy her, watch her.'

'Watch her attitude, you mean. Grace is always on about attitude, attitude, attitude. What does it mean?'

Angie thought for a moment before answering. The thing about attitude was that if you had to ask what it was you probably didn't have any and for most people that was no bad thing. But models weren't most people. If they were going to make it big they had to have something that enabled the camera to single them out and make them special. The very word attitude conjured up the look of a black rapper fresh out of jail giving her a whole lot of lip. Did Celestia look like a black rapper? No, of course she didn't, but her look and her general attitude towards anyone looking at her had the same forceful hard-to-ignore impact. Yet there was no way Tess could ever be described in that way and now that she thought about it, Angie realised there were exceptions up there at the top. Tess's look evoked the soft beauty of a red-haired Christy Turlington and what on earth was wrong with that?

'Tess,' she told her, 'forget about attitude. Just think about the way Celestia presents herself. If she were in here now she wouldn't be sitting hunched in a corner like this. She'd be over there chatting to everyone on the booking table. I'll say it again, Tess, she's a nice girl, very friendly and open. Swan's an upper-crust girl too and she's completely unspoiled, so they tell me. She goes out of her way to help other girls and she works unbelievably hard. Now, get rid of this silly chip on your shoulder and let's talk about what you're going to do before you go off to Milan. Oh, by the way, I had a postcard from Patrick and he asked after you. I think you really made quite an impression on my wayward brother.'

Following her father's frantic call about Patrick's disappearance, Angie had had to go home and reorganise her family's life. Grace and everyone else on the booking table had been incredibly supportive.

'Go and do what you have to do, Angie, but make sure you come back to us. You're special,' Grace told her to her delight. 'You're beginning to have a real eye for the kind of girls we want and the ones you're already looking after really adore you. They depend on you. You've become their best friend and that's part of what being a booker's all about, that and getting the girl the best possible deal. So off you go and come back soon.'

Angie was thrilled to hear she was doing well yet there was something that still niggled away at her. She knew Grace did not share her belief in Tess Tucker and that she felt the girl was still a potential problem. The problem was Grace was rarely wrong.

On the home front Angie didn't like the idea of her sisters and her little brother becoming latchkey children but she had no choice. Besides Mrs O'Connor, the merry widow from next door who had had her eye on Joseph Doyle ever since Angie's mother had done a runner, had volunteered to go in each day and get them their tea when they came home from school, and that made Angie feel a whole lot better. Kathleen then insisted she was old enough to do it and in the end Angie just let them get on with it together.

After about six weeks she had had word from Patrick that he was in Dublin trying to find their mother. For some reason he was convinced she had gone back to Ireland. Angie wasn't sure how she would feel if he suddenly wrote that he'd found her. She hated the hurt look on her father's face when she reported Patrick's news, and realised that Patrick had not been in touch with him.

'He's doing OK, Dad, he's got work, a job at a hotel called the Clarence, washing up in the kitchens.'

But her father just looked at her in silence.

The My Beautiful Laundrette shoot put poor Geraldine in yet another dilemma when it came to the captions. Celestia had turned up for the shoot begging to be allowed to wear her own clothes – or rather strip them off down to the underwear for the story. Her own clothes were nothing less than Demeule-meester, Margiela and the newest exponent of British decon-struction: Salisbury Plain. But Geraldine knew that if she put 'Skirt by Margiela' and then bra by the lingerie designer no one would give a toss about the bra. But if she put 'Clothes: model's own' everyone would recognise them and wonder why they hadn't been credited. There was also the question of whether Margiela and Demeulemeester were meant to be shoved into the washing machine. Perhaps it was best not to mention them by name. Then there were the Lawrence Corner pea coat and the backpacks and rucksacks; everyone was getting in on the act. The body piercer would want a credit next. She put everything on hold and switched to the photographer, a spiky young woman whose work had the media hailing her as the new Ellen von Unwerth one minute and the new Corinne Day the next.

When Grace Brown saw the sultry grainy black-and-white pictures she saw something she had not realised before: Celestia not only had more attitude than a knockout prizefighter, she was unbelievably sexy. Sprawled in front of a spin-drier, wearing nothing but a pair of white cotton briefs and sneakers, her cropped head thrown back as she chugalugged a can of Diet Coke, showing off her haughty patrician profile (and her pierced nose with the chain stretched across her cheek and running down to her lip), she had the long rangy body of an athlete with perfect muscle tone. There was an intended air of seediness about the background but Celestia herself came across on the page as an unmistakably classy piece of ass. Alice Johnson had already called to say she would be on the cover, and knowing that there would be one picture of Celestia reclining on the launderette bench in the nude, supposedly exhausted by the washing with the clothes scattered around her, and the controversy this was likely to cause, Grace knew her girl was on the point of a major breakthrough.

But Celestia had a problem looming that Grace did not know about. Prudence was jealous by nature and she was beginning to resent the attention being paid to her daughter.

She might plague Grace Brown with telephone calls like a maniacal stage mother but she had never really expected Celestia to get anywhere. The truth was that by introducing what she thought was her awkward, graceless hunk of a daughter into the modelling world, she had imagined that she would be able to make a comeback herself. The fact that it was impossible for her to make a comeback because she had never made it as a model in the first place entirely escaped her. She had never been anything more than a pretty woman in a frothy little blonde sort of way, totally lacking in the style and bone structure that made her mother-in-law and her daughter stand out. But of course she could never see that.

The last straw for Prudence was when Celestia didn't turn up for the *Hello!* story. Prudence had been writing the headline in her head for weeks: 'Lady Fairfax invites us into her husband's ancestral home, Trevane, and introduces us to her daughter, the Honourable Celestia, who has followed in her mother's famous footsteps by choosing a career as a model.' Then she found herself all decked out in her Lacroix in the Long Gallery, wondering what on earth she was going to say to the *Hello!* team when they arrived from their hotel in Tiverton. It had been bad enough that Hugo had refused to have them to stay in the house. Then Celestia had phoned to say she couldn't possibly come all the way down to Devon because she had a fitting. A fitting! It sounded as if she'd turned down *Hello!* for a visit to her dressmaker.

It was anything but. Fittings were a strange and necessary part of the business of being a model especially as, if she then got the job, she would often also be paid for the fitting. It was essential for Celestia to attend this particular fitting since it was for the Japanese, whose samples were notorious for their short sleeves. Western girls were often to be seen at fittings with their long arms hunched up at the shoulder, trying hard to fit into the sample sent from Japan.

Celestia was suddenly working flat out. Everyone wanted her. The Carter's launderette story caused an even bigger storm than either Alice or Grace had anticipated. The tabloid press alternated between fawning adulation: WHO NEEDS CLAUDIA, CINDY AND CHRISTY WHEN WE'VE GOT OUR OWN CELESTIA? to shocked outrage: PORNOGRAPHY MASQUERADING AS FASHION WITH TEENAGE MODEL. But Grace Brown didn't care. Celestia was being booked three or four times each week and one story shot at the notorious Thomas à Becket pub in the Old Kent Road, upstairs in its famous boxers' training gym, looked like it might be as controversial as the launderette story. The pictures had Celestia topless in boxer shorts sporting a black eye (courtesy of make-up) and an aggressive stare. It was a jewellery story and long ropes of pearls and heavy silver chains dangled between her bare breasts.

One day Grace called Celestia in a state of such excitement she could barely get the words out coherently.

'They want you in New York! They've seen the Carter's pictures and they want you at Condé Nast. You're booked on a flight out tomorrow morning. Come in here so I can brief you and then you can start packing.'

Celestia hung up and wondered why she wasn't over the moon. It didn't take her very long to figure it out. She couldn't think about going to New York because she had only one thing on her mind. Or rather, one man.

The controversy over Celestia's launderette pictures was rivalled only by the argument raging as to whether anyone should have dared to challenge the memory of James Dean and do a remake of Rebel without a Cause. Yet the advance word from America was that there was a new young actor

161

who was as close to the new James Dean as anybody was ever going to get.

Water (short for Waterfall) Detroit's parents had come of age in the 1960s when they moved from Michigan to California and set about raising five children in the hallucinatory Haight Ashbury area of San Francisco. Water's brothers were called Gulf and Storm, his sisters Stream and Flow. Flow later dropped the 'w' from her name and pretended it was short for Florence. All five were taught that the first thing they must find out on meeting someone, before even asking their name, was what their star sign was. Their mother baked a mountain of hash cookies every Friday for the weekend and Water spent most of his childhood semi-stoned.

When he was sixteen he suddenly woke up and ran away from home to Los Angeles. His parents barely noticed. He changed his name to Walter and got himself a job as a gofer in a talent agency on Sunset. Over the next few years both his heart and his body hardened up considerably. He had one ambition: to be a suit, a Hollywood shark, and as unlike his parents as he possibly could be.

But his bid to make baby agent status by the time he was twenty was blown by a casting director spotting him as a perfect candidate for *Torment*, the remake of *Rebel*. His real name was reinstated, or rather his real first name, since he had been born Waterfall Krantz. His parents had created the surname Detroit *en route* for California.

Etoile acquired tickets for the London première of *Torment* and sent along several of the girls on their books, including Celestia. The agency also put the girls' names on the guest list at Browns in Great Queen Street for the post-première party. Celestia arrived, minus her nose ring and chain, in a strapless scarlet fifties net dress from American Classics and a state of high excitement. She had sat through *Torment* in a complete trance, mesmerised by the image of Water Detroit. He was the most beautiful boy she had ever seen. He had a kind of brooding, ethereal quality about him that fascinated her. His face was fine-boned and almost wistful, his body slender and graceful; definitely not a hunk but with plenty of muscle tone. He seemed at once very young and very wise and a million miles removed from the chinless boy wonders from Eton and Harrow to whom she had been exposed before coming to London. Their clumsy fumblings, the way they came immediately she touched them and their pimply skin had not encouraged further sexual activity and since she had become a model, despite her wild exterior, Celestia had been surprised to find herself remaining extremely chaste.

All thoughts of chastity went straight out the window when she walked into Browns and saw Water Detroit standing there in the flesh. For the first time in her life Celestia was overcome by shyness. The idea was that the Etoile girls should be introduced to Water and pose for the press with him. The rest of her party was right there but Celestia slipped away to the upstairs bar and buried herself in a corner for the rest of the evening.

Down in Devon, Prudence Fairfax was plotting her revenge for the *Hello!* fiasco. Her daughter's career did not appear to be opening the right kind of doors for Prudence and the sooner Celestia was stopped from hogging the limelight the better. Headlines like PORNOGRAPHY MASQUERADING AS FASHION WITH TEENAGE MODEL had given her an idea. She had noted the byline of one of the stories: Lindy-Jane Johnson. She made a trip to the village store to buy a cheap lined exercise book out of which she tore a couple of pages. The letter she wrote was deliberately badly spelled in a backward-sloping childlike hand. The contents suggested, anonymously, that Lindy-Jane Johnson might like to think about the fact that the pornographic pictures in *Carter's* had been taken by another woman and that the Hon. Celestia Fairfax had had several crushes on other girls at her boarding-school.

Poor Prudence Fairfax was dumb enough to imagine that a potential supermodel could be brought down by a bit of scandal that she might be a lesbian.

Models aren't politicians, thought Lindy-Jane, as she wondered who had sent her the idiotic letter. Besides, what was so terrible if the girl was a lesbian? No, what was far more intriguing was the name Fairfax.

She had come across it recently in her research. If only she could remember where. . . .

British Airways Flight No. BA177 took off on schedule and Water Detroit slumped moodily in his first-class seat. When they said 'Champagne for you at all, sir?' he said no and asked for a Sol, changed his mind to Rolling Rock, St Pauli Girl, Meteor, Budweiser, Michelob, and Guinness before finally coming full circle and asking for a glass of champagne. Certainly, sir.

He had wanted to make the trip to London on Concorde but his agent hadn't been able to swing it. Water was pissed about that. He didn't know for sure but he figured guys like Keanu Reeves and Brad Pitt and Luke Perry and Christian Slater got a better deal than he did. OK so he'd only made one film but it'd been such a hit in America he reckoned it ought to give him brat pack superstar status.

London hadn't been the blast he'd hoped it would be. Wet and cold, and the English seemed like a bunch of slow unambitious people to him. Heavy on the politeness and not much edge. The party had been pretty pointless. No stars, no serious actors, just a bunch of ageing rock stars and DJs in fifties gear dragged out of semi-retirement. In fact the whole première seemed to have given the British some kind of excuse to indulge themselves in a bout of fifties nostalgia. In New York the première had been very nineties, with a party afterwards given by Miramax proprietor Harvey Weinstein. Water had been hailed as a star and fêted for a week. In London they'd just stood around and got drunk, slapped each other on the back and remembered the old days. That was the difference. In New York it was about *Torment* and now. In London it was about *Rebel* and then, and if you'd seen *Rebel* when it came out you had to be way into your fifties.

Water shrugged. In a matter of hours he'd be back in New York. He had decided he would reinvent himself. From now on he would live both on the West Coast and the East Coast, flying back and forth. In LA he would keep on his flaky, funky Laurel Canyon house and maintain his cool young brat pack image but in New York he would work at moving in with a more upscale crowd, more sophisticated, better informed, more literary. He might have fallen into acting but his ambition was to produce the films he appeared in and thus gain more control. To this end he had plans to focus his attention and his irresistible charms on young women working in publishing houses and literary agencies in order to secure an early look at commercial properties. It wasn't so much pillow talk he was after as bedside reading. Meanwhile he had plenty of reading matter to keep him going on the plane and he turned to the pile of newspapers and magazines he had brought with him.

He never read the newspapers. The girl on the cover of *Carter's* was to die for. To him her face was heartstopping, and he was someone who for the last few years had been trying to deny he had a heart at all. He sat staring at the face looking up at him from his lap, the wide apart grey eyes and long feathery lashes. The fine straight nose and exceptionally high cheekbones hollowing down to a deliciously full mouth. What he really loved was the way the chain running down to her mouth from her nose lifted her upper lip a little and gave her a slight sneer. Water brought the magazine up to his lips and kissed the mouth. He wanted to take that chain between his teeth and bite it off. So when he flicked through the magazine and found the pictures of Celestia semi-naked – and finally full frontal – in a launderette he had such an instant hard-on he had to get up and go to the john and deal with it.

He fantasised about what he would like to do to the girl, and then he fell asleep. He woke up in the middle of the movie feeling cramped and claustrophobic. They must have already served the food and left him to sleep. He got up to stretch his legs and and take a walk about the 'plane.

He saw her in coach, right at the back, smoking up a storm and plugged into her Walkman. He saw the chain running from her nose to her mouth. He imagined her pierced navel beneath her leather pants and her pierced pussy further down.

The seat beside her was empty.

'What sign are you?' he asked her, slipping into it.

There was no reaction whatsoever and Water was mad. Who did this chick think she was? He was used to beating girls off. Then he realised she had her music turned up so loud she hadn't even heard him. He leaned across and made an 'anybody home?' waving movement with his hand in front of her face. She turned and screamed so loud people started looking over the back of their seats to see what had happened. That was the problem with personal stereos. It distorted the volume of your own voice so you had no idea you were yelling when you spoke with the music plugged in your ears.

The stewardess arrived.

'Would you kindly go back to your seat at this time, sir.'

Water smiled up at her. It irritated him that she made no sign that she'd recognised him.

'See, here's the thing, I'm in First and I just want to sit with my friend here for a while. I'm also kinda hungry. Could you bring me some food? What do you have back here?'

The stewardess clearly thought it was all very irregular.

'I could bring you some braised Salisbury steak with pommes dauphinoises – on a bed of lettuce,' she added as if trying to make it sound more appetising.

'Clean sheets?'

She looked bewildered.

'On the bed of lettuce. Oh, forget it. I'm going to take my friend here up to First Class and get something there.'

'I'm not sure you can do that, sir.'

'Listen, honey, I am Water Detroit.' He looked at Celestia. 'What's your sign? When's your birthday?'

'June 25th.'

'Cancer. I'm Capricorn. Direct opposites. Great! Come on.'

The steward in First Class had seen it happen too many times before to be bothered to make anything of it. Fresh young rock star picks up girl, millionaire tycoon picks up girl, what difference did it make.

'What was your seat number back in coach, love?' he asked Celestia as he settled her in.

'Does it matter?' asked Water.

'Yes, sir. I'll have to make a note that the person in that seat moved to this one so if we crash – '

' . . . they'll know whose the charred body is. Awesome! What's your name?' he asked Celestia.

She told him and then almost passed out in shock as he reached over and began to kiss her hungrily. His teeth gave her chain a little tug.

'Does that hurt? Don't look so worried. At least I asked your name first. I don't always bother. Chill out a little, you're not as wild as you look, am I right?'

'I think you were just so wonderful in *Torment*. I'm your biggest fan. I never thought I'd actually meet you. I was such an idiot last week. . . .'

'Last week?'

'At the party after the première. I was so embarrassed, I couldn't bring myself to come and be introduced to you.'

'Well, I wish you had. I was bored shitless. So, you're a model, huh? How old are you? Don't lie now.'

'Seventeen.'

'Quite a grown-up. Ever been to New York before? No? Oh, I am going to have a great time showing you around.'

'Do you live with your parents?'

'Do I hell! I ain't seen them in years. I mean, would you live with your mom?'

Celestia thought of Prudence and shuddered. 'I'd live with my father, though.'

Water looked stunned. 'You would? Why?'

'Because he's the nicest man I've ever met. He's gentle and thoughtful and clever and he never pulls his weight. He's charming to everyone, whoever they are. I like that.'

' "You like that in a man": I must remember that. So what does your old man do?'

'He's one of Britain's most famous historians.'

'No shit? That sounds pretty grand. What does he think about the leather and the piercing?'

'I don't think he's noticed.'

'Jesus! Why do it then? Why cover up the real you?'

'It pisses my mother off no end. I swear she only married my father because he had a title. She's Lady Fairfax first, the

168

best Lady who Lunches in London second, and wife and mother decidedly last.'

'Now you're starting to make sense. The most my mom ever wanted for me was that I should live in a tent under the starry skies by a beautiful river and commune with nature along with forty other hippies in sub-grunge clothing.'

'And the most you ever wanted for yourself was what? To be a great actor?'

'Let's just say the *least* I ever wanted for myself was to be a millionaire by the time I was twenty-five and I'm rapidly downgrading that to twenty-one. Now shall I tell you what the most you should ever want for yourself is?'

'I just want you to give me another kiss,' said Celestia, and although she sensed it was not the kind of ambition he had in mind, she could tell he was pleased.

At JFK she was astounded to find him waiting for her in Arrivals when she finally got through Immigration and she accepted his offer of a lift in his waiting limousine with relief.

'My address is . . . wait a minute, let me look for it, it's a model apartment on Nelson Street, no, Horatio Street.'

'Put it away,' he told her, clasping her hand and drawing her to him in the darkness of the back seat. 'I'm taking you home with me.'

She fell asleep on his shoulder on the ride in and he woke her up to show her her first glimpse of the Manhattan skyline from the Triborough Bridge. The limo purred silently along the East River Drive, turned west across Manhattan right through to Fifth Avenue, going down it and then back in and up Madison.

'Hey, look,' said Water, 'there's a sight you ought to know. That's the Carlyle Hotel. If we're talking about what your ambition should be, it's to take over from Swan. Well that's where she lives, right up there in a penthouse apartment of

the Carlyle Hotel and I live right around the corner from
her.'

New York, 1994

Of course, it hadn't really been Molly Bainbridge at the lime kiln.

The likeness was uncanny and I could be forgiven for thinking she had come back from the dead. It was in fact her younger sister Sally. As I sat on the futon in the lime kiln and let them fuss around the old oven and serve me a surprisingly tasty stew, I reflected on the irony of several things. For the second time in my life I was witnessing the attentions of my beloved brother towards someone else, but this time I was older and more mature and I wasn't jealous. I could see he was truly in love with Sally Bainbridge and that his love was reciprocated and I realised that had he not encountered the dreadful Molly, who had succeeded in ruining a large part of his life, he might never have met the one person who was obviously bringing him untold happiness.

Harry had decided to start at the beginning in his quest for the truth about Molly Bainbridge's death: he had gone up to Liverpool to try and find her parents. Her father had died and her mother was in a home, but he had found Sally and abandoned his original plan to pretend to be someone else. He had told Sally who he was and she in turn had told him as much as she knew of Molly's side of the story. It seemed Molly had run away from home to be a model at the age of sixteen. Why she couldn't be a model in Liverpool, they had never been able to understand, but Molly had insisted on going to London. When her father said no, she ran away.

'She never came home again,' Sally told me quietly as we sat huddled in the kiln, eating our stew by candlelight. 'She sent postcards, the occasional letter, always full of how well she was doing, lots of work and that. We had an address for her and one day I went down to London to see her. It was about a year after she'd left Liverpool. I had finished school and I thought maybe she could give me a few ideas since she was doing so well. She'd told us she had a big flat and I imagined she'd let me stay for a few days. Well, as it turned out all she had was this tiny room in Paddington somewhere and she had to share a bathroom with at least five other people.

'She wasn't pleased to see me and she never once spent an evening with me. I don't know where she went at night but she really dolled herself up. Her make-up must have been an inch thick. After three days I couldn't take it any more. She lay around all day without bothering to get dressed, she smoked incessantly and then she went out in the evening. She hardly spoke to me and the place smelled of cabbage and I went back to Liverpool a very confused young girl. I never told our parents what I'd seen. I lied and pretended we'd had a great time. But Molly never wrote to us again and I think our mum suspected something because she never stopped asking me about it. We didn't hear a word except the odd Christmas card and then four years later she was dead. Murdered in your house.'

Since then Sally had determined to be as different from her older sister as she possibly could be. She had stayed in Liverpool and gone to art college there and now worked as a graphic designer at an advertising agency in London; she had a flat in Covent Garden. At weekends she came down to

Wiltshire to be with Harry. Together they had been searching for clues to Molly's life in London up to the time she arrived at the Boltons. They had gone back to the address in Paddington but there was nobody who remembered her. It was still a seedy rooming house for single loners and for a while Harry had taken advantage of the anonymity of the place to stay there in the hope of discovering something. I gathered that he had brought Sally down to Wiltshire intending to introduce her to our parents but she had talked him out of it at the last minute, more sensitive than he to the shock it would be to them not only to find that their son was indeed alive but that he had taken up with Molly Bainbridge's sister. He had insisted on showing her the lime kiln and then he had had the idea of turning it into his hiding place. As he had pointed out, nobody would think of looking for him right under his parents' nose.

'It was tough for him at first,' said Sally while Harry was outside gathering wood for the oven. 'He would see your father in the distance and long to call down the hill to him. But in another way he was able to see that they were all right and it was good for him.'

I watched her as she set about unpacking her weekend bag, taking out understated woollen jerseys with Fair Isle patterns, jeans, thick socks, plain white shirts and a Laura Ashley nightdress that buttoned up to the neck. She was a serious girl, totally devoid of her sister's sluttishness but with a gentler, prettier version of Molly Bainbridge's sexuality. This girl really could be a model, I thought, she has grace and style. And then I turned to Harry, bumbling about the place, knocking things over, his butterscotch hair falling over his face, and I was happy for him. I listened as Sally told him the news from London. Their situation was a strange one. For Sally, I thought, it must be rather like having an affair with a married man, a secret relationship she couldn't talk about. She had another life in London, one with friends and colleagues who knew nothing about Harry. I observed how Harry fell on her every word and I was impressed by the way in which she enabled them to 'talk shop' – he knew her world, after all – by giving him a blow-by-blow account of what had happened in the office that week and then listening while he talked about the people concerned as if he knew them. He knew her world; after all, he'd been a commercials producer before he had had to disappear. I realised this was a ritual between them and I felt like an intruder.

'But why haven't you been in touch with me?' I asked. 'You must have realised how frantic I've been.'

Again Sally spoke for the pair of them.

'You're not exactly easy to contact, Swan, always on the move, and you're very high profile, very protected. You always have a driver or a minder with you. We thought about it, I promise. I could have come on my own but to be honest I was apprehensive. You might be Harry's sister but you're also a world-famous celebrity. I could have brought you something of Harry's to prove I was telling the truth, that I was his friend, but we didn't know how to get to you without going through wall-to-wall people. And it wasn't as if we had anything to tell you. We wanted to wait until we had found out something. Please try to understand.'

Her words shook me because I knew there was a certain amount of truth in them. Had I really become so remote from the people I loved that they were nervous about contacting me? The more I thought about it the more I realised I had cut myself off. I had a frantic public life and an increasingly lonely private one. As I looked at Harry, I knew I was envious of him. I wanted someone in my life too. Maybe it was time to climb down from my supermodel pedestal into the real world.

I tried to offer Harry the money to get a place to live and some new clothes, and in doing so realised that by playing Lady Bountiful I had compounded my error. They did not want my wealth and my celebrity, they wanted me – the girl underneath the designer trappings.

But as I climbed into my chauffeur-driven car and allowed myself to be swept back up the motorway to London, I asked myself – was she still there?

I was slightly apprehensive about attending the Girl of the Year finals at the Plaza Hotel in New York. I was to host it with Charley Lobianco but it wasn't the thought of standing behind a lectern and reading out an idiotic script with Charley, like they do at the Oscars, that bothered me. It was the fact that one of the judges was to be Tatsuo Takamoto, the chairman of the Japanese company that owned SWAN. I had recently become somewhat disenchanted with my commitments as the SWAN girl and had even gone so far as to have Charley look at my contract and see when I could exercise my get-out clause. He had come back and told me I had another year to go if I wanted to opt out after three years instead of working the full five years of the contract but I had to give the SWAN board six months' notice. In other words, if I wanted to opt out I would have to tell Mr Takamoto – I never called him Tatsuo – in just over three months.

Mr Takamoto was an old man, amazingly well preserved but still easily old enough to be my grandfather. He claimed to remember the Tokyo earthquake of 1923. There were mutterings that he should have retired long ago but as far as I could see he was in full control of all his marbles and still very much in touch with what was going on. I found his old world courtesy quite charming and in many ways he did in fact remind me of my own grandfather. He listened to me with a benign expression on his face which made me feel like a small child and a wise woman all at once. I sensed that the smile was also one of embarrassment rather than of amusement and that the flashy world of modelling made him uncomfortable. I don't pretend to know anything about Japanese culture and society but I'm pretty sure the older generation don't like their women tripping down catwalks semi-naked.

When I was chosen as the SWAN girl and first introduced to Mr Takamoto, I was given a briefing by Charley on how to behave. It was explained to me that the Japanese resented any intrusion into their world, that they regarded themselves as unique and everyone else as foreign and that anyone who tried to understand the nuances of Japanese culture made them very uneasy. I interpreted this to mean that even though Mr Takamoto might appear to treat me with genuine warmth, he'd flip his lid if I turned around and tried to bond with him like I had with, say, Charley himself. Furthermore I should understand that self-assertion, while being an essential part of how to get on in America, was a cardinal sin in Japan, so even if Mr Takamoto came across as a modest, unassuming sort of fellow, I should never forget that he was hugely important to my career.

I happened to know that Mr Takamoto had been called out of retirement a few years ago following a few family problems. His son who had succeeded him as head of the company had been killed in a light aircraft crash. The next in line was Jiro Takamoto, the grandson, who had been sent to England and America for his education. When his father was killed Jiro was summoned home to Osaka to take over the running of the company. He had leapt at the chance of power, but his time in America had spoiled him and he proceeded to abuse it. He was a louche-looking, handsome young man, astonishingly tall for a Japanese and he had acquired the decadent habits of a western playboy. He drank, he did drugs, he womanised – he had even propositioned me shortly after I had become the SWAN girl. Jiro represented the blatantly competitive and materialistic new generation of Japanese, the so-called Crystal Generation, slaves to designer consumerism and anathema to old Mr Takamoto. But while he might be competitive, Jiro was no businessman and it was blindingly clear from the outset that he would be a disaster as head of the company. Old Mr Takamoto had no alternative but to step in and take over. Jiro was sent back to America and given a token position in the New York office; soon he was running riot once again.

I knew that because I liked Mr Takamoto so much, and had such a deep respect for him, I would have to tell him that I was thinking of stepping down. I owed him that much. He had always been utterly charming to me, constantly telling me that my ink black hair and ivory skin gave me a Japanese look – he said this despite the fact that Japanese skin is what they call 'wheat-coloured' rather than white – and that he liked to think of me as the daughter he had never had. I knew I couldn't live with myself if I didn't take the trouble to warn him of what I had in mind in person and left it to Charley to relay the news. It was ridiculous that I should think like this, given the cut-throat nature of the business we were in, but I couldn't help it. Tatsuo Takamoto was special in a world where not many people bothered to be.

I didn't really know why I wanted to give up being the SWAN girl. I suspected it was the beginning of my wanting to get out of modelling altogether. I could afford to. I had made enough money which, if properly invested, could probably keep me for the rest of my life – and Harry too, if it came to that. Whatever decision I made about my life, Harry was always part of the equation.

The Girl of the Year finals in New York was a much more fancy affair than the wild bash at the London Hilton. It was a black tie and evening dress occasion and there were no crowds milling around. It was just like the regular collections with everybody seated on gilt chairs below the catwalk and the only difference was that it was held at the Plaza Hotel instead of in the tents in Bryant Square behind the New York Public Library.

There had been over 300,000 entrants from all over the world and tonight's contestants had won national finals in over thirty-five countries. I knew the girls had been through exhausting dress rehearsals, a night out on the town and a run round Central Park with the paparazzi in tow. I knew they had also been subjected to complete makeovers in the hair and beauty department. For most of them it was their first visit to New York, and for many of the foreign girls it was their first visit to the United States.

I imagined the stars that must be floating in their eyes at the thought of winning the first prize of a $200,000 modelling contract with Etoile (or even the second prize of $150,000 or third prize of $100,000) and I thought of my own sudden disillusionment with the world where I reigned supreme.

I couldn't bring myself to say anything to Mr Takamoto. I could tell he was unbelievably embarrassed at having been asked to judge the competition. It wasn't his scene at all, but my limited knowledge of the Japanese way told me that he would rather go through with it than make Charley Lobianco lose face if he refused. We had our usual little chat. We reassured each other that we were in excellent health. I asked after Mrs Takamoto, whom I had never met, and was told that she was in excellent health. This prompted him to make his usual comment that it was high time I got married myself and then he concluded, as he always did, by asking me what I was reading. I was grateful to Mr Takamoto for introducing me to Japanese literature. He had sent me a gift of Junichiro Tanizaki's *The Makioka Sisters* for Christmas and I had sent him Kazuo Ishiguro's *The Remains of the Day*. We chatted about them and he asked my opinion of the film of *Remains of the Day* and of the new Japanese designer Koji Tatsumo who, like Ishiguro, lived and worked in London.

'You English,' he said and in those two words I understood he was issuing some comment on the fact that two successful Japanese men had elected to live with foreigners. I caught sight of Jiro lurching into the room, already drunk, and I thought of the pain his grandfather must feel at the way Jiro had turned out; I wanted to put my arms around Mr Takamoto's portly little frame and hug him as I would have done my grandfather, my father or one of my uncles. But such intimate behaviour was, of course, out of the question.

We were interrupted by Donald Trump. He owned the Plaza where the competition was being held and that seemed to make him an automatic judge. I had seen Ivana recently and she had regaled me with stories of how, following their divorce, her belongings had been stopped from leaving Trump Tower by Trump Security. I was not a particular friend of hers but I had always liked the warmth I saw in her brown eyes, and although her highly publicised role in life was as horrific to me as I was sure Donald Trump's was to Mr Takamoto, I admitted to a certain amount of respect for her. Whenever I looked at Donald I wanted to laugh. It wasn't him; it was his name. I always wanted to say something stupid to him like: 'Don't worry, Donald, something will turn up trumps.'

I was called to the podium at the head of the catwalk. The

show was about to begin. The Mayor of New York introduced the evening, then Charley and I read aloud from little pink cards.

'Hello Charley, hello everybody,' I read.

'You think they're ready to get started?' Charley read back.

'I think they are, Charley. They just can't wait,' it said on my next card.

'In that case, Ladies and Gentlemen, please welcome the top fifty-eight contestants for the final of Girl of the Year. . . .'

It seemed to take an age for the fifty-eight contestants to make their first trip down the catwalk, two by two. I didn't watch them. I know I should have but my mind was on other things. Harry. Sally Bainbridge. Should I give up modelling?

So when Amy La Mar came out I was in a kind of daze and barely noticed her until she was on her way back down the runway towards me. Poor Amy. She looked stunning but I suppose I sort of knew that she wouldn't win here.

Later, backstage, I went over to comfort her but she seemed perfectly cheerful, almost as if she'd expected the outcome. The winner was a blonde from Texas.

'Those Salisbury Plain pictures turned out really well and fashion editors and buyers are at long last beginning to sit up and take notice – they've even had a few orders. I'll get Willy to send some prints to you for your book. Where are you staying? Are you with Etoile New York?'

She told me she was going to see Barbara Harper at Grace's suggestion, and looking over my shoulder to make sure Charley wasn't listening, I told her she couldn't be in better hands.

'Barbara is a wonderful person and a terrific agent. If she takes you on she will really work her butt off for you. It may not go well for you at first, Amy, you have to be prepared. New York is a tougher place than London and you'll find out what I mean soon enough. But you'll win through, I know you will.'

I sounded more positive than I felt. I had seen so many black girls rejected. Barbara Harper might open a few doors for Amy but there were always going to be others further down the line that would be slammed in her face. I made myself a promise: one day I would go out of my way to help Amy La Mar. I would call Barbara the next day, see if she had taken Amy on, and ask her to keep me posted on Amy's progress and promise me that when a situation arose where my intervention would make a distinct difference she was to let me know.

I had returned to New York to spend a week or so relaxing before the onslaught of the collections in February and March and all that they entailed. I had a couple of jobs coming up in the Caribbean which didn't sound too arduous, particularly at this time of year, but in the meantime I intended to curl up in my apartment and read Michael Crichton's latest, *Disclosure*. But I had hardly finished the first chapter when the phone rang and an old friend of my mother's called Norah Nicholson was inviting me to a dinner party.

'Lavinia, darling, you absolutely must come. I'm giving it for a young writer called Rory Stirling. You won't have heard of him, his first book isn't out yet. And that heavenly creature who was in the remake of *Rebel without a Cause*, he's got a simply ludicrous name, what is it . . .?'

'Water Detroit,' I said wearily. Harvey Weinstein had invited me to an early screening of *Torment* and I confess I had not been very struck by Mr Detroit's abilities. He looked cute enough and that was presumably why everyone was in such a state about him, but as far as I was concerned he couldn't act for toffee.

'Thank you. Water! Whatever next? Well, he's bringing a new young British model. Everybody's raving about her. I thought you'd like to meet her.'

Darling Norah! Why did people always imagine that I wanted to spend my spare time with models? Still, if she was new and English I might know her anyway.

'What's her name, Norah?'

'Oh, heavens, I can't remember. But you know, the thing is, this young writer's just been jilted by his girlfriend and——'

'No, Norah,' I said firmly.

'Oh, darling, I didn't mean you. I thought this young model. . . .'

'But she's coming with Water Detroit.'

'So?'

'Norah, you're incorrigible.'

'Aren't I just? But it's such fun. Do come, Lavinia. It's a party for the young. No old fogeys, promise you. I'll put you next to Gene Pressman of Barneys. He adores you.'

'Norah, it'd make more sense for this young girl's career to put her next to him if he's got a new campaign coming up.'

'You're so right, so right. In that case I shall just have to put you next to Rory Stirling.'

Norah was a decorator who lived in a sumptuous ten-room apartment on Park Avenue in the Sixties. The elevator went straight into her apartment and I fought my way through the gigantic flower arrangements to say hello. So much for keeping the guest list to the very young. Due to pressure of work, and my own natural inclination not to go out when I did have a break, this was the first New York party I'd been to since *Vanity Fair*'s tenth anniversary bash at the old Stuyvesant mansion just a few blocks away, and I could tell at a glance that Norah had invited more or less the same crowd: Ivana, Tina Brown and Harry, Barry Diller and Diane von Fürstenberg, S.I. Newhouse, Helmut Newton, Anna Wintour and of course Chessy Rayner who was a friendly rival of Norah's. If the young British model had arrived I couldn't make her out, but I did see Water Detroit buttonholing an attractive man in his mid-thirties who had a great tan which was set off by his prematurely grey hair. I had always been attracted to young men with grey hair.

I eavesdropped on their conversation as I pretended to listen to Nick Dunne's description of Erik Menendez at the trial and where so-and-so had been when the earthquake struck.

'So when can I take a look at the manuscript?' Water Detroit was asking.

'I don't recall saying you could see it at all,' replied the grey-haired man.

'Aw, c'mon, man. I'm in town to look for properties. I need an early look. Help me out here.'

'Speak to my agent. That's Lynn Nesbit here and CAA on the Coast.'

'You just don't get it, I want to see the script direct from you. Oh, hey, there's Swan. Hey, Swan, over here. . . .'

I'd never met the little brat but out of courtesy I pretended I had and went over to say hello, whereupon the other man took the opportunity to slip away. But then just as Water was about to overpower me with his charm, Norah came round shepherding everyone in to dinner.

The room looked very pretty. There were about fourteen round tables each with a little stone cherub as a centrepiece with greenery arranged all around him as if he were standing in a wild garden. Looking closer I could see the cherub was in fact a jug and if you tipped him over he poured spring water from his mouth straight into a glass.

'Water for Water Detroit,' said Norah, seating him, mercifully, on the other side of the room. I found my place and sat down. The man with the grey hair was already there and rose slightly as I arrived.

'Rory Stirling?'

He nodded.

'Lavinia Crichton-Lake.' I held out my hand, wondering why I was giving my real name.

'That's quite a tan,' I commented.

'Yes.'

'Caribbean?'

'No.'

'Florida?'

He looked at me in horror.

'All right, California?'

'At this time of year? What is this? Twenty questions?'

'Looks that way.'

'Sorry. Africa.'

'Getting away from it all?'

'From what all?'

I began to lose patience. 'OK, be a surly old beggar, see if I care. They told me you'd had a girl walk out on you.'

'And you decide to bring it up the very first time you meet me. Your sensitivity is a little rusty, at least it would be if some girl had walked out on me. As it happens, it's just a line I spun everyone to make them leave me alone so I could get on with my book. "He went away to get over it." I expect that's what they told you. Bullshit! I sat in a tent by the Nile and wrote nearly 70,000 words.'

'You know you've been asked here tonight to meet a model?' I said, feeling suddenly wicked.

'What would I want with a model?'

'I can't imagine,' I said. It was refreshing to meet someone

184

who had clearly never seen my face before. Or was he just teasing?

'What do you do?' he asked.

'I'm a rocket scientist,' I deadpanned.

''Course you are. Read anything good lately?'

'*Disclosure.* Just finished it.'

'And?'

'Well, it was more like watching a movie than reading a book and the woman, Meredith Johnson, she was just awful.'

He looked at me in amusement. 'You know, eh, Lavinia, as little as two or three years ago that book would have been described as a computer novel, or just a virtual reality thriller. No one would have called it a sexual harassment novel.'

'Michael Crichton probably wouldn't have written it. I hadn't realised until now, you're not an American, are you?'

'You have a good ear. I've lived here for twenty years but I'm originally a Scot. But stop dodging the issue. What do you make of all this sexual harassment furore?'

'I wasn't dodging the issue. I was about to say I suspect I feel very British about the whole thing. I'm just not sure about the fuss that's being made about it all in America. I mean, I feel strongly about equality for the working woman and I hate all those creeps who come on to women at work. . . .'

'Come across a lot of them, have you?'

Did he know I was a model? As it happened there was no talk of sexual harassment in the workplace in the modelling business and this was probably because in order for somebody to sue they had to be directly employed by the person by whom they were being harassed. If a model was persistently harassed by a photographer she couldn't sue because he would not have been the one who had directly employed her. It would have been the client who had hired the ad agency or the magazine who had in turn hired the photographer and the model separately.

'No, not personally, but I've read about it. There was that case of that naval lieutenant, Paula Coughlin who was sexually assaulted at a naval convention, and Teresa Harris, the forklift operator . . .'

'Oh God, that was awful. Didn't she have to pick change from her employer's pocket to keep her job and fetch stuff off the floor when he threw it there? And you say the Americans have gone too far?'

'I can't explain. There's just a kind of PC hysteria. Have you ever seen the Office Rules for the American Man as laid down by that guy Sidney Siller of the National Organization of Men? If Sidney were to have his way you couldn't take me out to lunch if you were my boss.'

'Or if you were my boss? So us men have to be careful, is that it?'

I wasn't really listening any more. In truth I felt more strongly about racial equality than I did about sexual harassment. I had found myself thinking a good deal about Amy La Mar and the problems she would undoubtedly face here in New York. As in the case of sexual harassment, it was all about power and to a certain extent I had power in the modelling business. Power was supposed to be neither male nor female, black nor white, but that was a load of baloney, as they said over here. The one thing that had surprised me was that at the very end of the evening Mr Takamoto had come over to say good-night and murmured so quietly that I almost hadn't heard him: 'Shame about that girl. I liked her. She very honourable.'

Rory Stirling was looking at me quizzically.

'I'm so sorry,' I apologised, 'I was miles away. Listen, I'd better come clean. I don't know your work, what do you write about?'

'Well, the truth is I've yet to be published. I was at Bennington before even Bret Easton Ellis and Donna Tartt but I've taken a little longer to get down to writing. I just finished my first novel last year and it's being published any minute. Frankly, I'm pretty terrified. That's why I disappeared to Africa where no one could find me to try and start my second before I lost my nerve. Ah, something's happening. I think the model I've been asked to meet has arrived. Nothing like being fashionably late so she can make an entrance.'

Again I was glad I hadn't told him I was a model since he was so disparaging about them. Anyway I wasn't going to be one for much longer, was I?

There was a commotion outside in the hall and Norah came in with an incredibly striking girl. She had taken advantage of the punk revival in England and appeared to have pierced every available part of her body. She was wearing a black leather T-shirt with tiny holes cut out to show her nipples, and skin-tight black PVC trousers. I knew her as soon as I saw her. I'd seen her in the laundromat story in *Carter's*. Everyone had and they hadn't stopped talking about her since.

Norah came rushing over to me and dragged me to my feet. She was about to introduce me when the girl gave me the shock of my life by flinging her arms around me. We went in for a lot of kissy-kissy in the modelling world but even so this was a bit over the top.

'Lavinia, for heaven's sake. Don't you remember me? It's Celestia. Celestia Fairfax. Oh God, it was all so heavy, Cousin Oliver and your sister Venetia in that car crash. . . .'

· Celestia Fairfax. It wasn't possible! The girl who would have been Oliver Fairfax's cousin, had he lived. I remembered Oliver's aunt and uncle at the funeral, she heavily pregnant.

Celestia had been born later that year and we had all been invited to her christening, although I hadn't gone. My parents and Oliver's were friends in any case and they'd made a big thing of keeping in touch since Venetia and Oliver died. Oliver's family had a place on the Devon estate of Celestia's father and each year Lord Fairfax held a memorial service for Oliver on the anniversary of his death. We always tried to go because in a way Venetia was included in everyone's memories.

Apart from the wildness of Trevane, which had to be one of the most romantic and beautiful estates in England, one of the things that had always stood out in my mind about those memorial services was the sight of Celestia as she became old enough to attend. She was a proper little urchin who always refused to dress for the occasion but would ride up to the family chapel at Trevane at the last minute and leap off her pony, running in in her jodhpurs and riding boots and her hair cut short like a boy's. But she had these amazing bones and piercing eyes and you were compelled to look at her. Small wonder that she'd become a model.

'I've always felt as if I knew Venetia. Uncle Luke and Aunt Maria still talk about her. They were so devastated by what happened. They had great hopes for them as a couple even though they were so young. I think they were just so relieved that she came along and he dropped his old girlfriend. Apparently he was involved with a model, would you believe?'

'Perish the thought!' I said, laughing and glancing behind me to see if Rory Stirling was listening, but he had disappeared and I was surprised to feel a sharp jolt of disappointment. 'Who was it? Anyone we know?'

'Well, yes, as a matter of fact you must have known her. She had this really tacky reputation. Oliver's parents were quite appalled that he went out with her.'

'I'm sure. But why would I have known her? What was her name?'

'Oh, Swan, it was that girl who was found dead in your house. I always assumed you knew she'd gone out with Oliver, although I suppose the family did want to keep it hush-hush. She was obviously a complete failure as a model, because she became a nanny. Your nanny among others. Her name was Molly something, Molly Bainbridge.'

Milan, 1994

As the Alitalia flight to Milan thundered down the runway at Heathrow and lurched into the air with a shudder, Tess screamed out loud. She was terrified. She had never flown before and no one had warned her about the noise of the engines. She clutched her brand new passport and wished Bobby could be with her. He had had to go out ahead of her because the photographer he was assisting had a job on location outside Milan. He would not even be there at first when she arrived. Over and over again she reminded herself of the reasons Angie, Grace and Bobby had told her she was going to Milan. There were loads of magazines, those magazines came out very quickly and that way you could get masses of brilliant tearsheets for your book. Somehow the mantra she had adopted on the *Mrs de Winter* shoot to get her through her misery – the words Bobby had whispered in her ear: 'You're the most beautiful person I've ever seen' – had been replaced with 'Good for your book'. As the plane soared into the air and there was no going back, Tess repeated to herself: *good for your book, good for your book, good for your book* – and it made her feel a little better.

On a 747, Milan bound from JFK, Gigi Garcia was getting smashed out of her skull on Bloody Marys. The stewardess, unaware of Gigi's secret stash of Smirnoff hidden beneath her jacket, couldn't understand how the girl in 44A was getting so loaded when she was only serving her glass after glass of virgin Bloody Mary Mix. The mild-looking businessman trapped in the window seat beside Gigi was beginning to look decidedly worried but the plane was full and there was no chance of him moving to another seat.

'My boyfriend's sending me to Italy,' confided Gigi, leaning right across the man with half her blouse undone. 'His name's Charley. He's old enough to be my daddy, maybe. See, my daddy died when I was small and my mom abandoned me. Do you have children, mister? Would you abandon me? 'Course you wouldn't.'

She passed out eventually and slept in her seat until they arrived at Malpensa airport, where she went through immigration in a daze and emerged to be claimed by a taxi driver lying in wait for her who congratulated himself on ripping her off for double the fare into town.

Sitting in the back of her taxi on the ride in from Milan's other airport, Linate, Tess was beginning to feel distinctly uncomfortable. She could tell the driver was watching her all the time in his rearview mirror. Suddenly he drew in to the side of the road and stopped the car. He turned to face her and put a hand on her knee.

'Bella! Carina! Attrice? Modella?'

Tess flinched and pushed his hand away.

'Si, si, modella,' she snapped and moved to the other side of the back seat. 'Go on, go –' she gestured with her hand through the windscreen until he shrugged and started the car again. Yet she could still see him looking at her in the mirror and winking and licking his lips.

When she arrived at the agency on the via S. Vittore she was relieved to see it was not unlike the agency in London.

There was the same big circular table with the bookers sitting round it, chattering into their headsets. The only difference seemed to be the fact that it was computerised and there were far more men, and they all seemed to be dressed in what Tess thought of as slick suits. The girls too seemed to be far more elegant than in London. Tess thought fondly for a moment of Angie and her haphazard attempts to keep up with fashion which invariably went wrong. She looked down at her own clothes. Her father had been really brilliant and taken £250 out of his building society account so she could kit herself out for her Milan trip. She had rushed straight off to Jigsaw, Miss Selfridge and even Nicole Farhi, but these girls looked like they were all wearing Dolce e Gabbana.

She had been told to introduce herself.

'Hello, I'm Tess Tucker.'

'*Scusi?*' said a booker, still gabbling into her headset.

Tess began to feel very nervous.

Good for your book, good for your book, good for your book.

Of course: she should show them her book. She delved into her luggage and brought it out.

'Ah, *si*, Tessa. We are waiting for you.' The girl, a chic brunette, smiled with real warmth. 'I am Carla, and this is Francesca and Giancarlo and Simonetta and . . .' She went on and on round the table and Tess nodded and smiled and knew she wouldn't be able to remember half the names.

'Come,' said Carla, 'I take you to meet the owner, Signor Molino, Marcello.'

She knocked on a door and ushered Tess in.

'Tessa. Da Londra,' she said.

He was a big man with a beard, in his forties and dressed in a seriously expensive suit. To Tess he had a kind of god-fatherish feel to him and she meant the mafia movie kind rather than her Uncle Martin. He stood up and came around his desk.

'Buongiorno Tessa.' Everyone seemed to have rechristened her Tessa all of a sudden. 'Carla, you know she is really something.' He looked her up and down and touched her lightly on the chin, tipping it up slightly, but not in a sleazy way like the taxi driver, and to her surprise Tess was quite comfortable with it. He continued: 'She really has a chance. Her look is perfect for us – pure, Catholic, virgin pretty-pretty. She is going to need careful handling to get the best possible results. We must really persuade people to use her. They were right in London to send us this girl.' All this was said in heavily accented English so Tess could understand. It was wonderful. She had been in Milan less than an hour and someone was saying she was special. And a very important someone too, by the looks of things. 'Carla, I want you to take care of her personally, d'accordo?'

'Sure, OK. Come, Tessa.'

'Where am I staying?' asked Tess as they went back to the booking table.

'Later, later, first we must get you out on the road. This afternoon you have appointments at Donna, Moda . . .'

'Really?' Tess was thrilled. 'What about Glamour and Grazia and Lei and Amica?'

Carla was surprised. 'Not many English girls know so many Italian magazines the first time they come out here.'

'My father has a news-stand in London. It's in a very cosmopolitan part of town. He sells many foreign magazines and I love looking at them. Can't understand a word, of course.'

'That's a good story. Tell them that on your go-sees. It'll be something for you to say to break the ice and maybe it'll make them remember you. Now, let me explain about the trams and the metro and then I'll give you the addresses. Your last appointment's at five so be back here by six and then you can go and see where you're staying. So, first you go to *Donna*. . . .'

'Milan taxi drivers suck!' yelled Gigi as she charged into the agency. 'You guys are going to have to give me an advance. That guy really ripped me off. I think I'm almost completely out of cash.'

'And you are who?' Carla disliked her on sight let alone her attitude. Talk about In Your Face, or whatever it was they said in America.

'I'm Gigi Garcia. You're expecting me. Charley Lobianco has sent me personally.'

Like hell! thought Carla, and without bothering to introduce her to the other bookers, she steered her towards Marcello's office. They'd soon find out the extent of Charley's involvement in this monster. Gigi walked straight in.

'Hi, I'm Gigi, Charley sent me, y'know? Are you, like, the Charley of Milan?'

Marcello didn't get up. He nodded to Gigi, said to Carla, 'Ask her to wait outside please,' and Gigi found herself out in the corridor again.

'Carla, that girl is trouble. Charley called me about her. He *did* send her, but only because he wanted to get rid of her. You know the type, parties every night and then doesn't show up at the shoot. Apparently she was getting many many bookings to begin with but she wrecked all her chances. I have looked at her card already and now I see her in the flesh. She is a great girl but we have to keep an eye on her for Charley. But I don't want you wasting your time on her. Give her to Francesca, no, wait, give her to that new girl who came to us from Riccardo Gay who's so pleased with herself. What's her name? Simonetta? Paolo on the men's table told me yesterday that one of his male models is sleeping with her for free rent, she is so stupid. Let's give her Signorina Garcia and see if she is so smart she can handle her. If she can't, well, then she's out – and so is Gigi. Let's hope we can get her some work. That skin of hers is really dark.'

'D'accordo!' said Carla, laughing. This was going to be fun. Simonetta was already driving them crazy on the booking table with her fancy airs and graces. Let her see what she could do with Gigi Garcia.

Outside Gigi stepped back quickly as Carla came out. She hadn't liked Marcello's remark about her Latin skin. It had sounded almost racist.

Tess left the agency feeling more positive than she had in months. She recalled Angie's words to her before she left: 'Above all, Tess, remember that the agency is like your family, both here and whenever you go abroad. You'll feel lonely, it's natural. All the girls do. And the agency and your booker are always there to give you support just like your family would.'

It was true. She already felt the beginnings of a close bond with Carla and it was fantastic to have the support of Marcello. Yet Tess's first experience of Milan was a complete nightmare.

It began the minute she stepped outside the agency. As she began to walk down the street she became aware of the eyes. Men's eyes, everywhere, boring into her as if they could see right through her clothing to her naked skin underneath. As they passed her they always turned around and stared and whistled and made that horrible 'Sssss' noise. Now and again they let a hand drift against her as they went by.

In the metro it was ten times worse. They packed them in like sardines in England but the British reserve invariably prevailed and the English stood as stiffly as they could so as to avoid even minimal bodily contact. The Italians, Tess found, obviously thought it gave them *carte blanche* to grope her at every opportunity and she emerged from each *stazione* feeling as if she had been raped. Then she had to compose herself and appear at her go-sees calm and collected.

The fashion editors she saw were mostly solid, middle-aged women, elegantly dressed, who glanced quickly through her book and smiled dismissively when she tried to tell them her father sold their magazine at his news-stand in London. Sometimes she was asked to walk up and down and there was always a lot of muttering in Italian behind her back which she could not understand.

The old cobbled streets were hard to walk on and the weather was rainy and misty. She lost her way on the orange trams and by the time she arrived back at the agency Tess was almost in tears, but Carla had been on the phone to Angie in London and knew what to expect. Angie had explained that Tess was a girl with great looks but zero confidence who needed all the emotional support she could get. Carla was aware that Marcello thought Tess could make it in Milan and it was up to her to overcome Tess's crisis of confidence and break her through to success, which was why when Tess walked in looking thoroughly dejected, Carla left the booking table for half an hour and took the trouble to escort Tess in a taxi to where she was staying rather than send her out on her own again. She didn't go in with her, that would have been nannying her too much, but during the taxi ride she reassured her about the go-sees – 'I already called them at *Donna* and they loved you.' 'But they barely looked at me. . . .' 'They're professionals, they can see at a glance, that's all it takes. You've done well, Tess' – and from plummeting to the depths of depression, once again Tess's mood lifted as Carla dropped her off at the Darsena.

The Darsena, located near the Porto Genova and the canale

Darsena, was famous in the Milan fashion world as the place where the agencies put their models. It was a huge modern apartment block with rooms running from front to back of the building and balconies overlooking a central courtyard. Each apartment had two or three rooms, sometimes a single, a kitchenette area in the living room and basic furniture abused by the modelling industry over a period of time. It was conveniently located near the two big studios, Superstudio, an old converted workshop where they used to repair loco-motives, and Fabrizio Ferri's famous Industria complex.

Tess made her way around the nose-to-tail Ferraris parked in front of the building, wondering whose they could be. When she walked in, for one moment she thought she had entered a funeral parlour. The lobby of the Darsena was buried under a mountain of floral bouquets. Tess stopped to look at the cards and noticed they didn't even have anybody's name on them. Just room numbers, the words 'call me' and a tele-phone number. A group of girls came in behind her, giggling. They picked up their keys and disappeared towards the elev-ators. A man had followed them in. He asked the receptionist: '*La bionda? La camera, da che parte?*'

'*Numero trentecinque.*'

Tess watched as the man scribbled the room number 35 on a card followed by a telephone number, wrote the words 'Per La Bionda' and threw his bouquet on to the pile. As Tess went to collect her own key he eyed her up and down.

'Oh, no, you don't!' She turned and stared him out until he left. She wasn't going to have a complete stranger finding out her room number. 'Don't you give it to him if he comes back,' she warned the receptionist, who looked at her as if she was mad. Didn't this girl know it was almost part of her job to give out the models' room numbers to all the gigolos?

When she let herself into her room Tess found more

bouquets still in their cellophane wrapping, giant teddy bears and box upon box of gift-wrapped chocolates with kitschy pink bows piled halfway up the wall. What was going on? There were unwashed dishes in the sink and a musty smell wafting through the room. Tess opened the shutters in her bedroom, then the windows, and immediately wished she hadn't. From a building across the street two men were watching her, more gathered at other windows and the 'Sssss' noises of admiration started up again. She slammed the windows shut and went to the other end of the little apartment to open the doors and hide on the balcony.

The blasting sound hit her from every direction. People were hanging out on all the other balconies shouting to each other: 'Yo! Where you going tonight?' 'Maybe we should all hook up later.' 'There's an English DJ at that club we went to last night.' 'Are you going to Lizard tonight?' 'Yeah, and Shocking, then on to Hollywood.' 'I'm going to Plastic.' 'I heard there's a really hot Latin chick arrived at Etoile this afternoon.' 'I know, she's come in from New York and they've given her to Simonetta.' 'Didn't I see you with Simonetta's boyfriend last night? That English model?' 'She doesn't care. You know these Italian women: it's "I donta care whatta you do butta you gotta come home to me." He never actually sleeps with anyone but Simonetta.' 'It's only a matter of time. So what are we all going to do tonight?' 'P-A-R-T-Y!'

Tess went downstairs to ask for another room. The receptionist ignored her. Suddenly she was accosted in the courtyard by throngs of badly dressed young men all trying to press cards and tickets on her.

'Come to my club tonight. You won't have to pay for anything.'

'No, come to my club. Mickey Rourke will be there. Mel

Gibson always goes there when he's in town. Free taxi. Free entrance. Free drinks. I give you all free tickets.'

In the elevator Tess asked a girl what on earth was happening.

'Oh, it's just the PR guys from the clubs. The owners send them down to round up the girls. They compete with each other to lure the prettiest models to their clubs. It attracts the rich Milanese playboys, you see. We're just bait.'

Tess remembered the bank of Ferraris outside.

'Just remember,' called the girl after her, 'there's no such thing as a free lunch.'

Just as she had finished unpacking, a six-foot blonde came in, stripped off her clothes and left them in a trail behind her as she made for the bathroom. She didn't even notice Tess.

Then the door opened again and a voice announced:

'This place is a complete shithole.'

'I agree,' said Tess. 'I asked for a single room.'

'Well, I asked to be put in with the boys. Who are you?'

'Tess Tucker from London.'

'Gigi Garcia. This your first season in Milan?'

Tess nodded. 'I'm here with my boyfriend.'

Gigi looked around. 'No kidding? I don't see him.'

'He's away on a shoot.'

'Yeah? What's he like? Fucks you rigid, does he?'

'He's an angel,' said Tess, going into a kind of trance.

'So maybe they do it up there but it's not much use to you down here.'

Tess wasn't listening. 'He looks like an angel. He has long fair hair, all fine and silky, and his face is so pretty and soft.'

'Sounds like a faggot to me, darling. We on our own here or what?'

'No, there's . . .' Tess was gesturing behind Gigi. The six-foot blonde stood there stark naked drying her white pubic

199

hair with a towel. She had a very short feathery haircut, ice blue eyes, a turned-up nose, no breasts to speak of and her legs had to be at least 40 inches long.

'Hi, I'm Greta. I'm from Sweden.'

'Christ, that gurdy-gurdy-gurdy Scandinavian accent is going to drive me nuts,' muttered Gigi to Tess. 'I'm Gigi from Miami – ' she held out her hand completely unfazed by Greta's nakedness – 'how long you been here, Greta? Can I see your book?'

'Sure,' said Greta, handing over a bulging portfolio. 'About eight months. I *hade* it.' The gurdy-gurdy had acquired a mid-Atlantic slant along the way. 'I've done *Donna* and *Grazia* and catalogue, catalogue, catalogue all day long, and I've done shoes for Rinascente and today I had eleven appointments. Mondadori and Rizzoli are way out by the airport and you go out there for one appointment and then you find your next appointment is at *Vogue* and it's in the centre then it's back out to the airport for Rizzoli again and into town for *Amica*. I could kill my booker. I thought Simonetta, my old one, was bad enough and then she left and I thought at last I will be OK, but no, she's terrible, this new one.'

'I think I have Simonetta now,' said Gigi.

'Well, she's the worst, she's . . .'

'The booker from hell?' asked Gigi.

'Exactly!' said Greta and they both laughed. They completely ignored Tess, acted as if she wasn't there.

The phone rang and Tess grabbed it. It might be Bobby.

'Ciao, can I speak to Susan,' said a throaty Italian male voice.

'Susan?'

'Susan left yesterday,' said Greta, addressing Tess for the first time.

'Susan's gone,' explained Tess.

'Well, you, what are *you* doing tonight?' asked the voice without missing a beat. Tess slammed the phone down. Men, men, men everywhere. Men's eyes, men's voices. Why wouldn't they leave her alone?

The phone rang again immediately. Gigi picked up.

'Who? Maria? What, Greta? Oh, Maria left a week ago. What's that? Sure, I'd love to. Where? Oh, don't worry I'll find it, or why don't you pick me up here in the lobby? I need to take a nap, I just got off a plane from New York. OK. See you later.' She hung up. 'Greta, you know a club called Lizard?'

'Sure, maybe I see you there tonight.'

'What are you going to do tonight, Tess?'

'Oh, I'm going to wait in for Bobby to call and get an early night. I want to be fresh for my go-sees tomorrow.'

Gigi and Greta raised their eyes to heaven.

'Well, if my boyfriend calls from Oslo will you please tell him I love him,' said Greta.

'While you're out screwing someone else,' said Gigi and Greta laughed.

Tess felt completely left out. The misery was returning and 'good for your book' didn't seem to be much help against these two. There seemed to be no sign of the noise outside abating and her chances of an early night, or indeed of any sleep at all, seemed slim. Sitting on her bed after Gigi and Greta had left for the evening, she began writing a letter home to her parents, but after a while she realised it was sounding too miserable and would worry them. She picked up one of the giant teddy bears left for Greta by a playboy admirer and hugged it to her for comfort.

The phone rang. Tess eyed it nervously. Another predatory man. She picked it up on the seventh ring.

'Tess? That you?'

'Bobby! I can't tell you how pleased I am to hear your voice.'

'Baby, what's the matter? You sound gutted.'

Tess let it all come out in a rush – the flight, the men in the street, the go-sees, the Darsena, Gigi Garcia, everything. Typically, in her anxiety, she forgot to tell him the positive stuff about Marcello and the lady from *Donna*'s reaction to her. When Tess was down she never saw anything good.

'Hey, you've got to take it easy. This is Milan. All the girls go through this. It's part of a girl's modelling career, you've got to do Milan. You haven't even met the gigolos yet. There was this girl a few years ago, her gigolo gave her such a hard time, when she came home and found him in bed with some-one else, she shot him and she went to jail for it. Now, listen, I've got some good news. The photographer I'm working for has finished sooner than he expected and he's got to go back to London — '

'Oh, Bobby, please don't leave me here when I've just arrived. . . .'

'Just calm down and listen. I've been offered another job by an art director I've met, a guy named Roberto Fabiani, and here's the best part: he wants me to be the photographer, not just assist. It's my big break. But the very best part is that I showed him your card, which I just happened to have about my person, and he liked you. The job is a shoot for cashmere at Superstudio the day after tomorrow. He's going to call the agency for your book and set up a casting. The job's as good as yours. The perfect start. You'll be a big success here and we're going to be working together. Today working with Bobby Fox, tomorrow Aldo Fallai.'

'Who's Aldo Fallai?'

'Don't you know anything? He's mega here. One of Italy's biggest photographers. They gave him the keys to the city or some such honour and he never even showed up for the ceremony until it was all over. So sleep tight and don't let the Darsena bugs bite and don't forget to call the agency first thing and tell them to be ready for Roberto's call. I'll see you very very soon.'

After he had hung up Bobby walked naked through the expensive Milanese apartment full of chrome and black furniture to Roberto Fabiani's bedroom. He did not need to ask himself yet again if he was doing the right thing. He knew he was behaving despicably. His father had always told him he showed signs of becoming a weak man and he was proving him right. But it would mean a big break for his career to get this job so early. He wasn't going to get it any other way. He knew he wasn't that talented. But Tess was. She had what it took to go far. He was doing it for Tess. That's what he would tell himself. It would make him feel better.

Roberto was lying in bed, his bare chest visible above the fur rug he used as a bedspread.

'You took your time,' he growled. 'Come back to bed, and try to enjoy it a bit more this time otherwise I might just forget to call the agency about your little girlfriend. . . .'

The phone rang at six o'clock the following morning.

'Leave it,' Greta called from her room, 'it's only my father. He calls every morning from Oslo to wake me up so I get to work on time. He's my alarm clock.'

'What about us,' groaned Gigi who had come in at two. 'He'll wake us up every morning too.'

'Well, you'll be working too so it'll be fine for all of us.'

She was right about Tess, wrong about Gigi. Gigi might complain about how behind New York clubs Milan clubs were – 'all that fuckin' eighties house music!' – but she still stayed out every night till two or three. She had also gone wild about Italian food and was stuffing herself with pasta and *gelati*. Tess had been in the agency one day when Simonetta had translated what one of the fashion directors had said in Italian about Gigi in front of her at one of Gigi's castings.

'She take one look and she say, Simonetta, this girl, she fat like a peeg!'

'From what I hear she works it off on the dance floor and in bed,' murmured someone else.

For Tess, on the other hand, it seemed as if nothing could go wrong – except for the occasional spot when her complexion suffered from the horrible Milan pollution and the smog. She had rented a bicycle to get around so she didn't have to suffer the groping hands in the metro, and for the small distances she did have to walk along the street she wore mirrored sunglasses so she didn't have to make any eye contact with the lecherous Italians.

The shoot with Bobby had gone well. As he had photographed her, she had imagined him making love to her. She had loved the soft cashmere clothes and wrapped them lovingly around as if they were Bobby himself. Since then she had found herself working frequently at Superstudio. It was only a ten-minute walk from the Darsena on the other side of Porto Genova over a little bridge. The only thing she didn't like about Superstudio was the fact that there were always men wandering in on the shoots. In Milan, it seemed, if any guy knew anybody working at Superstudio he felt he had the right to stroll in and try and get an eyeful of a girl as she changed, a quick flash of a breast, a peek at her bush.

But knowing Bobby was there for her made all the difference to Tess, although in truth he wasn't there for her every day. He seemed to have suddenly become very much in demand in Milan and five nights of the week he said he had to work editing pictures. Still, Tess was happy, sitting in the room at the Darsena, writing letters home to her friends in London and her parents. She relished the calm when the other two girls were not there. She still could not get used to the noise outside. It seemed half the models, both male and female, wanted to party all night and keep awake the others who wanted to get a good night's sleep and be professional. Sometimes, however, a shoot ran far into the night and she wouldn't get home till one or two. On her return home she would sit on her bed and feel utterly alone. That, she was learning, was the price of modelling abroad. The pictures might be wonderful but every now and then you were stranded in a strange country with people all around you speaking a language you didn't understand and you had no one to turn to.

Tess made a point of trying to be professional. She always got to the shoot or the studio on time until Greta pointed out to her that it was pretty pointless in Milan. Italy – and possibly Spain – was the one place where you didn't really have to bother too much with punctuality. The Italians always got started late, and on her first shoot Tess was amused to find that the huge argument that took place amongst the crew for almost half the morning was not about the shoot itself, but about where to have lunch.

One day Marcello approached her at the agency.

'So, my pretty pretty virgin, you are doing very well for us. You are working nearly every day, Carla tells me. You see the pictures your boyfriend took of you already came out in a magazine. Soon your book will be fat like your friend Gigi. We have to do something about her. What about all this money you are making? Are you out there spending it on beautiful Italian clothes?'

'Oh, no, I'm saving it, keeping it right here in the agency till I can take it home to London.'

'Well anyway, I think you should have a little treat. Tonight there is a client dinner. The client, a big important man from Bergamo, he will pay for everything so I must put together a good table. You will come and so will Gigi, providing she does not eat too much. And Roberto Fabiani, and from the agency we will take Carla, of course, and maybe Simonetta so the client can see we have taken her away from her old agency. And Aldo Fallai, he will be very important to my client. I must ask Paolo from the men's table and get him to bring along a couple of his boys. I shall invite one of the fashion directors from the magazines. Then there are some sons of some friends of mine, young boys, very rich, you will like them.'

'Can my boyfriend come? Bobby Fox?'

'Ah, Bobby,' said Marcello knowingly, 'why don't you ask him? I do not think he will want to come.'

Tess couldn't believe it but Marcello was right. When she told him about it, he just said, 'I have some work to do at the labs. Another night maybe.'

'But Bobby, Aldo Fallai will be there. Wouldn't it be a fabulous chance for you to meet him? Marcello said I could invite you.'

'Big deal,' said Bobby. Tess didn't understand it. He seemed so morose. Could it be that he was jealous because she had been the one to get him invited instead of the other way round?

There was that, of course; Bobby's nose had been put a little out of joint, but the real reason was that he could not face being at the same table as Roberto Fabiani and Tess. Tess must never find out about his affair with Roberto. Affair! It was nothing but a seedy bit of prostitution that had enabled him to jump on the first rung of the ladder, and now he couldn't shake Roberto off.

206

Gigi teased Tess in the taxi all the way to the dinner.

'Little Cinderella out of the house at last. What have you done with your pretty Prince Charming, then? Going to run away to him when the clock strikes twelve, are you? Well, I wouldn't bother, honey, because his Prince Charming will be with us tonight.'

'What do you mean?' asked Tess.

'Oh, you'll find out soon enough. Now, Tess, watch out for the playboys. They'll come on very strong and you won't like it, but you've got to play the game tonight because the client's there and he's paying for it all, so don't go sobbing into your napkin.'

'There's no such thing as a free lunch,' said Tess, remembering what the girl in the elevator at the Darsena had told her.

'My, my, my, are you growing up at last, little girl?'

'Gigi, I think you're the one who needs to grow up. You're getting too fat to work and it's you who's going out with these playboys every night. Sooner or later you're going to have to pay a pretty big price. I worry about you.'

'Well don't,' snapped Gigi. 'I'm quite capable of taking care of myself.' But secretly she was beginning to worry that she wasn't getting any work.

At dinner she found herself sitting next to a young English male model. Tess was at the far end of the table surrounded by all the playboys Gigi would have liked to score with. She took a good look at the client, a shady-looking character to whom everyone was sucking up in a major way. Connected, thought Gigi. Laundering money through the fashion industry. This guy was clearly immensely wealthy. Had he made his money manufacturing cloth or did it come from Las Vegas? Did it matter, so long as it was coming her way? Gigi turned her attention to the large plate of risotto in front of her. It was the longest table she had ever seen and it wasn't long before the conversation took its traditionally bitchy turn.

'Simonetta, how did that girl get those pages in *Glamour*? She's so pock-marked it's like she's got craters all over her face.'

'What about that new English girl in *Carter's*? Did you see those pictures? Weren't they wild? I heard she's a dyke. Is it true?'

'See that pretty English girl up at the other end of the table, the one with the red hair, Marcello's latest discovery? See Roberto Fabiani sitting right next to her, sweet as pie? Well, of course, you know he's jumping her boyfriend, that pretty little photographer, Foxy Bobby. So who's going to be the first to tell her?'

'He's a shit photographer anyway, he's only a jumped-up assistant. She'd be well rid of him.'

'She's rather sweet. You know what she said in the agency today: "I'm going to one of Marcello's dinners just like a supermodel." What she doesn't understand is that you'd never catch a supermodel anywhere near one of these dinners! I imagine she doesn't have a clue what these playboys are going to want from her later on in the evening.'

'Oh, I wouldn't be so sure. Those quiet ones can sometimes go far and Carla's keeping a close eye on her.'

Gigi turned to the male model beside her.

'First season in Milan?'

'Yeah, yours too? Met many male models? We're not all gay, by the way. Hardly any of us, as a matter of fact. Men are much more into fashion than they used to be and they want to see heterosexual-looking guys in the magazines.'

'Is this a come-on?'

'Could be.'

'Well, you sure don't look like most of the models I see

around the Darsena. They're mostly American, that square-jawed-don't-I-look-the-business-in-a-suit look. Makes me sick, quite frankly. You're kinda cute, dark and gypsy looking. Are you sure you're English?'

'So it says on my passport. How's the work going?'

Gigi was caught off guard. Usually she had a list of lies to trot out about her amazing success since she had hit town but the way he was looking at her with his big brown eyes disarmed her.

'The truth is I haven't got very far. I'm having a bit of a problem with my weight.'

'And partying and staying up too late and not looking so good first thing in the morning on all those go-sees with all those dragon menopausal fashion directors? Tell me about it.'

'You mean you've got problems too?'

'Listen, I'm with Etoile in London. Paolo at Etoile here — see him down there at the end of the table — well, he faxed the men's table in London and said they were begging for me out here. There weren't any actual direct bookings but I flew out with my hopes as high as the Alps and well, basically, I haven't worked since. I've virtually run out of money and the mornings are getting harder to face each day.'

'Join the club,' said Gigi. 'What are we going to do about it?'

'Club. The magic word. I have the perfect solution,' he told her. 'Let's go and party at a club.'

Carla gave Tess a lift back to the Darsena and offered to drop Roberto Fabiani off on the way. He bowed flamboyantly, rather drunk as he stood on the pavement, before making his way unsteadily up the steps to the door of his building. As Carla drove away, the door opened and Tess saw Bobby help Roberto inside.

'Oh, look, there's Bobby. Poor Bobby. He couldn't come

tonight. He had to do some lab work. I didn't know his lab was in the same building where Roberto lives.'

It isn't, Carla started to say, then stopped herself. This girl was such an innocent but she was doing so well in her work that it would be the worst thing in the world if she were to be knocked off balance in her private life at this stage. With a bit of luck she could make it back to England without ever finding out about Bobby Fox and Roberto Fabiani.

Greta was away for a couple of days. The apartment was, for once, almost totally silent. Tess fell into a deep sleep to be awakened several hours later by a sound she couldn't identify. As she lay in bed, terrified, it dawned on her what she was listening to and her face turned red in the darkness.

The sounds were coming from the balcony. Tess tiptoed through the living room and peeked through the curtains. Gigi was on top of a naked man, her buttocks glistening in the moonlight. He rolled her over and began to thrust into her, banging himself down on her, bruising her as Tess watched, as fascinated as she was horrified.

Suddenly Gigi pulled away.

'Hey, I've got a great idea,' she said, 'let's play Bobby and Roberto,' and she turned herself over and offered him her butt as Tess stumbled away in sudden, sickening realisation.

The next morning she couldn't look at Gigi and it was only politeness that forced her to glance at the male model who was staying to breakfast when he said, 'Hey, you're English, aren't you? So am I. My name's Tommy Lawrence.'

New York, 1994

'Barbara, I've got Carl Sassoon on Line 1.'

'I'll take him right away.' Barbara Harper had just made it to the office after an hour's trek through bumper to bumper downtown New York traffic.

Nearly twenty years earlier, around the time when *Vogue* made Beverly Johnson the first black cover girl, Barbara too had been a model. It was a time when she was young and idealistic and her hopes had been high for the future of the black model. Then, as the years passed, she wised up. Advertising agencies were happy to use black girls – to sell products to black consumers. In fact even that didn't really apply. In the mind of the white person handling the booking, the image of a white model was often good enough for black people to look at too. The world of power was a white one inhabited by white people who were not necessarily thinking of black people. Something, thought Barbara, had to be done and there was no way she could do anything as a model.

So she switched to the other side of the booking table and became an agent. Around the table she was the only black booker. A client would call up and say, 'Hey, we've got this casting for a shampoo commercial. Send us five girls.'

Barbara would call three white girls and two black girls. The booker sitting next to her nearly passed out.

'Barbara, you can't send Mary and Jo. They didn't say they wanted black girls.'

'And they didn't say they *didn't* want black girls. All they said was five girls between eighteen and twenty and over five eight. They didn't say black, and they didn't say red haired or blue eyed either. If they specify "No blacks" then that's OK. That's fair. And sure, even if they don't they probably don't want them, I know that. But are you saying we're supposed to take the attitude of the client? Will you give me a break? You just have to keep sending black kids out as long as the client doesn't clarify specifically that they don't want them.'

Barbara's attitude was: the client's gotta get with it. The client was inevitably white and by habit the white agent wouldn't want to rub them up the wrong way by sending black girls. But how was a black girl ever going to see a client? She couldn't get a black model a half-a-day booking let alone a full day, and as for going on a trip – forget it. Definitely!

In the end there was only one thing to do: start her own agency. Barbara Harper Management was launched with white money and an all-white booking table in an old loft south of Canal Street in TriBeCa and Barbara embarked upon a crusade to educate her *bête noire*, the white liberal, who as far as she was concerned was constantly on the edge of racism. They didn't mean to be racist but they practised it every day. They weren't necessarily smarter than anyone else but they were often in power and therefore she had to help them think it through.

Carl Sassoon was a top New York designer on a par with Calvin Klein. Barbara shrugged off her coat, grabbed a quick sip of coffee and took his call.

'Barbara, I've got a job for you. I want you to find me a great dark girl.'

Barbara gritted her teeth and forced herself to keep her tone nice and light.

'That's good to hear, Carl, and I'm glad you called. I want to be the one to do this.'

'Well, God knows, Barbara, you're the one who can . . . after all, you're *the* black agent.'

She hated it when they said this. She was a model agent with her own agency. She had plenty of black girls on her book and plenty of white girls. Just because she herself was a woman of colour they branded her an agent for black models only.

'Well, Carl, I'm sure I could find you what you want . . .' she paused before putting the boot in, 'but did you hear what you just said?'

'What?'

'You said, find me a dark girl.'

'Yes.'

'How many white girls are you using in your show?'

'I don't know, thirty-four, thirty-five maybe.'

'Well, why do you want *a* black girl? Why don't you say I want you to find me some black girls? Why does it have to be just one? I tell you what I'm gonna do. I'm gonna send over my very best black girls and maybe a few of my white girls too. What do you say?'

'Oh, sure, sure, Barbara, believe me, I love black girls, you know I do. I don't have anything against black girls. I used to go out with a black girl. I took her to dinner, lovely girl. My daughter, she has black kids in her class at school. She brings them to our home. . . .'

''Bye, Carl, talk to you soon.' Barbara hung up. *I used to go out with a black girl. I took her to dinner, lovely girl.* Please! They only ever wanted one black girl when she had so many to offer. Still, four or five years ago the average New York

213

modelling agency didn't have any black girls on their books and the bigger agencies might have just a handful among hundreds and hundreds of white girls. Still, things were improving – at least in America. In London the line was still: 'Black girls really don't work over here. If you want to work, go to New York.' Agencies in Europe still only tended to have just one black model and the trouble was that there was no pressure over there to make them take more. The other problem with Europe was the collections. Barbara had difficulty getting girls of colour booked for both seasons. Over there the mentality seemed to be that black girls were better for summer clothes. It was, like, they didn't wear clothes in winter.

'Barbara, Lizzie Mayhew on two. . . .'

Barbara picked up. Lizzie Mayhew was a casting director for an ad agency.

'Hey, Lizzie!'

'Barbara, how you doing? Listen, I really like that girl of yours, Trina, for that soft drink campaign we talked about.'

'Lizzie, you have terrific taste.' Trina was a sensational new girl of colour Barbara had taken on six months ago.

'$1,200.'

'No, no, no, no, *no*!' Barbara couldn't believe she was hearing this. 'You know the rate is $2,500.'

'Not for this particular girl.'

'Why?'

'Well,' Lizzie was hesitant to come right out with it, 'this is a different market.'

'Well, I'm sorry, Lizzie, my girl works for $2,500. If you don't agree then I just don't think we can work together.'

'OK, Barbara, OK, but if I give your girl $2,500 please don't tell anyone that she's getting more than the other black girls.'

'No problem with me,' said Barbara. 'I don't have anyone else on this job but her.'

Why did it have to be like this? thought Barbara. Lizzie wants my girl to work on a campaign that's going to go right through the black community all over America; she wants to use the images but not pay the girl the money. It was such a vicious circle. She was prepared to fight for her girls of colour but often a black girl would go to a white agent thinking he would be better for her, have more power for her when in fact the greedy white agent would be more likely to look out for his white girls first.

'Barbara, don't forget you're seeing those new girls at eleven.'

She hadn't forgotten. One of them had come all the way from London. Grace Brown of Etoile London, a person for whom Barbara had enormous respect, had called her to tell her about Amy La Mar who had won their Girl of the Year competition and was coming to New York for the finals at the Plaza Hotel. Barbara went through to her office and sat at her desk for a quiet moment. Her office door had a glass window. Through it she could see the two girls come in and be asked to sit down and wait. They were both beautiful. One had platinum dyed hair cropped close to the head, very dramatic, and the other had a long streaked golden weave. Barbara recalled the days when she had a weave herself, her hair plaited in cornrows and the weave sewn in on top. She couldn't hear the girls' voices so she couldn't tell which one was the English girl. She guessed it must be the one with the weave.

She was wrong.

As Barbara saw it there were two girls of colour:

First, there was the girl with the fight and the bite – the 'don't fuck with me 'cos I got your number' type of girl – who seemed as though she was not afraid of anything because she had been raised by her family to believe that she was beautiful

215

and she should be proud of herself and she shouldn't let anybody tell her different. But behind the façade this girl was often insecure and had to come up with a little chip on her shoulder to get her through the door.

Then there was another kind of girl who knew both sides of the coin and knew that there was another direction to go in, a more humble, gentle, subtle approach. For Barbara knew only too well that the girl of colour had to be twice as humble as any other girl. She had grown up knowing she was in a minority, that she would always be going into a situation as a model to please someone else and for that someone she would not necessarily be the person of choice.

But this situation was not peculiar to black girls. With all models someone else was always going to decide their fate. All models went into a go-see hoping that the client would think they were the right girl for the job, but a black girl also had to hope that the client wouldn't judge her because of her colour.

It was only natural, Barbara felt, for a girl of colour to cower down inside. No matter how strong she was about herself on the inside, she had to know what was going on in the outside world. She had to hear the words 'No black girls, thank you' and no matter how hard she tried not to, she would sometimes have to take it personally. It could sound like, 'No, no, we don't want any dogs in here, thank you.'

Barbara knew from experience that humility worked better in the long run – with any model starting out, black or white – however much you might stand in front of the mirror and act tough and say to yourself, 'I'm going to go out there today and get that job, I'm the one they need', if you had your eye on the ball the best way to play it smart would be not to offend, to behave well, be polite and don't rock the boat. Let the model show humility and leave it to the agent to get tough.

As it turned out she had a perfect example of both kinds of girl waiting to see her.

Irma Washington was right in her face the minute Barbara opened the door of her office.

'Hi, here's my book. I put it together myself. I had someone take my pictures. I know what the score is. Can I start this afternoon, can I go to a magazine? I know this make-up artist who thinks I'm just fabulous.'

Barbara looked at the book. The pictures were terrible. They didn't do the girl justice at all. She was lithe and sexy and she knew it. She flaunted herself. She had attitude all right. Maybe too much of it, thought Barbara. Could be a problem.

The other girl, the English one with the short hair, was the complete opposite. She came in, she shook hands and then she yawned.

Her hand flew up to her mouth and her eyes widened in horror.

'I'm really sorry . . . I don't know what . . .' The girl was charming, natural, beautiful dark clear skin, an irresistibly captivating smile of embarrassment.

'Jet lag,' said Barbara, smiling. 'Happens to us all. Can I see your pictures, please.'

Amy handed over her book and sat quietly while Barbara looked through them.

'These are good. Who took them?'

'Oh, a friend of my boyfriend. He'll be so pleased you like them.'

'I certainly do. Turn your head to the left for me please, Amy, now to the right. Good. Show me your hands. Beautiful. Now, walk for me a little, up and down.'

She was a delight, a magnificent natural walker. Long legs, long arms, graceful movement.

'Were you nervous at the Girl of the Year competition?'

She nodded, green eyes wide again.

'You'll do OK,' Barbara reassured her. 'Whatever happens, just put it down to experience and remember it gave a whole load of people a chance to see you. Think of it as your first go-see. Now, you've seen the apartment where you're staying, you're happy?'

'Grace Brown found me this apartment on Spring Street. An English model just moved out and went back home and I can have her room. There's a couple on the same floor who she was friendly with and I'm supposed to go and introduce myself because they can keep an eye on me. I'm a little scared. I've never lived on my own before. I've never been away from home before.'

Barbara scribbled on a piece of paper.

'Here's my home number. You can call me whenever you want. I'm going to take you on and you're going to be coming by the agency all the time but this is just in case you need to reach me in the evening. I know the apartment where you're living. I suggested it to Grace. I've put girls there before; it's safe and I know the couple across the hall. She works on a magazine. I'll give them a call, tell them to look out for you. Go home now and get some sleep and come back tomorrow at ten and we'll figure out where to send you first.'

Outside Barbara introduced Amy to Irma.

'Hello,' said Amy immediately, smiling warmly and holding out her hand.

Irma took it but didn't return the smile.

Uh-oh! thought Barbara. She had seen it happen so many times: the paranoia among black girls in the same agency. The way the mentality of the outside world impinged on the girls:

218

there's only room for one, you want to be the only fish in the pond. Irma was already jealous of Amy and they hadn't even gone out on their first go-sees. It was the media's fault. They compared the girls of colour to each other all the time. Why did they have to compare Naomi with Tyra? Why couldn't they compare Linda or Tatjana with Tyra? Or Claudia with Brandi? Or Iman with Christy? It was the old slave mentality, the competition between the house Negro and the field Negro with the master shining up the one and keeping the other one down. The trouble was the black girls in New York were wise to the narrow mentality of the white people in power so when another black girl came on the scene, the original black girl had to feel threatened.

'I'm proud to have you two new girls join the agency,' Barbara told Amy and Irma. 'You're so different to each other, you're both going to be going all over the place.'

But Irma still looked uncertain and she walked out without saying goodbye to Amy.

Amy looked after her, a sad expression on her face. Then she said something so quietly that Barbara only just caught it.

'I'm going to pray for her. She needs our prayers.'

But you deserve them, thought Barbara, you deserve them.

Edward P. Ross was a black man in corporate America and he took care to preserve his position. He was acting divisional manager at ManuCom, a computer company, and he reckoned it was only a matter of time before the acting became a thing of the past and he became a major player in the white man's world.

But he was still a brother. He was still Eddie Cool like he'd been in school. He just divided his life a little. Everybody did. You compartmentalised your life and got the best of all worlds. He worked uptown and wore $800 suits to work – he only had two and he rotated them non-stop – and he had left the South Bronx ghetto of his childhood far behind; now he lived in SoHo in a little apartment on Spring Street and kidded himself on weekends that he was part of the fashion crowd. He'd crashed a gallery preview and befriended a designer.

Now the designer had asked him to dinner, told him to bring his girl, but Eddie didn't have a girl. At least not one he could take to dinner in a fancy restaurant. And if he was going to make it up the corporate ladder he was going to have to think about getting himself a woman to go with his new image. Eventually he was going to have to think about getting himself a corporate wife. Meanwhile, what to do about dinner? He was worrying about his problem as he let himself into his building.

'Just a minute. . . .'

She was coming up the steps behind him and gorgeous. Tall and leggy and good enough to eat.

'Absolutely. Come right on in. You live here?'

'I just moved in. Second floor. No, you call the ground floor the first floor, don't you? So I'm on the third floor.'

An English accent! And she'd moved into the model apartment. An English model. There couldn't be a more stylish person to take as his date to the dinner.

'You busy tonight, sister? What's your name, by the way?'

'Amy. Amy La Mar. Pleased to meet you.'

'Not as pleased as I am to meet you. I'm Eddie Ross. I want you to come to dinner with me tonight, meet some friends of mine.'

'Meet some friends of yours? I've only just met you. No, I'm sorry. Thanks.'

His arm was out across the doorway, stopping her getting through. He was a big man. His head was enormous, his face square and his lips thick and fleshy, crowned by his fine moustache. The gold caps on his teeth were almost as big as the gold ring on the pinky finger of his giant hand barring her way.

'Are you turning me down, sister?'

'Stop calling me sister.' Amy was agitated. She'd been literally shaking with nerves ever since she'd arrived in New York, starting with the flight over. It was the first time she had ever been in an aeroplane. She knew she was letting her imagination run riot regarding the menace she saw lying in wait on the streets of Manhattan but this great hulk of a man was more threatening than anyone she'd seen outside. 'Let me through. I need to get some sleep. I only arrived from London yesterday.'

'I'll let you go this time. Just this once. But you should plan on spending time with me soon . . .' and as she went up the stairs she heard the low hiss behind her—

'Sssssister!'

London, 1994

'I know this is kinda crazy but would you happen to know, by any chance, if a guy called Tommy Lawrence ever comes in here?' Cassie asked the man behind the bar at Joe's Café in Draycott Avenue in London.

The barman shouted out: 'Hey, do we get a Tommy Lawrence coming in here?'

'Thousands of 'em, all the time. Who's asking?'

'Young lady here. Take no notice of him, love,' he added hastily as Cassie's face lit up, 'he's just winding you up. Can I get you anything?'

'Oh, just a Diet Coke. I mean, you'd know, wouldn't you, if he was a regular customer?'

'Well, I'd know his face. I might not necessarily know him by name. Got a picture?'

That was the real problem. She didn't have a picture except the one in her head which was as vivid as it had been the day she tripped over him on Alice's Beach.

'You really want to find this bloke, don't you?' said the barman when Cassie shook her head, no, she didn't have a picture. 'What makes you think you'll find him here?'

It was still early evening and the place was quiet. He had time to listen and he had always thought of himself as a romantic, but as Cassie told him how she'd come all the way from New York to look for a man she'd only met twice in her life and who hadn't contacted her since, a man who could be anywhere in the world and had spun her a yarn about being part of the landed gentry and working in the City, a man, so she'd been told, who could be found in places like Joe's or Daphne's down the road or Foxtrot Oscar or Tramp or San Lorenzo or any of the other Sloaney watering holes, the barman reckoned he was listening to the biggest cock 'n' bull story he'd ever heard.

'Go home, darlin',' he advised, 'you'll probably find it easier to find the needle in the Manhattan haystack.'

If only she could go home, but Cassie knew she'd burned her boats with her family for the time being. From now on she was definitely Cassie Dylan. Cassie Zimmerman didn't exist any more. She could still hear her mother's voice repeating the same thing over and over:

'Don't upset your father. I'm warning you, Cassie, do not upset your father.'

It was ludicrous. The last thing she wanted to do was hurt her father. When she heard the news on the radio about the Los Angeles earthquake Cassie had left the model apartment and rushed straight home without even bothering to phone the agency first. She found her mother in a state of near hysteria, packing her suitcase to take the first plane out to California. As a result of the 'quake, Al Zimmerman had had a heart attack.

'His father went the same way,' was Doris Zimmerman's morbid comment.

Cassie's father pulled through but the experience enabled him to make up his mind once and for all. He was leaving California. He was moving back to New York and he wasn't going to wait a minute longer. The doctor was unequivocal in his instructions. Al was to have complete rest. He had had a lucky escape. On no account was he to be excited in any way; no stress, no arguments.

So when Cassie went to him and asked him to give her the money to go to London to pursue her modelling career (that was what she told him; the real reason was to find Tommy Lawrence) and he became angry and agitated at such an idiotic idea, Kari Zimmerman took her daughter aside and spoke to her in a new and direct tone of voice Cassie had not heard before.

'How can you do this to your father? You heard what the doctor said. You were there in the room. Has this ridiculous modelling caper gone to your head to such an extent that you no longer understand plain English? I am calling that agency tomorrow and I am going to tell them that you are no longer on their books. You will stay right here and help me look after your father. And you will not upset him. You will not!'

Cassie was not proud of what she had done next but she did not feel she was one hundred per cent to blame for her actions. Along with many other Beverly Hills kids, she had been raised a spoiled brat, but, she reasoned, it wasn't she who had done the raising, it was her parents. If she had emerged with a stubborn I'm-going-to-get-my-own-way-no-matter-what approach to life, she had learned it at her father's knee. Cassie knew she could wind Al Zimmerman round her little finger any time she wanted, and if she just worked on him a little longer he would give her the money to go to Europe, no problem. It was just a matter of explaining to him how much it meant to his little girl, how grateful she would be, and so on and so forth. Cassie had long since worked out that Kari did not have the same power over her husband. Still, in this instance she seemed determined to keep Cassie away from him. It was a new, tougher Kari Zimmerman

Cassie was dealing with here and new tougher tactics were required to deal with her.

'Has Grandma Zimmerman ever told you how much she wants to stay alive to see her great-grandchildren?' Cassie asked her mother casually one evening as they were preparing dinner together in Doris's kitchen.

'Of course, it's something of an obsession with her, you must know that.'

'I wonder how she'd feel if she knew what happened to her first great-grandchild?'

'Cassie . . . oh, no, I don't believe it . . . you wouldn't? Tell me you're joking. You never told her about the abortion?'

'Not yet.' Cassie pushed the carrots to one side and began slicing onions. 'My eyes are beginning to water. Don't you wish we were still in California and had Angelina to do all this?'

'Cassie, don't change the subject. Why are you raising this now? Grandma Zimmerman would be horrified. You mustn't tell her. Your father would die if he thought she'd found out.'

'Neat turn of phrase, Mother. I won't say a word. Just let me talk to Daddy about going to Europe.'

But Kari had changed more than Cassie realised. She cared desperately about her husband, but she also cared enough about Cassie to speak to Al herself and lay down certain conditions.

'I'm telling you this myself, Al, so that you should not upset yourself about it. Promise me you will not distress yourself. I hate to raise the matter again but you remember our daughter had a problem a few years ago. We won't name the problem nor will we deny it. I just want you to know that she feels strongly enough about going to Europe to use cheap, childish blackmail. She threatened to tell your mother about the problem. I know what that would do to you. She won't tell her, don't worry. We know Cassie. In her own way she's a sweet girl but the problem, it disturbed her, it's natural. Let us let her go to Europe. Pay her ticket, Al. You'll have to. I spoke with the agency and they were totally upfront with me. They don't rate her chances high enough to spring for the ticket themselves but they'll alert their London office and she can try her luck with them. But just give her enough money to stay for a month. If she has what it takes to make it then so be it, she'll make her own money. Otherwise she'll come home.'

Cassie never knew why her father suddenly presented her with an open return to London but she didn't hang around long enough to investigate his reasons. She jumped on the first plane.

In her first month in London she was more miserable than she had been at any time since the abortion. The tiny bedsit she rented in Earls Court with a hot-plate to cook on beside the washbasin, no fridge and a shared bathroom on the landing brought home to her the sheer luxury of Doris Zimmerman's apartment, let alone the Beverly Hills and Malibu palaces of her past. She began to imagine rats and other horrors lying in wait for her and sometimes she could not even bring herself to get out of bed in the morning. The only bright spot in her day was her visit to the news-stand at the bottom of the Earls Court Road to buy her paper. The vendor, Mr Tucker, always found time to have a chat with her. She was, he told her, about the same age as his daughter. He was very proud of his daughter. She was a model and he was looking forward to the day when her face would be on the cover of a magazine he'd sell. She was away in Milan apparently, doing very well according to her letters. Shame she wasn't in London, he'd have been happy to introduce them.

Cassie was too embarrassed to tell him she was also trying to be a model. She was also too proud to go to the Etoile agency in London. She knew from the way they hadn't come through with a ticket or any real support that she was on hold as far as Etoile was concerned, and if she could she was going to try and get somewhere on her own.

One day she was walking along Oxford Street when she saw a notice in a window saying *Wanted: Showroom Model, no experience needed.* She walked in.

'What size are you?'

'Twelve American.'

'Ten UK. Too small for us. Try across the road. They're looking for someone.'

They hired her for six weeks to walk up and down a room in front of buyers from stores, showing the designer's clothes for that particular season. It was boring but in a way it was useful. Cassie absorbed information she might otherwise never have learned. She noted which clothes Harrods and Fenwicks and Harvey Nichols thought would work for them and why. She watched as the clothes were ordered for the following season. She also learned to dress and undress very quickly, getting in and out of clothes in seconds. She learned, by watching the other girls, to start undressing as she was coming off the stage. Speed, she learned, was a real asset. There were only four models so she had to be ready and waiting as a girl was coming off stage. Afterwards she had to sort through the piles and piles of discarded clothes and hang them up again on the rails. For a girl who had once had a maid to do it for her it was a salutary experience.

Cassie hated it. She hated being stuck in the stuffy little showroom all day, sitting there waiting in case a buyer happened to stop by to see the collection, having to ask permission to go to the bank or go to the toilet. She got there every morning at nine and she was sometimes there till eight o'clock at night, when she would emerge dog tired to return to the little Earls Court bedsit. And she hated above all the constant lack of vision and the fact that if she ever did get to wear an exciting, daring new outfit, the buyers would invariably bypass it for a safe, basic design.

It was the other models who pushed her to go to the agency. Several of the girls were with Etoile and they confirmed it was the best agency in town.

'You shouldn't be stuck sitting in a showroom,' she heard over and over again, 'putting on the same outfits all through the day. It'll do your head in.'

She had to swallow her pride some time, but if she had known that Etoile London would send her straight off to Hamburg she might almost have stayed in the showroom.

'You know what the girls all say,' Angie, the New Faces booker told her, ' "Love those DMs!" The Germans will love you and they pay so well. All those Deutschmarks. They don't pay a fantastic daily rate but they'll book you for two or three weeks. They'll love your girl-next-door look.'

She shared yet another poky room in Hamburg – bunk beds – with a model from Holland who didn't speak much English and it was almost as bad as the Earls Court bedsit; but *Otto*, the big German catalogue, were so pleased with her they sent her to Tenerife where they'd built a massive open air studio in a round circle, concave, with sloping walls so there were no corners. While the sun went round Cassie was shifted round with it so that there was total all-day sunlight. The ultimate in German design but boy, did they work her hard.

Still, she came back to London with enough money to rent herself a proper apartment in Old Church Street, Chelsea, just off the King's Road. It was almost on the river and she loved the sound of the church bells ringing at the bottom of the street. She made friends with another model, who took her to Portobello Road where she picked up plenty of antique bargains with which to furnish her new home. She bought fresh flowers every other day and lighted scented candles in the evening. The only thing that kept her going was that one day she might bring Tommy back here and his first impression had to be perfect.

And at the agency she pestered them to tell her the places to go where she would find a young man who worked in the City and owned land in the country.

'Where in the City? Don't you have the name of the bank or wherever it is he's supposed to work? And where in the country? England may not be as big as America but we do have quite a large area of what you call country,' they told her, amused by her determination to find a boyfriend who could be almost anywhere. It was straight out of Mills and Boon. They gave her the names of likely bars and restaurants and tried not to laugh behind her back at the thought of her traipsing from place to place asking for him.

'Any sign of Tommy?' became the standard chorus each time Cassie walked into the agency.

'Well, they didn't know him at Joe's Café and they didn't know him at Daphne's but I'm going to try San Lorenzo tonight,' reported Cassie before she turned to study the briefs on the casting board.

'Girl: Long legs, blue eyes, blonde, must have very good teeth,' she read out. 'Boy: Tall, romantic, classy looking, dark hair, very English.'

'Hey, that might be something for you,' said Angie, 'it's for a dental floss commercial, wouldn't you know it? But they did ask if we had any American girls. They think American girls have good teeth. Want to give it a try?'

'Might as well,' said Cassie.

She walked out with the address in her hand. If she'd left five minutes later she would have heard Ashley on the men's table call out, 'Hey, Angie, give us the address of that dental floss commercial. They want a man and Tommy Lawrence is coming back from Milan after the weekend with his tail between his legs. He barely got a single job out there. We might as well send him along.'

'Well, at least we'll have found a Tommy for Cassie. What did she say her Tommy's last name was? I don't think she ever did tell us. . . .'

Lindy-Jane Johnson lay in a Badedas bath and listened to the tape of the interview she'd done down the line with Celestia Fairfax before she left for New York. She always recorded her telephone conversations. It was a legal requirement in England that the caller was able to hear a warning tone every fifteen seconds, a strange unidentifiable 'peep' which most people thought was her doorbell ringing in the distance.

The girl had spent most of the conversation going into ecstasy about Water Detroit, whom she appeared to have seen at a club. It had taken a great deal of Lindy-Jane's powers of persuasion to coax her into talking about herself and – more important – her family.

She hotly denied that any sexual relationship existed between herself and the woman photographer who had taken the *Carter's* pictures. Well she would, wouldn't she, thought Lindy-Jane, but she believed her all the same.

Lucy Fraser's revelation that Swan was a member of the Crichton-Lake family who had been involved in a near scandal when their son disappeared following the murder of a nanny in the family home in the Boltons had sent Lindy-Jane rushing to the library to dig up the cuttings from the time. The Crichton-Lake file had revealed more than she'd expected. There had, she learned, been an earlier tragedy in the family when the eldest daughter, Venetia, had been killed in a car crash on her eighteenth birthday with her boyfriend, Oliver Fairfax.

Oliver Fairfax!

It didn't take Lindy-Jane long to discover that Celestia and Oliver would have been related had he lived and this was what she had been building up to in the telephone interview.

'Oh yes, gosh, it was awful!' said Celestia, momentarily distracted from the thought of Water Detroit. 'Of course I wasn't born but yes, of course it was talked about. My aunt and uncle really really wanted them to get married. Cousin Oliver had been going out with an awful slut before.'

'Slut?' purred Lindy-Jane encouragingly. 'Surely not?'

'Oh, yes, he found her at an escort agency. Some prank he got up to in his last year at Eton.'

'Oh, no, I don't believe it. He'd never do a thing like go to an escort agency.'

'Oh yes he would, and did. It stuck in my mind because it posed as a modelling agency and you know my grandmother was a model. . . .'

'And your mother, of course. . . .'

'In a manner of speaking. Yes, Granny told me all about it. She was outraged that the place called itself a modelling agency, said it gave the modelling business a bad name.'

'Quite right. You don't happen to remember the name, by any chance?'

'You bet. I remember it because it was the name of my best friend at boarding-school. Cecile. We used to argue about which was the most exotic name, Celestia or Cecile. That was it: the Cecile Agency.'

When she got out of the bath Lindy-Jane hugged her towelling robe around her and flipped through the phone book. There it was: The Cecile Modelling Agency, with an address in Paddington.

She made a note to ring them first thing in the morning and called up the piece she was working on on her computer: her first story on Swan.

New York, 1994

For the first couple of months I woke up every morning and wondered what on earth I was doing in New York. I had seen enough violence on American TV shows and films to allow my imagination to run riot every night, imagining I was going to be murdered or raped at any second. The flight over had been bad enough. I had never been in an aeroplane in my life and the noise of the engines terrified me. Every morning I had to remind myself that the fact that I had won the Girl of the Year competition had enabled me to come to New York for free, something that just didn't happen to girls who grew up on the Portobello Court Estate, and then when Barbara Harper took me on it seemed to make sense to stay here and see if I could get work. But I missed Marcus all the time. Of course I missed Mum and little Tootie – Mum wrote that she was waking up in the night calling my name, she missed me so much – but I have to admit I missed Marcus most of all.

Before I left he'd sat me down and talked me through it like he always did. Marcus had been to America and he wanted me to understand the difference between racial prejudice in America and here, and how the roots are different over there, the guilt complexes are about what they have done to each other in the past whereas the guilt complexes here are not really about what is happening in England but how the English obtained their wealth from the colonies. The

234

notion of slavery is always going to be lurking somewhere in the Afro-American subconscious. In England it's predominantly in the inner cities where you'll find racism, and even then how often do you find black people standing in front of a line of police with machine guns, saying, 'We're going to do what we want to do' while they're being shot at? There are exceptions, but in England most of the time people will be nice to your face and smile although they probably do say 'black bastards, I wish they'd go back to where they came from' behind your back. But in America, Marcus warned me, the level of prejudice and the way it's acted out is much more blatant, more upfront and in your face. In history terms it's like only yesterday you were not allowed to enter certain places if you were black, it's still in everybody's memory.

Personally I prefer the American way. It's less hypocritical. It was a shock to find just how much colour was an issue, especially in the area of modelling. Barbara sent me out on at least ten castings a day. First of all I had to get acquainted with the city and work out the cross-streets and the buses and subway system. Sometimes I would walk thirty blocks in the rain to save a cab fare and then I'd walk in and show my book to someone who didn't even look up at my face. All the time I heard the phrase 'You're too strong for us', meaning you're too dark, too African looking. It's in my nature to be polite and not to rock the boat but time and time again I wanted to shake them and say, 'Why is it if you can't see it in my book that you can't imagine it? Why do you have no vision? Why are you all blind when it comes to looking at black faces?'

Another black model showed me a reader's letter printed in *Glamour* magazine in 1968 in response to the first black model they had put on their cover: 'Black is ugly – when I want to look at black faces, I'll buy *Ebony*.' There were times

235

when I felt that not very much appeared to have changed. One guy at a casting actually said to me, 'You look like a monkey, your lips are so huge.' I called Barbara about him because she had told me to let her know about any kind of unpleasantness, and by the time she'd finished with him, I wondered if he would ever work again.

Then, when I did start to get bookings things still went wrong. It's not that I don't enjoy modelling. I love it when I can get the work. It's not unlike when me and Tootie were kids, dressing up in Mum's clothes and prancing about the flat making everybody laugh. But it amazed me to discover that there are so many basic facts people who've been working in the fashion business for years don't know about when it comes to working with black models. There are probably forty shades of black skin and the make-up artists rarely seemed to understand that. A white base made me look too grey in my first pictures. From then on I took my own Naomi Simms base with me. Then I was frequently booked for shoots for no money in return for a credit in the magazines. This meant tearsheets for my book, so Barbara encouraged me to do it but inevitably the pictures never appeared in the magazines when they hit the stands. Another time at a shoot a photographer's assistant tried to spike my drink with drugs and I flipped out. I was so frightened during the whole shoot that when the pictures did appear I looked terrible in them, really uncomfortable.

Then came my first cover try. But even that never made it into the magazine because they had a feature in the same issue about a black sports celebrity and they felt that if they had a black girl on the cover it would make the magazine too black. Can you believe it? Have you ever heard of a magazine being too white? It's incredible but until I came to America the colour issue was never really a problem with me, yet each new day in New York brought it home to me more and more. For example, I couldn't get over the way they assumed Marcus was black without even asking.

All I could do was go home each night and pray to God for him to help me get a break. I'd curl up in front of the TV and write letters to Marcus or get out my sketch pad and work on my designs. I was getting terrific inspiration out on the streets of New York. On Sundays I went to dinner at Barbara's house along with other young girls from out of town. And then on Monday morning I'd crawl out of bed and begin the rounds of go-sees all over again.

There was something that was troubling me above all else and it had nothing to do with modelling. Mum hadn't mentioned it in her letters, but then her letters were all of four lines long, printed carefully like a child's.

DEAR AMY,
 WELL, HOW ARE YOU KEEPING? WE MISS YOU.
TOOTIE MADE A CAKE YESTERDAY. WELL, I
BETTER CLOSE NOW. LOVE
                                                    MUM

These were the first letters I had ever had from Mum. I had never realised she couldn't really write. But Marcus's letters went on for pages and pages. He was at college doing a business management course. He wanted to become a photographic agent – Joe would be one of his first clients – but instead of going straight to an agency and asking to be a runner or to be taken on for work experience, he wanted to learn the business side of things properly.

But his last few letters had been mostly about Leroy. It was stupid, but I had missed Leroy's arrival home by a fortnight. I hadn't seen my big brother for so many years. He was nearly nineteen. Marcus wrote that Leroy had come home a real Jamaican with dreads, the whole bit. He was out every night, he never stayed in with Mum and he had fast become part of the Grove gang. Marcus had only discovered this when he'd witnessed a fight at Ladbroke Grove tube station between the Grove boys and the Hackney boys. A knife was pulled. A boy was stabbed. It didn't stop there. Marcus suspected that Leroy was now hanging out with an even worse crowd: Yardies he'd known in Jamaica who were now over in London, dealing crack. He'd become an MC in a club notorious for its Yardie clientele.

I remembered my dream about Leroy being the Devil.

'Don't tell Mum,' I wrote to Marcus, although I couldn't help thinking she must have some idea. 'Shall I come home?' I asked at the end of each letter, but Marcus always said no, I should stay out here however much we missed each other, until I'd made some kind of breakthrough.

I felt bad because Marcus was being upfront with me about Leroy but I couldn't bring myself to tell him that I was having a tough time of it in New York. A couple of times I was so broke I didn't turn up at castings Barbara had fixed up for me because I literally did not have the money to pay for the bus or the subway fare to get there. When she called to bawl me out for not showing I had to tell her the truth. I hated to do it. I had my pride. From then on she insisted on giving me an advance from the agency to cover travelling expenses. As with many models, the agency became a kind of bank, making loans to me. I could pay it back when I started earning regularly.

But when would that be?

The agency had already advanced money to help pay my rent. My only regular income seemed to be from babysitting for the couple across the hall. Elaine and Jordan Franklin were, as Barbara described them to me, yuppies left over from the 1980s. He was a lawyer or a broker or something on Wall Street and she was a beauty editor on a magazine. He went out of his way to be politically correct. She couldn't give a damn. The kid, Katy, was five years old and a spoiled little brat but I liked her because she had cute little pigtails that reminded me of Tootie. She had a nanny who picked her up from nursery school, brought her home, fed her, bathed her and put her to bed. Then, if Jordan and Elaine were going out for the evening, I took over.

I had never been inside such a fancy home. It was called a duplex, I learned. The bedroom was fit for a princess, with a canopy above the bed and draped curtains coming down either side and loads of pretty little pillows scattered about. The bathroom had mirrored walls and an extra toilet, which Katy had to explain to me was 'not a toilet, silly, it's where you wash your pussy after you make babies'.

The first time I sat with Katy, Jordan and Elaine didn't come home till two in the morning and I had a casting at 8.30.

'Fucking black cab driver had no idea where to go, started taking us to New Jersey' – this was Elaine's way of apologising.

'Afro-American cab driver,' said Jordan.

'He was black, for Chrissakes, Jordan and he wasn't Afro. He was Haitian. He wasn't Korean or Chinese or Asian. He was black, like Amy.'

Jordan winced. 'Sorry, Amy.'

'That's OK,' I said. Actually it was fine with me. Elaine's attitude was perfectly healthy. Some black people she liked a lot, some she didn't, same as with the white people she knew. But Jordan wasn't about to let it go.

'If he'd been a white cab driver you would just have said "fucking cab driver".'

'I might have said "fucking Irish cab driver" or "fucking Jewish cab driver", I just like to be specific, Jordan. Why do you have a problem with that?'

She always teased poor Jordan like this and I couldn't help giggling, like when I first came down to meet them and she offered me coffee and asked me how I took it and I told her black and she asked Jordan to 'go make Amy a coffee of colour, would you, dear?' She was quite open about why she couldn't help me get any editorial work with her magazine.

'There's a policy, sweetheart, no black stories. They don't come out and actually say so, of course, but the word filters through somehow. See, I'm *a* beauty editor, not *the* beauty editor. When I get to the top job things will change – only if I see a black girl I like, of course.'

That was what I liked about Elaine. She wasn't into policies, but then again she wasn't into hiring a black person unless they were what she wanted.

It was comforting knowing the Franklins were such close neighbours. I was having terrible nightmares, always about fire. Elaine gave me a book she had about the interpretation of dreams and I looked up fire.

'An out of control blaze indicates that you should learn
to control that fiery temper, while kindling a fire may
mean you're about to seduce – or be seduced. . . .'

Well, I didn't have a fiery temper (although maybe I was suppressing anger at the New York fashion industry's attitude to black models) and Marcus was far away, so there was no chance of seduction.

Yet I knew full well how often my dreams came true.

I suppose I broke my resolve and said yes to Eddie Ross one

night because I was feeling so lonely and homesick and besides, I was so broke I could only afford to eat one meal a day and the offer of dinner in a restaurant was tempting. He'd invited me every week since I'd first bumped into him on the steps of our building, and I'd said no, thank you, every time. I was too young for him. I was just seventeen years old. What did he want with a kid like me? I guess I didn't realise that because I always kept myself looking good for my go-sees – and that was the only time he ever saw me, when I was coming in or out of the building – maybe I looked older, I don't know.

As it turned out, we didn't go to a restaurant. He'd ordered take-out and laid it out on the coffee table along with a bottle of wine, and candles.

'There's wings and ribs and all kinds of stuff. Just sit down and enjoy. Glass of wine?'

'I'll have a Diet Coke, please.' He looked disappointed.

'Baby, if we going to party you need to relax.'

'Diet Coke's fine. It's what I always drink.'

'OK, OK. Coming right up. Now, how come I ain't seen you on the cover of *Vogue* yet?'

'You're only ever going to see Naomi Campbell on the cover of *Vogue* and maybe then only once in a blue moon.'

'OK, I get you, so how come I ain't seen you on the cover of *Essence* or *Vibe*?'

As it happened I did have a job coming up with *Vibe*. Andrew Dushunmu, a stylist from Peckham in south London working in New York and Paris, and Geoffroy de Boismenu, a photographer, really liked my look and wanted to use me for the Xuly-Bët collection of the African-born Lamine Kouyaté. Barbara was always going on about how there just weren't enough people of colour working as stylists, photographers, make-up artists, hairdressers, location scouts – people on the

241

ground, foot soldiers who could influence thinking. The fact that Andrew had seen me and liked me was a big plus for me, she said.

I told Eddie about the job coming up and explained how hard it was for a young black girl.

'Well, of course, what did you expect? But let me ask you something. Why don't you get a weave? Nice long silky tresses 'stead of that short hair? That's what they'd like, white folks. You gotta look how they want, how they used to.'

'Because this is the way I wear my hair. If they want me to look different in the pictures, they can put the weave on or the extensions for the picture. Next you'll be asking me why don't I dye my skin lighter like *they* like.'

He laughed. 'Damn, baby, you're funny. C'mon over here and sit by me.'

I didn't move, so he did. Suddenly he was right there on the settee beside me, his arm around my shoulder and down inside my blouse, feeling my breast, pushing his tongue into my ear.

'Damn, baby, you're good. I've been thinking about you ever since you first arrived. Turn around a little so I can press up against you.'

I struggled to break free but his grip was strong. His bulbous lips fastened on mine and I could hear him breathing hard. He grasped my hand and put it between his legs and I could feel something hard and throbbing through his jeans.

'Feel me, baby, unzip me. Take me out.'

I knew what he had in there but because I wanted to stay a virgin until I was married, Marcus and I had never gone in for this sort of thing. Whenever Marcus became too excited, I left him until he calmed down. I wriggled out of Eddie's grasp.

'It's not for me to tell you what you should do but I think fornication is wrong,' I said.

He looked at me like I was completely crazy.

'You mean this AIDS thing?'

'Not only that. I just don't, that's all.'

'You mean you're a virgin?'

I nodded.

'Sister, you do not know what you are missing.'

'Oh, I know it's good but I can wait, that's all.'

'Until when? Doomsday?'

'Until I'm married.'

'You really mean it, don't you? What would happen if I led you into temptation?' He ran his hand up the inside of my leg.

'I'd scream the place down.'

He let go immediately. 'They have this date rape shit over in England?'

'I don't know what you mean.'

'Well, just don't go telling anyone I tried getting anywhere with you. I stopped, right? You said no and I stopped.'

I didn't know what he was talking about. At least I'd had some good food but now I wanted to get out of there. I had realised what my nightmares about fires were all about – being seduced.

But I was wrong.

Katy wouldn't go to sleep. She'd listened to four of her bedtime story tapes in the cassette player by her bed and still she was wide-eyed and demanding attention.

'Tell me 'bout Tootie, tell me 'bout Tootie!' she demanded. She loved to hear stories about my little sister. I had shown her a picture of Tootie and she had amazed me by saying, 'She looks just like me.'

The truth is she was right only I hadn't seen it because – well, because Katy was a white kid and it had never occurred to me that a white kid could look like a black kid. Just goes to show it works both ways.

She went off to sleep finally and I went into the kitchen to fix myself some supper. This was another bonus about babysitting. I knew I'd always get a meal. Also Barbara had told me to ask for double the rate if they came in after midnight.

'You need it. They can afford it. Do it,' she said firmly. Since Elaine could party all night if Jordan would let her I was doing pretty nicely out of the Franklins (providing I didn't have an early photo call the next morning). I knew they'd be in really late so I stretched out on the couch and dozed off.

They said later that the fire must have broken out about one in the morning. It started in my apartment – no one knows how – and if I had been there I might well have been suffocated by the smoke. All anyone knows is that it moved really fast, sweeping across the hall to the Franklins'. I awoke to the smell of scorched plastic and the smoke pouring out of the kitchen. My first thought was that I had left something on the stove while I was cooking my supper but then I saw the smoke pouring under the door of the burning hall.

Katy!

Her room was right by the hall. I dashed to the bathroom, drenched a towel in water and held it to my face as I ran into her room. At first I thought she was already dead, but I picked her up in any case and carried her limp body to her parents' room. I laid her on the ground and tried to open the window.

It was stuck fast. I picked up a chair and hurled it through the glass. My arms were cut as I lifted Katy out on to the fire escape and ran down it with her in my arms. A crowd had already gathered below and someone had called the fire brigade. There were cheers as I neared the ground and wolf whistles. The wolf whistles might have been for Eddie Ross, who was ahead of me with a buxom blonde, both of them completely naked.

It was just one of those fickle fingers of fate, or whatever they call it. God had finally heard my prayers and had answered them by sending a fire.

The press were waiting for us. Katy was not dead and I had saved her life. Before we were bundled into an ambulance they asked me who I was and what I did.

'Amy La Mar. I'm a model.'

I'll never know what made me add, almost as an afterthought, 'with Barbara Harper Management', but I did and they printed it in the paper the next morning – ENGLISH MODEL SAVES CHILD FROM BURNING BUILDING – alongside an unbelievably striking picture of me. The photographer had caught the triumphant look in my face when I looked up at them as I reached the last step of the fire escape. But what really came across was the look of innocence in my un-made-up face. It was natural black beauty and I looked stunning. Plus I was in black and white, which helped.

Suddenly I was a heroine. Barbara was besieged by calls about me. My own apartment was destroyed and so I moved in with her. Within days someone had come up with a new slant on the fire escape fashion story and I was booked as the only model. My *Vibe* shoot earned me a cover, and within two months I was on the cover of a major fashion magazine. I was invited to go to Paris to model there for Xuly Bet but meanwhile there were the castings for the New York shows.

My breakthrough had come at last.

New York/Lake Como, 1994

I loved shooting at Fabrizio Ferri's Industria, the photo studio complex on Washington Street, because it always seemed to me to be a little piece of Italy just a couple of blocks in from the West Side Highway.

In summer it was a real gathering place with models, stylists, photographers, fashion editors standing around outside eating and drinking. This was the first time I had worked there in winter. We'd had nearly two feet of snow and roads were closed all over New York. Cars were abandoned, buried under snow, and everyone was worrying that if there was a freeze, the snow would turn to ice and they'd never be able to get the vehicles out until the thaw. The city's sanitation department was in the process of clearing the roads with snow ploughs chugging about the place, and my cab took nearly an hour to get from East 76th Street all the way down to Industria between Jane and West 12th Street. I was going to be late.

Once we arrived I then had to walk half a block before I could find a place where a gap had been cleared through the snow to the sidewalk. It was a fine crisp freezing cold morning with brilliant sunshine and a clear blue sky. Down here on Washington it was as if I were a million miles removed from uptown New York. I was in the middle of the meat-packing district and slipping on the ice were men carrying giant carcasses of beef, fighting their way through the snow alongside

246

leggy models making their way into Industria. You never saw anything like that where I lived on Madison Avenue.

I tore up the cement ramp to Studio 5 (there are eight in all) and apologised profusely before going into make-up. I was doing a *Vogue* silk kimono-style evening wear story for which my slightly Japanese look had been an obvious choice. We worked hard all morning and then wandered down to Braque for lunch. Braque is quite wonderful. It's the café to the right of the entrance to Industria which handles all the catering for the shoots. To an outsider it might not appear to be anything special. Indeed, it was the fact that it was so unpretentious that made me like it so much. It had an adobe feel: yellow brick walls on which were hung black-and-white photographs of aeroplanes, guitars, trees and pampas, and an orange ceiling. There was a bar and along the opposite wall there was a banquette with just two big tables, one wooden and a marble one on a cast-iron stand. A Taittinger champagne bucket was stuck in a corner left over from some night-time rave, for Industria was used for parties by the cognoscenti – Eddie Murphy, Ralph Lauren, Madonna, Leo Castelli, people like that. Models wandered in and out from shoots in their curlers and someone might come running to tell the woman chef that 'Studio 2 is coming down' and the big wooden table would be hastily laid and there would be a lot of activity in the kitchen at the end of the café. Soon everyone working on the shoot would be tucking into soup, salad, home-made pizza and pasta and white truffles made the night before by Karen, the overall manager of the studio who just felt like doing some cooking.

There was a new guy behind the bar. I sat on one of the bar stools and ordered an espresso. He smiled at me as he handed it to me.

'You're new here?'

He nodded. 'Name's Mayo.'

I detected an English accent. 'You're English? Do you have a first name?'

'That's it. It's a nickname. Like Swan.'

'But why Mayo?'

'Because he makes such great mayonnaise. Better than Hellmann's,' shouted someone.

We chatted for a while. I liked him. He was just a kid who wanted to get into fashion like they all did. He seemed to know quite a bit about modelling from his time spent chatting to the girls when they came down from the shoots, but he didn't seem to have expertise in any other area. Except maybe cooking. If he made sensational mayonnaise then maybe he was an ace cook. For some time now I had been contemplating indulging in the luxury of hiring someone to come into my apartment at the Carlyle and cook for me. Of course, I could always order Room Service whenever I wanted and sometimes I even enjoyed pottering in the kitchen myself, but I had grown up in a household with a cook. I was spoiled. I liked the notion of someone preparing tasty home-cooked meals and leaving them ready for me to eat when I came home exhausted from a day's work. The reason I loved Industria was because of the delicious comforting food I could run down and eat in Braque.

I knew if I didn't take it up with him there and then, I'd never get around to it. I slipped away and asked the chef if he ever cooked for her.

'He's incredible! He cooks it all at home. He lives with his parents right across the street in the Westbeth apartment building and he brings it over. Here, you can taste some of the quiches he made for today.'

They were out of this world. I decided this man could change my life. I went back to the bar and put it to Mayo that he could moonlight as my private cook. He looked completely taken aback and said he'd have to think about it and could he call me? I said, 'Sure, but make it soon', and went back to work.

The next day I realised why my suggestion had taken him so much by surprise. The phone rang and a woman's soft Irish/American voice said, 'Me name's Bridie Reilly. Me son Mayo asked me to call you. We have a bit of a confession to make but I beg you not to tell anyone else what I'm about to tell you. Mayo can't cook. He can't even boil an egg, as far as I know. I'm the cook. He takes the food I've prepared over the road to Braque and they think he's cooked it. It was a way of getting him a job. Where's the harm? But, y'know, I could come and cook for you if you'd like?'

I liked.

Bridie was a gem. And, of course, the Irish doormen downstairs at the Carlyle took to her immediately. There was always quite a long pause between the moment when they rang to say she was on her way up and her actual arrival. I imagined the New York Irish mafia gossip going on in the lobby or at the back entrance, or wherever they let her in. She made soda bread, which I hadn't had in years. She made delicious nourishing vegetable soups. She made extraordinarily tasty vegetarian dishes. Her cooking was very health conscious and she understood that while I adored food I had to watch my weight. We spent a couple of immensely pleasurable hours discussing all the delicious things she would make while I was away on trips, and store in the freezer for my return.

For I was getting ready to take off again – Italy, London, Italy again, Paris, the Caribbean and back to New York for the shows at the end of March. A successful model was always on the move. Bridie tut-tutted about it all the time.

'How you're going to find yourself a good man to look after

you if you're always running round the world like this I don't know.'

How indeed? Hanging on to boyfriends was always one of the challenges of a model's life. It was either a question of outgrowing the boy next door, who had been your sweetheart before you became a model, because he was no longer part of your world; or, if you found someone in your new world, the chances were that he was jealous because you were earning more than he was. Then you were always away somewhere and the constant separation often ruined the relationship.

If only we had known, as Bridie bustled about in my tiny kitchen, that when I came back from my trips I would be sharing her meals with the new man in my life.

Charley had been on at me for months to do some TV and he'd finally persuaded me to do the *Today* show. I was leaving for Italy at the end of the week for a brief vacation at his mother's holiday villa on Lake Como before the shows started and he caught me in a weak moment when I was in a state of excitement at the thought of some time off and I went and said something reckless like, 'Fine, fine, set it up this week before I go.'

I shunned publicity like the plague, especially TV, but Charley looked after me very well and every now and then I felt obliged to give him a break and let him wheel me out on show. I had to get up at some unearthly hour to go to the studio for the interview but it wasn't as if I'd never had to do that before. Early calls were part and parcel of a model's daily life. I didn't like the guy who interviewed me. It was instinctive. He was probably a household name in America but I never watched morning television so he was a complete stranger to me. His face was friendly enough but some sixth sense told me not to trust him.

I'll never know what made me do what I did next. Maybe it was because I was in a frivolous mood, looking forward to my holiday. He had a list of questions in his hand and just as we were about to go on air I reached over and plucked it away from him. For a split second he looked devastated but he recovered his composure in time to introduce me to the viewers as 'Swan, the most famous supermodel in the world – but how long can she retain her position?' So that was how he was going to play it. Charley might have warned me.

I handled it pretty well, taking the 'there are so many wonderful young girls coming up and so many talented new designers and clients throughout the world, there's plenty of room for all of us' line. Had the man got wind of the fact that I was planning to relinquish the SWAN contract? He was obviously building up to something, but surely Charley wouldn't have said anything and he was the only one who knew what was on my mind. The interview dragged on with predictable questions like was I looking forward to doing the collections? and I realised that without his precious list he was ad-libbing desperately. No mention of SWAN. It was almost nine o'clock. The show was drawing to a close. I sank back on the sofa, lulled into a false sense of security, totally unprepared for his final question.

'It must be terribly hard to maintain such a high-profile career following the tragedies that have occurred in your life?'

I stared at him, alarm bells clanging in my head.

'What tragedies?'

'The tragedies that hit your family. The death of your sister in a car accident. The disappearance of your brother following the death of a woman in your family home in London. Do you think you will ever see your brother again, Swan?'

My alabaster skin must have blanched for the first time in my life. I was dumb, pleading, tears welling up in my eyes. I shifted in my chair, knowing that the camera was undoubtedly moving in for a close-up, and he must have realised I was on the point of getting up and leaving the studio.

'Swan, you will find him. I know you will. Thank you for

being with us this morning. That's it for *Today*. The news and weather are upcoming on the hour. . . .'

He waited till we were off the air before saying, 'I guess you don't know what's happened. There was a story last night in a London evening paper and the New York press picked it up and are running with it this morning. We were pre-warned. It was too good an opportunity to miss. Here, take a look. This is the British paper where the story appeared last night.'

I looked at the front page of the *Standard*.

SWAN'S FAMILY IN SUPERSCANDAL, read the headline. I looked for the byline.

Who on earth, I wondered, was Lindy-Jane Johnson?

I crawled into bed once I arrived back at the Carlyle and spent the morning staring at the papers spread out before me. It was a cut-and-paste job, telling me nothing I didn't already know and Lindy-Jane Johnson, whoever she was, had obviously had herself a ball in some clippings library and regurgitated all the stories the English press had run at the time. But why had she done it now? Did she know more than she implied in her piece?

I called my mother as soon as it was a reasonable hour in London. She sounded calm enough, which was more than could be said for my father, apparently.

'He's locked himself away. He wouldn't come down to dinner last night and we haven't seen him at all today. He's mortified. The truth is he's been like this for some time. I don't want to worry you, darling, but I fear this horrible newspaper story has tipped him over the edge. If only we had some news of Harry. But more important, how beastly it must be for you. Are they hounding you in New York? Do you want to come over and hide in Wiltshire?'

There was nothing I would have liked better but it would be madness. The last thing I wanted to do was to lead the press anywhere near my parents. It was so sad. There was Harry living just down the lane, and they had no idea. As soon as I had been to Milan I would go on to London and make some kind of progress with Harry. We had to do something to put our parents out of their misery.

'Mummy, that's really sweet of you but I'm actually leaving tomorrow to go and stay with Laura Lobianco, my New York agent's mother. She's got this divine villa on Lake Como. It'll be peaceful and utterly private. Has Granny seen the newspapers?'

'No. It's not really a problem unless she speaks to someone in London. It was only in the *Standard* last night and the sleaze tabloids this morning, which of course she doesn't get. Nor do we, I hasten to add, but I drove into Salisbury this morning and sneaked a look at a few copies. Quite disgusting, but God knows we've been through it all before and survived. Are you coming to London soon?'

I held my breath for a second. For years I had felt suffocated by my parents' desperate need to see me but now I wanted to spend time with them again, yet at the same time didn't know if I could face the strain of keeping Harry's proximity a secret.

'Yes, Mummy, I expect I'll come on after Italy. I'll call you then. Tell Daddy I love him. You too. 'Bye now.'

I had to hang up. I could feel the tears welling up inside me. I walked into my closet and reached up to the shelf above my clothes for my disguise. It was just a silk headscarf and dark glasses, but somehow I felt safer going out looking as anonymous as possible. It had come as a shock to me when I had begun to be stopped on the street. I had never seen myself as a celebrity but that was what I had become. I had to get out now. My apartment felt claustrophobic despite the breathtaking view over the city.

Downstairs in the lobby I was stopped by Michael, my absolute favourite of the Carlyle's Irish doormen.

'Don't think you ought to go out the front, Miss Swan,' he said, taking my elbow and turning me right around, 'they're waiting for you. Let's slip you out the back.'

Mummy had been right. The beastly press hounds were baying for blood already. I saw them as I slipped across 76th Street at Madison. I refused to let them force me to alter my routine. I crossed Madison as I always did to go and look in Givenchy's window. They always compared me to Audrey Hepburn's Givenchy-clad Holly Golightly in the film of *Breakfast at Tiffany's*, and I suppose I did sort of have something of her dark-haired elfin look.

After Givenchy I crossed back to the south side of Madison, nipped past the Whitney and scuttled into the sanctuary of Books & Co., my favourite bookstore, with the intention of finding something to read on holiday. I headed for the children's section at the back with the little painted wooden rocking chair. Every time I saw it I wondered if I would ever have any children of my own. I liked the back of the store, with all the photographs of the writers who had given readings there. I barely knew any of them unless they actually had a book they had written in their hand to identify them. I recognised Norman Mailer, of course, and I thought the one with the cracked glass was of Fran Liebowitz but other than that, I was lost.

I pushed one of the ladders idly along the shelves, barely aware of what I was doing. There was a slightly different atmosphere and I couldn't quite put my finger on it. Then it dawned on me. The place was empty. And yet it wasn't. There might not be anybody downstairs but there appeared to be some kind of commotion upstairs. Of course! A reading was in progress. It was a welcome distraction. To be honest, I didn't really like readings. I found them pretentious and superfluous. I liked to read the book myself, not have it read to me as if I were a child. Poetry maybe, but nothing else. Still, it would amuse me to go up and see who it was. The reader's voice was familiar as I reached the top of the stairs and turned. The place was packed and I could only see his head and shoulders at the lectern over the crowd.

His grey head. It was Rory Stirling.

I dropped my bag in surprise and as I stooped to pick it up the silk scarf slithered from my head. Everyone turned to see who was making the terrible clattering. Rory Stirling paused for breath, looked up and straight at me.

I turned and ran down the stairs.

That afternoon as I was packing for Italy Michael rang up from the lobby to say a package had been delivered for me from Books & Co.

It was a small book. I believe they call the format large crown. It was beautifully produced, thick pages almost like blotting paper with jagged edges. It was a novel. The title was *Coming Out Fighting*, the subtitle: *The Memoirs of a Sensual Delinquent*. By Rory Stirling. Inside was a card.

He had a strong, flowing hand and he used a fountain pen with black ink. It looked rather like something out of the last century.

'I am asking Books & Co. to deliver this to you as I do not have your address. Why did you rush off? Is my reading so terrible? Can I buy you dinner? Please call me. Rory.'

I walked around the room staring at his number for so long that by the time I finally came to dial it I had memorised it.

'It's me, Swan,' I said when he answered, then realised that I'd called myself Lavinia when I'd last seen him.

'I'm so glad you called. Why did you rush off like that?'

'I might ask you the same question. I turned around at Norah Nicholson's that night we were there and you had disappeared.'

He sighed down the line. 'I'm no good at those things. I don't know why I went at all and I only stayed as long as I did because I met you. When I saw that your attention was going to be focused elsewhere, I cut out. It was rude, I know. I wrote Norah a very apologetic note the next day and I felt so guilty I couldn't even bring myself to ask her for your number. But listen, I saw the papers this morning. You must be feeling terrible.'

'It's pretty awful, but my biggest worry at the moment is that the press are downstairs in the lobby and I doubt they'll go away. I'm leaving for Italy tomorrow so it's just a question of slipping past them and out to the airport without them knowing I'm leaving the country.'

'Maybe I can help.'

'How?'

'Drive you to the airport. I have a Cherokee jeep. It's pretty beat up. It's not exactly the stretch limo they'd be expecting you to leave in. What time's your plane and where do you live?'

He made it all so easy for me. I alerted Michael that Rory was coming and he was sent up as soon as he arrived. When I opened the door to him it was the most natural thing in the world that we should embrace and kiss, and he kept his arm around me as I showed him the apartment. He left me only to place both hands on my telescope and turn it in another direction.

'Is there any way we can fix it so it stays exactly in this position at all times?'

'Why would we want to do that?'

257

'Because if you look through here you can see my window in the Gainsborough Building on Central Park South. If I were there you'd be able to see me. You could call me and I could go to the window and you could look through your telescope and see me blowing you a kiss.'

He was like a little boy but he was fun, and when it was necessary he took charge of me.

'Now call the bellman and get him to take down your bags. Michael's got the Cherokee into the garage below the hotel.'

It was like a real movie getaway. I lay along the front seat of the jeep with my head resting in his lap as he revved up and charged up the ramp and was off down the street before anyone had noticed. I didn't sit up until we were halfway over the Triborough Bridge and that was only because I love to look at the breathtaking long-distance view of the Manhattan skyline you get from it. I have this love-hate relationship with New York. I am English to the core but I love living in New York. My job takes me away enough for me to never get tired of the place, and each time I cross the Triborough I wonder if I will actually get to come back. Manhattan always looks so surreal, it's like I look back at it and think: do I really live there?

'Writers are usually pretty nosy people,' Rory told me once we were over the bridge. 'Put your headscarf on, someone might recognise you from a passing car. Now, why didn't you tell me who you were when we first met?'

'I didn't think you'd be interested.'

'Listen, I was interested enough to come to the dinner in the first place. I wanted to take a look at you close up.'

'You mean you knew who I was all along?'

'Of course I did. Norah asked me to meet you. She'd been to my apartment and seen all those tearsheets from magazines

258

I have of you plastered all over the wall of my study. She's no fool. She knew you were in town and—'

'She set me up? Norah? The scheming old bat! She told me she was asking you to meet Celestia.'

'Well, of course she did, otherwise you wouldn't have come. She told me how reclusive you were. It made you all the more attractive to me.'

It was a clever wheeze, coming on to me in the confined space of his jeep where there was no way we could take it further and I was about to get on a plane and leave him far behind.

'You were saying writers are curious people,' I said to change the subject.

'I was wondering what really happened with your family – that's if you want to tell me about it?'

It was such a release to talk about it. For years and years it was something I could only discuss spasmodically with members of my family. For years I had had to keep it bottled up inside me and I suddenly realised as I was talking to him that I had never let anyone in before, I had subconsciously kept people at bay in case they got too close to me and I let something slip.

For years I had been so, so lonely without ever really knowing it.

He was a great listener. Occasionally he reached out and patted my hand lying on the seat beside him, to indicate his sympathy. I told him everything, even where Harry was hiding and how I was going to be seeing him in England soon.

'You're going on to England from Italy? I have to be there week after next. My book's coming out there too and they want me for publicity.'

I gave him Grace Brown's name and number and told him

259

he could find out from her when I would be coming in from Milan.

'So can I call you while you're in Italy? Can you give me a number?'

Suddenly I went into panic. I barely knew this man. I had met him precisely twice. I didn't know anyone who knew him except Norah. He could have all kinds of reasons for driving me to the airport and pumping me with questions. He might be a journalist as well as a novelist, he might have set the whole thing up with a very different agenda in mind. . . .

'I think I need a little breathing space. Can you understand that?'

'Of course. You have my number in New York so you know where to find me if you want to.' He looked genuinely disappointed.

He kissed me at the gate, pressed his lips hard against mine, bruising them.

'I know you're a model and I should take care of your skin but you aren't working for a week and I wanted to do that.'

As the plane took off I sat in my window seat sipping my champagne and realised I had wanted it too, and when I reached Italy the first thing I did was to call Norah and ask her about him. It took a while to steer her away from the subject of the newspaper stories but finally I managed it.

'Rory Stirling? My dear child, what are you saying? I've known him since he was a child. He's perfectly adorable. The worst you can say about him is that he's a complete loner. Never goes out. Disgustingly anti-social. A hostess's nightmare. But the truth is, I've had him in mind for you for months but I knew if I ever so much as hinted to either of you you'd both run a mile. I'm simply delighted I've finally got you together. It's a marriage made in heaven.'

It was just an expression, something people said all the time about all kinds of relationship.

But it started me thinking.

Laura Lobianco's villa on Lake Como is to die for. Her family has owned a textile company in Como for decades and she spent her childhood holidays at the Villa Luini. Milan owes a good deal to Como for its development into one of the fashion centres of the world. The silk factories of Como and the accompanying fabric knowledge were an integral factor in the success of the ready-to-wear designers. Both Armani and Versace worked closely with Laura's family in interpreting their ideas into beautiful fabric but, more importantly, they backed the new designers financially at the start of their careers and in the competitive world of ready-to-wear fashion this support gave them a much-needed edge against the French.

Laura also backed me right from the start of my career. Charley brought me to meet her here at the Villa Luini soon after he had taken me on and I have always suspected that he relies heavily on his mamma's judgement of the girls he selects.

I have always loved the Italian lakes, the pines, the oaks and chestnuts on the steep wooded slopes coming down to the water, the stone houses linked together by old arched bridges, and the way the little boats in the harbours of the fishing villages rock alarmingly on the waves caused by the passing of a steamer. I love the literary heritage of the area. Virgil was nuts about the place and was it Longfellow who asked: 'Is there a land of such supreme and perfect beauty anywhere?'

I always arrive at the Villa Luini by speedboat. From the lake you can see the snow-capped Alps in the distance and palm trees along the shore. As we approach I always stand up to catch my first glimpse of the terracotta tiles on the roof before disembarking at a little lichen-covered landing dock below a pair of huge eighteenth-century wrought-iron gates hung between stone pillars bearing statues of lions just like the ones outside our old house in the Boltons. The key to the gates has been lost for years and you go around the pillars and walk through knee-high lavender and daisies up to the house: this too reminds me of walking through the fields right up to the house in Wiltshire. Approaching the villa you walk through a tunnel of cypresses, glimpsing landscaped gardens with balustraded terraces, lily ponds bordered by stone cherubs, hedges of azaleas and rhododendron bushes, box trees and yews on either side.

Laura's family house is seriously grand and proportioned like a Florentine palazzo. The walls are covered with delicate eighteenth-century frescoes. The grand salons on the ground floor are stiff with marble floors, ornate mirrors, consoles, crystal chandeliers and endless doors opening on to balconies with views to the lake. There is a small pergola overlooking the garden and the lake where we eat most of our meals, which is a little more relaxed, and I love the great big terracotta urns filled with pink geraniums. The *piano nobile* with Laura's bedroom and sitting room and the guest rooms is a completely different story. Here Laura has mixed and matched with modern Milanese and Italian Renaissance furniture, thrown loads of books, flowers, paintings and beautiful tapestry cushions all over the place, left the doors with the hand-painted panels, loaded up the logs in the fireplaces and suffused the rooms with soft warm lighting from elegant table lamps.

We holed up on the *piano nobile* in front of blazing fires to ward off the February cold. My first evening we ate supper on trays: piping hot minestrone alla Milanese followed by osso bucco, a salad, panettone for dessert and some delicious cheese, Gorgonzola, Mascarpone and Stracchino. We had barely made inroads into the osso bucco when I began to tell Laura about Rory Stirling. She let me talk for some time without interrupting, her elegant frame encased in a soft floor-length cashmere cardigan over a silk shirt and wide woollen pants. She had cut her almost white hair very short and her proud aquiline profile carved an impressive candlelit shadow on the wall behind her. Hers was a haughty beauty, strong, defiant, but I knew that her temperament was warm and romantic.

Suddenly she interrupted me.

'Tell me, do you believe in *il destino*?'

Did I believe in destiny? I nodded. Yes, after a fashion.

'You have to grab the moment. Is that how you say it? You know when you find the right man. No one else can tell you. You have to know it yourself, and you do. You know when you find him. He is like no one you have met before. Young girls think they are in love over and over again. At fifteen it begins, maybe even at twelve these days, who knows? But when you meet the right one you realise that all those times before you have been deceiving yourself. It sounds to me like you are lucky, Swan. Many women, they never meet him. They never experience passion. Or they marry one of the boys they think they are in love with and then they go and meet the right one and they divorce, making everyone unhappy. From the passion in your voice it seems your Stirling is the right man.'

264

'My Rory. Oh, God, what am I saying? He's not mine. I haven't even—'

'You haven't fucked him yet?' Laura laughed. 'Don't look so shocked. I am sixty years old but I still fuck my husband. It's very, very important. You have to fuck him, Swan. If it's no good with him in bed you must forget him. It won't last. You have to fuck him. My family never understood why I ran off with Charley's father but it's so simple. If I could have found a man from Milan or Como or Bergamo who fucked like he did, I would have stayed here. Charley's father, he was amazing and he still is. So his business in America is a little, how can I put it, connected? So I don't look too closely. He makes me happy, in bed, out of bed, it's all I ask. Find Signor Stirling and take him to bed. And Swan. . . .'

'Yes?'

'Call me and tell me how he is. Every last detail!'

'Are you coming back for the shows in Milan?' Laura asked me as we drove along the narrow road that connected all the lakeside villages. She had to ask me several times before I took in what she was saying. I was in a complete dream. The night before I had sat up until the small hours reading Rory's book, *Coming Out Fighting: The Memoirs of a Sensual Delinquent*. It was about a young boy in his late teens who had a strange passion for older women, not just one but several. Without being in the least bit cruel, somehow Rory had delivered a series of brilliant protrayals of a group of divorced, insecure yet still desirable women in their forties who were desperate for both sex and love. Rory's earthy young immigrant hero was able to provide both but what made the book wonderful was the marvellous descriptions of the different sensual education he received from each of the women. I couldn't stop wondering how autobiographical it was. Nor could I wait to see him again since if he was only half as sensual a lover as his hero, Rory Stirling was a treat in store! We were on our way to lunch at the house of a friend of Laura's, whose son had a house party of weekend guests up from Milan. Among the guests there were several models, a photographer or two and the usual crowd of young playboys who preyed on models in Milan, the sons of rich, well-connected families who might just as easily have made their money in olive oil or tomatoes as in the rag trade. The Porsches and Ferraris scattered around in front of the villa told their own story.

'I always do Armani,' I told Laura. 'Will you be coming to Milan for that?'

'Probably. I haven't been to his shows for a while but I think he'll always keep a place for me. I remember years ago he showed in New York and I was in town and I was sent a ticket and I walked in very late. There was no placement and all the seats were taken. Then a girl got up from a seat in the front row and gave it up to me. I was astonished, then I saw that a large part of the front row was occupied by the little girls who were sales assistants in the store and each time a special customer came in, up they jumped and relinquished their seat. They were human reserves. Isn't that sweet? Now, here we are. Let's hope it's halfway amusing. If not, we'll leave as soon as we can and go back to our books by the fire.'

I was left to fend for myself as Laura's friend whisked her away for a quiet lunch à deux in another room while I was ushered into a large rustic dining room. I nearly walked straight out again. An art director called Roberto Fabiani was there. There are many gays in our business and most of them are a girl's best friend. Not Roberto. I have always detested him, sensing him to be trouble. He was slimy, insinuating, gossipy, altogether a thoroughly nasty piece of work. Mercifully, as he came towards me, I was rescued by Suzy Davis, a wacky Texan girl I had worked with in New York.

'Swan, ah had no idea you'd be coming. Come and tell me what's happenin' in New York.'

Typical Suzy, far from listening to anything I might have to tell her, she dragged me over to sit beside her and proceeded to amuse me with scandalous gossip about everyone else in the room.

'See that girl over there? She's called Gigi Garcia. Comes from the wrong side of the South Beach tracks. You come across her in New York?'

I shook my head. The girl was a knockout of the sultry Latin variety. She oozed sex appeal from every pore and I imagined the camera must absolutely adore her. I wondered why I hadn't seen her pictures anywhere.

'Believe me, you don't need her. She's held up more shoots than Bonnie and Clyde held up banks plus from what ah heard, with her it's like she won't get into bed for less than $10,000 a day, not out of it. And see that kid beside her? Well, he's an assistant photographer and they say he slept with Roberto Fabiani to get a shoot of his own. He's cute, isn't he? Ah'd go for him myself but he already has a girlfriend, and I don't mean Roberto.'

'That girl Gigi?'

'No, an English kid, real pretty, red hair. The Italians are crazy about her. She's doing real well here. Beats me what she's doing with a weak jerk like Bobby Fox.'

'Is she here?' I liked the sound of this redhead and it would be nice to talk to someone English.

'No. She ain't. She was asked but ah heard she knows about Bobby and Roberto and when she found out Roberto was going to be here, she quit at the last moment. They says she's embarrassed by the whole thing.'

'Well, don't sound so surprised, Suzy. Wouldn't you be? No, on second thoughts, I suppose you'd lap it up in one gulp. So did this Bobby come up here with Roberto?'

'No. That's the wildest thing. He drove up with Gigi Garcia, and Gigi is his girlfriend's roommate.'

Throughout lunch I watched as Gigi Garcia became seriously drunk. There was something rather pitiful about her. It was as if she had no control and had some wanton desire to self-destruct yet at the same time she came across as an unhappy child. She was at once abusive and flirtatious with everyone she talked to. She was voracious, probably as much with sex as she was with food. I watched her shovelling forkloads of pasta into her mouth. She should watch it. She was no waif and I suspected she was already getting a little too plump for photographic comfort.

Over coffee she suddenly turned her attention on me.

'What makes you so special?'

Everyone was suddenly silent. I was, after all, a supermodel and this was a kid waiting for a break. I pretended not to have heard her. It seemed the kindest thing to do.

'I said: what makes you so special? You're with Etoile, right?'

'Yes.' I answered the second question, again ignoring the first.

'Me too. Did you ever, you know, make it with Charley?'

This was outrageous but she went on without even waiting for my answer.

'See, Charley's crazy about me. He's taking care of me. I'm his special protégée. He sent me here to Italy. He's gonna be waiting for me when I get back. Could be you're history, Miss High and Mighty Swan.'

I forced myself to remember that she was just a kid, probably very insecure. Laura and our hostess had just come in. Very soon I would be out of there. If I could just keep myself in check for five more minutes.

'Who's the old witch you came with, Swan?' Gigi's question was perfectly audible to everyone in the room.

I lost it.

'That, if you did but know it,' I hissed, 'is your precious Charley's mother.'

'Shit!' said Gigi. Realising she was in too deep to get out, she went on the defensive. To everyone's horror she lurched drunkenly up to Laura and said:

'Your little boy's in trouble. Know why? There's a little fourteen-year-old girl called Victoria Parrish who's expecting a baby, and I know a maid at a Miami hotel who saw her there with Charley. Looks like Charley fucked an underage cookie and you're going to be a grandma!'

That night we called Charley in New York.

'Of course, what you have to remember is he's his father's child as well as mine,' said Laura as we drove home from lunch. 'There could be some truth to her story. There's definitely something wrong in Charley's life right now. Every time I've spoken to him over the last couple of weeks he has sounded very down, very distracted. I'm not a complete ostrich, you know. His father was always in trouble when he was young and he has introduced Charley to some pretty shady people in his time. I know all about Charley's reputation with women. The trouble is, so does everybody else. Somebody may be using this woman as bait of some kind.'

'We're not talking about a woman here by the sound of things,' I pointed out.

'I appreciate that. But you know these days it's easy to make a mistake. When I was a girl we looked our age. Now a child of twelve can sometimes pass for twenty, and that's only a slight exaggeration. From what I have seen of the modelling world, they even encourage it. I have discussed it with Charley. I disapprove strongly and he just accuses me of being old-fashioned.'

Charley was evasive on the phone. Laura was right. He didn't sound himself. He admitted he could easily have been in Miami at the same time as the girl. Mrs Parrish had been back to see him again and brought her daughter with her. Charley conceded that Victoria Parrish was familiar but he couldn't recall ever having slept with her. She claimed he had done so in a Miami hotel and the dates she gave coincided with the time the maid Gigi had talked to had seen them.

'Charley, where did you pick up that girl, Gigi?' I asked when Laura handed me the phone.

'Again, in Miami. I barely remember it but she claims I saw her in a hotel room as I was walking down the corridor and told her to enter our beauty competitions when she was older. Then she wound up in New York and when I saw her in my office, I didn't even recognise her.'

'But Charley, that's obviously what happened with Victoria Parrish, only she probably didn't win any beauty competitions and now she's resentful. Is she pretty? Could she model later on?'

'I doubt it. She has pretty short legs. My guess is her parents yanked her back to New York and never let her out of their sight and this is some kind of rebellious stunt she's pulling to make me notice her. But it could get ugly. Etoile doesn't need this kind of scandal if the press get hold of it.'

'You mean, no parent would ever let you take on their daughter as a New Face?'

'You know, the saddest thing is there are some parents who probably still would even if it was true about Victoria. I've seen really ambitious mothers who'll go to extraordinary lengths.'

'Will you dump Gigi Garcia?'

'No. She might just make it if she ever gets her act together, if she gets a break of some sort. Get her to show you her book. Those pictures Marlon Warner took of her are pretty amazing. Her look has what it takes to stand out. It may happen. She's perfectly capable of destroying both her career and herself all on her own and I'm not going to make it easy for her by dumping her. She'll either self-destruct or we'll have a supermodel in the not too distant future inasmuch as you can be a supermodel without being a showgirl. That she's never going to be!'

But if Gigi Garcia wasn't ever going to make it on the catwalk, when I walked into Etoile Milan I saw a girl who had runway potential written all over her. She was a tall willowly redhead with fragile white skin, porcelain-coloured like mine but with a smattering of lightly dotted freckles. Her voice told me she was English and suddenly I knew who she was: Bobby Fox's girlfriend.

Carla confirmed this.

'Si, Tessa. A wonderful find. She has been working ever since she arrived, nearly every day.'

'But how did you find her, Carla?' I asked.

'They have this fantastic new booker in London called Angie. She found her. It's interesting. Grace called me and she warned me. She said: Angie is sending you a girl who is very shy with no confidence. We are in despair over her. She's coming with her boyfriend. It's the only way. With him she is confident. Do what you can. Then Angie called and she told me how to handle Tessa, how to be very gentle with her, how to encourage her all the time and she's right. Here is a beautiful girl who is working all the time but still she is not confident. It's better but we are not there yet.'

'I understand there was a scandal with the boyfriend. The usual problem with Roberto Fabiani.'

'Si, and now it is worse. For the first time Tessa confided to me this morning. She came home last night and she found her roommate, Gigi, in bed with Bobby. They had been away for the weekend together. They arrived back in Milan, they went to bed, Tessa walks in. Today Tessa says she wants to go home to London. What do I do?'

'Do you have her booked for any of the shows?'

'She's just starting to go on the castings this week. She has a few today but she wants to go home. This is her chance to be a showgirl and she wants to go home.'

'You know she'd be perfect for Armani,' I told Carla. 'Why don't I have a word with Giorgio, tell him to look out for her. Meanwhile you get her name on the list and send her off to the casting. What that girl needs is a massive boost to her ego. Just persuade her to have one more try here in Milan before she goes home.'

I stayed a night in Milan in order to have dinner with Marcello and Carla and discuss which of the shows I would come back and do, then I flew to London. It was London Fashion Week and I was booked to do the new young designers' shows. I always supported British fashion. But the shows weren't till the middle of the week. I had time to go down to Wiltshire and see Harry – and, if they would let me, visit my parents for the first time in ages.

But when I landed at Heathrow all the plans I'd been making on the plane flew straight out of my head: there waiting for me in Arrivals, standing beside my minder from Etoile, was Rory Stirling.

Milan, 1994

On her way to the Armani casting in his palazzo in the via Borgonuovo, Tess tried to keep her mind on what lay ahead but her thoughts kept straying to the scene she had witnessed the night before: Gigi and Bobby.

She didn't need to go to this stupid casting, because what nobody knew was that she had finally earned enough money to pay for her mother's new wheelchair. She had taken it out of the agency ready to take back to London and rather than leave it at the Darsena, she carried it around with her at all times. She wanted to get back to England as fast as she could, away from the probing eyes of the Italian men and the salacious invitations of the Milanese playboys, and take her parents off to the showroom. Then she could start thinking about what to do with her life. She knew her mother would want her to return to school and try for her A levels but she wasn't sure she'd still be able to. In any case the last thing she needed was another humiliating casting and she was only going along as a favour to Carla, who had been so terrific to her while she had been in Milan.

She walked a little faster. She knew she had to get there between twelve and 12.15. At 12.15 they shut the doors and if you were one minute late they didn't let you in.

There were loads and loads and loads of girls going all round the block.

273

What Tess didn't know was that Gigi Garcia, aware that she had to get her act together, had been one of the first to arrive. Her name was not on the list, of course. There was no way Carla would have suggested Gigi for Armani. But by being there early Gigi was able to gatecrash by giving the name of another girl on the list, and when the doorman ticked off that name Gigi went in.

When Tess finally got in the first person she saw was Gigi.

It was extraordinary. A few minutes ago she had had a problem taking the casting seriously. One look at Gigi and she was suddenly filled with a rage she had never known before. This little tramp had taken Bobby from her and Tess was angry. It was an entirely new experience and it gave her new-found energy. She walked past Gigi, head held high, cutting her dead, and was rewarded by the look of astonishment on Gigi's face.

What happened next was the single most exhilarating experience of Tess's entire stay in Milan. The girls were asked to strip down and put on a flesh-toned body and flat shoes.

'Flat shoes?' grumbled Gigi. 'Whatever for?'

She soon found out.

The reason the girls were asked to put on flat shoes was to ascertain that they were truly 5 feet 8 inches and over. Gigi wasn't, and in the line of girls waiting to go up on stage, without her four-inch heels, she stood out as being smaller than the rest. They asked her to leave.

This time as Gigi passed her Tess smiled radiantly and in uncharacteristic fashion-speak called out, "Bye darling, catch you later.'

Just before the girls went up on to the catwalk they had an Armani jacket slipped on to them.

'No books, just two cards please.'

And so Tess walked down the catwalk, coolly elegant, her

strawberry blonde hair falling around her shoulders, the Armani jacket fitting perfectly and her legs, naked except for tights, long and shapely. At the end of the catwalk she was aware of Armani himself sitting there with three or four people. She reached the end of the catwalk. There was complete silence. They were all looking her up and down and then looking at a magazine. Tess could see it was a copy of *Carter's*. It must be her *Mrs de Winter* shoot.

Tess had heard that if they liked you they asked you to walk up and down again.

'Walk for us again, please.'

Then, Tess had heard, if they really liked you, they took your picture.

She turned at the end of the catwalk.

'Wait a second. . . .'

A man was taking pictures of her with a Polaroid camera.

'Thank you very much,' he said eventually.

And he smiled at her.

On the way back to the agency Tess was torn. They loved her here in Milan. Yet she wanted to go back to England. If they loved her in Milan, they'd learn to love her in England too. She was on her way. But she didn't want to be a model any more. She wanted to buy her mother the wheelchair and move on. She had the money, she only had to . . .

She felt a man brush against her and stepped aside in exasperation. Every single time she went outside she was accosted.

It wasn't until she arrived back at the agency that she realised that for once the man had not been after a cheap grope. All the money she had saved for her mother had been pickpocketed.

London, 1994

Tommy Lawrence went home from Milan with his tail between his legs. He had barely worked at all. It had cost the agency nothing; they hadn't paid for his ticket. He had gone out there at his own expense in response to a fax sent by Etoile Milan.

Growing up in Croydon, a south London suburb where his parents' idea of a good time was a visit to a classical music concert at the Fairfield Halls or a trip to the Whitgift Shopping Centre, Tommy was bored out of his skull and retreated into an almost Walter Mitty dream existence. One week he would convince himself that his real father was not Alan Lawrence, accountant, but a distant relative of Prince Rainier of Monaco and that his real name was Tomas Grimaldi, rightful heir to the little principality. Another week would find him fantasising that he was a young hotshot in the City and he could be seen walking around Croydon holding an imaginary mobile phone to his ear, buying and selling commodities for astronomical prices.

Inevitably it dawned on him that he might be able to put this ability to fantasise to good use by becoming an actor, but in typical Tommy fashion he spurned the notion of attending drama school in England and blew the cheque his parents gave him for his eighteenth birthday on an aeroplane ticket to Los Angeles. Here he loped around trying to 'break into movies' without success. In the meantime he worked in super-markets, as a poolman, waiting tables, wherever he could get cash-in-hand work without a work permit. The closest he came to landing a part was when he auditioned for the remake of *Rebel without a Cause*. Tommy looked nothing like James Dean but there was a brooding, arresting quality to his looks that prompted the casting director to give him a screen test. For a whole week Tommy was on tenterhooks until he learned that he had been passed over for a nerd who went by the ridiculous name of Water Detroit. By way of consolation the casting director told Tommy he ought to try modelling.

A male model? Bunch of bloody faggots, thought Tommy and left town in disgust to go back to London.

He was quite wrong. Now that more and more men were fashion conscious and read magazines, the look that was required was often just as much a hetero as a homosexual one. It was when he began to read about Kate Moss's brother Nick being fêted as a male model that Tommy started thinking seriously of taking the casting director's advice. He'd been at school with Nick Moss who had been a few years behind him, for God's sake. But the good thing about male models – probably the only good thing since they could never hope to earn anything like as much as the girls – was that they could start later and go on longer. Tommy Lawrence was twenty when he walked into the Etoile offices for the first time. He lucked into Ashley on the men's table who had had a morning of mothers on the phone to him who were, as he put it, 'wild about their child', convinced their gangling schoolboy sons would be perfect male models. The relatively mature Tommy Lawrence put Ashley in mind of a British Marcus Schenkenberg, a handsome Swede and the closest man the world of fashion had to a male supermodel, and Tommy's arrival was like a breath of fresh air.

The first thing they did was to cut his hair. Tommy was far from being the typical square-jawed handsome Gillette male model, but with his black hair cut short and spiky suddenly he had a new and different masculine waif look without his face losing its male strength. He had a good smile, not too cheesy and a long way from a smirk. He could lift an eyebrow, frown a bit and deliver the sexy sort of male look everybody wanted. He had a masculine sensuality and exuded a certain kind of serious confidence within himself. If he was in a picture chatting up a girl at a bar he always looked as if he was going to get her.

It was hard to learn. Tommy spent hours practising his look but when he went in front of the camera he became self-conscious and instead of being natural he would become too smiley, over the top, too exaggerated. But perhaps the best thing in his favour was his gift of the gab. In London, even if all he had in his book was a Xerox of his face, they always remembered because he made them laugh. Ashley reckoned sadly that it was because he hadn't been able to give them the chat-up in Italian that he'd been passed over in Milan.

Still, he was back now and he'd landed the dental floss commercial right away, so things were looking up.

Cassie couldn't get over it. She'd been in hair and make-up for nearly three hours and now she was looking at the result. She had been made up to bear an uncanny resemblance to the Princess of Wales and while the short wig in the celebrated style certainly helped, Cassie was amazed at how much her violet eyes and the shape of her face resembled the princess's.

She looked at the script. She would not say the words herself because of her American accent. They would be dubbed on later.

'When you have a new man in your life, you want to be sure to look your best always – especially for the big clinch.'

She read it out loud and giggled at how stupid it sounded.

'No spinach between your teeth once you go in for the big close-up, eh?' said a voice behind her.

Cassie turned and squealed in sheer delight.

'Tommeeeee!'

'That's me. Thought I'd come and say hello. We're going to be doing this together. I'm Tommy Lawrence. They never gave me your name.'

She suddenly realised he couldn't possibly recognise her, dolled up as she was as the Princess of Wales.

'It's Cassie. Cassie Dylan, or Cassie Zimmerman as you knew me.'

'Did I?' He looked baffled.

'I've been searching for you everywhere. I never knew which bank you worked at or where your country house was. What are you doing here? Do you own the dental floss company or something?'

'I'm a model. Like you. I'm doing this commercial with you. I don't own any country house or a company. I think you've got me confused with someone else.'

'I haven't. I recognise you, I recognise your voice.'

She nearly said 'I want to kiss you like we did last time I saw you.'

'Well, I'm awfully sorry but I don't think I've ever seen you before.'

'Weren't you in California? Eighteen months ago? On Alice's Beach.'

'As a matter of fact, yes. I mean I can't remember which particular days I went to Alice's but I did live in LA for a while. Is that where you're from?'

Cassie was beginning to feel very strange. She was deliri-

279

ously happy to have found him again but she was deeply hurt he didn't remember her. She was saved from any further awkwardness by the director coming over to get them to rehearse.

The action was fairly simple. Cassie and Tommy had to walk along the street arm in arm while she gazed up at him adoringly and laid her head on his shoulder. They entered a restaurant. They sat opposite each other over a candlelit dinner obviously enjoying their food. There was a shot of Cassie on her own cleaning and flossing her teeth and then finally she went into Tommy's arms and looked over his shoulder to camera in a dazzling smile showing all her teeth pristine clean. It was left to the viewer's imagination as to whether this clinch was in the bedroom the same night or at a later date.

Throughout the day Tommy teased her.

'Perhaps your Royal Highness would like a sausage roll?' he said at lunch, 'or a cheese sandwich?'

Then, when they wrapped at the end of the day: 'Perhaps your Royal Highness would like to join me for dinner. Won't be anything fancy. This is the first job I've had in months.'

The Pizza Express in the Fulham Road was a bit of a comedown from Le Caprice or Daphne's where Cassie had imagined herself dining with Tommy, but being able to feast her eyes on his gorgeous face across the table and knowing that she had finally found him made it all worthwhile.

Afterwards he said, 'I think I'd better see you home and make sure you floss all that extra peperoni away.'

He stayed the night, of course. He'd had it in mind all along. It was a real drag going all the way back to Croydon every night and until he could afford to get his own place, Old Church Street, Chelsea was as good a place to kip as any.

Besides, he rather liked this open, friendly Californian girl even though she was clearly a bit of a flake to come running halfway across the world after some guy she'd only met once. Still, it was pretty flattering and it made him almost misty-eyed for the time he'd spent there when he'd had a different California girl virtually every night. He'd be moving on soon anyway. Not for him the quiet life by the fire. The good thing about modelling if he could succeed at it was that it meant a great deal of travelling and as the last thing Tommy wanted to do was to settle down with a wife and family, this suited him just fine.

If he had known that by staying in the little Chelsea flat with Cassie he was prompting her into planning their wedding, their honeymoon and most of all their first baby, he would have run a mile.

So it was ironic that he found himself – and his career – bound inextricably to Cassie in an entirely unexpected way.

The commercial was transmitted the same week as Tommy was sent by Etoile to a film première as the escort of a young actress appearing in the film. It was a PR exercise. The actress needed a walker. Tommy needed his face seen.

It wasn't a royal première but the Princess of Wales was there by invitation. Afterwards she met the cast. When she shook hands with the young actress, Tommy was standing right beside her.

The next morning Tommy was on the front page of every single tabloid.

'IT'S HIM!' screamed the headlines. They had cropped the photograph to show just the Princess of Wales and Tommy and beside it they ran a shot from the commercial of him and Cassie looking just like the Princess. The caption echoed the words of the commercial: 'When you have a new man in your life. . . .'

Suddenly Tommy was catapulted into the public's consciousness as the new man in the Princess of Wales's life.

The commercial went through the roof. Every country in the world wanted it. Angie spent days on the phone negotiating the buy-outs.

Cassie and Tommy were going to be very, very rich. . . .

London/Wiltshire, 1994

I was stunned to see Rory standing there. Naturally I had been thinking about him non-stop but it never occurred to me that he had also been thinking about me.

My wonderful minder, Brian Murphy, a Robert Mitchum lookalike, tactfully closed the glass partition as Rory and I snuggled together in the back of the limousine. Brian had driven him out to meet me, I learned to my amazement. Grace Brown had given Rory the details of my flight, he told me.

Grace Brown! Grace normally protected my privacy as if it were a soon to be extinct animal. She never ever divulged details of my whereabouts. How on earth had Rory managed it?

'Simple. I invited her to lunch. I called Etoile in New York and they told me Grace Brown looked after you in London so I called and told her you were very special to me and that I'd like to take her to lunch to discuss it. She said you were very special to her too and she couldn't think of a nicer way to spend her lunch break than discussing your specialness over a bowl of pasta.'

He had just told me a couple of very important details.

1. He thought I was very special.

2. Grace thought he was very special, otherwise she would never have let him come and meet me. And I trusted Grace's judgement probably more than my own.

He was staying at Blake's. I was booked into the Halkin. Blake's came first on the way in from the airport. I got out with him and asked Brian to take my bags on to the Halkin. We were just in time to go downstairs to Blake's' tiny little dark bar and have a drink. Pools of light from the fierce spots illuminated occasional areas. It was one of the most romantic bars in London. You could huddle there for hours virtually unseen, which we did, and several glasses of champagne later we made our way into the dining room to have dinner.

Inevitably we began to talk about Harry.

'Of course, in America he wouldn't have a problem these days,' said Rory.

'Why's that?'

'Well, everyone's a victim in America. You're not guilty even if you've slaughtered fifty-nine people in broad daylight witnessed by a capacity crowd at Shea Stadium. All you have to do is remember – and if you can't your lawyer will remember for you – how badly abused you were as a child and that's why you're the monster you are today.'

'I should have made that point on the *Today* show. But Harry didn't commit any crime.'

'Of course not, but I should think if you're even suspected of one you'd do well to come up with a bit of hanky-panky in the family skeleton department. Are you going to go and see him while you're here?'

'Absolutely. My only real worry is whether to descend on my parents or not. They are so paranoid about me, with first Venetia being killed and then Harry disappearing; they get so nervous when they see me and when it's time for me to go they can barely stand it. We sort of came to a silent understanding some time ago that the less they saw of me, the more they were able to cope. What about your parents?'

'Just my father left. He's pretty old. My mother had me late in life. There are times when I wonder if it wore her out. She died of cancer about five years ago.'

'Do you get on with your father?'

'Yes, I do as a matter of fact. Don't see him all that often. He lives out in Montana of all places, a very rugged existence. It reminds him of Scotland. He hates New York. He's pretty anti-social.'

'I heard you were a bit that way yourself.'

'I'm just picky about the company I keep. Nothing wrong with that.'

'What about your mother?'

'She specialised in passive hostility. Hated confrontation. My father was an angry man but he was real, you knew where you stood with him. My mother went in for a lot of pursing of lips and looking disapproving but never actually saying anything so you couldn't have an argument with her and clear the air.'

'Sounds pretty frustrating.'

'It was. I remember, there was this time when. . . .'

We sat there, chatting about our families and ourselves as naturally as pie. As we reached the coffee stage I realised what it was about him that made him different. He didn't seem to have an overriding need to impress me as most men I went out with did. He didn't bore me to tears going on about his BMW, his yacht, his duplex in Sutton Place, his place in the Hamptons, his seat on the board, his affairs with movie stars. He wasn't competitive with me. I'd had a few problems in that area in the past. Most men were uncomfortable with the fact that I probably earned way more than they did, but Rory Stirling was secure in himself.

He also turned out to be far and away the best lover I had ever had. He delighted in my body in a way no man ever had before. He laid me out on his bed upstairs in his room at

285

Blake's and examined me from top to toe, stroking my feet, the insides of my thighs, running the palm of his hand lightly over my stomach, cupping my breasts, smoothing the skin on my arms, letting his finger wander round and round the inside of my palm. Then he took my face between his hands and stared at me for an eternity before lowering his head and raining kisses all over me. As he moved about above me I caught glimpses of his massive erection waiting, ready to perform. When he finally entered me, easing himself in then slowly pulling out again, in, out, in, out, I felt as if my entire body had been turned to liquid, a torrential river into which he was plunging as deep as he could go.

Afterwards he brought a towel from the bathroom and wiped me down before turning me over and beginning a new examination of my back, culminating in his long-limbed frame lying on top of me and entering me from behind.

We slept for a while then it was my turn to sit astride him, on him, dipping my breasts to allow his mouth to suck on my nipples till they hardened. When I bent my head to do the same to him he completely lost control and exploded as I rocked his penis up and down inside me. I let him sleep and woke him by gently squeezing his balls and massaging his cock until he was ready for me again.

By morning we were dripping in sweat, and under the shower I shampooed the grey hair that had first attracted me to him, while he washed my pubic hair and knelt to tongue me there.

We tried to look innocent for Room Service when they brought us breakfast and I know we failed. I was wearing one of his shirts and I didn't fool anyone. We had a problem when we went out because the minute we touched each other accidentally, we couldn't stop. I thought he was going to have sex with me up against the Michelin Building when we came out of the Oyster Bar after lunch, but I managed to bundle him into a taxi just in time. It was only a five-minute ride back to the hotel but he put a hand under my skirt and made me come twice before we arrived.

By Monday morning I ached all over. My eyes could barely stay open, so little sleep had we had. We had got to the stage of all red-hot new affairs where we had to spend a few hours apart to recover our energy.

I caught a cab to the Halkin and rather sheepishly checked in three days after Brian had delivered my bags. Then I had him drive me to Etoile. Before going into the agency I put on my dark glasses and headscarf and slipped into a café for a quiet cup of coffee in a booth at the back, to collect my thoughts. It was already nearly lunchtime and two girls came and sat down in the next booth. I had my back to them so they couldn't see me and I couldn't see them, but I could hear their conversation quite clearly.

It has always been a mystery to me why people discuss what are obviously highly confidential matters in public places like restaurants, always assuming people at neighbouring tables will never know who they are talking about. For example, I pricked up my ears immediately when I heard the words:

'Have you told Grace yet?'

'Of course not. I haven't even said I'll accept the job offer yet. I'm still thinking.'

'But the money, Angie – you can't say no to that. Your dad would kill you if he found out you'd turned down that kind of money. What's the name of the other agency again?'

'Tempest.'

'Would you be able to take any girls with you?'

'Tess Tucker might come with me. I discovered her, after all, and she's been doing really well in Milan. They want her in Paris and before that she'll do some shows for London

Fashion Week. She's really dependent on me. The thing is, I'd feel terrible leaving her if she didn't come with me.'

'What about that one who did that nude story in a launderette?'

'Celestia. You make it sound like a porno mag. It was a fashion story. Anyway, she's way out of my league. She's gone off to New York and she's bound to go straight to Paris from there. No, my big coup might be this new American girl, Cassie. You must have seen her in the Princess of Wales dental floss commercial? She's earning a fortune out of that one commercial. It's not winter or summer orientated so it'll run all year round and she gets royalties each time it's shown, plus it's running internationally. There have been buy-outs for the right to show it in different countries for a percentage of the BSF—'

'BSF?'

'Basic Studio Fee. There's an option on her at the moment for a French TV commercial filming in the South of France. It won't be shown in the UK, just in France, so if Cassie does it – and they want her on the strength of her success in the Di commercial – she'll be working for a BSF of £1,000 a day and she'll automatically get a minimum of 500 per cent on top of that for the French exclusivity, for transmission in France only. I've got offers like that coming in for Cassie every day. The problem is she's smitten by this bloke she did the Di commercial with. Would you believe, she even met him on a beach in California and came over here to look for him. We're saving that press story for the right moment.'

'What's the problem?'

'She doesn't want to go off on her own and leave him. On the other hand, he *does* want to go off on his own and make his mark independently and of course she doesn't know that, poor thing. On top of everything the ad agency want another dental floss commercial – the ongoing story – with the two of them. Anyway, I was the one who got Cassie the commercial in the first place so she'd probably be loyal and stick with me – except I don't want to leave. I love it at Etoile. We've got a really strong table. They've brought in a new girl to do the New Faces, I've moved up. I adore Grace. She's being so supportive at the moment. I'm having this really hard time with this rubbish girl called Gigi who's been dumped on us by Etoile New York. She really blew it in Milan and she's dead pushy, she goes, when am I going to be doing this, when am I going to be doing that? down the phone all day long. I had to laugh, I got her this casting with this German company, right, and they said she must bring a bikini and she must be able to ride a bike. Well, they only had her pedalling round Soho in a bikini in the rain while they videoed her. And she attracts really weird people too. She's got this guy who keeps calling the agency asking for her number. He begged me for a signed Z card of her so I got her to send him one. Anyway we've stopped her doing anything for three weeks until we can get her weight down. She really has a problem there. . . .'

'Do you ever see Swan? She's one of yours, isn't she?'

'She's in town at the moment, actually. I'm really worried, as it happens, there's this journalist keeps ringing up asking all sorts of questions about her.'

'About that stuff in the *Standard* the other day, her nanny getting murdered?'

'Yeah, it's the same woman. Lindy-Jane Johnson. It's funny because it's not Swan she's really interested in – it's her brother. Harry. The one who disappeared right after that girl died. I don't like the sound of what she's insinuating, I tell you. . . . She called this morning. She saw Swan in the Oyster Bar having lunch with some man at the weekend, she wanted to know who he was. As if I would tell her, even if I did know!'

'So, you wanted to tell me something about your family?'

'It's my brother, Patrick. I just don't know what to do. He was working at the Clarence Hotel and then in his last letter he told me he had a new job starting soon in Bono's club, the Kitchen, when it opens so I told a girl who was going over for a shoot in Dublin to go and look him up. She went there and they told her he'd left and gone to America and no one had heard from him since. . . .'

I had stopped listening to the conversation. Lindy-Jane Johnson had seen us at the weekend! I had to phone Rory and warn him. He was in the hotel doing interviews for his book. I nipped across the road to Etoile, hugged Grace and winked at her to let her know the weekend had gone well. But when I called Blake's they told me Mr Stirling had asked not to be disturbed during his interviews.

I forced myself to concentrate on what Grace had lined up for me. I had London Fashion Week ahead of me, then back to Milan and on to Paris. I insisted on Grace handling all my bookings. It was a question of loyalty. Etoile London was my mother agency. Speaking of loyalty. . . .

'Grace, I've been hearing some good things about a girl you've got on the booking table. Angie someone.'

'Angie Doyle. She's a star. She'll be head booker alongside me before too long. You must meet her.'

'If someone else doesn't poach her first.'

'You been hearing anything I should know about?' Grace was no fool.

'Could be. Time she had a raise, maybe? Before she gets a bit, how shall I put it, tempestuous . . .?'

'Gotcha. Thanks, Swan. Can't imagine who you've been talking to. You must mix in very dubious company.'

That reminded me about Lindy-Jane Johnson. I was pleased to have done something about Angie Doyle. I hadn't even seen her face properly but she'd been talking a lot of sense to her friend at lunch, from what I could hear. Tess Tucker and Cassie, whoever she was, were lucky to have her.

I ignored the Blake's Do Not Disturb signs and burst in on Rory's interview with a thin-lipped, stringy-haired woman whose face fell open at the sight of me.

'Darling, this is Jane Smith,' he introduced me. I winced at the 'darling'. That was a dead giveaway, much as I liked the sound of it.

'A plain name for a plain girl,' I commented as she left to make way for the next reporter. I wasn't usually so bitchy but she had had a particularly mean expression. I slipped into the bedroom to wait while Rory did his next interview. After all, we'd undoubtedly wind up there before long and I didn't want another journalist to see me.

'Hello, I'm Ruth Picardie to do the piece for the *Independent*. What was she doing here, if I may ask? I wouldn't have thought your publishers would let someone like her near you. It's not as if she writes for the book pages or anything.'

'Jane Smith? She writes for the *Guardian*.'

'The *Guardian*, my foot! Her name's not Jane Smith. She's called Lindy-Jane Johnson and she writes for the tabloid sleaze. I hope you stuck to your book and didn't tell her anything about yourself or you're really in trouble.'

I sank back on the bed. Lindy-Jane Johnson. And this was the second time she'd seen me with Rory!

We made an odd foursome, sitting together, huddled round the fire burning in the old oven in the lime kiln. Rory had his arm around me to keep me warm and Sally Bainbridge nestled close to Harry. We were like children who had sneaked out to have one of those incredibly uncomfortable midnight feasts in a forbidden place where you would rather die than admit it wasn't exactly paradise while you tucked into soggy sandwiches and tried to keep out the cold, secretly wishing you were back in your nice warm bed.

In our case it was a nice warm four-poster bed in one of the most romantic little hotels in England: At the Sign of the Angel, an old coaching inn at Lacock, the other side of Wiltshire. Rory and I had booked in there for the weekend and I confess I feared for the durability of the four-poster bed after we had finished with it on our first night there.

I had been nervous about introducing Harry and Rory. First I didn't know how Harry would feel about my having told Rory about him, and then there was the question of how my brother would respond to the first serious love of my life. For I knew by now that I had fallen in love with Rory. But I need not have worried. Rory handled it beautifully. The minute he shook hands with him, Rory slipped an arm around Harry's shoulder and led him away from us, talking urgently. I don't suppose I shall ever know what he said to him but whatever it was, it worked. When they returned Harry was positively beaming.

'Jolly nice chap, your Rory.'

My Rory! That's what Laura Lobianco had called him – which reminded me, I owed her a call to let her know what Rory was like in bed. I giggled at the thought of what I would tell her.

'Honestly! Listen to her . . .' said Harry in mock exasperation, 'she always did that when she was a kid, giggled away to herself at some private joke. Come on, Skinny, spit it out. What are you thinking about?'

'Don't call me that!'

'See. Outraged as ever. She'll never grow up. You don't know what you've let yourself in for, Rory.'

'Oh yes, I do,' said Rory.

'Still, it is hard to remember you're a world-famous supermodel seeing you sitting there in a baggy sweater, jeans and a ponytail, giggling to yourself like a naughty schoolgirl,' said Sally, laughing. Indeed, she was infinitely more elegant in her Edina Ronay sweater and Paul Costelloe trousers. She was more relaxed than when we had last met, and I sensed that her relationship with Harry had deepened considerably.

'Well, I won't be much longer,' I told them.

'*What?*'

'I want to start thinking about lowering my profile. I am going to quit as the SWAN girl. Charley's going to tell Mr Takamoto after the shows. I have to give him six months' notice.'

'Then what are you going to do? Settle down and get married?' Harry blurted it out in typical tactless fashion before Sally could stop him.

'Well, that's certainly an option,' I whispered and felt Rory's hand give mine a squeeze. 'But Harry, we're not here to talk about me. There's something I want to clear up. I met Celestia Fairfax in New York. You remember Oliver Fairfax's Aunt Prudence and Uncle Hugo? Well, they had a daughter after Venetia and Oliver died. She's become a model. She's quite fabulous, actually, all punky and wild, but that's neither here nor there. She told me Oliver used to take out Molly Bainbridge before he started going out with Venetia. Tell me, Harry – and Sally too, for that matter – did either of you know this?'

Sally shook her head.

'Oliver Fairfax was a creep!' said Harry suddenly and I leaned forward to see his face in the firelight. I knew that tone

293

of voice. I only heard it when Harry – bumbling, charming, easygoing Harry – was really upset. 'OK,' he continued, 'you might as well know. I'll tell you the whole story. Are you sitting comfortably? It was a dark and stormy night and . . .'

The old mischievous Harry had returned.

'Get on with it, Harry,' I warned.

'I was at Eton with Oliver Fairfax, as you probably remember. That's how Venetia met him, through me. Not that I planned it. He was such a swine. He had plenty of other bits of fluff on the side when he was taking out Venetia. What I do recall is that in his last year he went up to London with a whole crowd and they went to this escort agency. I mean, it was obviously a brothel but it called itself an escort agency. I even remember the ridiculous name it had: the Cecile Agency. All we heard about for the rest of that term was Oliver's prowess at the Cecile Agency. Made me sick.'

'Jealous?' I couldn't resist asking.

'Oh, shut up, Skinny!'

'Give it a rest, you two. Try to behave like grown-ups. I know it's hard being in this place. It must have such memories for you both.' As ever Sally's was the voice of reason.

'Oliver became obsessed with one particular girl. He claimed she was better than the rest, came from a respectable family. He didn't go around declaring undying love for her or anything like that, but he was obviously smitten in a kind of schoolboy's first fuck crush kind of way. Then I introduced him to Venetia and I think he realised what an ass he'd been making of himself with this prostitute. I'm sorry, Sally. It was Molly. This is the reason that I've never mentioned it before. I didn't want you to find out your sister was a tart. But what Oliver hadn't bargained for was the fact that she was a pretty tenacious woman. She obviously reckoned she was on to a good thing with Oliver and she didn't want to let him go.

She kept calling him. It sounds a terrible thing to say, but if he hadn't gone and got himself killed I think she would have caused him serious trouble. She was all set to gatecrash Venetia's birthday party, that I do know.'

'So you knew her when she came to be my nanny?' I was stunned.

'I'd never actually met her but I knew who she was when she arrived. She told me. She said she'd always had her eye on me. You see she'd been spying on Oliver and Venetia around town and she'd seen me with them.'

'You mean she applied for the job of Swan's nanny to go after you?'

'It certainly looked that way to me at the time. Yet there was something else. I can't quite put my finger on it but she seemed scared, as if she was seeking shelter in some way. Whoever it was couldn't get at her in the Boltons.'

'Who couldn't get at her?'

'I don't know.'

But he did know. I have always been able to tell when Harry was lying. He has such an open honest face and he always looks you straight in the eye to the extent that it can be pretty exhausting. But when he knows he's done something wrong, he looks away.

'Well, we'll just have to see if this Cecile place still exists and pay them a visit.'

'It doesn't,' said Harry quickly. 'Closed down years ago.'

But I knew he was lying again.

Rory and I went for a walk, down through the woods and along the narrow river path until we came in sight of the old rose-brick house bathed in the faint winter sun, and then suddenly there was the crunching of twigs behind us and my father stood there.

295

I hadn't seen him for a very long time and nothing my mother had said had prepared me for the way he had aged. He had sort of slumped over as if he'd been hit from behind. He was wearing a flat cap, the kind he always liked to wear in the country, and his old tweed jacket now had leather patches on the elbows. His sweater had holes in it, his shirt collar was frayed, his twill trousers had seen better days. He had the appearance of someone who had given up on life.

'Lavinia, my dear, there you are,' he said as if he'd only seen me a week ago, but then I realised he probably thought he had.

'Daddy!' I flung my arms around him. 'Daddy, this is Rory, Rory Stirling, a very dear friend.'

'Jolly good,' said my father. 'Down from London, are you?'

'Yes, sir,' said Rory.

'We're staying in Lacock, Daddy.'

'Pretty abbey. Discovered photography there. Something like that. Seen your mother?'

'No, not yet.'

'Better come up to the house for tea. Remind me what you're doing these days, Lavinia. Memory's terrible. Terrible!'

What could I say? They would never believe it in New York. I'm the world's most famous supermodel and my father can't remember what I do.

'I'm a model, Daddy.'

'Jolly good. You're an artist then I take it, Mr Stirling?'

'No, Rory's a writer. His book's just been published here in England.'

'Penguin?' asked my father hopefully, obviously plumping for the only publisher whose name he could remember.

'Secker & Warburg.'

'Jolly good.'

My mother saw us coming across the fields from her bedroom window and rushed outside to meet us. She couldn't control her tears as I introduced her to Rory.

'Do forgive me, I am so sorry. It's the shock. A wonderful shock but I wasn't prepared, we haven't seen her for so long, do forgive me. . . .'

'Rory's an old friend of Norah Nicholson, Mummy.'

'Oh my heavens, I know exactly who you are, you must be Annabel Stirling's son. Poor Annabel. I was so sorry to hear about her death. Now do come inside and have some tea and tell me all about your dear father. I hear he's gone and locked himself away in Montana although, heaven knows, Lavinia, your father might just as well be in Alaska for all we see of him.' My father had wandered off and was shuffling towards the french windows leading to his study. 'I imagine it was a bit of a shock seeing how dotty he's become, but I did try to warn you.'

I could tell Mummy adored Rory. He charmed her ruthlessly till I became quite jealous. We stayed to dinner and my father emerged from his study halfway through to join us. He picked at his food and drank whisky instead of wine. After dinner we had coffee in the library, which was really an extension of his study, and it was here that my father began to pay serious attention to Rory. Not because of anything he said. Rory owed his popularity to nothing more than the fact that my father's ancient black labrador, Golly (short for Gollywog, the most politically incorrect name ever bestowed upon a dog), took a shine to him and ambled over to lick his hand. This was rare. Golly was usually locked in the scullery when my parents had visitors because of his propensity for charging at them with bared teeth. He always missed them by a mile since he was almost totally blind, but it didn't give a very good impression. But Rory was clearly flavour of the month. Golly wouldn't leave him alone, even going so far as to try and climb into his lap.

'Golly!' scolded my mother, 'how many more times do I have to tell you: you are not a lap dog. Get down!'

But my father sat watching happily. If Golly liked this young man of mine then he must be a good chap.

Which was all to the good, for when Rory dropped his bombshell on me just as we were about to go back to our four-poster bed, and, standing bolt upright, shaking just a bit, approached my father and said, 'Sir, I should like to ask you for your daughter's hand in marriage,' all my father said was:

'Jolly good.'

The first thing I did when we got back to London was to look up the Cecile Agency in the phone book. It was there in bold.

'You'll have to go,' I told Rory. 'Pretend you're a punter. They'd recognise me and then it'd get in the papers.'

'It'd make a pretty good story if I went. Supermodel sends fiancé to brothel on first day of engagement.'

I hit him with a pillow but we did then sit down and agree to keep our engagement strictly private. I telephoned Mummy and asked her if it would be a problem for her and Daddy to keep it quiet.

'I'll do whatever you want, darling, and as for your father, don't be too sad but I'm afraid he barely remembers you were here.'

'We thought we'd get married in London secretly after the shows. Will you and Daddy come up? It'll have to be somewhere private. . . .'

'Of course I'll come, I can't speak for your father. But listen, I have a better idea. Why not do it at the Fairfax chapel at Trevane? I'll have a word with Hugo and Prudence, they'll keep it quiet, do it all in the family. It's the most private place I know.'

'That's a wonderful idea. Ironically, I've just met Celestia again in New York.'

'I'll organise it. Don't worry. If banns have to be read there's enough time while you're away at the shows.'

I was so excited I forgot all about Rory's mission until he came home and told me that they had denied all knowledge of Molly Bainbridge's ever having worked at Cecile's, that they had become suspiciously enraged by his questions, and refused to believe he was nothing to do with the journalist who had been there a week ago asking questions about Molly Bainbridge – whoever she was – and someone called Harry Crichton-Lake.

I didn't need to ask the name of the journalist. I knew who it was: Lindy-Jane Johnson.

New York, 1994

Water was away in California and Celestia was secretly rather relieved. She was pretty wild about him but sometimes he took himself rather more seriously than she did. Celestia was uncomfortable on the Upper East Side, which was something Water simply could not understand. She knew he saw her as a classy upper-class Brit. He did not, she realised, like the British although apart from his trip for the *Torment* première, he'd only ever been there once before about eight years ago as a backpacking tourist kid with his parents. She'd seen the endless photographs he'd taken, all neatly mounted in a special album.

But he liked her British image, especially when it was matched with that of a potential supermodel, yet he didn't seem to be able to see beyond it to the rebellious teenager still lurking beneath the surface. Water was into money. She was into fun – and the only time she managed to have some seemed to be when Water went away.

Her model apartment had turned out to be in the West Coast building down on Horatio Street, conveniently located a block away from Industria Superstudio where she found herself working a good deal of the time. In time, when she had enough money for the down payment, she would get herself a loft south of Canal Street in TriBeCa. There was a building on West Broadway that housed several of the world's best-known supermodels.

But not Swan.

Celestia mused for a while about Swan. They weren't related. If Oliver and Venetia had lived and married, Swan and Celestia would have been some sort of second cousins by marriage. She knew her parents were still friends with the Crichton-Lakes, more so in fact than Oliver's parents were, yet Swan herself had been absent from the family get-togethers in recent years. It was as if she had gone off and become a model and no one had seen her since. Celestia's mother had accused her of becoming 'too grand for the likes of us, thank you very much. I wrote to her to ask her to help me get back into modelling and she never replied.' Celestia had been tempted to comment that Swan was obviously too smart to waste time on the impossible.

She was rather worried about having talked to that journalist in England before she left. She wondered if she ought to call Swan about the recent stories in the press, but they told her at Etoile that Swan was away in Europe. It could wait till she got back. Water had been on at her to introduce him properly to Swan. It was all part of his plan to get his mitts on the screen rights to Rory Stirling's new bestseller *Coming Out Fighting*. From what Celestia could gather, when she bothered to listen, CAA, Rory Stirling's agents on the Coast, were not terribly interested in talking to Water since they had had expressions of interest from Tom Cruise, Liam Neeson, Dan Day-Lewis and Tom Hanks, to name but a few. Water simply could not get it through his head that he was not yet as bankable as these guys. It was as if she, Celestia, with one *Carter's* cover behind her, now thought she could command a multimillion-dollar beauty contract. Saying things like: 'Dream on, Water. Give it a rest, let's go to a club' was

301

pointless. Water's idea of a night out was very Californian: to eat an early dinner at some French or Italian restaurant and then climb into bed with a pile of scripts.

He had begun to get persistent about Swan when he had, so he claimed, seen Rory Stirling driving out of the Carlyle garage in a Cherokee jeep. His interrogation of the Carlyle doormen failed to reveal whether or not Rory was staying there, but when he went as far as the desk they told him Mr Stirling was not a guest. Water spent a few days hanging out of the windows of his apartment, since he could see the entrance to the Carlyle from there, but there was no sign of Rory. He began to wonder who Rory might have been visiting and then he remembered that Swan had also been at Norah Nicholson's party. Rather belatedly he rang Norah to thank her for her party and dropped hints about Rory and Swan. Norah, delighted, dropped even heavier hints without divulging anything. That did it.

'When I come back from California I want you to call up Swan and invite her over here,' he told Celestia. 'I'll get to Rory Stirling that way, meet him through Swan, convince him I have to play Ralph in *Fighting* and that I have to produce and direct as well.'

Etoile had sent Celestia's book ahead of her to New York. For the first couple of months she would be working illegally until they could get her a work permit. She was not to go through Customs with a diary or a portfolio or anything that indicated she was going to be working in New York. From the word go she had ten go-sees a day, and within a month she was booked for a GAP campaign, Russell Bennett, Joan Vass, Mark Eisen, and Cuban-born Manolo, the Vivienne Westwood of New York. She started to make money and learned the basic difference between England and America. In America she had to hand over 50 per cent of everything she earned to the agency and they turned 30 per cent of that straight over to the IRS. In England she handed over 20 per cent to the agency and took care of her own tax. Soon she was able to apply for a work permit by going to see a lawyer with ten tearsheets and a sponsor – her agency. She paid $1,200 and it took three weeks. Nothing, it seemed, could go wrong with Celestia's career, but her private life was becoming a little schizophrenic.

Uptown with Water she was the movie star's English girl-friend moving with a grown-up crowd, going to dinner parties in apartment blocks that had doormen, introduced to people by Water as an old family friend of Swan. It was all about upgrading her cachet with the type of social climbers Water wanted to impress: bankers, publishers, lawyers, agents, CEOs, presidents, vice-presidents, money, money, money. . . .

But this wasn't her. She hated this hard, chic, predatory crowd and she suspected Swan probably did too. Everything Celestia had heard about Swan as she was growing up had made her feel as if she would like her. Her father had always told her that of all the people who had come to stay at Trevane, Swan had always loved it the best.

'She was a strange child, kept herself to herself. Wasn't even particularly pretty as a little girl. Venetia was the one, God rest her soul. Swan was always in her shadow but the funny thing is, if you go back and look at the family photo albums, you find yourself drawn to the pictures of Lavinia more than anyone else. She had a photographic quality even then but we never dreamed she'd turn out to be so famous. We none of us saw it, except of course my mother. It used to drive Prudence mad when my mother said Lavinia ought to think about modelling. You see, your grandmother never believed your mother when she said she'd been a model. But there's something tragic about those Crichton-Lakes. Lavinia was the only one who liked coming here to Trevane. It suited her. She used to walk for miles, just like you do, and when that brother of hers disappeared I had her to stay for a week. Prudence was away, thank God. The poor girl was devastated. I don't think she ever got over it and that's when she started to become something of a recluse. You can see it in her eyes in the photographs of her in those fashion magazines your mother leaves lying around the house. She's a lost soul, Celestia. Tragic.'

It was a long speech for her father to make and Celestia had never forgotten it. It put paid to all the notions she had had about her father, much as she loved him, being a dusty old historian. Hugo Fairfax was clearly far more perceptive about the people around him than people realised, least of all his wife.

Celestia felt a strange affinity with Swan but the last thing she wanted to do was to presume on their tenuous family connection and inflict herself upon her for the sake of further-ing Water's wretched career. Already she was beginning to see the vast cultural divide between what she saw as innate American pushiness and natural English reticence. Every American she met said they were absolutely deliriously happy to meet her, especially when they found out she had ties to Swan, and she found it unreal. She began to realise that Swan clearly did not hang out with this crowd and that, like Water, these people saw Celestia as a possible entrée into Swan's world. Suddenly Celestia understood why Swan hid herself away in an apartment at the Carlyle where she was constantly protected. She would, she decided, invite her to visit when she returned from her travels – but not to Water's immaculately decorated apartment on Madison. Celestia would invite Swan down to Horatio Street or for an espresso in Braque at Indus-tria. Somehow she was sure Swan would prefer that. . . .

So Celestia liked it when Water went away. She escaped back down to the West Coast Building, home to masses of other models and hairdressers and fashion people. She loved hanging out in SoHo with its cobbled streets and dark green and red buildings with the fire escapes zigzagging down them and the big banners hanging out over the stores and galleries. She loved the galleries, and the bookstores, and Anna Sui and Agnès B and she lived off macrobiotic Japanese food at Nosmo King on Varick or Souen on the corner of Sixth and Prince. She joined the art scene when she ran into her old friend Caroline who had been at boarding-school with her at St Mary's, Calne, back in Wiltshire and who was now working in a gallery on Spring Street.

She kept her smart designer clothes in a closet in Water's apartment uptown and on Horatio Street she wore her real clothes which she found in a warehouse in Brooklyn for $1.50 a pound. She would dig through piles and piles of clothes and drag home to Horatio Street a whole new wardrobe in a huge garbage bag for under ten bucks. Most of it was stinking and disgusting until she washed it, but then she had the basic materials – gas station attendant shirts and work pants with chains – to put together the right cool, baggy look.

And then, of course, she went clubbing.

Water had his uses. He got her into the Limelight, an old church on 20th Street, first time round but after that she went to Disco 2000 on Wednesday nights on her own. Sushi and Astro Earl and the other club kids were soon letting her in as a matter of course. She could have stayed in the VIP room but she preferred the techno and progressive house they played in the bigger rooms. On the whole she avoided the rave parties, but like everyone else, if Moby was spinning anywhere she'd turn up because he was especially good for hard-core techno. A lot of the dialogue on the telephone between the models in the West Coast Building was about how to get on the lists for clubs. Here again, Celestia found herself being hit on to use Water's name to get into places. Sometimes she sneaked off to hear bands play at the Knitting Factory on Houston, so called because the ceiling was made out of knitted sweaters.

She might go to clubs but Celestia was disciplined. New Yorkers, she learned, were far more professional than anyone else. There was no overtime. Studios were booked nine to five and everyone worked to get the job done, because the client didn't want to pay any more than was necessary. Besides, she was happy here. Hard work by day. Clubbing by night. Mixing with artists and models in galleries, cafés and on the streets of SoHo the rest of the time.

Until Water came back to New York.

He was pretty high and full of himself. Celestia had gone uptown and let herself into his apartment, changed into a bit of all-American Bill Blass he'd bought her at Bergdorf's and which made her look at least twenty-six, and was ready and waiting when he came in from the airport.

'Come on, we're doing dinner with Mike Ovitz. He's in town for a second. I didn't get to see him on the Coast but it's all set up for tonight.'

It wasn't. There was no sign of the legendary agent when they arrived at the restaurant and Celestia never discovered who the suits they dined with were. They were very impressed by her and she wondered what Water had told them; probably that she was going to be on the next cover of *Vogue*. They kept asking her if she was going to do the upcoming shows in Paris and Milan, and when she told them she'd had options put on her for both, Water suddenly went very quiet.

Then, in the cab going home, he turned on her and went ballistic.

'Why didn't you tell me? *Why didn't you tell me?* I didn't know you were going to Paris. I didn't know you were going to Milan. Suddenly you're big time.'

So that was it, thought Celestia. He wants me to be the fancy model girlfriend, providing he can keep me in my place, providing his career is in better shape than mine. Mike Ovitz blew him out. He can't get near Rory Stirling's book. But I might just be a big hit on the runway and he doesn't like it one bit. Well, tough!

Water was not exactly a soft and gentle lover. Celestia sensed that he would be rough with her if he could get away with it. But she was a model and models couldn't turn up to castings with their bodies and limbs bruised and marked. The irony was that for a would-be tough control freak, Water had a puny, awkward body like a shy little boy's. It brought out the maternal instinct in Celestia and this further enraged Water.

After they had made love, she stroked his protruding rib cage and ran her finger along his pelvic bone.

'You'd make a good model,' she told him, 'this is just what they want. You're the perfect waif, just right for the baby doll look.'

It was a stupid thing to do. Water took himself far too seriously to stand being teased. He leapt out of bed and grabbed the first thing he could find, which happened to be Celestia's big black leather model bag. Perfect! Water raised it by its straps and prepared to whack Celestia's naked body.

She escaped to the bathroom as the bag came hurtling down towards her and the contents cascaded out all over the bed. She sat down on the toilet and smoked a cigarette, staring at her flushed face in the mirror. She'd stay there for a while. Make him sweat. Let him think he'd really upset her. Make him feel guilty.

307

'Jesus Christ, this shit is amazing!'

She was curious.

'What is?'

'This stuff in this notebook. Open the fucking door and I'll read some to you. Can you hear me? Listen to this:

"They make the girls watch.
The clients are killed and they make the girl watch the whole thing. . . ."

Hey, Celestia, what you doing?'

Celestia was out of the bathroom and had snatched the book away from him.

'Water, don't you ever, *ever* go through my bag again, do you understand? That book is private.'

'Hey, baby, chill out. I'm sorry. I swear. I'm sorry. I had no idea you were into that kind of stuff. You only had to tell me. . . .'

'I'm not. I'm absolutely not. How could you even think I might be?'

'But you just like to take a peek at those pages every now and then? Gives you a thrill? Who wrote that stuff anyway?'

It turned him on, she could see. She let him fuck her again to get him off the subject of the notebook. There was no way she could ever let him find out whose it was.

She had found it in the attic at Trevane. After her father had told her about Swan's photogenic qualities coming out in the family album, Celestia had gone to take a look for herself.

'You'll find the albums in a box marked Crichton-Lake. Prudence put everything to do with the family up there at the time of Venetia and Oliver's accident. She'd had a letter from Oliver that day – he'd been to stay the previous weekend and it was probably to thank her – and it completely unnerved

308

her. She just piled everything to do with that family into this box and asked me to take it away.'

Celestia had found the unopened envelope addressed to her mother. She had opened it immediately with a child's curiosity and read the contents. It was a standard bread-and-butter thank-you letter: Dear Aunt Prudence, thank you so much for having me and Venetia for the weekend. We did so enjoy ourselves. It was so good to see you and Uncle Hugo on such good form ... blah blah blah ... lots of love, Oliver. It was the PS that had caught Celestia's attention.

PS Sorry to be a bore, Aunt P, but I left a rather important notebook by my bed. Little navy book with a red binding. I do my accounts in it and I do need it. Could you be an angel and post it to me.

Prudence got as far as finding the notebook, bringing it downstairs and putting it in a drawer, intending to post it. Then she forgot all about it. By the time she found it again Oliver was dead, and she sent it up to the box in the attic, unread.

Celestia read it all – and wished she hadn't. At the time she hadn't understood very much but as she studied it over the years, she learned the sickening, horrible truth about her 'cousin' Oliver.

It was a kind of diary, not a day-to-day account of his life, but notes made about a place called Cecile's where he obviously spent a good deal of his time. Celestia realised that Oliver had been making notes about the place in order to show them to someone. He seemed to be trapped in a situation he couldn't get out of. It wasn't really clear whether or not he had actually worked at Cecile's or whether he was a customer. Celestia suspected he had started off as a customer and had got himself sucked into something bigger. The name Murray came up over and over again, and someone called Molly was clearly Oliver's informant about what was going on. Many of the pages began with the words: 'Molly told me today . . .'

Gradually Celestia came to understand that some men who were clients at Cecile's actually died and that Murray, whoever he was, had warned the girls who were made to watch that if they ever went to the police they would be the ones who would be accused of murder, despite the fact that a third party was always standing by to administer the ultimate strangulation.

The last entry was the most horrific.

'I have to get Molly out of there. They have video cameras in all the rooms. They are making films of all these men dying and the girls are in the films. Molly is too frightened to do anything for herself. I can't handle this any longer on my own. I have told Harry everything.'

It was dated the day before Oliver died.

Harry knew everything. Why had he never said anything?

Celestia didn't really need to ask. She knew the answer. It was the same reason she had kept quiet about Oliver's notebook for all these years. The Crichton-Lakes and the Fairfaxes didn't need another scandal to add to their tragedy. Yet Celestia had always known that she would have to face up to it some time. She knew that was the reason why she had let slip the name Cecile to that journalist. If the place still existed, let Lindy-Jane Johnson flush out the dirt.

Meanwhile Celestia would figure out a way to tell Swan about her brother Harry's involvement. There was no hurry. It wasn't as if poor Swan even knew where her brother was.

A week later Water came home from a meeting and casually told Celestia:

'It's cool. I'll let you go to Paris for the shows. I'm going with you. I just got cast in *Prêt-à-porter*, Robert Altman's fashion movie he's shooting there. We'll probably be in the movie together.'

Competitive little shit! thought Celestia. He knows perfectly well they haven't actually confirmed me for any of the Paris shows yet. Well, let him put me down while he can. When it comes to showtime, I'll show him!

Paris, 1994

Sitting hunched in her window seat on an Air France flight to Paris, Gigi spent forty-five minutes taking stock of her life. She was not exactly doing well. She'd made a mess of Milan. They hadn't liked her there, the bookings had been non-existent and to crown it all she had gone and behaved like a jerk in front of Charley Lobianco's mother. The only person who had been remotely nice to her was Bobby Fox.

She'd heard the gossip. They thought she'd driven back from Como and jumped into bed with him. They were so wrong! Well, yes, she had got into bed with him but what they didn't realise was that Bobby was in the process of coming out. He might have slept with Tess Tucker. He might have slept with one or two other beautiful, gentle, non-threatening girls but in reality Bobby Fox was gay. The reason Gigi had finally crawled into bed with him was because she had sensed that it was going to take a long time for him to finish unburdening himself on to her – a conversation that had begun in the drive down from Como – and it was more comfortable curled up beside him. There was no sex between them. Bobby was just a confused boy who was gradually beginning to work out in his mind that while he abhorred sex with the reptilian Roberto Fabiani, his adventures with more attractive men were leading him in the direction he wanted to go. Gigi had listened to his problems with his father, his concern about his career and what to do next, his guilt about leading Tess on, how it had been Grace Brown's fault; Grace had made him persuade Tess to go to Milan and from the work point of view it had been the best thing that could have happened to her. And then Tess had walked in and found them.

Gigi hadn't seen her since. She had left the next day and gone to London and the minute she walked into Etoile in Covent Garden she knew it wasn't going to work there either. She was put with a booker called Angie who disliked her on sight, and it was mutual. Gigi was shrewd enough to know that if your booker didn't like you, your chances of working were slim. The booker would not be hustling for you and your name was not going to be the first to come to her mind when the castings came in.

Then Gigi hit a stroke of luck. The owner of Etoile Paris, Daniel Mercier, was in town. Gigi did not know Daniel from Adam and when he walked quietly in and sat down on the big leather sofa between the two booking tables to wait for Grace to finish her call and be ready for him, Gigi ignored him and carried on with her conversation with another model.

'Listen, baby, you got an approach from Tempest, why don't you ask them for more money and go right over there? It's your chance. You told me last week Kari B wants to move from Models One. Everyone's moving. I even heard Tempest were after my mumsy little booker, Angie, only she was headed off at the pass by Grace offering her more money to stay here. I was in Iceni last night and this girl tells me she wants to move to Etoile and what can I do about it? I mean, what am I, a model scout?'

Daniel Mercier had approached her later in the day, a French version of Charley Lobianco in New York and Marcello Molino in Milan; late thirties, expensive suit, very smooth. He wanted her in Paris, he said, he'd squared it with Grace Brown, Gigi was to leave the next day.

And here she was, about to land at Charles de Gaulle airport, with a strange premonition that this was her last chance to make something of her life. She took a cab to Montparnasse where good old Swedish Greta from Milan had come up trumps with a low-rent apartment in the rue Broussais.

'They'll try to put you in Henri's apartment block,' Greta had told her on the phone.

'Who's Henri?'

'He's this very rich playboy who had the bright idea of buying a building off the Avenue de L'Opéra near the Etoile and Ford agencies, a really expensive neighbourhood where a carrot costs twenty francs, perfect for poor struggling models with one booking a week. His reputation is notorious amongst us Scandinavians. He goes off to Scandinavia, Sweden mostly, and he picks these blonde chicks off the streets and he says, 'Come to Paris with me, I will buy you everything', and off they go expecting the world and finding nothing. He runs these convenience-built apartment blocks for models, close to the agencies, studio rooms, split level, two single beds, little kitchenette in the cupboard and floor to ceiling mirrors everywhere.'

'Uh-oh. . . .'

'That's right, and there he sits on the other side of the two-way mirrors watching the girls and they have no idea. Maybe he's even got video cameras set up to film them, who knows? He's got *carte blanche* to go in and out of those apartments, he's the landlord, and those poor girls are at his mercy. He lays on all these drugs and if the girls aren't wise to the whole scene they go under very fast. You come and stay with me, Gigi, and we'll organise our own partying.'

Greta might have been in town only a month but she'd wasted no time finding the action. She'd come to Paris following a shoot she did in Milan which landed her on the cover of French *Glamour*. She introduced Gigi to everyone and before she even thought about sorting out her portfolio, Gigi bought herself a little code book. To get into an apartment building in Paris at night you had to know the building's code. Only then did you have access to the entrances to the apartments upstairs. If a guy invited her over to his apartment at night and she couldn't remember the code to his building, she would be stuck downstairs in the street with no way of reaching him. She could barely remember her own code and on top of everything her crazy London fan had followed her to Paris and was calling her at all hours of the night. What she couldn't figure out was how he'd got her number in the first place. He was obviously smarter than she'd thought. But there was no way he was going to get the code to enter her building. Yet if he'd managed to get hold of her number. . . .

So Gigi ran around town at night and trekked round go-sees by day and began to wonder if anyone would ever book her. After the fiasco at Armani in Milan, she knew she wouldn't get booked for any of the forthcoming shows. She had to face up to the truth: she wasn't a show-girl. She hated the castings, going into a room with seven people all gabbling away in French so she couldn't understand, then turning to her with a sniff, going, 'Oui, merci, au 'voir' and that was it. She wondered why on earth Daniel Mercier had arranged for her to come to Paris in the first place and it wasn't until Greta took her to the notorious Bains Douches club that she was able to find out. No one arrived at clubs until at least one o'clock in the morning. Greta's building had plenty of models living in it and they invariably came home from work, cooked dinner and then fell into bed for a sleep before going out after midnight. Between twelve and one the building became hectic with those who were going out putting on their best threads and getting their look together, and those who weren't and had an early call the next day pleading '*Keep it down!*' and being ignored.

When Greta and Gigi arrived at the Bains Douches there was a line going round the block. A blonde lady with a concrete face was working the door. There was no list, just two huge bouncers and the ferocious blonde who suddenly called out to Greta, 'Hey you! You were on the cover of *Glamour*. You can come in.'

And suddenly the Red Sea parted and they were inside.

'The dance floor's downstairs. Let's go up and have a drink at the bar first,' said Greta.

Daniel Mercier had a table. It reminded Gigi of Marcello's dinner party in Milan. Heavy clients and a scattering of beautiful girls. She hovered, not certain whether she should automatically go over, and then he saw her and beckoned. He made room for her beside him and ordered her a vodka tonic. Gigi recalled what Greta had told her.

'Gigi, you want to drink at the Bains Douches, you got to have serious money. It's at least £10 for soft drinks, maybe £80 for a bottle of vodka . . . go easy!'

Daniel put his arm around her and introduced her to the table. Most of the names whizzed past her too fast to remember except for the odd movie star and fashion editor she recalled seeing but who was too grand to remember her. Suddenly Gigi felt out of her depth. Greta had disappeared. Gigi was on her own, the little South Beach Orphan Annie on the outside looking in.

'So, Gigi, have you been making lots of new friends in Paris?' Daniel ruffled her dark curls. She nodded. 'Good, good. That's what I want you to do. Make friends with all the other models and find out who is unhappy.'

'Unhappy?'

'You keep your ears open at all the castings you go to. You find out who wants to leave us. Who is doing well at another agency but is unhappy there and who might like to come and join us. Who is sleeping with which photographer. And everything you find out, and don't forget the private apartment numbers, you come and tell Uncle Daniel at the Bains-Douche. Do we have a deal?'

'What do I get out of this deal?' Gigi's streetsmarts surfaced automatically.

'Presents. Whatever you want. I don't know what you're into. You have to tell me. Or tell one of my friends.' He gestured round the table. Gigi got it in a second. These were rich young playboys just like in Milan, moving around Paris in packs like wolves. One of them was probably the famous Henri, owner of the mirrored model apartments Greta had warned her about.

Gigi didn't like it. She preferred Milan with all its upfront sleaziness. Paris seemed to be a lot more subtle, loaded with the chic, opulent fashion crowd who were so in love with themselves on the surface but just as sleazy once you scratched a little. Still, Gigi had adopted a new philosophy for survival: beggars can't be choosers. And Daniel had chosen well. Gigi was a natural spy. It was in her nature to weasel out the truth from all the girls she encountered, find out who was becoming really successful and what it was that bothered them about their own agency. Then she ran to Daniel and whispered in his ear, giving him the ammunition he needed to poach the girl for Etoile.

Just as Paris Fashion Week was about to start the Americans

began to arrive, there was a new crowd at Daniel's table and Gigi was introduced to the sexiest man she had ever met.

Until she saw Jiro Takamoto, Gigi never realised that she actually found beefcake unattractive. Big men with bulging muscles were a turn-off for her. What she wanted was a sensual emotional-looking type with a mean streak running through him. Jiro was tall for a Japanese, long-limbed and supple like an elegant sapling. He wore an expensive suit with a white shirt, open at the neck, tie askew. There was an air of dangerous languour about him. He looked louche. His eyes were barely visible black dots but they seemed to miss nothing. He balanced a cigarette precariously on his lower lip. If it weren't for his oriental features he could have been a Frenchman, a Japanese Alain Delon. Gigi could see him on screen, whipping out a .45 and blowing Daniel's table away. That's what attracted her: his air of menace. A Park Avenue/Tokyo gangster.

Jiro ordered her a Black Russian and asked her where she came from. Without thinking twice about it Gigi told him about her father's drowning, her mother running back to Cuba, her adoption by Elena, her childhood in South Beach.

'And you?'

'Not so different. I was born in Osaka. My family's business is there. Very big. My grandfather is Tatsuo fucking Takamoto. We take over American companies every day. SWAN is owned by Takamoto, for example.'

'So you work for your father?'

'My grandfather. My father was killed when our company jet went down. But I don't miss him. I miss my mother. She still lives in Osaka so I don't see her that often. My grandfather wants me to get married and have children, heirs to carry Takamoto into the twenty-first century, but I have never met

318

a woman who will look after me like my mother did. Women now, they are so independent. I want a slave.'

Gigi realised he was very drunk. She had heard the gossip in New York about Tatsuo Takamoto's disreputable grandson. He had a reputation for being very un-Japanese. The stories about the noise coming out of his Columbus Avenue apartment every night were legion. In order not to allow the Japanese to lose face, seasoned New Yorkers knew that standard etiquette for dealing with noisy Japanese neighbours was to knock on their door, say 'Good evening, good evening' several times back and forth, wait for them to say 'How can I help you?' at which point you explain you are having trouble sleeping. 'Oh, really?' 'Yes.' And it was up to them to say eventually, 'Oh, perhaps it's my music that's disturbing you?' 'Well, maybe it is, yes.' 'Shall I turn it down?' 'Oh, yes, that would be most gracious of you.'

Jiro apparently opened his door and yelled 'What the fuck do you want?' before anyone could say anything. The Japanese code of behaviour was formal and polite, never to say no or make any demands. Jiro was non-stop arrogant, demanding and, to some people, irresistibly charming.

'If you like,' said Gigi, laughing, 'I will be your slave.'

She saw it as a challenge. It was so out of character for her to play the humble handmaiden and be submissive that for a couple of nights she quite enjoyed the novelty. As they lay together in bed she liked to look down on their bodies, noting in the warm light of his bedside lamp the way their colours blended perfectly, hers a dark coffee-cream, his a golden wheat. When they embraced, naked, in front of the mirror she liked the way their black hair merged into a single raven head.

It was his cruelty that brought her Latin blood back to boiling point. Their lovemaking at first was sensual and slow then, on the third night, instead of flicking his ash into the ashtray it landed on her bare buttocks. She thought it was an accident until she looked up and saw his lip curling. She reached up and scratched his face with her blood red talons while he shouted a word at her in Japanese which she subsequently discovered meant slave. Yet it was the minute she had stopped being his slave and started fighting back that he had become seriously excited.

And so had she.

London, 1994

In the end Armani didn't book Tess for his show but she flew home for the castings for London Fashion Week where to everyone's delight she was booked for Amanda Wakeley, the New Generation designers' show at Harvey Nichols, John Rocha, Tomasz Starzewski, Ally Capellino, Salisbury Plain and Helen Storey. At Harvey Nichols they had transformed the fifth-floor restaurant, running a catwalk down the middle, right next to the food market where Swan's minder, Brian Murphy could be seen doing her shopping. Backstage Tess met a rather dreamy American model called Cassie who pounced on her when she heard her name.

'I know you, your dad has a newspaper stand at the bottom of Earls Court Road. He was so sweet to me. I was in the depths of depression. I had just arrived in London. I had no work. I hadn't found Tommy. . . .'

'Tommy?'

'Tommy Lawrence. My boyfriend, see, over there. He's the tall dark waify-looking one with a bit of stubble and a nose ring. My mom and dad would die if they knew I was going out with someone with a nose ring! We've done this mega commercial together and we've become like this media item. I've made so much money I can hardly believe it.'

And I've just lost so much money I can hardly believe it, thought Tess. But she didn't resent Cassie's success. This apple-pie American girl was so non-competitive it was hard to begrudge her anything.

'Which shows are you in?' Tess asked.

'None. Tommy's doing Copperwheat Blundell. He gets to wear a woolly hat and a coarse linen shirt. I'm just happy to be here to support him. It's his first show. He's been booked for Paris too.'

Cassie was also backstage at the John Rocha show in the big tent outside the National History Museum. Here Tess got her first taste of the big-time runway, longer and more powerful than the little catwalk at Harvey Nichols. Tess suited the John Rocha clothes perfectly. Her russet hair and pale skin blended beautifully with his distressed sheepskin jackets in earth brown over the finest chiffon tops and his chocolate suede boleros with sheepskin collars and cuffs. Tommy did this show too with the weird new male models Jerome and Mat Rose and wide-eyed, skinny Keith Martin whom Paul Smith had used in the past. After the show Cassie suggested Tess join them for dinner that night.

'I can't,' sighed Tess, 'I've got a date.'

'Hope he's worth it,' said Cassie.

'He's not. He's history but I have to give him a chance to tell me his side of the story.'

'Sounds like a long one,' said Cassie.

'It is. I'll tell you another time.'

'Maybe in Paris?'

'I can only hope,' said Tess.

'There speaks a true model. Isn't that what we do all the time? We have so little control over our own destiny, all we can ever do is hope. 'Bye, Tess, it was nice meeting you.'

Bobby Fox had called right in the middle of supper her first night back. Tess's parents had been so overjoyed to see her that her father had even closed his stall early for the first time ever so he could come home and not miss a second of her stories about Milan.

'We knew you'd do it, love. We knew that Bobby would see you right.'

Tess said nothing.

'You should have seen yer dad when that *Carter's* story came out with you in that graveyard,' her mother told her. 'He had the magazine pinned back open at the page with your pictures and he stuck it up all over the stall. Every customer he had he tells them: "That's my girl!" He was so proud of you, Tess. Me and all.'

You would have been a lot prouder if I'd come home with enough money to buy you that wheelchair, thought Tess.

'Hey, Bobby's on the phone,' called her father from the hall.

Bobby! She hadn't spoken to him since she'd walked in and found him in bed with Gigi.

'Hello, girl,' he said quietly when she walked into the wine bar on the Fulham Road where they'd arranged to meet. He was sitting on his own in a corner and there, right at the next table, was a group of her schoolfriends. Tess couldn't believe it. She hadn't seen them since she'd started modelling. They must have all left school by now themselves.

'Jenny, Susie, Lynda, how are you? How've you been? How's Gary? Are you still with him? What happened with your GCSEs, Lynda? Still going to college? I've been in Italy.'

'We know, your dad told us,' said Lynda.

'Thanks for the postcard,' said Jenny. 'I suppose supermodels don't have time to remember their humble friends back home.'

'I've got my friend Bobby over there, shall we join you? Let's all go out together. Are Gary and the boys coming?' Tess looked around for a chair. As if on cue a scruffy-looking boy came in wearing a beat-up leather jacket, followed by two boys in sweatshirts with the hoods up trying to look cool.

'Tess! Great! Look at you! Saw your picture in the magazine, and what about that story in the paper with you all naked in the bath?'

To her own amazement Tess laughed. A couple of months ago she would have been freaked out by them mentioning the Lindy-Jane Johnson story but now she could toss it off as nothing. That's how far she had come. What she didn't realise was that she had left her girlfriends far behind. They were glaring at her now, angry at the attention she was getting from Gary and the other boys. Who did she think she was? their looks said, coming in here and thinking she could take over their boyfriends just because she'd become a model.

'Why don't you go and join your own boyfriend and leave ours alone?' hissed Susie.

'What, that little poofter? He's not her boyfriend, is he, Tess?' Gary was looking at Bobby.

Tess was shocked, both at Susie's tone and by the fact that Gary saw instantly that Bobby was gay.

'Well, no,' she admitted, 'but he is my friend. Well, I'll leave you to it. See you.'

'You won't see them again, you know that, don't you?' said Bobby when she sat down beside him. 'I've seen it happen over and over again. When a girl makes it, the ones she thought were her friends are suddenly threatened. And by the way he's right, you know, I am a poofter.' He was looking her straight in the eye, appealing to her to make it all right between them.

'And I'm just a little innocent. It's crazy,' said Tess, 'those girls think I've become all sophisticated and yet I didn't even clock you for being gay. You must have thought I was stupid.'

'Never! And you know why? Because I hadn't even come

to terms with the fact that I was totally gay myself those times we slept together.'

'We slept together . . .' repeated Tess. 'Did we, I mean, have you . . .?'

'It was safe sex. You know we used a condom every time. You have no need to worry about that.'

'And Gigi? Did you use a condom with her?' Tess's tone became sharp as she remembered the last time she'd seen him.

Bobby explained everything to her as best he could. He was impressed by the new Tess but he could see the old vulnerability was still there and it wouldn't take much to unnerve her. When he had finished, he said:

'I know I've hurt you and the only way I can make it up to you is by becoming your best friend, if you'll let me. You need someone to look after you, Tess, and I can be that person. You're working in a tough world. You've made terrific progress. Grace Brown and Angie were only saying yesterday how much more positive your attitude has become, but you've got a long way to go. Let me help you.'

Tess began to cry. She couldn't help it. She buried her face in Bobby's shoulder and let him pat her on the back and go 'There, there' as if she were a baby. After all the tension in Milan, his unthreatening gentleness was such a relief. Finally she dried her eyes and looked up into his face.

'I never thought I'd ever say anything like this but I love you, Bobby Fox, not in the way I thought I did but as my best mate!'

'Well, in that case you can go and do your best mate a favour and make sure you're a hit with all the designers at the show castings in Paris so we can do Paris Fashion Week together. I'm going to be there assisting Willy O'Brien, no less.'

'It's a deal,' Tess grinned. "Bye, Gary,' she called on her way out and ignored her girlfriends.

'Stupid stuck-up cow,' said Susie. 'What does she think she's got that we haven't?'

'Everything,' Bobby told her as he followed Tess out.

'I have everything,' Tess told herself two weeks later as she looked at herself in the mirror of her new Paris apartment off the Avenue de l'Opéra. She had been an instant hit at her Paris castings, booked not only for Sonia Rykiel and Claude Montana but also for Valentino. She could hardly believe it. Bobby was here, staying in a hotel with Willy O'Brien, and he was going to show her Paris by night. 'But I have to hang on to it. . . .' she reminded herself. She pulled her CK vest over her head, shook her long red hair and stared critically at her naked reflection.

And on the other side of the two-way mirror, Henri stared back.

I adore going to Paris. Ironically, it's probably where I can be the most private. I never stay at a hotel. I have this little apartment off the rue de Clichy in the 9th *arrondissement* just below Montmartre, not far from Pigalle. It's not an especially fashionable area of Paris but it's pretty unspoilt and old and quiet and if I want to, I can walk to l'Opéra, the Place de la Concorde, the Jardin des Tuileries, the Louvre and even across the Seine to the Left Bank.

The entrance to the building is typically Parisien with double doors leading to a courtyard from the street and a staircase leading to the upper floors. My little apartment has four rooms and is what they call in America a railroad apartment. The rooms all lead into one another. Each room is painted white and has a marble fireplace with a tall framed mirror above it and that wonderful wood panelling on the lower walls. The windows have little balconies and awnings and there's a bar/café downstairs where I often have breakfast or hot chocolate.

I didn't walk to the shows. They sent a driver to pick me up each day. I went downstairs to my car because I didn't want him to see Rory, who had come with me to Paris. While I had been busy doing the London shows, Rory had returned to Wiltshire to stay with my parents so they could get to know their future son-in-law. And while he was there he had

327

been to see Harry to tell him about his visit to Cecile's. I was scared by Harry's reaction. Rory told me my brother went into a state of near panic when he confronted him with Cecile's existence and had clammed up completely, saying he would only talk to me. Since there was no phone at the lime kiln this would have to wait until my wedding day.

For we had decided that Harry should be reunited with my parents at the wedding at Trevane.

Most of the collections were now shown at Paris's newly built fashion showcase, the Carrousel du Louvre, a £40 million, 250-metre underground gallery beneath the I.M. Pei pyramid at the Louvre. Gone were the days of fashion editors fighting their way through rain-soaked crowds to sodden tents. It was typical that just as New York began to show in tents, Paris converted to underground modernistic salons. It did make life much more simple although I was always rather nostalgic for the old days when I wasn't grand enough to have a car and driver and used to hop on the back of the little scooters they had ready to transport us from show to show.

It was Wednesday, 9 March and we were all doing Valentino at 12.30 – me, Claudia, Naomi, Linda, Christy, Helena, Cecilia, Brandi, Nadja. There was an additional excitement at the shows this year because the acclaimed American director Robert Altman, famous for M.A.S.H, *McCabe and Mrs Miller*, *Nashville*, *The Player* and most recently The Oscar nominated *Short Cuts*, to name but a few of his movies, was making a fashion epic called *Prêt-à-porter*. He was known for his documentary approach and there had been roving cameras among the show audiences, not to mention backstage. He had Sophia Loren, Lauren Bacall, Sally Kellerman and Tracey Ullman sitting in the front row and there was a lot of sniping among the fashion press about the fact that those people playing fashion editors never wrote anything down and didn't even appear to be holding notebooks. Reports came back to us each day from the rushes via our resident spy, Water Detroit, Celestia's boyfriend, who was in the movie. No one knew exactly when they were being filmed or when what they said was being recorded. Backstage we were particularly vulnerable and there was apparently a hilarious scene where three famous supermodels had been caught putting their heads together and declaring very seriously, 'Now let's talk about politics.' This angered me. Why did everyone always have to assume we were all so thick?

But by Valentino Altman had finished filming the shows and we could all relax. Celestia was there. She'd had her short hair dyed platinum blonde and she looked stunning. The supermodels' clothes rails were in a line just behind the stage with our names written in huge black childish writing on pieces of cardboard. The other girls were on the other side of a big gap and at first I couldn't see Celestia through all the clothes. In any case it was a crazy scrum with girls getting changed and the dressers squealing things like: 'What do you mean, your shoe size is 40? They told me 38 and it's the only pair I've got' just before you're about to go on stage. We had these huge pony-tail hair extensions which were very strange to walk in, and for one outfit I had to undo twenty-five buttons of a black evening jacket before I came to the end of the runway and they just would not come undone! I was still fiddling with them as I came off stage.

Still, for all the panic, the show was an amazing success. We ran down the runway at the end with Valentino, clapping away, and afterwards those who could get past security came backstage for loads of air-kissing and congratulations.

Celestia came across to my rail and stood there shyly while I was changing into my day clothes. I noticed she was shaking slightly. I hugged her.

'How was it?'

'Amazing. It's the only show I've done here at the Louvre. It's just so huge. I did Dries van Noten, Ann Demeulemeester, Vivienne Westwood, Martine Sitbon, Jean Colonna but they were all elsewhere. This show was sort of major. As I was about to go out on the catwalk I thought I was going to throw up. I had to stop for a second and remember my grandmother and everything she taught me.'

'She was one of the all-time greats. You couldn't have had a better training,' I told her. It was true. Fiona Fairfax was a legend. Celestia had told me about the sessions in the Great Hall at Trevane. Soon I would be having my own show there: my wedding.

'I'm getting married,' I told Celestia on impulse.

'No! Who to? I don't believe it.'

'His name is Rory Stirling. He's a writer. In fact you've met him. He was at Norah Nicholson's party.'

'Of course! He's divine. Then Water was right.'

'What do you mean?'

'Water saw Rory Stirling driving out of the Carlyle one day and he wouldn't rest until he could figure out what he was doing there. He's desperate to get to Rory because he wants to buy the film rights to his book. In fact, I'm supposed to get you together when we get back.'

'No. Celestia, you mustn't tell anyone about Rory and me. Not even Water. We want to keep it very private. But I would love you to come to the wedding if you can. You'll hear about it anyway from your parents. We're getting married at Trevane, in the chapel. Why don't you be my matron of honour or whatever they're called? But I'm sorry, I don't want you to bring Water. I sort of don't trust him somewhere.'

'Oh, don't worry, nor do I. I just have a good time with him. It's nothing serious as far as I'm concerned. He's driving

330

me crazy at the moment. He's so jealous because I appear to have a bigger role in *Prêt-à-porter* up there on the catwalk than he does actually being in the film. He's very insecure at the moment. He can't handle this improvisation thing they're doing where there's no script and he doesn't quite know when he's being filmed, do they have his best profile and so on and so forth. But Lavinia, I mean Swan, I'd adore to come to your wedding. There's just something I have to show you first.'

'Of course, what is it?'

It was bewildering. She suddenly thrust a little blue and red notebook into my hand and ran away. Literally. I peeked inside. There was a folded slip of paper and a single-line handwritten note: *This is Oliver's diary. Talk to me when you've had a chance to read it. Celestia.*

I dropped the notebook in shock and a hand reached out and picked it up for me. I looked up and saw the pretty redhead from Milan, what was her name? Tess someone.

'I wanted to thank you. Carla told me you suggested me for the Armani casting.'

'I certainly did,' I told her. 'How did you get on? I know I saw you around at the London shows.'

'Well, Armani didn't pick me but I've done so many shows here in Paris.'

I looked at her for a second. This girl was radiating beauty and energy. I recognised the look. She was falling in love.

'You look fabulous. Do I detect a special glow?'

She giggled. 'I ran into him at the Gaultier show just last Sunday. He was just this weird-looking boy Gaultier saw on the street here in Paris, the way he does, not a model, and he got him to be in his show. It's just so reassuring to have him around, I can't explain.'

'You don't have to. I know the feeling.'

Love was in the air. Speaking of which, I had to meet Rory

for lunch at one of my favourite restaurants, a little place on the quai Voltaire where the couple who ran it grew all the vegetables they served in their own garden.

But I could barely concentrate on my *consommé en gelée* and my *carré d'agneau aux haricots*, let alone my beloved Rory, because I couldn't wait to read Oliver Fairfax's diary and find out why Celestia had suddenly given it to me.

It was just as well that Celestia managed to go as Water's guest to the dinner given by Polly Mellen and Linda Wells for *Allure* magazine at the pretty little restaurant Marie et Fils in the rue Mazarine in the Quartier Latin. Polly Mellen is an institution in the fashion world, a legendary if not daunting former fashion editor on *Vogue* in New York, and someone who has always been very kind to me ever since I arrived in New York. I was so thrilled that she had just been given a Lifetime Achievement award. She so deserved it. I remember someone telling me he had been going up in the elevator with Polly at Condé Nast and she told him she wept every time she saw a beautiful dress at the shows.

I don't know what I would have done if I had had to wait another day to talk to Celestia about Oliver's book. As it was I had to wait all evening. It was a very A-list fashion dinner – Anna Wintour, Gene Pressman of Barneys, Ellin Saltzman of Bergdorf Goodman, Helmut Newton and his photographer wife Alice Springs, Andree Putman and André Leon Talley, Creative director of *Vogue*, Natasha Fraser of *W Fashion Europe*, Suzy Menkes, masses of designers like John Galliano, Sonia Rykiel, Agnès B, Jean Colonna, Martine Sitbon, Eric from Chloé plus a smattering of writers and actors like Sandra Bernhardt and her girlfriend, Billy Norwich, Rupert Everett, Diane von Fürstenberg and last but not least, there in his own right and nothing to do with me, the new hot young writer, Rory Stirling. We arrived separately so as not to arouse suspicion. When he came through the door I had to stop myself flinging my arms around him. I was listening to a crazy conversation going on between Helmut Newton and Rupert Everett who were both reminiscing about a shoot for Anna Wintour (who had just said hello crisply).

For once Celestia had abandoned her young-style rebel look and was wearing a beautiful Todd Oldham strappy number and with her new platinum hair and huge grey eyes she looked almost other-worldly. She was on one of the round tables at the back. I was at the front on Polly's table, seated between Helmut and André Leon Talley, and I couldn't get to her all evening. To my horror, I saw that Water was on the same table as Rory and was looking decidedly predatory. The chat was all about Fashion Week, whose clothes had worked and whose hadn't, Valentino had started forty-five minutes late, one designer had been so bored by the questions posed backstage by a journalist from British *Elle*, he had fallen asleep mid-interview, on and on it went. Normally I would have loved it all but I had so much else on my mind. We didn't sit down till after 10.30 but as soon as we had finished dessert and people were starting to get up and table-hop, I rushed over to Celestia.

'Come on, we're leaving,' I hissed. 'Tell Water and maybe he can invite Rory; that way I can have Rory with me.'

'Where are we going?'

'To the Arc club near the Etoile. Tell your taxi to follow mine.'

I had had a call from Cher who was in town staying at the Club St James, and she had told me to meet her at the Chrome Hearts party. When we got there, however, there was no sign of Cher but the dark ambience of the club provided the perfect spot for Celestia and I to sit in a corner and discuss Oliver's diary. Poor Rory had to fend for himself with the dreaded Water but I had hurriedly whispered to him why I had asked them to join us and I knew he understood.

I clutched Celestia in the semi-darkness.

'I knew Harry was lying. I just knew it. He told me Oliver went to this escort agency called Cecile's but he said it closed down years ago. It hasn't. Rory went to check, but when he confronted Harry with it Harry went nuts. Rory said he was seriously frightened and said he would only talk to me. As soon as the shows are finished I'm going straight down to Wiltshire to see him.'

'You mean you know where your brother is?' Celestia was so surprised her voice came out as a squeak. I realised I had let the proverbial cat right out of the bag without thinking. I had to tell Celestia the whole story.

'That's incredible,' she said when I had finished. 'I don't know what prompted me to show you Oliver's book after all this time but I'm so glad I finally did. We have to get to the bottom of it all when we get back to England. Can I help, Swan, from now on? Please say I can. I feel so terrible for not showing you this before. I really want to help.'

'Of course you can,' I told her. 'The first thing I'm going to do is ask Harry for some details about this Murray character.'

But when we got home to the rue de Clichy there was a message waiting for me on my answering machine.

'Swan, it's Sally. Sally Bainbridge. Listen, I hope it's all going well. I just thought I should ring you. I don't know what to do. It's Harry. I went down to Wiltshire, to the lime kiln, last weekend and he'd gone. There was nothing there. He's taken all his things and I haven't heard a word from him. He's completely disappeared again.'

Alice Johnson tottered on to the escalator at the entrance to
the Carrousel du Louvre. She was decked out in her one and
only Chanel suit. Unfortunately it was now much too small
for her and she bulged rather, but if one was going to the
Chanel show, one had to wear one's Chanel. Didn't one?

Alice clattered along the underground shopping mall and
cheesed at Suzy Menkes of the *International Herald Tribune*,
who completely ignored her (hardly surprising since Suzy had
never seen Alice in her life before). Silly cow, thought Alice,
and why does she always have that ridiculous hairdo? Alice
had never actually seen Suzy Menkes before either but she felt
as if she had, having seen her picture in so many magazines.

She would rather die than admit it but this was Alice's first
time at the shows and to make matters worse she'd arrived in
Paris and immediately come down with a bug. This was her
first day out of bed. She hoped Geraldine and Lindy-Jane
would be all right. They had left her her ticket for Chanel
the night before and gone off to the Chrome Hearts party,
whatever that was. Alice assumed Chrome Hearts was a band
of some kind but their sniggering when she'd mentioned this
made her think perhaps she'd got it wrong.

She arrived at the entrance to the halls and flapped her
ticket as she went through.

'S'il vous plaît, s'il vous plaît, Madame, *Madame!*' A man

335

with a mobile telephone had come rushing after her and was guiding her, horror of horrors, back behind the cord and leading her round to a long line of people to one side waiting to get in.

'But I have a ticket. See? With my name on it.' She displayed the black card with CHANEL in gold lettering.

'Yes, Madame, but you do not have a seat. You are standing only.' And he walked away.

Alice could hardly bear it. She had to stand there with the plebs and watch while the élite (with a seat) sailed past her triumphantly. Actually none of them even glanced at her but Alice assumed that Anna Wintour, John Fairchild, André Leon Talley, Alexandra Shulman, Anna Harvey and, of course, Suzy Menkes were all laughing their heads off at her. Then she saw Geraldine and Lindy-Jane. They had their tickets out; they were waved through.

'Geraldine! Over here! Here I am.'

But they ignored her and suddenly it dawned on her. Geraldine had switched the tickets and given Alice her own standing one.

The crowd pushed and shoved behind her as more and more people arrived and then, finally, when they were let in, at the next entrance they had to show their passports. Alice hadn't brought hers with her. She rummaged in her bag and brought out the first thing with her name on it: her Blockbuster video membership card and then, just as the man was studying it intently, she was thrust forward by the crowd and the barrier broke. Alice ran. What did it matter if she lost her Blockbuster card if it meant getting into Chanel?

Inside she was confronted with a dilemma. Her high heels were agony and not meant for an hour's standing, but if she took them off she would be too small to see above the crowds. She looked about. The place was packed. She saw a row of

Japanese men snoring quietly, and fumed. She saw women in very recent Chanel suits take their seats clutching motorbike crash helmets. She saw Geraldine bouncing up and down in her seat and waving at people who, Alice was pleased to see, didn't wave back. She saw Eileen Ford, doyenne of model agents, whose girls would soon be adorning the catwalk, yawning. The lights went down and suddenly Alice was nearly thrown off her feet by the floor below her reverberating with the loudest disco music she'd ever heard. Whenever she tried to write anything her pencil wobbled.

It was a sportswear collection with workout suits covered by giant national flags for the models. Swan had a Union Jack draped around her, Linda Evangelista the red and white maple leaf of her native Canada and Claudia Schiffer the yellow, black and red German flag. There was a lot of fake fur and the accessories were very witty: little picnic sets with bottles of water, little fur handbags, mobile telephones, ski goggles and rubber boots with the double C logo.

'Chanel wellies,' wrote Alice dutifully, 'fluffy mittens, hats with fluffy octopussy tentacles.' It didn't sound quite right. She'd have to get Geraldine to smooth it out a bit. She glanced at Geraldine. That girl had it coming! Her gaze wandered to Lindy-Jane. Alice simply could not believe it. Lindy-Jane was not even watching the show '... and after all the trouble I went to to get her tickets!' raged Alice. Her sister was hunched over in her seat, totally absorbed in a little red and blue notebook. It looked like Lindy-Jane was reading somebody's diary!

She was.

Lindy-Jane had had quite enough of her sister, whose vocabulary had suddenly become limited to only two words: fluidity and deconstructed. Alice thought that if she uttered these words in every sentence, people might be fooled into

337

thinking she actually knew something about fashion. As soon as she was able, Lindy-Jane made her escape.

At the Chrome Hearts party the night before, she had muscled her way in and sat watching Swan and Celestia in their corner. She had seen them poring over the notebook. She had heard Water Detroit telling Rory Stirling it was pretty sexy stuff and then, when no one was looking, she had reached into Celestia's voluminous model bag and taken the notebook.

Now she couldn't believe what she had. She would photo-copy it and return it to Etoile Paris for Celestia's attention with a note saying it had been found on the ground somewhere.

She was still reading it when the show had finished and she was distracted only by Alice shaking her arm.

'Come along, my girl, time to go. Last time I'm giving you a helping hand. I had to bloody stand. Now, for God's sake, come and do something about Geraldine. The wretched girl suddenly thinks she's Anna Wintour and is trying to get backstage.'

There was a very different atmosphere on the runway now. Where Linda, Helena, Tatjana, Naomi, Claudia *et al.* had been only minutes before, bouncing about and clapping Karl Lagerfeld going down the runway in his little ponytail, now there was poor Geraldine being punched in the face by a security guy. Admittedly he had been aiming at a photographer and Geraldine had got in the way. She went down like a ninepin and to Alice's everlasting mortification, the last sight the Paris fashion world had of her was as she lurched down the catwalk dragging her semi-conscious assistant along behind her.

By way of punishment, Alice appropriated Geraldine's invitation for that night's party and gave it to Tess Tucker. She had Tess lined up to do some stories in Paris for *Carter's* after

338

the shows. The *Mrs de Winter* story had been a triumph. The girl deserved it even if she did have a rather odd-looking new boyfriend she insisted on bringing with her.

The party was at one of Paris's oldest and most establishment restaurants, Ledoyen in the Champs-Elysées, and it had been taken over by Bulgari the jewellers for the evening; their name was emblazoned across the top of the entrance in a giant neon sign.

The bash was being thrown by Bulgari for the benefit of Robert Altman's cameras for his film *Prêt-à-porter*. The entire cast was there including poor Sophia Loren who was made-up and ready at 7.30 p.m. and still hadn't been called when they finished filming at three in the morning. The actors were miked for sound so anyone wandering up to talk to them was supposed to call them by the name of their character in the film. Except nobody knew the names of the characters.

'Rupert, you look terrible, why aren't you wearing your kilt?' asked Jean Paul Gaultier of Rupert Everett, who always wore his family's Maclean tartan (on his mother's side) kilt at evening functions.

'Shhhh! You're supposed to call me Jack. I'm playing Jack Lowenthal, son of Simone Lowenthal, who was originally based on Sonia Rykiel.'

'Darling, may I kees you?' enquired Gianfranco Ferre, going up to a woman with a short bob and fringe and dark glasses, who was bending over, sitting in a corner shovelling hors-d'oeuvres into her mouth. He nearly fell over backwards when she looked up. She was huge. He had thought she was the skeletal Anna Wintour. He backed away hurriedly, saying 'Sorry, sorry!' but whoever the large lady was, she was on her feet instantly and pursuing him.

'Darling, *run*' yelled the large lady's companion. 'He has a house to die for on Lake Como and if you become his new best friend we can all come and stay.'

Designers Agnès B, Vivienne Westwood, Christian Lacroix, Claude Montana, Sonia Rykiel and Jean-Charles de Castelbajac rubbed shoulders with Marcello Mastroianni, Lauren Bacall, Kim Basinger, Rossi de Palma, Lyle Lovett, Tracey Ullman, Richard E Grant in thigh boots with stacks, a high hat and a frocked coat, and Stephen Rea mooching around in a red velvet jacket. The security guys ran round instructing the guests, 'Regardez pas le caméra!'

This was pretty hard since there was a camera in someone's face every five seconds.

Water Detroit was extremely pissed off yet again, since Tommy Lawrence had been such a hit on the catwalk in the Dries van Noten and Gaultier shows that Altman had put him in the film for the party. Water, on the other hand, was just a guest. Cassie was thrilled to bits. As she kept telling everyone, it was like a real Hollywood party back home.

Then she remembered that Hollywood was no longer home. To make matters worse, she ran into Ute Lemper who was playing a character called Albertine in the film. Albertine was a model who was contracted to do the shows for a designer in the film but who had showed up eight and a half months pregnant. Cassie looked at her stomach protruding through her clinging slinky evening gown, and sighed. Then she dissolved into tears.

'Hey, hey, hey,' said Tess, coming upon her suddenly, 'what's all this?'

'Her,' gulped Cassie, pointing at Ute Lemper, and she proceeded to tell Tess all about her abortion and how she was desperate to have a baby to make up for it.

'Well, why don't you?' said Tess. 'Tommy looks like he would make a great father.'

'Yes, he would, wouldn't he,' said Cassie and made a mental note to throw away the Pill.

Ute Lemper's mike recorded the whole conversation.

After the party, the cast went on to the Bains Douches and Cassie and Tommy went with them.

The first person Tommy saw when they walked in was Gigi, who rushed up to him and flung her arms around his neck.

'Where did you get to? I heard you'd gone to London and done that amazing commercial. Wowie, Tommy!' She kissed him smack on the lips.

This struck a raw nerve with Cassie, vulnerable as she was following her confrontation with Ute Lemper's pregnancy. She had thought she would never see this little hustler again and here she was kissing Tommy. Tommy was *hers*. She strode across and shoved Gigi out of Tommy's arms.

'Wait a second, what's going on here? Cassie, honey, it's me, Gigi.'

'Keep away from Tommy.'

'Why should I do that? We go back a long way, right, Tommy?' She hooked her arm through Tommy's.

Cassie laid into her again, this time slapping her around the face. Gigi let go of Tommy's arm and clawed back at Cassie's face. Nails dug deep into Cassie's soft peachy skin, drawing blood. Cassie pounded Gigi's left breast and there were gasps from the crowd now gathering. Cassie's blouse was ripped from her back, exposing her lacy bra. Gigi withdrew for a second and returned to headbutt Cassie like a fiery little Latin bull. Cassie went down. Gigi stood over her, raining blows. Cassie's hand flew out and scratched Gigi's thighs below her micro skirt. Gigi kicked her. Somehow Cassie managed to get to her feet again. She was taller than Gigi. She always had been. It was the all-American blonde against the immigrant Hispanic. It was war.

Both girls were breathing heavily. By now the crowd had found out their names and were cheering them on.

'*Allez*, Gigi!'

'C'mon, Cassie, hit her upstairs!'

Gigi stood on tiptoe and spat full in Cassie's face, blinding her for a second. Then she reached out and ripped what was left of Cassie's blouse from her, leaving her breasts exposed and falling out of her bra. Gigi pulled her leather jacket tightly around her own breasts and withdrew from the scene, blowing kisses to the crowd, responding to the wolf whistles, milking her audience for all it was worth. This was her terrain, her people.

As Tommy led away a weeping Cassie, Gigi sidled into the banquette beside Daniel Mercier.

'OK for one night,' he said, 'it'll be all over the papers internationally tomorrow. I called the press over to watch. They got a few pictures. YANKEE GIRLS IN NIGHTCLUB SUPERBRAWL OVER BRIT MALE MODEL. But that's it. I don't want to see you doing anything like that again, not while I'm looking after you. Who's the blonde, anyway? Someone I should know about?'

'She's a hopeless model. She didn't work at all in New York. I shared an apartment with her. She's so unreliable, she turns up late for every shoot. She misses castings. She gets fat. She's on drugs. You don't want anything to do with her, Daniel. Believe me,' Gigi lied away cheerfully.

'Thanks for the tip,' said Daniel. 'Keep up the good work. Here's Jiro come to take you home. Go easy on her, Jiro, she's had a bit of a beating here tonight. Nothing she couldn't handle but she might be a bit fragile.'

Jiro took Gigi back to his hotel and ran her a bath.

'That last remark of Daniel's, does he know what we get up to?' asked Gigi, lazily soaking in the tub.

342

'Of course he does. He told me you'd like it.'

'But how did he know? I didn't even know myself.'

'Daniel always knows. But listen, I've got a bit of real gossip, something that's going to cause shock waves round the modelling world.'

'Ooooh! Tell me, tell me,' Gigi was sitting up with soapsuds on her nipples. Jiro couldn't resist tweaking them off. Hard.

'I spoke to my father. Charley Lobianco of Etoile New York's been on to him. Swan's giving us notice. She wants out of her contract. We're going to be looking for a new SWAN girl. . . .'

That's something I really do have to tell Daniel as soon as I can, thought Gigi. I wonder where he is.

It was four o'clock in the morning. At 'Ultra' night at Folies club in the place Pigalle, the place was packed. A lot of people from Karin's agency were there. And one from Etoile. Bobby Fox, abandoned by Tess in favour of her new man, was amused to be cruised by none other than Daniel Mercier.

London/Devon/New York, 1994

I went into a minor panic when Charley called to say *Vanity Fair* wanted to do a cover story about me. Why now of all times? Did they know about Rory? Had they discovered Harry hiding somewhere? But further investigation by Charley revealed that it was all perfectly innocent, and I had to smile at the irony of the timing. If only they knew what a story they might have had: Swan gets married! I let Charley in on my secret because I knew he could be relied upon to keep quiet. Besides, I wanted to invite him and Laura. I had decided to relax and ask a few very special guests to my secret wedding. For example, Norah Nicholson absolutely had to come. She was the one who had introduced us!

I was in Grace Brown's office (and of course I had to ask her) when she took a call from Barbara Harper in New York. When she got off the phone she told me about Amy La Mar's freak success.

'The thing is,' pondered Grace, 'she needs something really big in the publicity department to put her in the public eye internationally. I mean, that fire might have got her some work in New York but it doesn't mean beans to anyone over here.'

It started me thinking. I had always told myself that one day I would do something major to help Amy La Mar and

344

now I saw what I could do. I called Barbara Harper, who was an old friend.

'Barbara, I've had an idea. Tell me what you think. They want me for a *Vanity Fair* cover story. What if I were to tell them I would only agree to do it on condition they bring Amy into the piece and put her on the cover with me, like they did with Cindy Crawford and k d lang? I could make the focus of my interview about modelling in general as opposed to just about me. . . .'

' . . . and you could let Amy have her say about black models. Swan, would you really do that?' Barbara was overjoyed.

I would and did. They weren't too happy about it to begin with but after a while they got the point. They couldn't photograph us until I was back in New York for the shows. Apparently Amy was also going to be doing them. She wouldn't do Paris and Milan until the following season. A time for the interview was set up for a date in April – by which time I'd be a married woman, only they wouldn't know it. But they'd have one coup: it would probably be my last major interview as a working model and they'd have the story about my quitting as the SWAN girl. They interviewed Barbara at my request and she got in her bit about the fact that the New York City's Department of Consumer Affairs had done this study on the lack of black people in print advertising but that when they pointed out what they had found to magazines and ad agencies, none of them would agree to sign a pledge to depict people of colour more accurately on their pages or in their advertising.

Barbara was ecstatic when she called.

'You've done us proud, girl, you really have. There's no way they can leave out what I told them 'cause they know I'll just go right out there and say they left it out. Thank you, Swan.

345

Amy and I thank you from the bottom of our hearts. We truly do!'

So of course I had to go ahead and invite them to the wedding too.

Celestia and I went down to Trevane four days before the wedding. Rory was to follow on the eve of the Big Day. Celestia and I were in adjacent rooms and our behaviour reverted to that of schoolgirls sharing a dormitory at boarding-school. We sat up all night exchanging gossip about the mod-elling world, gossip upon which we had embarked at the dinner table and quickly abandoned as it became clear that, as with all shop talk, it was unspeakably boring to outsiders. We even went as far as having a midnight feast, raiding the kitchen for chicken legs and smoked salmon and taking them up to the attic, where Celestia unearthed the old photograph albums where she had first seen my picture.

Once you start looking at old photographs it's very hard to stop, and soon we were giggling at snaps of the entire family. I was a little shaken to come across pictures of Oliver with Venetia, looking so young and blissfully happy together. I turned the page quickly and clutched myself in shock. There was a page of snapshots of Oliver at Eton and in several pictures he was standing with a tall, sardonic-looking youth whose sneering face made me cringe. But it was the caption that gave me the biggest jolt: me with Murray. Murray and me at Fourth of June. Murray and me at Exeat.

Murray!

Charley arrived to stay, bringing his mother and Norah Nich-olson. Charley was on splendid form and had some wonderful news to tell us.

'That naughty little girl, Victoria Parrish, they caught her at it in Miami. Her parents take her there on vacation all the time and she sneaks into the Park Central and throws herself at these guys. I mean, I was probably one of them but I see so many girls, I couldn't remember her. My problem wasn't that I couldn't remember doing anything with her but that I couldn't remember not doing anything with her, if you get my drift. Anyway, what I'm trying to say is that there are guys coming out of the woodwork she's been coming on to and now they've learned she's only fifteen or whatever she is, they're all prepared to say she was the one who wanted it. They wanted nothing to do with her. That baby she's pregnant with, the father could be anybody. She got caught soliciting – in an upscale way, but soliciting all the same – by a detective in the hotel. Mrs Parrish is so embarrassed she doesn't know where to put herself. Now she thinks I'm the one who's going to press charges. Jesus!'

We were all so relieved, we couldn't stop laughing.

Trevane was so huge there was plenty of room for everyone to stay. I was so happy having all the people I loved around me and the only bit of unpleasantness occurred when Barbara Harper arrived with Amy and her boyfriend Marcus and Marcus' brother who had brought a sound system so we could have some music to dance to afterwards. I was crossing the hall with a huge vase of flowers when I heard Prudence's voice and my heart nearly stopped.

'Good God, Celestia, there are some coloured people getting out of a taxi. And there's another in a big van. Run and tell them they've come to the wrong place before the taxi leaves.'

I went back into the hall.

'Actually, Prudence, they're my guests.'

'Don't be silly, child. Please don't try teasing me now, I've got far too much to do.'

'I'm not teasing you.'

'But, my dear girl, why ever didn't you warn me? What am I going to do?'

I suppose if I'd thought about it for one second it might have dawned on me that Prudence Fairfax would be a racist. She probably thought all black people ought to be shot like Hugo's pheasants. There was only one thing to do: keep her as far away from them as possible. As far as Barbara, Amy and Marcus were concerned, Celestia would be their hostess.

'Prudence, I'll deal with them, show them to their rooms. There's a man from the caterer's in the kitchen and I think he's ruffling Cook's feathers a bit; her domain and all that. Perhaps you'd better go and sort that out.'

'Oh, all right, Lavinia. Oh no! Do look, they've brought a child, for heaven's sake!'

My bridesmaid. There was no one young enough in the family so I had told Amy she could bring her little sister, Tootie, to be my bridesmaid. I couldn't believe the exuberant little creature dressed in pink organza, who ran into the hall and mimed walking along behind me holding a posy of flowers.

'Are you Swan? Do I do it like this? Can I sing while I'm walking up behind you? My voice is brilliant. Listen. . . .'

Prudence fled.

The main reason for Tootie's excitement, I discovered, was that this was the first outing of her new hair. Every little black girl wants to be able to have long flowing hair that they can swing around their head like white girls do. Unplaited, Tootie's spiky little pigtails turned into a mop of coarse frizz barely covering her ears. Now, as a special treat, Amy had taken her to Shepherd's Bush market and bought her some long fake hair extensions, which she'd had sewn into her real hair. Tootie's hair now hung halfway down her back and she spent a lot of time shaking her head like a pony and making her new hair fly around the place.

I could tell Amy wasn't quite herself. I sent Marcus off with Barbara and Tootie to walk round the grounds and took Amy upstairs for a chat. It seemed her brother Leroy was in trouble. She suspected drugs. In any case he'd disappeared. (Join the club! I felt like saying, but restrained myself.) The police had come round and her mother was in a terrible state.

'Oh, goodness, I should have invited your mother. Is she all on her own?'

'She's fine. She's having a nice peaceful couple of days all to herself.'

Then everything seemed to go into a haze because Rory arrived, with his great big bear of a father who had come all the way from Montana, and I couldn't think of anything else but him. I even stopped worrying about Harry for half a second. Celestia introduced herself to Amy and I could see they were going to become firm friends. Water Detroit was back in New York. It was a funny relationship between him and Celestia. She seemed perfectly happy to have a few days away from him but I knew they did have something good going when they were together.

It was a brilliant March day, my wedding day. The winds were strong but there was plenty of sunshine too. I stood at my bedroom window watching everyone making their way across the fields and down the narrow path flanked by rows of daffodils to the little chapel, the women holding on to their hats in the wind. Tootie, Celestia and my mother were with me, helping me get dressed. I was wearing an ivory silk suit with a tight-fitting, boat-necked jacket, long narrow sleeves and the back tapering to a point dipping over the skirt. The skirt was skin tight, ankle length with a band of fake fur around the hem matching the fur of the muff I carried.

A beautiful halo of white roses sat on my jet black hair and my grandmother, too frail to make the journey, had sent her pearl choker as a wedding present.

My father was waiting downstairs, resplendent in his grey morning suit. Golly the black labrador had a white ribbon tied round his neck, which Tootie was using as a lead.

'Jolly good,' said my father predictably as I came downstairs but when I saw the look of pride and affection in his eyes I knew I had made him terribly happy. Willy O'Brien had come down to take the pictures and he took a group photo outside Trevane of Daddy and me flanked by Mummy and Celestia, with Tootie standing in front of me waving a little Union Jack she had insisted on carrying and Golly nearly pulling her over.

We reached the chapel and there was Rory waiting for me. As I walked down the aisle towards him I held my head high and knew that this performance was better than any I had ever given on a runway. Old Uncle Matthew, the only member of the family who had ever taken holy orders, had been woken up and brought out of mothballs to conduct the service. I don't know what made me do it but as he cleared his throat for the twentieth time and began to intone, 'Dearly beloved, we are gathered together here in the sight of God, and in the face of this congregation, to join together this Man and this Woman in holy Matrimony . . .' I turned my head and looked back down the aisle in time to see Harry slip in at the back of the chapel and hide behind a pillar.

Of course by the time the service had finished and I had thrown back my veil and was walking triumphantly back down the aisle on Rory's arm, he had vanished.

We had a high old time back at Trevane. There were fewer than twenty of us but we threw back the rugs in the Great Hall and danced to the most incredible West Indian music coming from an impromptu sound system Marcus' brother had rigged up at the last moment. It was their wedding present to us. Tootie sang to us whenever she got the chance and we managed to get Prudence pissed for the first time in her life so that she too joined in the dancing, shaking her petticoats while Willy took her picture. My only sadness was that while Harry had managed to be present for the wedding service itself, he had missed out on all of this. And I hadn't been able to invite Sally because I would have had to explain who she was.

Rory and I left on our alleged honeymoon around two in the morning. I say alleged because in fact we were driving to Heathrow to take a flight to the Caribbean, not for a holiday, but because I had a shoot there. We had just driven through the main gates when a figure leapt into the middle of the road, caught in the glare of the headlights.

Harry!

He climbed into the back of the car, I said the name Murray to him, and on the long drive back to London he told me everything.

'Guy Murray. Horrendous fellow. You remember the March-Wentworth's son, Toby? Poor little sod fagged for Murray at Eton.'

'What did you say?' asked Rory, nearly swerving off the road.

'It's a barbaric custom at English boys' public schools. The older boys have what are called fags who clean their shoes, make their beds, run errands, act like servants and generally do absolutely everything for them. It's frightful but I'm afraid it probably exists to this day,' I explained.

'Guy Murray was a loathsome bully,' continued Harry, 'it was awful, he had some kind of hold over Oliver. Oliver idolised him to begin with then I think he realised what a creep he was, by which time it was too late for him to get away. It was Murray who introduced Oliver to Cecile's. When Oliver told me what went on there, I told him he had to cut loose from Murray. Then Oliver was killed and I thought that would be the end of it. Sorry to put it like that, but you know what I mean. What I wasn't prepared for was Molly Bainbridge. Murray had terrorised her. She worked there for years before she could summon up the courage to try and break away. She approached me. I didn't know what to do. I felt responsible for her somehow. I told her that my parents were looking for someone to take care of you, Titch. . . .'

I let it go. I was a grown-up married woman. I could afford to overlook these irritations now. Besides, what Harry had to say was riveting.

'I thought if she was under our roof I could protect her, but I was wrong. She told me Murray had tracked her down. She reckoned he had part ownership of the club. She said he threatened her, said she was to come back or else. Well, I'm afraid it was a case of "or else". I walked in on them. He was there, on the top landing at the Boltons, suffocating her with a pillow. I tried to pull him away but she was already dead. He was wearing gloves. He said there was no way I could prove he was the one who did it. There were no witnesses. And he said if I ever told anyone I'd be dead myself within the hour.'

I shivered, half expecting Guy Murray to suddenly sit up in the back seat like they do in movies and blow Harry's brains away.

'Anyway, how do you know about Murray?' he asked suddenly. 'I never told you about him.'

I told him about Oliver's notebook and the photo albums in the attic at Trevane.

'Oliver's diary! That'll do it. Let me see it. Have you got it?'

Then I remembered. Oliver's diary had been lost in Paris. Celestia had mislaid it after I had given it back to her.

'Don't worry,' said Rory, 'we're getting there. Can you and Sally try and track Mr Murray down and then when Swan and I are next in the country we'll all pay him a visit, even if it means storming that club of his.'

Harry was going to go to ground in London in the flat upstairs from Sally in Covent Garden which had come up for rent. I rang Sally from the airport and told her to get some money for the rent from Grace Brown out of my account at the agency. I gave her details of the wedding to pass on to Grace so Grace would know she was dealing with someone who knew me well.

Then Rory and I flew off to Saint Barts. It turned out to be a honeymoon after all since there was some nightmare problem at the airport with the carnets for the photographic equipment and the clothes and they never arrived so we couldn't do the shoot. While we waited for it to be sorted out I scampered off to Rory, who was staying in a separate hotel, and discovered what bliss it was to be Mrs Swan Stirling.

The flight back to New York was less than blissful. Rory wasn't flying with me and sitting next to me was a man they call the Poacher – I can't even remember his real name – who is a scout for a rival model agency to Etoile. He travels the world trying to persuade top models to leave their own agency and join whichever poxy agency he scouts for. We all know him. He's a pest. He books first-class seats next to supermodels on long haul flights to places like Australia and then bends their ear non-stop from take-off to landing. I took one look at him and popped a sleeping pill.

As I arrived back in New York and let myself into the Carlyle apartment I realised Rory and I hadn't discussed where we were going to live. I supposed until our marriage was out in the open we would have to keep our separate apartments. One good thing was that Rory had installed a telescope over on Central Park South so we could look closely at each other through our respective lenses.

Bridie had left me plenty of goodies in the fridge and an apologetic note on the kitchen table. It seemed she wouldn't have quite as much time for me in the next few weeks. Her son Mayo had upped and gone to Paris and she had had to come clean with Industria about the fact that it was she who had been doing the cooking. She was now working part time there in his place until he returned. He was due back any day now.

I wandered into my bedroom, dejected, tired after the long flight, missing Rory already. The red light on the answering machine was flashing. Maybe he'd called me already. I rushed to flick the switch.

I was just about to sling my bags into the upper closet when a low seductive voice, faintly familiar, began to talk to me.

'Swan? You there? Did you have a good trip? I sure hope so because what I have to tell you may upset you just a little. It's too bad *New York Magazine* did that pictorial profile on you recently. . . .'

What pictorial profile? I wondered. One of those cut-and-paste jobs, probably. Whatever it was I knew nothing about it, but it was quite easy for someone to collect together photographs from various libraries and run a story.

I went on listening to the stranger's voice, hypnotised into obeying his instructions mindlessly, as I would be in months to come – for this was the first time I heard from the Messenger.

Part 3

The Messenger 1994-1995

New York, 1994

Six months later, in October, I flew in from the Paris shows to hear the Messenger tell me:

'Remember the first time I ever called? Remember what I asked you to do? Well, I'm going to ask you again to go and look through your mail till you find another blue airmail envelope postmarked London Heathrow. I mailed it to you before I – and you – left for Paris. It should be there by now. Inside you'll find a photograph, just like before. Don't worry, it's not of you this time. I'll call again in about a week, give you time to think. In my next message I'll tell you why I'm sending it to you. Switch off now and go and look.'

At the beginning of his message he'd told me the gunshot that had shaken me so badly as I walked along the runway in Paris had been just a tape recording. This guy was a real freak. He had to be obsessed with tapes, on or off answering machines.

The photograph inside the envelope was a mystery to me. I knew who she was. Another model, a seriously pretty girl I knew slightly, but why her? Well, there was nothing I could do. I'd find out in a week's time when he called again. *If* he called again. Meanwhile, Mr Takamoto had told me they were getting close to making a final decision about my replacement as the SWAN girl.

I had been rather impressed with the way Takamoto Inc.

had gone about replacing me as the SWAN girl. They had turned the whole thing to their advantage by launching a kind of *Gone With the Wind* publicity stunt, comparing the search for SWAN II with the casting of Scarlett O'Hara in the film. They were, they said, looking for a relative unknown. The castings took place, as Japanese castings often did, in a New York hotel suite with practically the entire board of Takamoto Inc. flying in from Osaka and clustering round one end of a long table while the girls presented themselves at the other. Needless to say the final shortlist they drew up comprised five models who, if not exactly household names, were not completely unknown to the market.

I was appalled by the inclusion of Gigi Garcia but I understood she was Jiro Takamoto's girlfriend, if not his fiancée, and he had pulled strings with his grandfather to see she was included. All well and good, provided she didn't actually replace me. I was surprised to find I had a rather unpleasant desire to sabotage her chances by having a word with old Mr Takamoto, but I resisted such a childish temptation.

Cassie Dylan was an understandable choice as her sensational Princess of Wales dental floss commercial had been a huge success in Japan and she was, if I can be forgiven for such an awful pun, very much flavour of the month.

Tess Tucker was a pretty obvious choice. Her look was the type the Japanese went for as a matter of course. She had done really well in Paris, they liked her 'English rose with freckles' look. She'd done all the standard Paris shoots: sitting in one of those little sidewalk cafés ordering a coffee or standing at the side of the road hailing a taxi, and she'd been worked to death in what we call Paris Daylight Studio No. 1 – the Place de la Concorde. Poor girl, I'd heard from Milou, the location bus driver, that they'd whacked out quite a few catalogues with her in the Place de la Concorde. She'd had a few bits of bad luck, I'd heard, the usual thing: you brag away about the spreads you're going to be getting in a magazine because you're so excited and your agency's telling you 'when those pix come out watch your rate soar!' and then the magazine hits the stands and your picture's the size of a postage stamp, no use at all for your career. But apparently she was sailing through it all quite happily because she was so hooked on the new boyfriend. It was quite a surprise who it turned out to be. She'd been in New York for some time now, trying her luck here and doing pretty well by all accounts, and I'd run into her at Industria when we'd both been doing a shoot there. Mayo was back behind the bar, and who should walk in and give him a passionate embrace but Tess. It turned out he'd gone to Paris for a holiday and Jean Paul Gaultier had spotted him wandering down the street, whisked him away and put him in one of his shows last spring. Now that I thought about it I recalled her telling me about him backstage at Valentino. It was just that she'd never mentioned his name. Mayo! Who would have thought?

My own personal favourite was Amy La Mar and I was simply delighted she had made the shortlist. Our *Vanity Fair* piece had certainly helped place her firmly in the public eye and she was a beautiful girl as well as being an interesting and original model. I confess that I had let slip to Mr Takamoto at some stage that I thought they ought to consider her and without making too much of it, I had hinted at the points they would score in the political correctness arena by having a black model on their shortlist.

Then finally, there was Celestia. Of course she was almost family so I was delighted for her. She had been such a huge hit on the runways in Paris, and then in New York last season, plus she was so much the darling of Condé Nast that she was almost a cinch. In a way she was most like me. Same background. Same swan's neck.

It was going to be a pretty close run thing between the four of them. I couldn't bring myself to include Gigi seriously. Indeed I was pretty relieved when Mr Takamoto called again to tell me:

'Swan, I wanted you to be the first to know. It was very hard decision to make but we have finally chosen Cassie Dylan as the new SWAN girl.'

The very next day the Messenger called again and told me that the girl in the photograph he had sent me was his fiancée and if I did not manage to secure her the SWAN contract then he would release the photograph he had taken of me and Harry to the press.

For months I had agonised over who the Messenger might be. Now I was almost certain I knew. He could have been any one of the five men associated with the girls on the SWAN shortlist.

The picture of me and Harry had been taken in 1987 in England and whoever it was had to have had access to the Paris shows.

Gigi was supposedly engaged to Jiro Takamoto and, of course, Jiro had been educated in England as a boy. He was also always at the shows for Takamoto Inc.

Cassie was with Tommy Lawrence. He was English and he'd grown up there. And as a top male model he had access to the shows.

Tess was in love with Mayo. Well, he had an English accent, and Gaultier had called him back for the recent shows although in the end he hadn't used him. Still he'd been around in Paris.

Amy was engaged to Marcus. They were both English and Amy had got passes for Marcus for all the shows she was in. But surely the Messenger couldn't be wonderful, reliable Marcus?

Water Detroit was going around telling the world that he was engaged to Celestia. I had long ago decided that I would believe that one when I heard it from Celestia herself but they were still together and that had to mean something. And I recalled him boring me to death at some point with details of some trip he'd made to England with his parents when he'd been a kid. As part of the Hollywood movie brat pack he was assured a front row seat at the shows if he wanted one.

I stared at the girl in the picture and thought about the voice of the Messenger whose identity I now knew. It all fell into place. The voice had always been faintly familiar but it had always had a strained quality to it, as if the person was trying to disguise his real voice.

Cassie Dylan had been picked as the new SWAN girl but the girl in the picture the Messenger had sent me was Tess Tucker. What was I going to do now?

London, 1994

The day Takamoto Inc. called Etoile to begin negotiations for Cassie's contract as the new SWAN girl, Cassie decided she couldn't delay telling Tommy she was pregnant any longer. She was beginning to show. She had thrown away her pills right after the Paris shows last season – but she hadn't told Tommy. She hadn't become pregnant right away. It had taken two months but now that she was nearly four months gone they'd already guessed at the agency, because the fitters had been complaining she was up a dress size every time she had a job.

But she didn't want to tell Tommy just yet. It was amazing that he hadn't even noticed, but then he had had a lot on his mind. It was because he was so preoccupied that she didn't want to add to his troubles. Having refused to hire his own father as his accountant, Tommy was now in terrible trouble with the taxman and that was all he could talk about. But why should the news of a forthcoming baby add to his troubles?

What was she thinking of? It would be a joyous surprise for him. As for Cassie, it was her dream come true, the compensation for the baby she had lost back in California. Her mother would be thrilled for her. For an instant she reached out for the phone to call Kari in New York. But no, she must tell Tommy first.

Etoile beat her to it. They didn't mean to but he was in the agency and Grace assumed he knew about the baby.

'Hey, Tommy, can you believe it? Cassie's been picked as the new SWAN girl. We haven't mentioned the baby but at some stage we're going to have to.'

Tommy looked thunderstruck

'I know,' said Angie, 'it's amazing, isn't it? A major, major contract. Take a deep breath. We had to when we first heard.'

'Not that . . .' stammered Tommy.

'Oh, shit, you mean you didn't know about the baby? Hold on a sec . . . Mr Pearson, yes, hello, it's me, Angie Doyle. Look, I'm afraid I've told you before, your daughter will be perfectly all right. She's nineteen years old. That's quite old for a model starting out these days, and besides she's a very together girl. She's only going to Switzerland not South Central Los Angeles, she doesn't need a bodyguard, I promise you. I really do. Please, Mr Pearson. Oh, all right, talk to Grace Brown but she'll tell you the same thing . . . Grace? It's that over-anxious father again, wants his bloody daughter to have a bodyguard. She's only been modelling two months, anybody'd think she was Claudia Schiffer, the way he's carrying on. Anyway, Tommy, yes, about the baby. You'd better have a chat with her. Seriously. I mean, we've known for a while and they even want you to do another dental floss commercial together, this time while she's pregnant, and then there'll be another one with the baby - like an ongoing story. It's been such a success all over the world they want to keep it running as long as possible.'

Tommy was trapped.

They didn't want him to do the commercial without Cassie. It wouldn't be the same. They'd start a completely new couple off on the same theme if they couldn't have Cassie and Tommy again. So if Cassie didn't do another commercial with him he was out of a job – and facing a gigantic tax bill.

Etoile fully expected Cassie to be overjoyed about the SWAN news and they were pondering how to tell Takamoto Inc. that she was pregnant, and could they hold off for a while till she'd had the baby? Swan herself was still the official SWAN girl until the end of the year.

Cassie surprised everyone. She opted for the commercial. The script was a teeny bit racy and controversial. She appeared pregnant and the script called for Tommy to propose to her in order to give the child a name. The dental floss element was now more or less a given, the couple were so famous. The press picked up the story: will he marry her for real? There was tremendous public demand for Tommy to do the right thing, and in the end he succumbed.

Cassie lost the SWAN contract because the baby would come just at the wrong time, but she didn't care. What she had meant far far more to her. Even Tommy was pleased. As long as these commercials kept going he was in clover financially. But he'd have to do something about that interview he'd done with a magazine about what male models got up to with female models on shoots and how their girlfriends felt about it. He'd got a bit drunk with the pretty blonde girl interviewing him and told the truth – a different girl on every shoot. Cassie wasn't going to like it. . . . Well, he could always go back to Croydon and bond with his dad. Heaven knows, he needed an accountant.

Mr Takamoto called Swan for the second time.

'You heard the news, my dear? Sad, but such an honour for her to have a baby. I think you will be pleased about our next choice. I hear she is almost like family to you. Another beautiful English girl, honourable too: Celestia Fairfax.

When Grace Brown at Etoile received the news, Celestia was sitting in a suite at the Château Marmont hotel in Los Angeles surrounded by gift-wrapped bottles of champagne, boxes of chocolates, and outsize bouquets of flowers. They were offerings from 'her friends' at CAA, William Morris and ICM. Celestia looked at the names: Guy MacElwaine, Ed Limato, Michael Ovitz. She didn't know anything about them except that they were agents. All she knew was that she had been approached by a Hollywood studio to play the lead in a movie they were making and she didn't have a theatrical agent to negotiate her deal. If she was interested in taking it further she needed a Hollywood agent.

If she was interested! She'd read the script and she loved it. She was fed up with modelling. Her natural rebellious tomboy instincts were surfacing and she wanted to move on to something else. Standing around in a studio all day was so boring! The location shoots were quite fun but you never got to see much of the country you were in and then it was off to the next job. The only thing she really enjoyed doing was runway work but that didn't happen all the time.

The film they wanted her for was about a young American woman who inherits an English stately home from her uncle and decides to turn it into a rehabilitation centre for young drug addicts and alcoholics in recovery. Everything goes fine until a beautiful young man arrives from New York. She falls in love with him and he tries to lure her back with him on to drugs. It was the setting Celestia was drawn to; not the drug world but the house her character inherited. In the script she got to ride around the grounds on horseback and Celestia realised that was the life she was missing.

'Sounds like the Betty Ford Clinic set in *The Secret Garden*,' said Water, his voice loaded with sarcasm. 'You do realise, Celestia, that all these agents are not actually interested in you personally? They just want to beat each other to get to you.'

Celestia ignored him. She knew he was jealous because they were in Los Angeles because of her and not him. Ever since he'd finished shooting *Prêt-à-porter*, he'd been like a bear with a sore head. Nobody was taking him seriously as a producer. He couldn't get to first base with any of the studios, he couldn't get his hands on the kind of properties he wanted, someone always beat him to it, nobody wanted to power-lunch him, nobody wanted to even do lunch with him, and to top it all here was Celestia being pursued all over town. The only way he could even get arrested was by attaching himself to her and that was why he had begun spreading rumours that they were engaged.

Celestia was not stupid. She had become addicted to Water in a strange kind of way. She didn't necessarily want to marry him. She wasn't ready to marry anybody yet. Yet she wanted to have him around.

She went with Ed Limato at ICM in the end because while she had never heard of him before, he looked after Richard Gere and Mel Gibson and Michelle Pfeiffer among others and she'd heard of them. Water was seething with envy.

'Just get me into a meeting with him,' he kept begging her.

He wanted Ed Limato to look after him too instead of the nerd-with-no-clout he was currently with.

Ed Limato did an amazing deal for her and sent her off to a drama coach, and a dialogue coach for the American accent, for the pre-production period. When Grace Brown called to say she had been picked as the new SWAN girl, Celestia was at a lesson and Water took the call. He freaked. They were casting for the male lead opposite Celestia in the movie, the role of the young American addict who tries to lure the heroine into his world, and he was up for the part. The studio liked the publicity angle of the new hot young model and her fiancé, the brat pack actor, starring in the same movie. Apparently Takamoto Inc. had a problem with Celestia appearing in a film with a drugs-related background *and* being the SWAN girl. She was going to have to make a choice. And if Celestia pulled out of the movie, then he'd probably be out too.

But he needn't have worried.

Celestia had entered the modelling world in order to pay homage to the memory of her grandmother, and now she was ready to leave it. There was a lot of money being dangled with the SWAN contract but what nobody ever seemed to have taken into account (least of all Water, who didn't even know) was that she was heiress to Trevane and the Fairfax fortune. What did she care?

She also had the last laugh on Water. He was on a real high about landing the lead playing opposite her – all the other brat pack actors had been after the role – until he discovered that he'd been chosen not only for the publicity-with-Celestia purpose, but because his shit-for-brains agent had agreed he'd do it for scale. Celestia was getting a fortune; he was getting virtually zip! Take it or leave it.

'Christ,' said Grace Brown when Celestia said no, 'there's five girls on this SWAN shortlist. It's getting like ten green bottles. . . . If one green bottle should accidentally fall . . . oh well, two down and three to go.'

London, 1994

It was no ordinary funeral. They weren't lowering the coffin into the ground but bringing it up again. Suddenly they threw it in the air and it landed on a catwalk. The photographers in the pigpen at the end leapt up and began to prise it open. All along the runway fashion editors and buyers, their faces shrouded in black lace veils, leaned forward in their front-row seats and craned their necks to identify the body.

'It's me, it's me!'

I woke up screaming but I knew that even as I regained consciousness, the dusky-skinned girl rising from the coffin was not me but Gigi Garcia.

Tootie rushed in and jumped on my bed. Ever since I had come home she had been sleeping in Mum's room instead of sharing with me like she used to do. I tried to explain to Mum that I hadn't changed, I was happy to have Tootie around, but Mum said I needed my own room now. I had become quite the neighbourhood celebrity since the *Vanity Fair* issue with Swan and me on the cover had appeared. I was pleased with the interview I'd done and grateful to Swan for giving me the opportunity to voice what I felt. I'd been able to raise the fact that so few black models were used on magazine covers and when they had pointed out that this was because if a black face appeared on a magazine, circulation dropped considerably that month, there were statistics to prove it, then I was really able to go to town.

'Well, of course circulation's going to drop because it's such a shock to the system of the public. Having a black face on the cover of *Vogue* or *Harpers* or whatever is so rare that if they were to use a black model everyone would assume it wasn't *Vogue* or *Harpers* but a magazine targeted only at a black market, and if they were looking for *Vogue* they'd pass it by unless the face was that of a supermodel or a celebrity. An unknown beautiful black girl would not do.'

'So you understand the need of the magazines to bow to the pressure of their advertisers and keep black models off their covers, that they must respect what the public demand?'

The interviewer had walked straight into my trap.

'No, I don't think that at all,' I had replied. 'I think if the public became used to seeing black covers all the time, there would be no problem. If they were used to it, if they were expecting to see a black cover on *Vogue* every couple of months like they're used to seeing black actors on TV and in the movies, and it didn't come as a shock to them, then the circulation would be perfectly healthy. It'd be tough in the beginning but the editor who is brave enough to break down the barriers will go down in history.'

They had been sceptical but I had made my point and they printed it. I was secretly amazed at myself. Just over a year ago I had been just another young girl on the Portobello Court Estate. Now here I was with the confidence to speak out for my race in an international magazine. Marcus had given me a quote from Marcus Garvey which I carried around with me at all times:

If you have no
Confidence in self you

370

Are twice defeated in
The race of life. With
Confidence, you have
Won even before you
have started.

That's what modelling could do to you: give you a crash course in sophistication.

Yet it could also bring out your worst insecurities. I didn't really know the girl in my dream, Gigi Garcia, but what I had seen of her I rather liked. She was a Cuban, or rather she was a Cuban-American. If I didn't like it when people didn't take me for an English girl just because I was black, I had no right to call Gigi just Cuban. She wasn't that dark but she wasn't pure white either. She had told me that her parents had brought her to America with the Mariel boatlift. Marcus had told me that since Cuban exiles were mostly white, people often assumed that all Cubans were white, but this was not the case. Cuba had always been heavily black and mulatto and with so many of the white population having fled the island, and a higher birth rate among the Cuban blacks who remained, the population was now about 70 per cent black. When I asked Gigi about her father, she didn't volunteer the information whether or not he was black – and why should she? But the more I saw of her the more I sensed that here was someone who really did have a complex about her colour. Yet I liked the way she seemed to be fearless and always came right out and said what she thought. She put people's backs up but she was passionate and fiery and vibrant and I admired her spirit. She was insecure about her colour and her background but she wasn't going to let it get her down. I played the game and didn't rock the boat. She rocked it every chance she could and her career was set to self-destruct at any second.

But she was exciting!

Yet things were getting a little too exciting around my own family. Even though he was older than me, Leroy was just a confused kid playing Boyz 'n the Hood meets Yardie gangsta-rapper and getting himself in one great big muddle. No one knew where he was. Marcus and I tried to persuade Mum to go to the police but she'd lived in the area too long for that course of action to come naturally to her. She distrusted the police but she was going crazy and trying hard not to show it for Tootie's sake. And it was poor little Tootie who took the brunt of Leroy's stupidity. Marcus and I came home one afternoon to find her locked in a cupboard. She was shaking so much and her teeth were literally chattering in fright that it was a good five minutes before we were able to calm her down and get her to tell us what had happened.

She'd been alone in the flat. She was supposed to go over to a neighbour's until Mum got back from work but the neighbour hadn't been in and Tootie had let herself into our flat with her own key. When the doorbell went a few minutes later she ran to open it, despite what Mum had always told her about never answering the door when she was on her own. Tootie thought it would be the neighbour come to get her. Instead in walked a bunch of heavies from the Grove gang who started putting the frighteners on her about her brother. Where was he? When had she last seen him? Only when they realised she genuinely didn't know where Leroy was did they push her into a cupboard and leave her locked in.

'Crack, crack, crack . . .' went Tootie in a high, squeaky voice, 'that's what they said – crack, crack, crack.' She giggled in near hysteria and I hugged her to me. Did she mean they'd been pointing a gun at her or had they made her little bones crack by holding them tightly?

'Don't be daft,' said Marcus, 'I told you Leroy was involved in something. He must be dealing crack for them. Let's hope he hasn't been stupid enough to do a runner with some of their stuff. If they catch him I don't fancy his chances.'

We left a note for Mum and took Tootie down the police station before anything else happened. And Leroy surprised us. He'd been in police custody all the time but they'd been keeping quiet about it because he was helping them with their inquiries. They'd been keeping their eye on me and Mum – nice to be told after the event, so to speak – but they hadn't anticipated anybody paying little Tootie a visit. Leroy had found himself in too deep. When he'd been picked up by the police on what turned out to be a false arrest he had panicked and begun to squeal. On the information they were extracting from him drip-drip fashion every day, they were getting closer and closer to a major crack house bust in Notting Hill. In return, Leroy wanted police protection.

'It's a lab, man. You put me out on the streets before you get them they going to kill me.'

We had to go home and tell Mum. On the one hand she was relieved; on the other she was sad. The first time I had seen my brother in ten years he was in a police cell.

Life went on. Leroy was the gangsta wannabe, Tootie was very soon back to being the entertainer in our family and Marcus and I were just enterprising young black people trying to make a go of it as best we could, be it in a black world or a white world. Whatever. I had enrolled to do a foundation course at my local polytechnic and then I would apply to do my fashion degree at St Martin's or Central St Martin's College of Art and Design as it's now known. I had saved a fair bit of money from my modelling just as Marcus had said I would.

The fact that I was on the shortlist for the SWAN contract didn't seem real until something unpleasant made me take it seriously. I went into Etoile to talk to Grace and Angie about a possible job coming up and, of course, to speculate about the SWAN contract. Grace Brown was on the phone to Jiro Takamoto. She was frowning.

'You can't go around saying things like that, Jiro, not in this day and age.'

'What things?' said Angie when Grace had put the phone down.

'I'm sorry, Amy, but he says they'd never give the SWAN contract to a black girl. It was just a PR exercise putting you on the shortlist.'

'I don't believe it!' said Angie.

'Call Gigi and ask her. She was with him while he was talking to me. She must have heard.'

I can't say I was amazed. I was just relieved I'd never got my hopes up about it. By the time I was on my way out to dinner with Marcus, I'd almost forgotten all about it. Marcus had a friend who was going out with a white guy, and his older sister, a lawyer, had invited us all round to her place for dinner. Georgina was fair haired and blue eyed and warm and welcoming. She owned her beautiful house in West Kensington. She was clearly successful. I started to feel a little niggle. If I had got the SWAN contract I could have bought her house two or three times over. I was brooding about this as we sat down to eat in her kitchen and it was a few minutes before her conversation penetrated my thoughts.

'I've got this case at the moment,' she was saying. 'There's this Italian girl who was working for a bank when it was taken over by the Japanese. They're letting her go, the Japanese I mean, because they say she does not have a "British" face. They've bought a British bank, they want everything British. The Italian girl is suing the bank for racial discrimination.'

It was the word Japanese that made me sit up and listen. Marcus, sitting beside me, sensed my interest.

'Go on,' he said, 'tell her what happened to you.'

'I'm on – or rather I was on – the shortlist for a beauty contract for a Japanese company, Takamoto Inc.'

'Oh, yes, I've heard of them. They've got an English end,' said Georgina. 'Don't tell me it's the SWAN contract they had that highly publicised search for?'

'Exactly. Today one of the executive officers, I think that's his title, anyway he's the grandson of the owner, he said I would never actually get the job because I was black.'

'What were his exact words?'

'Well, I didn't hear them direct but I'm told they were: "we'd never give the contract to a black girl".'

'There's a witness?'

'There was someone with him when he said it, yes. And he was talking down the phone to someone else.'

'I think you have a case,' said Georgina, leaning forward, pushing her plate away. 'A claim for race discrimination can arise from being refused a job if we can show that a person – in this case you – was not selected for a job because of their colour in circumstances where a GOQ did not apply.'

'GOQ?'

'Sorry, legal jargon, stands for "genuine occupational qualification" – in other words when the job requires a particular race for authenticity. Now if they selected you for the shortlist, that implies they were leading everyone to believe they didn't necessarily specifically require a white girl.'

'And the witness is not entirely white.'

'Think about it and give me a call if you want to take it further,' said Georgina. 'Now, that's enough shop talk. Marcus, fill up my glass please.'

I talked to Grace Brown the next day. She couldn't deny

what Jiro had said to her. She called Gigi in and we asked her to corroborate his words.

'Listen, what the fuck is this? The guy's my lover. I don't need this kind of shit right now. It might jeopardise my own chances, has anyone thought of that?'

'Gigi,' I said, taking her aside, 'when you look in the mirror do you see a lily-white face?'

It was the meanest thing I'd ever said to anyone in my life but I was disappointed in her. Just when I needed her usual in-your-face attitude she was going to let me down.

'Just let me think about it, OK?'

'OK.' It was all I could say.

But she called me a couple of days later.

'Amy? I decided I'm gonna help you out. Maybe. You get yourself a lawyer and I'll talk to him.'

'Her.'

'Whoever. Just talk. Off the record. Then we'll see.'

That was when I knew I was going to take on Takamoto Inc. I called Georgina and set up my first meeting with her.

And that night I dreamed about Gigi's funeral. What had I got her into?

Paris, 1994

'*Fuck you and the donkey you rode in on!*' yelled Gigi down the phone. She was going to have to do something about this guy, whoever he was. How had he got her phone number? Since she had come back to Paris he had been calling her every couple of days, pleading with her to meet him, threatening her when she said no. She still didn't know who he was. He said he was her biggest fan, that he'd seen her at a shoot, he slept with her signed Z card under his pillow and he wanted to get to know her better. He wouldn't even give his name, he just kept pleading with her to meet him.

And then he did something that really scared her, that showed her he meant business.

She went to the country for a job and when she came back she found a note from him in her apartment. Not only did he now have the code to get into her building but he had a key. He'd been staying there, sleeping in her bed, using her shower. She told Jiro and he just laughed, but then Jiro was becoming pretty weird these days. His sexual sadism was getting worse and she was no longer enjoying it, it was becoming scary.

She had one ray of sunshine in her life to hang on to and give her hope. She had always known what Amy had just discovered: that her presence on the SWAN shortlist was just a charade. Jiro had pulled a few strings and put up her name

377

because in his own way he was as obsessed with her as the fan who kept calling her. But she hadn't a hope in hell of getting the contract. She knew that perfectly well.

However, the agency had called one day and told her they'd sent a stack of cards to J. Walter Thompson, who were doing a worldwide campaign for a new French perfume, and they'd requested to see her. She went along to the agency, was shown into a room on her own, offered a drink of water. Water! As soon as she was alone again Gigi reached in her model bag for an Evian bottle filled with Bacardi and took a quick swig. Then the art editor and a couple of people handling the account walked in. Gigi enjoyed the respect with which she was treated. They weren't looking at her as if she were just any old model, they were looking at her as the potential girl for their campaign so they were treating her as if she already was that girl. And they were looking at her all the time.

She had a couple of callbacks and finally they called the agency to say she was the one they'd chosen. Her option was confirmed. She flew down to the South of France for the shoot; waiting for her at the hotel was a team of twelve people all there for the sole purpose of getting her ready for the shot. Gigi's entire modelling career up to now had been a sham. She'd worked intermittently but she'd never hit the big time. Her name on the SWAN shortlist had helped get her a go-see for this job and suddenly she began to experience the thrill of the undivided attention of a team of people who knew that if they made her look right, she might become a star. Everyone knew this was the platform for the new perfume. If the shoot went well then everything might just go bang!

The photographer, a German, talked her through his philosophy of how he wanted to do the shoot, what look he wanted to get out of it, and for the first time Gigi listened intently. Then they went up to a villa overlooking the town where they had virtually rebuilt the garden as the set, with plants brought in from all over the place, an entire nursery. There was a little seat and a little table and Gigi sat there for two days while they photographed her.

When she returned to Paris the agency told her she was going to be a star. They now had a platform on which to sell her even though the campaign wasn't out yet. Suddenly everyone wanted her and the next thing she knew she was booked on a flight back to London for two days of castings. JWT had reported back that the advertising people in the office of the perfume company had loved the shoot, but the company was family owned and they just had to run it past the family, something they always did, no problem. After all, it was a week before release; what could possibly happen now?

Gigi was in the air on her way to London when the word came back that the family had said no. No particular reason, they'd just looked at her face and decided it wasn't right for their product.

She was on a real high when she landed at Heathrow. Etoile had said they would send a car for her as a celebratory gesture for the perfume campaign. She went through Arrivals and looked for her name amongst the sea of chauffeurs holding up cardboard notices.

There it was: GIGI GARCIA.

The driver wasn't wearing a uniform but, Gigi consoled herself, they didn't much now, did they? They'd just sent a minicab instead of the limo she'd been expecting. Well, all that would change once the campaign was actually released.

The driver didn't say a word as he picked up her bags and led her to the car. Once she was settled in the back seat he turned to her and said, 'So, I finally got to meet you at last.'

She recognised the French voice immediately as her obsessive telephone fan.

London, 1994

What we would never know was whether or not my nightmare about Gigi's funeral had in fact come true. Was she still alive? Or was she lying dead in a ditch somewhere?

To begin with Grace and Angie had just been exasperated that yet again Gigi Garcia hadn't turned up for an appointment. It seemed she had quite a reputation as a no-show. Then, of course, exasperation turned to genuine concern especially when Angie remembered the crazy fan who had kept calling when Gigi was in London, and a junior working at Etoile in Paris confessed to having given out Gigi's number to someone whose name she had not bothered to ask.

The saddest thing was that Gigi appeared to be all alone in the world. She had no family to be contacted. She had bluffed her way through the modelling world for less than two years, leaving havoc in her wake, and now she seemed to have vanished without trace and everyone was filled with a strange sense of loss and foreboding. She had that effect on people. When she was around she was infuriating but now she was gone she was still there, under our skin, the image of her striking smouldering looks embedded in our subconscious just like a supermodel's should be.

And there was another devastating consequence of her disappearance which I felt guilty even thinking about: I had lost my prime witness.

'Don't worry,' said Grace. 'I taped the conversation with Jiro.'

And Georgina had been making progress in quite another direction. Swan had called me to tell me that old Mr Takamoto was very upset by the charge of racial discrimination, so much so that he was coming to London. Georgina had made it clear to the Takamoto lawyers that she had a case and she had two cast-iron witnesses. At that time poor Gigi had still been around. Georgina advised them to settle out of court. Swan explained to me that Mr Takamoto was furious with Jiro for what he had said and very worried about the fact that Takamoto Inc. might be seen to lose face if they were taken to court and lost. Much better to settle out of court.

So in the end I did have some money to be invested in my future as a designer although not quite in the way that Marcus had predicted. It wasn't a huge amount – about £25,000 – and I didn't invest it in the way Marcus had envisaged. I used it to obtain a mortgage for a bigger flat for Mum where she and Tootie and Leroy could each have their own room. Meanwhile I was going to live with Marcus. I knew I was going to marry him and I felt ready to sleep with him. He didn't want to actually get married until he'd set up his photographic agency and got it off the ground.

But I could wait. The nightmares were gone. I was getting new ideas for designs every day and besides, we had a new model in the family: whenever I had the time to run up one of my creations on Mum's old Singer, Tootie, who had shot up in the last year and whose early-teen figure was gently ripening, was the ideal model for them, and as I watched her parading up and down, and flipped through the fashion magazines I was now able to afford at the newsagent's and saw the glossy spreads, I could hardly believe that for one brief year I had been part of that world. It all seemed so far, far away.

Yet, if my new dreams came true, and I was determined that they would, I would be part of it again – only this time I'd have control of my destiny – black or white.

London, 1994

Alice Johnson still hadn't had her revenge on Geraldine for switching the tickets for the Chanel show in Paris, but a crafty little plot was hatching itself in her less than original mind.

Geraldine had been in a state all week about what to wear to a dinner she was going to that evening. She hadn't been invited in her own right. She was going in Alice's place – on Alice's ticket again as it were, only this time with Alice's blessing – as the *Carter's* representative at a dinner being given by a new manufacturer who wanted to play big industrial entrepreneur and produce all the top designers' clothes and was therefore courting the fashion world for all it was worth.

The reason Alice wasn't going herself was that she was otherwise engaged: she had finally landed herself an invitation to a very grand dinner party in Eaton Square. These days upward social mobility was becoming rather important to Alice and suddenly, darling, she was deciding that the rag trade, darling, could take a back seat in her journey through life. Eligible husbands did not grow on shoe trees. Meanwhile, she had Geraldine to deal with.

'Geraldine darling, it's terribly simple. Why don't you have a little peep in the fashion cupboard? I'm sure you'll find something perfectly suitable.'

'Oh, I thought we weren't supposed to, I mean . . . may

384

I?' Geraldine was breathless with excitement. In the fashion cupboard she could have her pick from a dozen little numbers from Flyte Ostell, Anouska Hempel, Calvin Klein, Alexander McQueen, Helen Storey or Ben de Lisi. She'd have to be careful. The dresses had been used in fashion shoots and were due to be returned to the designers next week. Geraldine selected an Anouska Hempel – when would she ever be able to afford an Anouska Hempel herself?

The first person she saw – as Alice Johnson had known she would – when she walked into the dinner was the PR person from Anouska Hempel, the person who had sent the dress over to Alice and Geraldine for use in a *Carter's* shoot and who was expecting it back, unused except by the model, the next day. Poor Geraldine knew she had been caught in the act of committing a serious blunder and something told her that if she tried to explain that Alice had said it was all right, Alice might just deny having said any such thing.

Enjoying a teensy-weensy lie-in the morning after her dinner party, having drunk rather more than she should have done and slept till noon, Alice picked up the phone to call Lindy-Jane at the office. It amused her to keep her sister abreast of her social calendar. She sensed that it irked poor Lindy-Jane that try as she might – and heaven knows Alice did everything to help her – Lindy-Jane was unable to make any headway herself, either in her career or socially.

They told her Lindy-Jane wasn't there; hadn't, in fact, been there all week. Alice allowed herself to feel worried for a split second. Lindy-Jane hadn't been picking up messages on her answering machine for over a week. Where was she?

If Alice only knew!

At that precise moment Lindy-Jane was watching a partially clothed man lying on a bed being strangled.

She had only worked at the club for a week. Months ago she had gone to Cecile's and asked for a job in order to further her investigation, only to be told they were closing down. But the manager had kept in touch with her and when the club reopened – as Brigitte's – she had begun what they were calling her training week.

She had heard stories from the other girls. When they really trusted you, you had to hold your man down and distract his attention while someone else came in and finished him off – for good. And they taped the whole thing – so you better stand out the way.

Somewhere, Lindy-Jane figured, they had to store those videos.

There was an office at the back of the building on the ground floor that was always kept locked. When she asked whose it was the manager told her it was Mr Murray's, and when she asked who Mr Murray was she was told she didn't need to know – which immediately told her that she did. The trouble was, the club was open twenty-four hours a day. It operated as a kind of hotel. Lindy-Jane watched the back office closely. No one seemed to go near it. She smeared the door handle with hand cream and checked it at various intervals. It was untouched. She left it on all night and at eight o'clock the next morning she found it had been used. The cream had been wiped off. One night, hiding in the corridor after she was meant to leave, she stayed all night and at 7.30 in the morning a man let himself in the front door of the building, made his way to the back office, used a key to unlock it and reappeared seconds later, locking the office behind him. He was tall, very slender, fair hair slicked back and dressed like an old-style City gent in a pinstriped suit, wide stripes, double-breasted jacket, watch and chain, buttonhole, well-

386

shined shoes. He carried an overcoat with a black velvet collar. A real city slicker, thought Lindy-Jane.

She kept up her vigil for several days in order to establish that he came every day at the same time. After three days she was rewarded for her perseverance. He came out of the office with the pigskin briefcase he always carried, and dropped it. It wasn't properly fastened and all the contents fell out. Among the papers were videos.

Lindy-Jane resolved to go home and get a few good nights' sleep and then go back, smash the glass on the door, break into the back office and have a good look round.

When she went back Guy Murray, he of the pinstriped suit and the pigskin briefcase, was waiting for her.

It had been disastrous timing when I had received the Messenger's ultimatum because we still hadn't nailed Murray. The main problem was that Cecile's had suddenly closed down. One day it was there and the next it was all shut up. When I had flown straight back to New York from Saint Barts after our wedding, Rory had returned to London to link up with Harry and confront Murray. That's when they had discovered Cecile's was no more. Harry couldn't very well put out feelers about Murray with his Eton chums through the old boy network since no one was supposed to know where Harry was. He had given Rory a few pointers but so far Rory hadn't been able to turn up anything. Murray seemed to have vanished into thin air along with Cecile's.

In the end we had Sally Bainbridge to thank for tracking down Guy Murray. At the ad agency where she worked she overheard one day one of the twitty little Sloaney secretaries yacking down the phone – thus preventing the switchboard from being able to put through important calls to her boss – for twenty minutes to a friend about a 'simply dreamy new boy who's moved in to The Laurels. His name's Piers Murray and he's got a sister called Marietta and he's actually about eighteen months younger than me, he's in his last year at Eton, but I don't care, we danced all night at....'

It was the combination of the phrase 'in his last year at

Eton' and the name Murray that had made Sally look up from what she was doing and eavesdrop on the conversation, which she relayed to Harry that evening. Harry called me and we decided it was a long shot but all we had to go on. Harry had been playing supersleuth, going to spy on all the Guy Murrays he could find in England but he hadn't recognised any of them. There was only one he hadn't actually seen and that was a Guy Murray who had suddenly moved without leaving a forwarding address. Nobody in the area he had left seemed to know much about him except that he had worked in the City. Harry had always thought that eventually he might have to go trailing round the City searching for the elusive Murray but to do that would only draw attention to himself. There was only one thing to do: Sally went down to the village where the Murrays had lived and asked if they had had any children. Yes, was the answer, two: Piers and Marietta. Finding out where the twitty little secretary in Sally's office lived was easy. Now we had the name of the village and the Murrays' house: The Laurels. More eavesdropping on Twitty's phone chats with her girlfriend revealed that the Murrays went to church every Sunday.

'Mummy and Daddy simply can't understand it. First of all I'm coming home every weekend and then I'm coming to church with them too. The Murrays all come – their father's really religious apparently – and they have the pew opposite ours so I can take peeks at Piers all through morning service. Yummy!'

I desperately wanted to come over on the next plane and stride into church in the little village in Oxfordshire, along with Harry, Sally and Rory, to see if we'd found our man. But my face was far too well known and would have drawn attention to us. If he was the Guy Murray we wanted then he must know my real name; correction, my real maiden name.

When Harry called to tell us it was him, I did something I had never done in my entire career as a model: I cancelled a job at the last moment. I knew I was letting people down but I couldn't help it. I was about to confront a demon that had been haunting my family for fourteen years.

Guy Murray hadn't seen Harry in church and Sally had made equally sure she wasn't spotted by the secretary from her office. The following Sunday we all drove down to Oxfordshire – Harry and Sally, Rory and I – and waited in the car as the congregation came out of church. We watched Guy Murray shake hands with the vicar, all smiles and good-will, and then we saw him walk down the road with his wife and two children and enter a drive off to the right. The Laurels.

I was dressed to kill in Armani. I love Armani but I save it for special occasions as it always gives me added confidence. I know I'm supposed to be this glamorous supermodel but most of the time I feel like a perfectly ordinary young woman inside; I think we all do. But when I wore Armani I always felt as if I could conquer the world. I had added my dark glasses even though it was November. I wanted to add a bit of mystery to my appearance.

Rory too had an Armani silk bomber jacket over his jeans, Harry was in an old Barbour of my father's that I'd pinched for him, and Sally was in her usual Fair Isle jumper and pretty pale green tweed jacket and skirt.

When Guy Murray opened the door to us with a glass of sherry in his hand, Harry came straight out with it.

'I'm Harry Crichton-Lake and you haven't seen me in quite a while. You'll probably recall when you last saw me and where. We'd like to come in and ask you a few questions about a club called Cecile's. You see we've—'

Guy Murray reached behind him, snatched some car keys off the hall table and pushed through us to his car, throwing the sherry glass on the gravel. He had a Mercedes 300SL and it was backing down the drive before we'd even realised what he was doing.

'Quick!' yelled Harry, 'after him!'

We piled back into Sally's BMW and gave chase. About ten miles down the A40 Rory told Harry:

'Stop the car.'

'But we'll lose him.'

'We sure will with you driving. Now stop the car and let me take over.'

I learned something new about my husband. He was a budding racetrack driver. Guy Murray was driving very fast, and since we'd parked our car round the side of the church, he probably didn't know we were following him. Once we left the motorway it took some expert driving to keep on his tail and Rory was amazing.

Murray led us to a building in a seedy part of King's Cross.

Harry went round the back on his own and had a snoop through a couple of windows. He came back pretty quickly.

'Find the nearest phone box and call the police,' he told Sally. 'Get them here as fast as you can. There's a body lying on the floor in a room at the back.'

When they arrived he told Sally and me to stay in the car while he and Rory went with the police to the front door of the building. There was no answer, so they broke in. Guy Murray was in the process of making his escape but they caught him and restrained him. In his hand was a pigskin briefcase full of videos.

The woman lying on the floor, bound and gagged and severely beaten, was Lindy-Jane Johnson who had, she told the police, quite a story to tell.

London/Wiltshire, 1994

At Etoile they were all of a twitter because the selection of the SWAN girl had been settled once and for all. Tess Tucker was not pregnant, had no plans to become a movie star, was not about to sue for racial discrimination or go over to the other side and become a designer and, barring any unforeseen accidents, was still very much alive and kicking. Furthermore she had decided that, after a shaky start, she really loved being a model. It was just a question of confidence. As soon as Tess began to see that people thought she was worthy of their attention, she blossomed. The press were having a field day with her. They loved her story that she had gone into modelling in the first place in order to buy her mother a new wheelchair. Mr Takamoto was flying in that afternoon to be photographed standing between me, his old SWAN girl and Tess, his new one. It would be an interesting picture, since the top of his head would barely reach our ribs.

'I have to say,' said Grace during a rare moment of quiet on the booking table, 'credit where credit is due. Angie, stand up and take a bow. If it had been left to me I would never have taken Tess on, I freely admit it. It's all due to Angie's faith in Tess that we've landed ourselves a multimillion-dollar contract.'

'And I have to freely admit that that new boyfriend of hers has to take some of the credit,' said Angie. 'I don't know who the hell he is but she's really taken on the proverbial new lease of life since she met him. Let's hope he stays in the picture.'

I didn't know what to do. It was something that was worrying me to death. I knew who he was and because he had sent me Tess's picture I knew he also had to be the Messenger. And because he was the Messenger he had to be some kind of sicko, the last kind of person Tess needed in her life. Somehow I was going to have to bring what I knew out into the open and Tess was going to have to deal with it. I understood what Angie had just said. Tess might now know she was a successful model but she was still probably quite vulnerable emotionally. To learn that Mayo was less than perfect might damage her at the very time when she needed to be at her best. Still, I had to do something. Now that Guy Murray had been caught, the Messenger no longer had a hold on me. Then another thing struck me: what was I going to say to Bridie?

'I know Tess's boyfriend,' I said quietly. 'He works at Industria in New York, I met him when I was working there. He serves behind the bar in the restaurant. His name's Mayo.'

I was about to go on when I saw Angie's face. She was looking completely shellshocked.

'Mayo?' she whispered.

'Yes,' I said, 'crazy name, isn't it? They called him that at Industria because he makes such sensational mayonnaise.'

'He never made mayonnaise in his life,' said Angie.

'Actually, you're right, how did you know that? It's his mother who makes it. She's this marvellous cook, she cooks for me in fact, and he takes what she's made in to Industria.'

'His mother?' Angie was incredulous.

'Yes, he lives with her, right across the street in this great big apartment building in New York overlooking the West

393

Side highway. Angie, do you know this man?' I was beginning to get suspicious.

'I don't know,' said Angie slowly, 'but I just might.'

Then she knocked us all dead by saying, 'Grace, can I take some time off and go to New York to meet this Mayo? It's sort of important to find out a bit more about him given Tess's circumstances. Tess told me he had gone back there yesterday.'

'Angie, as far as I'm concerned you can do whatever you want,' said Grace. 'If you're going to New York to case this guy I wouldn't exactly call it time off.'

'Thank you,' said Angie. 'I'll just go home and sort out what to do with the kids while I'm away and then I'll get on the first plane.'

'Angie, do you have a place to stay?' I asked.

'Oh, I expect Stacey at Etoile in New York will be able to find her somewhere,' said Grace.

'No,' I said, 'I insist she stays with me. I'm flying out tonight. I'll be there waiting for her.'

'Thank you, Swan,' said Angie, 'I'd really appreciate being with you. I mean, I barely know you, are you sure?'

'More than sure,' I said and smiled. 'I'll look forward to it and as for barely knowing you, this will give us a chance to get to know each other, won't it?'

Lindy-Jane Johnson was very lucky to be alive. She had gone back to Guy Murray's office, broken in and found him waiting there. He had summoned someone to knock her unconscious and bind and gag her. What she hadn't known was that the man had been told to come back and kill her after Murray had left but we had arrived first.

Murray owned Brigitte's. He had co-owned Cecile's in the end and the reason that had been closed down so suddenly was because Murray had had his partner killed. His partner

394

had been about to blow the whistle about the snuff video line. Murray had simply disposed of him and moved the operation elsewhere. Only it wasn't just his ex-partner who was running scared. Only a handful of girls worked the Death Rooms, as they were known. Videos were made all the time and collected daily by Murray who wanted to make sure they didn't fall into the wrong hands and liked to pass them on to the fence personally. A death video was made very rarely. The client/victim had to be carefully selected: no one with a family or someone in his life who would come looking for him. The girl who serviced him had to be specially trained. Only four people on the staff were involved: the girl, the person operating the video camera, the man who entered the room to do the killing and Murray himself.

Murray liked to watch.

It was all so disgustingly gruesome I could barely bring myself to think about it. He liked to stand and watch while someone was strangled to death. And then he had had the bodies buried in his garden in the country. That was why he had had to move. He'd run out of room. When they went to investigate, they found fourteen bodies. It had been bad enough with the The House of Horror in Gloucester at the beginning of the year. Murray had been planning to start again at The Laurels in Oxfordshire.

It was the videos themselves that trapped him. The video camera operator had taken the protection of ensuring that occasionally Murray himself was captured on tape, standing in the doorway watching. He had kept those videos to himself. When Murray was arrested he came forward and presented them to the police. When Murray was made to watch them he collapsed and confessed everything, including Molly Bainbridge's murder. At long last Harry's name was cleared.

Whether or not Harry would have to give evidence at the

trial remained to be seen. Poor Harry! He had finally cracked up. The strain of being in hiding for so long and the final shocking outcome had taken its toll. Sally was something of a stoic so it was hard to tell just how worried she really was but none of us could ignore the terrifying depression into which Harry had sunk. Rory predicted that he would need hospitalisation but mercifully my doctor, to whom we took him, prescribed a long rest in the country.

It was obvious where we should take him: back to Wiltshire. But not, as before, to his secret hiding place in the lime kiln. This time we would drive up to the house and be welcomed by our mother. She would be prepared, inasmuch as she could be prepared for such a highly charged emotional reunion. The horrific story of Guy Murray's murders had been all over the papers for days and Molly Bainbridge's name had been included in the list of his victims. Rory and I had already been down to explain to her about Harry, where he had been and about his involvement with Sally. We had decided to let him tell her himself that he had actually been hiding in the lime kiln. Nevertheless, as we approached the house with Harry and Sally holding hands in the back seat, we were all feeling decidedly apprehensive.

Of course it would turn out to be the one time where Golly, defending his castle and barking furiously at Harry, hurtling out of the house at him at full tilt, didn't miss. Poor Harry, weak and worn out as he was, went down like a ninepin. But in a way it was probably meant to be. My mother, instead of awkwardly greeting the son she hadn't seen in years, rushed without thinking to help him to his feet and shepherded him into the house. Rory and I followed with Sally, bringing the bags, by which time my mother and Harry had disappeared. She had taken him straight up to his room.

She did not come down for two hours and when she did it

was as if her face had shed twenty years. She was once again the relaxed, beautiful woman I had known as a child. But the real surprise was my father. My mother told us that he had taken the news of Harry's reappearance surprisingly well.

'In fact,' said my mother, 'I think it's brought him back to life, that, and your wedding, which he can't stop talking about. He's been reading all about Guy Murray in the papers every morning. You know your father, how he used to be, he keeps crackling the pages and bellowing things like "stands to reason, his father was always a rotter. Chips Murray, he was in my house, absolute rotter, fellow cheated at cards!" I try to point out that if you cheat at cards it doesn't necessarily mean your son's going to turn out to be a kinky mass murderer but of course in your father's eyes it's a given.'

There was another problem, however, that in my anxiety over my parents' reunion with Harry I hadn't actually anticipated. Sally Bainbridge. I became aware of it over dinner. My mother had put Harry to bed in his old room. A bed for Sally had been made up in the guest room. For the first time in ages my father's conversation dominated the dinner table.

'Jolly good thing Harry's turned up. Going to get him to help me with clearing out the attic. Lot of papers up there.' My father spoke as if Harry had come down for the weekend after an absence of about a month.

'I could help you with that, sir,' said Rory rising to the occasion.

'Reading all that nonsense in the newspapers made me think about it. Got to do away with the past. Venetia's death. Young Fairfax. That Bainbridge girl. Kept the newspaper clippings up there out of my wife's sight. Time to throw it all away now. Make a bonfire, what do you say?'

'Jolly good!' we all chorused.

Except Sally.

397

She hadn't said a word throughout dinner and I noticed my mother casting furtive glances her way. I cursed myself for having been so insensitive. She was Molly Bainbridge's sister and neither she nor my mother knew how to handle it. On the way to the library for coffee I waylaid Rory.

'Take Daddy up to the attic now. Take him down to the orchard. Dump him in the river, do whatever you like, but distract his attention. I want to give Sally and Mummy a chance to get to know each other without Daddy wittering on. I don't know what's got into him but whatever it is I'm going to ask you to deal with it. Please, Rory. For me?'

'See you later,' was all he said, kissing me on the nose before leading my father firmly away from us.

My mother was pouring coffee in the library. Sally was perched nervously on the end of the sofa.

'Do you take cream?' asked my mother.

'I really do love Harry,' said Sally at the same time.

'And if it hadn't been for Sally, Harry would never have had the strength to carry on,' I blurted out. 'Sally's been the most amazing support for him. We owe her such a lot, Mummy, you have no idea.'

My mother sat back in her chair for a second then she stood up and went over to Sally with outstretched arms. For one ghastly moment as they embraced I thought Mummy was going to say something terribly corny like 'I might have lost one daughter but I can see I've found another.' Then I realised that the only person being corny was me for even thinking it.

My mother coaxed Sally to talk about herself and by the time Rory and my father could be heard stomping down the stairs, the two women had grown infinitely closer. Sally pleaded tiredness and asked if she might go up to bed.

'I've put you in the guest room but if you go to the end of the corridor and turn right, Harry's room is the first on the left,' said my mother. 'Sweet dreams, Sally dear, and may I just say, belatedly, how terribly sorry I am about your sister's death and, at the same time, how delighted we are to welcome you into our family.'

I wasn't aware that I had actually heard that Harry and Sally were getting married but my mother seemed to assume it was definitely on the cards.

'A dear girl. Quiet. Determined. Just what Harry needs now. And to think he might never have met her if her sister hadn't died in our house.'

'And I might never have become a model,' I said.

'Do you regret it?' asked my mother.

'Not at all.' I was surprised at the vehemence of my response. 'It's a wonderful life for a girl if she keeps her feet on the ground and doesn't allow it all to go to her head.'

'I kept worrying about you. . . .'

'You never said anything.'

'Well, I didn't want you to worry about me worrying, if you see what I mean. But, well, people don't really seem to take models very seriously. Quite often I had to defend your intelligence to those who thought just because you were a model, you must be stupid. Of course, they didn't actually say so to me but I could tell that's what they were thinking. And all those stories one hears about partying and drugs.'

'I don't know about drugs, but you can still have a good time partying and live to tell the tale,' I protested. 'You're only young once. Common sense applies as much in modelling as it does in any other profession. You can have fun, you can earn a ton of money, you can travel the world in a way that most young girls would never have the chance to do. All you have to do is remember that it won't last forever.'

'Will you miss it?' asked my mother.

'No. Yes. Oh, I don't know. Parts of it I shall miss terribly but I can't pretend I'm going to miss spending days on aeroplanes and hours and hours hanging around waiting for a photographer to be ready for me. I'll miss all the people, the make-up artists who've become my friends, the hairdressers, all those people I'd never have had a chance to meet if I hadn't become a model. But I'm lucky, I'm getting out while I'm still ahead of the game and I've got Rory.'

'And you've got us. You've got your family,' said my mother.

And I knew that that was one of the most important things for a model, wherever they were in their career.

As Rory and I drove away the next day to catch our plane back to New York, leaving Harry to be cosseted back to health by my mother and Sally, I leaned back in my seat and watched the Wiltshire downs rolling past, secure in the knowledge that my troubles were now finally over. The threat of the Messenger was out of my life forever. For a brief moment I wondered what would become of Mayo but as the car picked up speed on the motorway back to London and the airport, I told myself it was nothing to do with me any more. That whole area of my life was a thing of the past.

Yet somewhere deep down inside me a voice said: don't be too sure!

New York, 1994

When our plane landed at JFK we were both so exhausted by the week's nightmare events and the flight that we decided to have an early night – apart. Now we really could bring our marriage out in the open and live together but for tonight we'd go our separate ways. We agreed to say goodnight to each other the way we always did when we were at our own apartments. On the dot of eleven we would each look through our telescopes – Rory had installed one at the Gainsborough – and blow each other a kiss.

Rory dropped me off first and Michael took me up to my apartment.

'There y'are, Miss Swan. Call down if you need anything.'

The red message light was blinking furiously but it no longer held the threat it once did. I listened to my messages. As I had expected there was nothing from Mayo the Messenger.

I took a long bath and slipped into my nightdress. I was just about to go over to the telescope to kiss Rory goodnight before I went to bed when I heard a horribly familiar sound. It came from the living room. I hadn't even been in there. Then it came again. And again.

Gunshots.

Someone was firing a pistol of some kind in my living room. As I reached for the phone to call security the shots grew louder and louder, as if someone was turning up the volume.

I replaced the receiver. I could deal with this on my own. There was no pistol. Someone was turning up the volume – on a tape recording of a gunshot.

I put on my long towelling robe and went into the living room. Mayo was sitting on the sofa playing with a tape recorder.

'Hi, Swan,' he welcomed me cheerfully. 'I used my mother's key. Don't mind, do you?'

'No, of course not, Mayo. Can I get you anything? Cup of coffee?'

'No, stay right here.' Suddenly he looked frightened. 'Don't leave me.'

'I wouldn't dream of it. I'm not going anywhere.'

He was like a big awkward baby, sitting there. His long clown's face had an almost Modigliani-like beauty, bathed as it was in the moonlight. I hadn't turned on the lights but the drapes were open and behind him the New York skyline glittered.

'Mayo, why did you leave me those funny messages?' I asked him as gently as I could.

'I met Tess again. Back in London I knew she liked me but then she went off with this Bobby chap. I wanted to show her who I was. I wanted to show her I could get her the contract. She was so impressed by you, always talking about you. She was the one who showed me that story about you in the magazine and that's when I realised I'd taken a photo of you when I was a kid. It was this camera my mother left me. I saved every picture I ever took to show her. And I did, all except yours. And with my mother coming here and all and having the telephone number, it was so easy. I've always been a bit of a joker. No one took me seriously back home, you see. I had to prove to my family I was . . . I was . . .'

'Powerful?'

'That's it. Someone to be reckoned with. Angie and my dad, they never took me seriously. That's why I had to get away and look for my mother. She was the only one who would take me seriously until I could get Tess back. It worked, didn't it? She's got the contract. She's the new SWAN girl.'

He was looking at me anxiously, seeking my approval.

'Yes, Mayo, she's got the contract. I didn't know you knew Angie? Is that the same Angie who's Tess's booker?'

'Yes, but Tess knows she mustn't tell Angie about me. It's our secret.'

'But how do you know Angie, Mayo?'

'How do I know her? How do you think I know her? I grew up with her. She's my sister.'

When Rory arrived minutes later, Mayo was asleep in my arms on the sofa. Rory had dashed right over because I had not come to the telescope at eleven o'clock. He spent the night with me and we left Mayo in the living room. The next morning we took him home to Bridie and broke the news to her that her daughter was on her way to New York.

'Bridie,' I asked her, 'how on earth did Angie know that Mayo was her brother Patrick?'

'Well, I suppose she couldn't be sure, but how many people go by the name of Mayo? It's what I've always called him. He was born in County Mayo in Ireland, you see. It's where I'm from and it's what we all called him when he was a boy. As he grew older his father started calling him Patrick, which is his real name, sure, and the other children followed suit but I've always had my special name for him, and when he turned up here looking for me he asked me to call him that again.'

I looked at Bridie, taller than Angie but with the same black curly hair and cornflower blue eyes, and I saw the resemblance. I realised I'd always looked at Bridie and seen a cook. Now I was seeing a beautiful woman, a little on the heavy side, inevitable with all that cooking perhaps, but an extraordinary face all the same. She would have made a marvellous model. . . .

'Bridie, may I ask you something, and do please tell me if it's none of my business – why did you leave your family?'

By way of answer she opened a door and called:

'Felix!'

A tall man with a grey beard came in. His face was warm and weatherbeaten and it lit up when he saw me. A man who appreciated beautiful women.

'Love,' said Bridie, 'I left my family for love. I wasn't in love with Joseph Doyle. I thought I was when I married him but I was very, very young. I had all the kids then I felt trapped. Then I met Felix here. I didn't plan it. He was my escape. An Irishman on his way to America to seek a new life. I'm a romantic, Swan. Look how happy I was when you found your Rory. It's the real thing, I can tell. Just like Felix. I knew when he came along I'd have to go with him. If I hadn't left then, I would have left sooner or later. I knew it, and so does Joseph, no matter what he told the children.'

'But you never kept in touch?'

'Better to make a clean break of it. If the children wanted to find me there were plenty of people they could ask who would point them in the right direction. Look at Mayo here, took him no time at all. Now you say Angie's on her way. We'll have a grand reunion. Now what'll we be eating? I'd better start planning the feast.'

I don't know what happened when Angie was reunited with her mother. It can't have been easy. Maybe it was for the best that mother and daughter had been separated while Angie was growing up. They were not alike – Angie was practical

404

and down to earth with her father's determination, and Bridie was a feckless, irresponsible romantic (and a damn good cook) – and no doubt there would have been many a struggle of wills and Angie would probably have wound up looking after her brothers and sisters anyway. Who knows?

The person who did surprise me was Tess. I called her that night in London to tell her about Patrick. She had known about him all along; everything, that is, except for his role as the Messenger.

'I ran into him again in Paris and we became like brother and sister. He's so gentle, Swan, and so confused just like I've been for so long. Seeing what a mess he was in made me realise how strong I had to be to help him. I do love him, Swan. He's ill and he needs me. In a way I owe a lot to him. Besides Angie, he was the one who gave me hope right in the beginning. We used to go out for coffee and talk for hours and hours and I always felt so uplifted afterwards. I know I hurt him when I went off to Italy with Bobby. He's vulnerable, Swan, far far more vulnerable than I am. I hope Angie will understand. I think when she falls in love herself, she may. Patrick needs treatment and now we can all see that he gets it, but just because a person is emotionally unstable that doesn't mean you can't love them. It means they need your love even more, you must all see that.'

Except she wouldn't be there for him. Didn't she realise that? Now that she was the SWAN girl her life was going to change beyond all recognition. She was going to be working all the time and travelling more and more. She was going to be meeting all kinds of men, most of them a lot more glamorous than Patrick. Would she really stand by him?

But then the more I thought about it, the more I realised that if anyone would, Tess would. There was a steadfastness to her that might just enable her to evade all the piranhas waiting for her out there.

London, 1995

Tess's first ad as the SWAN girl appeared early the following
year and she looked staggeringly beautiful in it, but I must
admit as I looked at it I did feel a tiny pang of regret. I had
given up a lot and I still did not really know what I was going
to do next.

It happened quite by chance, as everything always does in
my life. I was walking down the King's Road in Chelsea and
I happened to glance down a side street and see a FOR SALE
sign. I knew immediately what it was: the little bookshop
where I had worked and where both Willy O'Brien and Harry
had discovered me. Within the month it was mine. Within
two months the shop was up and running again. I worked
there three days a week and I was as happy as Larry. I did a
roaring trade giving the local Dillons and Waterstones a run
for their money. Swan's Bookstore became something of a
tourist attraction. Everyone flocked to get a close-up view of
the former supermodel. Well, let them, I thought, as long as
they buy a book. The only thing I refused to do was sign
books for them. We only had one author in the family and
that was Rory.

Rory and I had moved into the house in the Boltons. We'd
divided it into two wonderful apartments, one for us and one
for Harry and Sally, who are getting married this summer. We

have added another stone lion by the steps and he is called Stirling, naturally.

And at Christmas, when the baby comes, we shall be adding a little stone lion cub.

Or should it be a cygnet?